"*The Christmas Box* will probably appeal to most readers . . . who already believe in the magic of Christmas. But the message of love and the importance of cherishing family is for everyone."

—*Winston-Salem Journal* (NC)

"[A] memorable tale. . . . The book's timeless message is appropriate for any season . . . *The Christmas Box* is an artful blend of fiction and inspirational writing."

—*Orlando Sun Sentinel*

TIMEPIECE

"Like the titular treasure chest of Evans' bestselling *The Christmas Box*, the eponymous timepiece—'a beautiful rose-gold wristwatch'—of this heart-plucking prequel fairly vibrates with sentimentality. . . . The nation's supply of Kleenex is bound to deplete after this book hits the shelves."

—*Publishers Weekly*

"A jewel of a book . . . this exquisitely crafted story is wonderful reading for everyone."

—*The Pilot* (Southern Pines, NC)

"Richard Paul Evans is a good writer. His style is crisp and uncluttered."

—*The Star* (Chicago)

"A touching story that reminds readers of the connections binding one generation to the next."

—*Baton Rouge Magazine* (LA)

"A love story. . . . For those who don't mind a thoughtful and leisurely journey, it has much to offer along the way."

—*Detroit News*

THE LETTER

"In a day when popular fiction often fails to inspire goodness, *The Letter* is refreshing. . . . Evans' story manages to wrap warm hands around its readers, instilling in them a hunger for goodness to prevail. . . . Evans' writing is excellent. . . . The enchanting plot dares the reader to put the book aside."

—*The Daily Universe*

"*The Letter* is a delight to read."

—*Chattanooga Times*

"A sweet and tender love story. . . . On one of these cold winter nights find a comfortable place and settle down and read *The Letter* . . . . When it is over you will feel warmed and enriched by the story you have shared."

—*The Daily Sun*

The
Christmas Box
Collection

Richard Paul Evans

The Christmas Box Collection

POCKET BOOKS
New York London Toronto Sydney Singapore

This book is a work of fiction. Names, characters, places and incidents are products of the author's imagination or are used fictitiously. Any resemblance to actual events or locales or persons living or dead is entirely coincidental.

These titles were originally published individually in hardcover by Simon & Schuster, Inc.

 POCKET BOOKS, a division of Simon & Schuster, Inc.
1230 Avenue of the Americas, New York, NY 10020

The Christmas Box copyright © 1993 by Richard Paul Evans
Timepiece copyright © 1996 by Richard Paul Evans
The Letter copyright © 1997 by Richard Paul Evans

ISBN: 0-671-02764-6

First Pocket Books printing November 1998

18 17 16 15 14 13 12 11

POCKET and colophon are registered trademarks of Simon & Schuster, Inc.

Printed in the U.S.A.

For my sister Sue.
Whom I love and I miss.

CONTENTS

The
Christmas
Box

CONTENTS

◆

No little girl could stop the world to wait for me.

—NATALIE MERCHANT

CHAPTER ONE
THE WIDOW'S MANSION

It may be that I am growing old in this world and have used up more than my share of allotted words and eager audiences. Or maybe I am just growing weary of a skeptical age that pokes and prods at my story much the same as a middle-school biology student pokes and prods through an anesthetized frog to determine what makes it live, leaving the poor creature dead in the end. Whatever the reason, I find that with each passing Christmas the story of the Christmas Box is told less and needed more. So I record it now for all future generations to accept or dismiss as seems them good. As for me, I believe. And it is, after all, my story.

My romantic friends, those who believe in Santa

Claus in particular, have speculated that the ornamented brown Christmas Box was fashioned by Saint Nick himself from the trunk of the very first Christmas tree, brought in from the cold December snows so many seasons ago. Others believe that it was skillfully carved and polished from the hard and splintered wood from whose rough surface the Lord of Christmas had demonstrated the ultimate love for mankind. My wife, Keri, maintains that the magic of the box had nothing to do with its physical elements, but all to do with the contents that were hidden beneath its brass, holly-shaped hinges and silver clasps. Whatever the truth about the origin of the box's magic, it is the emptiness of the box that I will treasure most, and the memory of the Christmas season when the Christmas Box found me.

◆

I was born and raised in the shadow of the snow-clad Wasatch range on the east bench of the Salt Lake Valley. Just two months before my fourteenth birthday my father lost his job, and with promise of employment, we sold our home and migrated to the warmer, and more prosperous, climate of Southern California. There, with great disappointment, I came to expect a green

Christmas almost as religiously as the local retailers. With the exception of one fleeting moment of glory as the lead in the school musical, my teenage years were uneventful and significant only to myself. Upon graduation from high school, I enrolled in college to learn the ways of business, and in the process learned the ways of life; met, courted, and married a fully matriculated, brown-eyed design student named Keri, who, not fifteen months from the ceremony, gave birth to a seven-pound-two-ounce daughter whom we named Jenna.

Neither Keri nor I ever cared much for the crowds of the big city, so when a few weeks before graduation we were informed of a business opportunity in my hometown, we jumped at the chance to return to the thin air and white winters of home. We had expended all but a small portion of our savings in the new venture and, as the new business's initial returns, albeit promising, were far from abundant, we learned the ways of thrift and frugality. In matters financial, Keri became expert at making much from little, so we rarely felt the extent of our deprivation. Except in the realm of lodging. The three of us needed more space than our cramped, one-bedroom apartment afforded. The baby's crib, which economics necessitated the use of in spite of the fact that our baby was now nearly four, barely fit in our bedroom, leaving less than an inch between it and our bed, which was already pushed up tightly against the far wall. The kitchen was no better, cluttered with Jenna's toy box, Keri's sewing hutch, and stacked cardboard boxes containing cases of canned foods. We joked that Keri could make clothing and dinner at the same time without ever leaving her seat. The topic of overcrowding had reached fever pitch in our household just seven weeks before Christmas and such was the frenzied state of our minds when the tale of the Christmas Box really began, at the breakfast table in our little apartment, over eggs over-easy, toast, and orange juice.

"Look at this," Keri said, handing me the classifieds:

Elderly lady with large Avenues home seeks live-in couple for meal preparation, light housekeeping, and yard care. Private quarters. Holidays off. Children/ infants welcome. 445–3989. Mrs. Parkin

I looked up from the paper.

"What do you think?" she asked. "It's in the Avenues, so it has to be large. It's close to the shop and it really wouldn't be that much extra trouble for me. What's one extra person to cook and wash for?" she asked rhetorically. She reached over and took a bite of my toast. "You're usually gone in the evenings anyhow."

I leaned back in contemplation.

"It sounds all right," I said cautiously. "Of course, you never know what you might be getting into. My brother Mark lived in this old man's basement apartment. He used to wake Mark up in the middle of the night screaming at a wife who had been dead for nearly twenty years. Scared Mark to death. In the end he practically fled the place."

A look of disbelief spread across Keri's face.

"Well, it does say private quarters," I conceded.

"Anyway, with winter coming on, our heating bill is going to go through the roof in this drafty place and I don't know where the extra money will come from. This way we might actually put some money aside," Keri reasoned.

It was pointless to argue with such logic, not that I cared to. I, like Keri, would gladly welcome any change that would afford us relief from the cramped and cold quarters where we were presently residing. A few moments later Keri called to see if the apartment was still vacant and upon learning that it was, set up an appointment to meet with the owner that evening. I managed to leave work early and, following the directions given to Keri by a man at the house, we made our way through the gaily lit downtown business district and to the tree-lined streets leading up the foothills of the Avenues.

The Parkin home was a resplendent, red-block Victorian mansion with ornate cream-and-raspberry wood trim and dark green shingles. On the west side of the home, a rounded bay window supported a second-story veranda balcony that overlooked the front yard. The balcony, like the main floor porch, ran the length of the exterior upheld by large, ornately lathed beams and a decorative, gold-leafed frieze. The wood was freshly painted and well kept. A sturdy brick chimney rose from the center of the home amid wood and wrought-iron spires that shot up decorously. Intricate latticework gingerbreaded the base of the house, hidden here and there by neatly trimmed evergreen shrubs. A cobblestone driveway wound up the front of the home, encircling a black marble fountain that lay iced over and surrounded by a snow-covered retaining wall.

I parked the car near the front steps, and we climbed the porch to the home's double door entryway. The doors were beautifully carved and inlaid with panes of glass etched with intricate floral patterns. I rang the bell and a man answered.

"Hello, you must be the Evanses."

"We are," I confirmed.

"MaryAnne is expecting you. Please come in."

We passed in through the entry, then through a second set of doors of equal magnificence leading into the home's marbled foyer. I have found that old homes usually have an olfactory presence to them, and though not often pleasant, unmistakenly distinct. This home was no exception, though the scent was a tolerably pleasant combination of cinnamon and kerosene. We walked down a wide corridor with frosted walls. Kerosene sconces, now wired for electric lights, dotted the walls and cast dramatic lighting the length of the hall.

"MaryAnne is in the back parlor," the man said.

The parlor lay at the end of the corridor, entered through an elaborate cherry-wood door casing. As we entered the room, an attractive silver-haired woman greeted us from behind a round marble-topped rose-wood table. Her attire mimicked the elaborate, rococo decor that surrounded her.

"Hello," she said cordially. "I am MaryAnne Parkin. I'm happy that you have come. Please have a seat." We sat around the table, our attention drawn to the beauty and wealth of the room.

"Would you care for some peppermint tea?" she offered. In front of her sat an embossed, silver-plated tea service. The teapot was pear-shaped, with decorative bird feathers etched into the sterling body. The spout emulated the graceful curves of a crane's neck and ended in a bird's beak.

"No, thank you," I replied.

"I'd like some," said Keri.

She handed Keri a cup and poured it to the brim. Keri thanked her.

"Are you from the city?" the woman asked. "I was born and raised here," I replied. "But we've just recently moved up from California."

"My husband was from California," she said. "The Santa Rosa area." She studied our eyes for a spark of recognition. "Anyway, he's gone now. He passed away some fourteen years ago."

"We're sorry to hear that," Keri said politely.

"It's quite all right," she said. "Fourteen years is a long time. I've grown quite accustomed to being alone." She set down her cup and straightened herself up in the plush wingback chair.

"Before we begin the interview I would like to discuss the nature of the arrangement. There are a few items that you will find I am rather insistent about. I need someone to provide meals. You have a family, I assume you can cook." Keri nodded. "I don't eat breakfast, but I expect brunch to be served at eleven and dinner at six. My washing should be done twice a week, preferably Tuesday and Friday, and the beddings should be washed at least once a week. You are welcome to use the laundry facilities to do your own washing any time you find convenient. As for the exterior," she said, looking at me, "the lawn needs to be cut once a week, except when there is snow, at which time the walks, driveway, and back porch need to be shoveled and salted as the climate dictates. The other landscaping and home maintenance I hire out and would not require your assistance. In exchange for your service you will have the entire east wing in which to reside. I will pay the heating and light bills and any other household expenses. All that is required of you is attention to the matters we have discussed. If this arrangement sounds satisfactory to you, then we may proceed."

We both nodded in agreement.

"Good. Now if you don't mind, I have a few questions I'd like to ask."

"No, not at all," Keri said.

"Then we'll begin at the top." She donned a pair of silver-framed bifocals, lifted from the table a small hand-written list, and began the interrogation.

"Do either of you smoke?"

"No," said Keri.

"Good. I don't allow it in the home. It spoils the draperies. Drink to excess?" She glanced over to me.

"No," I replied.

"Do you have children?"

"Yes, we have one. She's almost four years old," said Keri.

"Wonderful. She's welcome anywhere in the house except this room. I would worry too much about my porcelains," she said, smiling warmly. Behind her I could see a black walnut étagère with five steps, each support-ing a porcelain figurine. She continued. "Have you a fondness for loud music?" Again she looked my way.

"No," I answered correctly. I took this more as a warn-ing than a prerequisite for cohabitation.

"And what is your current situation in life?"

"I'm a recent college graduate with a degree in business. We moved to Salt Lake City to start a formal-wear rental business."

"Such as dinner jackets and tuxedos?" she asked.

"That's right," I said.

She took mental note of this and nodded approvingly.

"And references." She glanced up over her bifocals. "Have you references?"

"Yes. You may contact these people," said Keri, handing her a scrawled-out list of past landlords and employers. She meticulously studied the list, then laid it down on the end table, seemingly impressed with the preparation. She looked up and smiled.

"Very well. If your references are satisfactory, I think we may make an arrangement. I think it is best that we initiate a forty-five-day trial period, at the end of which time we may ascertain if the situation is mutually favorable. Does that sound agreeable?"

"Yes, ma'am," I replied.

"You may call me Mary. My name is MaryAnne, but my friends call me Mary."

"Thank you, Mary."

"Now I've done all the talking. Have you any questions that I might answer?"

"We'd like to see the apartment," Keri said.

"Of course. The quarters are upstairs in the east wing. Steve will lead you up. They are unlocked. I think you will find that they have been tastefully furnished."

"We do have some furniture of our own," I said. "Is there some extra space where we could store it?"

"The doorway to the attic is at the end of the upstairs hall. Your things will be very convenient there," she replied.

I helped myself to a cracker from the silver tray. "Was that your son who answered the door?" I asked.

She took another sip of her tea. "No. I have no children. Steve is an old friend of mine from across the street. I hire him to help maintain the home." She paused thoughtfully for another sip of tea and changed the subject. "When will you be prepared to move in?"

"We need to give our landlord two weeks notice, but we could move in anytime," I said.

"Very good. It will be nice to have someone in the house for the holidays."

CHAPTER TWO
THE
CHRISTMAS
BOX

t is not my intent to launch upon a lengthy or sanctimonious dissertation on the social significance and impact of the lowly box, well deserved as it may be. But as a box plays a significant role in our story, please allow me the indulgence of digression. From the inlaid jade-and-coral jewelry boxes of the Orient to the utilitarian salt boxes of the Pennsylvania Dutch, the allure of the box has transcended all cultural and geographical boundaries of the world. The cigar box, the snuff box, the cash box, jewelry boxes more ornate than the treasure they hold, the ice box, and the candle box. Trunks, long rectangular boxes covered with cowhide, stretched taut, and pounded with brass studs to a wooden frame. Oak boxes, sterling boxes; to the delight of the women, hat boxes and shoe boxes; and to the delight of all enslaved by a sweet tooth, candy boxes. The human life cycle no less than evolves around the box; from the open-topped box called a bassinet, to the pine box we call a coffin, the box is our past and, just as assuredly, our future. It should not surprise us then that the lowly box plays such a significant role in the first Christmas story. For Christmas began in a humble, hay-filled box of splintered wood. The Magi, wise men who had traveled far to see the infant king, laid treasure-filled boxes at the feet of that holy child. And in the end, when He had ransomed our sins with His blood, the Lord of Christmas was laid down in a box of stone. How fitting that each Christmas season brightly wrapped boxes skirt the pine boughs of Christmas trees around the world. And more fitting that I learned of Christmas through a Christmas Box.

◆

We determined to settle into the home as soon as possible, so the following Saturday I borrowed a truck from work and my brother-in-law, Barry, the only relative living within two hundred miles, came to help us move. The two of us hauled things out to the truck, while Keri wrapped dishes in newspaper and packed them in boxes, and Jenna played contentedly in the front room, oblivious to the gradual disappearance of our belongings. We managed to load most of our things, which were not great in number, into the truck. The rest of the boxes were piled into our Plymouth—a large pink-and-chrome coupe with graceful curves, majestic tail fins, and a grill resembling the wide, toothy grin of a Cheshire cat. When we had finished clearing out the apartment the four of us squeezed into the cargo-laden vehicles and together drove off to our new residence in the Avenues. I parked the car out front and met Barry in the driveway.

"Just pull it around back," I shouted, guiding the truck with hand gestures. He backed around to the rear of the house, pulled the parking brake, and hopped out.

"You're moving into a mansion?" he asked enviously.

"Your blue-blooded sister found it," I replied.

I released the tailgate while Barry untied the straps securing the canvas tarpaulin we had used to cover the load.

"Here, give me a hand with this wicker chest. We'll take it straight up to the attic." Barry grabbed hold of the handle at one end of the chest and we lifted it down from the truck's bed.

"Only one person lives in this house?" he asked.

"Four now, counting the three of us," I replied.

"With all this room why doesn't her family just move in with her?"

"She doesn't have any family. Her husband died and she doesn't have any children."

Barry surveyed the ornate Victorian facade. "There's bound to be a lot of history in a place like this," he said thoughtfully.

We made our way up the stairs, through the kitchen, down the hall, then up the attic steps. We set the chest down at the top of the landing to catch our breath.

"We'd better make some room up here before we bring the rest of the things up," Barry suggested.

I agreed. "Let's clear a space against that wall so we can keep our things all in one place." We began the chore of rearranging the attic.

"I thought you said she didn't have any children," Barry said.

"She doesn't," I replied.

"Why is there a cradle up here then?" Barry stood near a dusty draped sheet revealing the form of a shrouded cradle.

"Maybe she's storing it for someone," I suggested.

I lifted a small stack of boxes and set them aside. "I haven't seen one of these for a while," I said, displaying my own discovery.

"What is it?"

"A tie press. It must have been her husband's."

Barry hoisted a large portrait of a man with a handlebar mustache posing stoically for the picture. The portrait was set in an elaborate gold-leafed frame.

"Look," he said, "their banker." We laughed.

"Hello, look at this," I said, as I gently lifted what looked to be an heirloom. It was an ornate wooden box of burled walnut, intricately carved and highly polished. It was about ten inches wide, fourteen inches long, and a half foot deep, large enough for a sheet of stationery to lie flat inside. It had two large brass hinges crafted in the form of holly leaves. Two leather straps ran horizontally across the lid and buckled securely into silver clasps on each side. The lid had a skilled and detailed etching of the Nativity. Barry walked over for a closer look.

"I've never seen anything like it," I said.

"What is it?" Barry asked.

"A Christmas Box. For storing Christmas things in.

Cards, baubles, things like that." I shook it gently. There was no rattle.

"How old do you think it is?" Barry asked.

"Turn-of-the-century," I speculated. "See the craftsmanship?"

While he took a closer look, I cast my eyes around the room at the work remaining to be done.

"We better get on with this," I lamented. "I have a lot of work to catch up on tonight."

I set the box aside and we went back to organizing space for our things. It was dark outside by the time we finished unloading the truck. Keri had long finished unpacking the kitchen boxes and dinner was waiting for us on the table when we came down.

"Well, Sister, what do you think of your new home?" Barry asked.

"I could get used to all this room," Keri said, "and the furniture."

"You should see some of the things up in the attic," I said.

"Mom, how will Santa find our new house?" Jenna asked anxiously.

"Oh, Santa's elves keep track of these things," she assured her.

"The trick will be how Santa's reindeer will land on the roof without impaling themselves," I joked.

Keri cast a sideways glance toward me.

"What's impaling?" asked Jenna.

"Never mind your dad, he's just teasing."

Barry laughed. "Aren't you supposed to be making dinner for the lady?" he asked.

"We officially begin our arrangement on Monday. In fact, she is making dinner for us tomorrow. At least she invited us to dine with her."

"Is that right?" I asked.

"She was up here just before the two of you came down."

"This should be interesting," I decided.

We finished the meal and, after thanking Barry profusely for his help, we cleared away the dishes. Then I dove into a pile of receipts and ledgers, while Keri put Jenna to bed.

"Can Daddy read me a story?" she asked.

"Not tonight, honey. Daddy has a lot of work to do."

"It doesn't have to be a long one," she pleaded.

"Not tonight, honey. Some other time."

A disappointed child was tucked under the covers and went to sleep yearning for "some other time."

THE
BIBLE
BOX

 unday was not proclaimed the "day of rest" by a mother with a family to ready for church, but such is the irony of piousness. Upon our return home at the conclusion of the day's "churching," we reveled in the discovery of a glorious new lifestyle. In our last apartment we had had such little space we found ourselves looking for ways to spend our Sunday afternoons outside the home. Now we defiantly spread our things, and ourselves, throughout our quarters. I napped in front of the drawing room fireplace while Keri read in the bedroom and Jenna played quietly in the nursery. What we may have lost in family togetherness we more than made up for in sanity.

At quarter to six Keri woke me, and after washing up, we descended the stairs to Mary's dining room. It smelled wonderfully of roast beef and gravy and freshly baked rolls. The dining room was spacious and, in typical Victorian style, the floor was covered with a colorful Persian rug that stopped short of the walls, leaving a border of the polished hardwood floor exposed. The room was built around a large, rectangular, white-laced dining table. A Strauss crystal chandelier hung from the ceiling directly above the center of the table, suspended above a vase of freshly cut flowers. The east wall had an elaborate built-in china closet displaying the home's exquisite porcelain dinnerware. On the opposite wall was a fireplace, as ornately carved as the parlor fireplace, but of lighter wood. The mantel extended to the ceiling, and the firebox and hearth were tiled in marbled blue-and-white patterns. To either side of the fireplace were walnut side chairs with Gothic carved backs and tucked haircloth upholstery.

Mary met us at the doorway and thanked us graciously for joining her.

"I'm so glad that you could come!" she said.

"The pleasure is ours," I assured her.

"You really shouldn't have gone to so much trouble," said Keri.

Mary was a hostess of the highest order and would not feel the affair worthwhile had she not gone to a lot of trouble.

"It was no trouble at all," she said instinctively.

The place settings were immaculate and beautiful, and the china plates were trimmed in 24-karat gold.

"Please sit down," she urged, motioning us to some chairs. We took our seats and waited for her to join us.

"I always pray before I eat," she said. "Would you please join me?"

We bowed our heads.

"Dear Lord, thank you for this bounty which we have during this blessed Christmas season. Thank you for these new friends. Please bless them in their needs and their desires. Amen."

We lifted our heads.

"Thank you," I said.

Mary uncovered a woven basket of steaming rolls, broke them apart, and placed one on each of our plates. She then filled our goblets with water and the food-laden platters were passed around the table.

"So how are your quarters?" Mary asked. "Have you moved in all your things?"

"We have," Keri replied.

"There was enough room in the attic? I was afraid it might be a little cramped."

"Plenty," I assured her. "We don't own much furniture." I lifted another spoonful from my plate then added, "You really have some beautiful things up there."

She smiled. "Yes. That's mostly my David's doing. David loved to collect things. As a businessman, he traveled all around the world. He always brought something back from each journey. In his spare time he became very knowledgeable about furniture and antiques. A few years before he died he had started collecting Bibles."

I bobbed my head in interest.

"See this Bible over here?" she said. She motioned to a large, leather-bound book sitting alone on a black lacquer papier-mâché table inlaid with mother-of-pearl. "That Bible is over two hundred and fifty years old. It was one of David's favorite finds," she shared joyously. "He brought it back from Britain. Collectors call it the 'wicked' Bible. In the first printing the printer made an error, and in Exodus they omitted the word 'not' from the seventh commandment. It reads 'Thou shalt commit adultery.' "

"That's deplorable," Keri chuckled.

Mary laughed out loud. "It's true," she said. "After supper you're welcome to look it up. The British crown fined the printer three hundred pounds for the mistake."

"That was a costly mistake," I said.

"It was a very popular version," she said, smiling mischievously. "In the front parlor is a French Bible with what they call fore-edge painting. If you fan the pages back there is a watercolor of the Nativity. It was a unique art form of the period. Upstairs in the attic is a Bible box that David bought for it, but I think the book is so beautiful that I leave it out."

"The Christmas Box," I said.

She looked surprised at my familiarity with the box.

"Yes, there is a Nativity scene etched in the wood— of the Madonna and the Baby Jesus."

"I saw it up there. It's very beautiful."

"It's not from France, though," she explained. "I believe it was from Sweden. Fine box-making was an art in the Scandinavian countries. When David passed away I received not a few requests to purchase the Bibles. Except for the Bible I donated to the church, and the three that I still have, I sold the rest. I just couldn't part with these three. David took such joy in them. They were his favorite treasures."

"Where is the third Bible?" I asked.

"I keep it in the den, for my personal reading. I'm sure there are some collectors that would have my head for doing so, but it has special significance to me." She looked down at Jenna.

"But enough of these old things, tell me about your sweet little three-year-old," she said kindly.

Jenna had been sitting quietly, cautiously sampling her food, largely ignored by all of us. She looked up shyly.

"Jenna is going to be four in January," Keri said.

"I'm going to be this many," Jenna said proudly, extending a hand with one digit inverted.

"That is a wonderful age!" Mary exclaimed. "Do you like your new home?"

"I like my bed," she said matter-of-factly.

"She's glad to get out of her crib," Keri explained. "We didn't have room in our last apartment for a bed. She was devastated when she found out that she was the only one in her dance class who slept in a crib."

Mary smiled sympathetically.

"Oh, speaking of dance," Keri remembered, turning to me, "Jenna's Christmas dance recital is this Saturday. Can you make it?"

I frowned. "I'm afraid not. Saturday is going to be a busy day at the shop with all the December weddings and Christmas formals."

"It must be a very busy time of the year for your type of business," Mary offered.

"It is," I replied, "but it drops off in January."

She nodded politely then turned to Keri. "Well, I, for one, am glad that Jenna likes it here. And, if you're wanting for company, I would love to take Richard's place at that dance recital."

"You are more than welcome to join us," Keri said. Jenna smiled.

"Then it's a date. And," she said, looking at Jenna, "for the little dancer, I made some chocolate Christmas pudding. Would you like some?"

Jenna smiled hungrily.

"I hope you don't mind," Mary said, turning to us. "She hasn't finished her supper."

"Of course not," Keri said. "That was very thoughtful of you."

Mary excused herself from the table and returned

carrying a tray of crystal bowls filled with steaming pudding. She served Jenna first.

"This is very good," I said, plunging a spoonful into my mouth.

"Everything is delicious," Keri said. "Thank you."

The conversation lulled while we enjoyed the dessert. Jenna was the first to break the silence.

"I know why flies come in the house," she announced unexpectedly.

We looked at her curiously.

"You do?" Mary asked.

Jenna looked at us seriously. "They come in to find their friends . . ."

We all stifled a laugh, as the little girl was in earnest.

". . . and then we kill them."

Keri and I looked at each other and burst out laughing.

"My, you are a little thinker," Mary said. She chuckled, then leaned over and gave Jenna a hug.

"I'd like to propose a toast," Mary said. She raised a crystal glass of wine. Following Mary's lead we poured our glasses half full of the rose liquid and held them in the air.

"To a new friendship and a wonderful Christmas."

"Hear, hear," I said emphatically.

"A wonderful Christmas," Keri repeated.

The rest of the evening was spent in pleasant conversation, punctuated with laughter. When we had finished eating, we lavishly praised Mary for a wonderful meal and transported the dishes to the kitchen. Mary firmly insisted on cleaning up the dishes herself, so reluctantly we left her to the chore and returned upstairs to our wing.

"I feel like I've known her all my life," Keri said.

"Like a grandmother," I observed.

Jenna smiled and raced up the stairs ahead of us.

◆

The ritual of cohabitation took on a natural and casual openness welcomed by all. It soon became clear to Keri and me that Mary had solicited a family to move in with her more for the sake of "family" than real physical need. She could easily have hired servants, as there obviously had been in the past, and she seemed to trouble herself immensely to make our stay amiable, to the extent of hiring out any chore that Keri or I might find overly tedious or time-consuming, except when said chore would invoke a vicarious act of a familial nature. Bringing home the Christmas tree was such an occasion. Mary, upon finding the largest, most perfectly shaped tree in the lot, offered to purchase a second pine for our quarters. She was absolutely delighted when Keri suggested that we might all enjoy sharing the same tree together. We brought the tree home and after much fussing, the fresh scent of evergreen permeated the den. Not surprisingly, the room became a favorite place for us to congregate after supper. We enjoyed Mary's company as much as she desired ours, and Jenna accepted her readily as a surrogate grandmother.

◆

Some people were born to work for others. Not in a mindless, servile way—rather, they simply work better in a set regimen of daily tasks and functions. Others were born of the entrepreneurial spirit and enjoy the demands of self-determination and the roll of the dice. Much to my detriment, I was born of the latter spirit. Frankly, that spirit was just as potent a draw to return to my hometown as the quaint streets and white-capped mountains I had grown up loving. As I said before, Keri and I had left Southern California for the opportunity to operate a formal-wear business. Though formal-wear rental is quite common now, at the time it was new and untested and therefore exciting. The opportunity came by way of a friend who found himself in a small town just north of Salt Lake City, called Bountiful, for a wedding. That is when he met my future partner, an enterprising tailor who had begun leasing elaborate bridal gowns, and soon discovered a greater need for suitable accoutrements for the bride's and bridesmaids' counterparts.

As necessity is the mother of profit, he began renting a line of men's dinner jackets with great success. It was at this time that my friend, while dressed in one of those suits, had, unbeknownst to me, engaged the proprietor in a lengthy discussion on the state and future of his business. Having been impressed with expectations of my marketing prowess, the owner called me directly and after many long-distance phone conversations offered to sell me a portion of the new company in exchange for my expertise and a small cash outlay, which Keri and I managed to scrape together. The opportunity was all we could have hoped for, and the business showed signs of great promise.

Under my direction, we increased our market by producing picture catalogs of our suits and sending them to dressmakers and wedding halls outside of the metropolitan area. They became the retailers of our suits, which they rented to their clientele, and received no small commission in the transaction. The paperwork of this new venture was enormous and complex, but the success of my ideas consumed me and I found myself gradually drawn away from the comparatively relaxed environment of home. In modern business vernacular, there is a popular term: "opportunity costs." The term is based on the assumption that since all resources, mainly time and money, are limited, the successful businessman weighs all ventures based on what opportunities are to be lost in the transaction. Perhaps if I had seen my daughter's longing eyes staring back at me from the gold-plated scales, I would have rethought my priorities. I adroitly rationalized my absence from home on necessity and told myself that my family would someday welcome the sacrifice by feasting, with me, on the fruits of my labors. In retrospect, I should have tasted those fruits for bitterness a little more often.

CHAPTER FOUR

THE DREAM,
THE ANGEL,
AND THE LETTER

don't recall the exact night when the dreams began. The angel dreams. It should be stated that I am a believer in angels, though not the picture-book kind with wings and harps. Such angelic accoutrements seem as nonsensical to me as devils sporting horns and carrying pitchforks. To me, angel wings are merely symbolic of their role as divine messengers. Notwithstanding my rather dogmatic opinions on the matter, the fact that the angel in my dream descended from the sky with outspread wings did not bother me. In fact, the only thing I found disturbing at all about the dream was its frequent recurrence and the dream's strange conclusion. In the dream I find myself alone in a large open field. The air is filled with soft, beautiful strains of music flowing as sweet and melodic as a mountain brook. I look up and see an angel with wings outspread descending gradually from heaven. Then, when we are not an arm's length removed, I look into its cherubic face, its eyes turn up toward heaven, and the angel turns to stone.

Though I have vague recollections of the dream haunting my sleep more than once after we moved into the Parkin home, it seemed to have grown clearer and more distinct with each passing slumber. This night it was alive, rich in color and sound and detail, occupying my every thought with its surrealism. I awoke suddenly, expecting all traces of the nocturnal vision to vanish with my consciousness, but it didn't. This night the music remained. A soft, silvery tune plucked sweetly as a lullaby. A lullaby of unknown origin.

Except tonight the music had an origin.

I sat up in bed, listening intently while my eyes adjusted to the darkness. I found the flashlight kept in the pine nightstand next to our bed, pulled on a terry-cloth robe, and walked quietly from the room, following the music. I felt my way down the hall past the nursery where I stopped and looked in at Jenna. She lay fast asleep, undisturbed by the tones. I followed the music to the end of the hall, pausing where the melody seemed to have originated, from behind the attic door. I grasped the handle and opened the door slowly. The flashlight illuminated the room, creating long, creeping shadows. Apprehensively, I climbed the stairs toward the music. The room was still and, except for the music, lifeless. As I panned the room with the light, my heart quickened. The cradle was uncovered. The dusty, draped sheet that had concealed it now lay crumpled at its base on the attic floor. Anxiously, I continued my examination, until I had centered the light on the source of the enchanted disturbance. It was the ornate heirloom box that Barry and I had discovered the afternoon that we had moved in our belongings. The Christmas Box. I hadn't known at the time it was capable of music. How odd it should start playing in the middle of the night. I looked around once more to be sure that I was alone, then balanced the flashlight on one end so that its beam illuminated the rafters and lit the whole attic. I lifted the box and inspected it for a lever with which to turn off the music. The box was dusty and heavy and appeared just as we had seen it a few days previous. I inspected it more closely but could find no key and no spring, in fact no mechanism of any type. It was simply a wooden box. I unclasped the silver buckle and opened the lid slowly. The music stopped. I moved the flashlight close to examine the box. Inside lay several parchment documents. I reached in and lifted the top page. It was a letter. A handwritten letter, brittle with age and slightly yellowed. I held it near the flashlight to read. The handwriting was beautiful and disciplined.

December 6, 1914

My Beloved One,

I stopped. I have never been one to revel in the intrusion of another's privacy, much less inclined to read someone else's correspondence. Why then I was unable to resist reading the letter is as much a mystery to me as was the parchment itself. So strong was the compulsion that I finished the letter without so much as a second thought into the matter:

How cold the Christmas snows seem this year without you. Even the warmth of the fire does little but remind me of how I wish you were again by my side. I love you. How I love you.

I did not know why the letter beckoned me or even what significance it carried. Who was this Beloved One? Was this Mary's writing? It had been written nearly twenty years before her husband had passed away. I set the letter back in the box and shut the lid. The music did not start up again. I left the attic and returned to my bed pondering the contents of the letter. The mystery as to why the Christmas Box had started playing music, even how it had played music, remained, for the night, unanswered.

The next morning I explained the episode to an only slightly interested wife.

"So you didn't hear anything last night?" I asked. "No music?"

"No," Keri answered, "but you know I'm a pretty heavy sleeper."

"This is really strange," I said, shaking my head.

"So you heard a music box. What's so strange about that?"

"It was more than that," I explained. "Music boxes don't work that way. Music boxes play when you open them. This one stopped playing when I opened it. And the strangest part is that there didn't appear to be any mechanism to it."

"Maybe it was your angel making the music," she teased.

"Maybe it was," I said eerily. "Maybe this is one of those mystical experiences."

"How do you even know the music was coming from the box?" she asked skeptically.

"I'm sure of it," I said. I looked up and noticed the time. "Darn, I'm going to be late and I'm opening up today." I threw on my overcoat and started for the door.

Keri stopped me. "Aren't you going to kiss Jenna good-bye?" she asked incredulously. I ran back to the nursery to give Jenna a kiss.

I found her sitting in a pile of shredded paper with a pair of round-edged children's scissors in hand.

"Dad, can you help me cut these?" she asked.

"Not now, honey, I'm late for work."

The corners of her mouth pulled downward in disappointment.

"When I get home," I hastily promised. She sat quietly as I kissed her on the head.

"I've got to go. I'll see you tonight." I dashed out of the room, nearly forgetting the lunch which Keri had set by the door, and made my way through the gray, slushy streets to the formal-wear shop.

◆

Each day, as the first streaks of dawn spread across the blue winter morning sky, Mary could be found in the front parlor, sitting comfortably in a posh, overstuffed Turkish chair, warming her feet in front of the fireplace. In her lap lay the third Bible. The one that she had kept. This morning ritual dated decades back but Mary could tell you the exact day it had begun. It was her "morning constitutional for the spirit," she had told Keri.

During the Christmas season she would read at length the Christmas stories of the Gospels, and it was here that she welcomed the small, uninvited guest.

"Well, good morning, Jenna," Mary said.

Jenna stood at the doorway, still clothed in the red-flannel nightshirt in which she almost always slept. She looked around the room then ran to Mary. Mary hugged her tightly.

"What are you reading? A story?" Jenna asked.

"A Christmas story," Mary said. Jenna's eyes lit up. She crawled onto Mary's lap and looked for pictures of reindeer and Santa Claus.

"Where are the pictures?" she asked. "Where's Santa Claus?"

Mary smiled. "This is a different kind of Christmas story. This is the first Christmas story. It's about the baby Jesus."

Jenna smiled. She knew about Jesus.

"Mary?"

"Yes, sweetheart?"

"Will Daddy be here at Christmas?"

"Why of course, dear," she assured. She brushed the hair back from Jenna's face and kissed her forehead. "You miss him, don't you?"

"He's gone a lot."

"Starting a new business takes a lot of work and a lot of time."

Jenna looked up sadly. "Is work better than here?"

"No. No place is better than home."

"Then why does Daddy want to be there instead of here?"

Mary paused thoughtfully. "I guess sometimes we forget," she answered and pulled the little girl close.

◆

With the approach of the holidays, business grew increasingly busy, and though we welcomed the revenue, I found myself working long days and returning home late each night. In my frequent absence, Keri had established the habit of sharing supper with Mary in the downstairs den. They had even adopted the ritual of sharing an after-dinner cup of peppermint tea near the fire. Afterward Mary would follow Keri into the kitchen and help clean up the supper dishes, while I, if home by this time, would remain in the den and finish the day's books. Tonight the snow fell softly outside, contrasted by the sputtering and hissing of the warm fire crackling in the fireplace. Jenna had been sent up to bed, and as Keri cleared the table, I remained behind, diving into a catalog of new-fashioned cummerbunds and matching band ties. Tonight Mary also remained behind, still sitting in the antique chair from which she always took her tea. Though she usually followed Keri into the kitchen, sometimes, after she had finished her tea, she would doze quietly in her chair until we woke her and helped her to her room.

Mary set down her tea, pushed herself up, and walked over to the cherry wood bookshelf. She pulled a book from a high shelf, dusted it lightly, and handed it to me.

"Here is a charming Christmas tale. Read this to your

little one." I took the book from her outstretched arm and examined the title, *Christmas Every Day* by William Dean Howells.

"Thank you, Mary, I will." I smiled at her, set the book down, and went back to my catalog. Her eyes never left me.

"No, right now. Read it to her now," she coaxed. Her voice was fervent, wavering only from her age. I laid my text down, examined the book again, then looked back up into her calm face. Her eyes shone with the importance of her request.

"All right, Mary."

I rose from the table and walked up into Jenna's room, wondering when I would catch up on my orders and what magic this old book contained to command such urgency. Upstairs Jenna lay quietly in the dark.

"Still awake, honey?" I asked.

"Daddy, you forgot to tuck me in tonight."

I switched on the light. "I did, didn't I. How about a bedtime story?"

She jumped up in her bed with a smile that filled the tiny room. "What story are you going to tell?" she asked.

"Mary gave me this book to read to you."

"Mary has good stories, Dad."

"Then it should be a good one," I said. "Does Mary tell you stories often?"

"Every day."

I sat on the edge of the bed and opened the old book. The spine was brittle and cracked a little as it opened. I cleared my throat and started reading aloud.

The little girl came into her papa's study, as she always did Saturday morning before breakfast, and asked for a story. He tried to beg off that morning, for he was very busy, but she would not let him . . .

"That's like you, Dad. You're real busy too," Jenna observed.

I grinned at her. "Yeah, I guess so." I continued reading.

"Well, once there was a little pig—" The little girl put her hand over his mouth and stopped him at the word. She said she had heard the pig stories till she was perfectly sick of them.

"Well, what kind of story shall I tell, then?"

"About Christmas. It's getting to be the season, it's past Thanksgiving already."

"It seems to me," argued her papa, *"that I've told as often about Christmas as I have about little pigs."*

"No difference! Christmas is more interesting."

Unlike her story's counterpart, Jenna was long asleep before I finished the tale. Her delicate lips were drawn in a gentle smile, and I pulled the covers up tightly under her chin. Peace radiated from the tiny face. I lingered a moment, knelt down near her bed and kissed her on the cheek, then walked back down to finish my work.

I returned to the den to find the lavish drapes drawn tight, and the two women sitting together in the dim, flickering light of the fireplace talking peacefully. The soothing tones of Mary's voice resonated calmly through the room. She looked up to acknowledge my entrance.

"Richard, your wife just asked the most intriguing question. She asked which of the senses I thought was most affected by Christmas."

I sat down at the table.

"I love everything about this season," she continued. "But I think what I love most about Christmas are its sounds. The bells of street-corner Santa Clauses, the familiar Christmas records on the phonograph, the sweet, untuned voices of Christmas carolers. And the bustling downtown noises. The crisp crinkle of wrapping paper and department store sacks and the cheerful Christmas greetings of strangers. And then there are the Christmas stories. The wisdom of Dickens and all Christmas storytellers." She seemed to pause for emphasis. "I love the sounds of this season. Even the sounds of this old house take on a different character at Christmas. These Victorian ladies seem to have a spirit all their own."

I heartily agreed but said nothing.

She reflected on the old home. "They don't build homes like this anymore. You've noticed the double set of doors in the front entryway?"

We both nodded in confirmation.

"In the old days—before the advent of the telephone . . ." She winked. "I'm an old lady," she confided, "I remember those days."

We smiled.

". . . Back in those days when people were receiving callers they would open the outer set of doors as a signal. And if the doors were closed it meant that they were not receiving callers. It seemed those doors were always open, all holiday long." She smiled longingly. "It seems silly now. You can imagine that the foyer was absolutely chilly." She glanced over to me. "Now I'm digressing. Tell us, Richard, which of the senses do you think are most affected by Christmas?"

I looked over at Keri. "The taste buds," I said flippantly. Keri rolled her eyes.

"No. I take it back. I would say the sense of smell. The smells of Christmas. Not just the food, but everything. I remember once, in grade school, we made Christmas ornaments by poking whole cloves into an orange. I remember how wonderful it smelled for the entire season. I can still smell it. And then there's the smell of perfumed candles, and hot wassail or creamy cocoa on a cold day. And the pungent smell of wet leather boots after my brothers and I had gone sledding. The smells of Christmas are the smells of childhood." My words trailed off into silence as we all seemed to be caught in the sweet glaze of Christmastime memories, and Mary nodded slowly as if I had said something wise.

◆

It was the sixth day of December. Christmas was only two and a half weeks away. I had already left for work and Keri had set about the rituals of the day. She stacked the breakfast dishes in the sink to soak, then descended the stairs to share in some conservation and tea with Mary. She entered the den where Mary read each morning. Mary was gone. In her chair lay the third Bible. Mary's Bible. Though we were aware of its existence, neither Keri nor I had actually ever seen it. It lay on the cushion spread open to the Gospel of John. Keri gently slipped her hand under the book's spine and lifted the text carefully. It was older than the other two Bibles, its script more Gothic and graceful. She examined it closely. The ink appeared marred, smeared by moisture. She ran a finger across the page. It was wet, moistened by numerous round drops. Tear drops. She delicately turned through the gold-edged pages. Many of the leaves were spoiled and stained from tears. Tears from years past, pages long dried and wrinkled. But the open pages were still moist. Keri laid the book back down on the chair and walked out into the hall. Mary's thick wool coat was missing from the lobby's crested hall tree. The inner foyer doors were ajar and at the base of the outer set of doors snow had melted and puddled on the cold marble floor, revealing Mary's departure. Mary's absence left Keri feeling uneasy. Mary rarely left the home before noon and, when she did, typically went to great lengths to inform Keri of the planned excursion days in advance. Keri went back upstairs until forty-five minutes later, when she heard the front door open. She ran down to meet Mary, who stood in the doorway, wet and shivering from the cold.

"Mary! Where have you been?" Keri exclaimed. "You look frozen!" Mary looked up sadly. Her eyes were swollen and red.

"I'll be all right," she said, then without an explanation disappeared down the hall to her room.

After brunch she again pulled on her coat to leave. Keri caught her in the hall on the way out. "I'll be going out again," she said simply. "I may return late."

"What time shall I prepare supper?" Keri asked.

Mary didn't answer. She looked directly at her, then walked out into the sharp winter air.

It was nearly half past eight when Mary returned that evening. Keri had grown increasingly concerned over her strange behavior and had begun looking out the balcony window every few minutes for Mary's return. I had already arrived home from work, been thoroughly briefed on the entire episode, and, like Keri, anxiously anticipated her return. If Mary had looked preoccupied before, she was now positively engrossed. She uncharacteristically asked to take supper alone, but then invited us to join her for tea.

"I'm sure my actions must seem a little strange," she apologized. She set her cup down on the table. "I've been to the doctor today, on account of these headaches and vertigo I've been experiencing."

She paused for an uncomfortably long period. I sensed she was going to say something terrible.

"He says that I have a tumor growing in my brain. It is already quite large and, because of its location, they cannot operate." Mary looked straight ahead now, almost through us. Yet her words were strangely calm.

"There is nothing that they can do. I have wired my brother in London. I thought you should know."

Keri was the first to throw her arms around Mary. I put my arms around the two of them and we held each other in silence. No one knew what to say.

◆

Denial, perhaps, is a necessary human mechanisim to cope with the heartaches of life. The following weeks proceeded largely without incident and it became increasingly tempting to delude ourselves into complacency, imagining that all was well and that Mary would soon recover. As quickly as we did, however, her headaches would return and reality would slap our faces as brightly as the frigid December winds. There was one other curious change in Mary's behavior. Mary seemed to be growing remarkably disturbed by my obsession with work and now took it upon herself to interrupt my endeavors at increasingly frequent intervals. Such was the occasion the evening that she asked the question.

"Richard. Have you ever wondered what the first Christmas gift was?"

Her question broke my engrossment in matters of business and weekly returns. I looked up.

"No, I can't say that I've given it much thought. Probably gold, frankincense, or myrrh. If in that order, it was gold." I sensed that she was unsatisfied with my answer.

"If an appeal to King James will answer your question, I'll do so on Sunday," I said, hoping to put the question to rest. She remained unmoved.

"This is not a trivial question," she said firmly. "Understanding the first gift of Christmas is important."

"I'm sure it is, Mary, but this is important right now."

"No," she snapped, "you don't know what is important right now." She turned abruptly and walked from the room.

I sat quietly alone, stunned from the exchange. I put away the ledger and climbed the stairs to our room. As I readied for bed, I posed to Keri the question Mary had asked.

"The first gift of Christmas?" she asked sleepily. "Is this a trick question?"

"No, I don't think so. Mary just asked me and was quite upset that I didn't know the answer."

"I hope she doesn't ask me, then," Keri said, rolling over to sleep.

I continued to ponder the question of the first gift of Christmas until I gradually fell off in slumber. That night the angel haunted my dreams.

◆

The following morning at the breakfast table, Keri and I discussed the previous evening's confrontation.

"I think that the cancer is finally affecting her," I said.

"How is that?" Keri asked.

"Her mind. She's starting to lose her mind."

"She's not losing her mind," she said firmly. "She's as sharp as you or me."

"Such a strong 'no'," I said defensively.

"I'm with her all day. I ought to know."

"Then why is she acting this way? Asking weird questions?"

"I think she's trying to share something with you, Rick. I don't know what it is, but there is something." Keri walked over to the counter and brought a jar of honey to the table. "Mary is the warmest, most open individual I've ever met, except . . ." She paused. "Do you ever get the feeling that she is hiding something?"

"Something?"

"Something tragic. Terribly tragic. Something that shapes you and changes your perspective forever."

"I don't know what you're talking about," I said.

Suddenly Keri's eyes moistened. "I'm not so sure that I do either. But there is something. Have you ever seen the Bible that she keeps in the den?" I shook my head.

"The pages are stained with tears." She turned away to gather her thoughts. "I just think that there is a reason that we're here. There is something she is trying to tell you, Rick. You're just not listening."

CHAPTER FIVE
THE
STONE ANGEL

My conversation with Keri had left me curious and bewildered. As I gazed outside at the snow-covered streets I saw Steve in his driveway brushing snow off his car. It occurred to me that he might have some answers. I ran upstairs to the Christmas Box, removed the first letter from it, and scrolled it carefully. Then stowing it in the inside pocket of my overcoat, I quietly slipped out of the house and crossed the street. Steve greeted me warmly.

"Steve, you've known Mary a long time."

"Pretty much all my life."

"There's something I want to ask you about."

He sensed the serious tone of my voice and set the brush down.

"It's about Mary. You know she's like family to us." He nodded in agreement. "There seems to be something troubling her, and we want to help her, but we don't know how. Keri thinks that she might be hiding something. If that's the case I think that I might have found a clue." I looked down, embarrassed by the letter I was holding. "Anyway, I found some letters in a box in the attic. I think they're love letters. I was hoping that you could shed some light on this."

"Let me see it," he said.

I handed the letter over. He read it, then handed it back to me.

"They are love letters, but not to a lover."

I must have looked perplexed.

"I think you should see something. I'll be over at Mary's Christmas Eve to visit. I'll take you then. It'll be around three o'clock. It will explain everything."

I nodded my approval. "That will be fine," I said. I shoved the letter back into my coat, then paused. "Steve, have you ever wondered what the first gift of Christmas was?"

"No. Why do you ask?"

"Just curious, I guess." I walked back to my car and drove off to work.

As had become the norm, it was a busy day spent helping brides-to-be match colorful taffeta swatches to formal-wear accessories; choose between ascot or band ties; pleated, French-cuffed shirts with wingtip collars or plain shirts with colorful ruffled dickies. I had just finished measuring and reserving outfits for a large wedding party. Upon receiving the required cash deposit from the groom, I thanked them for their business, waved goodbye, and turned to help a young man who had stood quietly at the counter awaiting my attention.

"May I help you?" I asked.

He looked down at the counter, swaying uneasily. "I need a suit for a small boy," he said softly. "He's five years old."

"Very good," I said. I pulled out a rental form and began to write. "Is there anyone else in the party that will need a suit?"

He shook his head no.

"Is he to be a ring bearer?" I asked. "We'd want to try to match his suit to the groom's."

"No. He won't be."

I made a note on the form.

"All right. What day would you like to reserve the suit for?"

"We'd like to purchase the suit," he said solemnly.

RICHARD PAUL EVANS

I set the form aside. "That may not be in your best interest," I explained. "These young boys grow so fast. I'd strongly suggest that you rent."

He just nodded.

"I just don't want you to be disappointed. The length of the coat cannot be extended, only the sleeves and pant length. He may grow out of it in less than a year."

The man looked up at me, initiating eye contact for the first time. "We'll be burying him in it," he said softly.

The words fell like hammers. I looked down, avoiding the lifeless gaze of his eyes.

"I'm sorry," I said demurely. "I'll help you find something appropriate."

I searched through a rack of boys suits and extracted a beautiful blue jacket with satin lapels.

"This is one of my favorites," I said solemnly.

"It's a handsome coat," he said. "It will be fine." He handed me a paper with the boy's measurements.

"I'll have the alterations made immediately. It will be ready to be picked up tomorrow afternoon."

He nodded his head in approval.

"Sir, I'll see that the jacket is discounted."

"I'm very grateful," he said. He opened the door and

walked out, blending in with the coursing river of humanity that filled the sidewalks at Christmas time.

◆

As I had spent the morning measuring out seams and checking the availabilities of jackets, Keri was busy at her own routine. She had fed, bathed, and dressed Jenna, then set to work preparing Mary's brunch. She poached an egg, then topped a biscuit with it, dressing it with a tablespoon of Hollandaise sauce. She took the shrieking teapot from the stove and poured a cup of peppermint tea, set it all on a tray, and carried it out to the dining room.

She called down the hall, "Mary, your brunch is ready."

She went back to the kitchen and filled the sink with hot, soapy water and began to wash the dishes. After a few minutes she toweled off her hands and walked back to the dining room to see if Mary needed anything. The food was untouched. Keri explored the den but the Bible lay untouched on its shelf. She checked the hall tree and found Mary's coat hanging in its usual place. She walked down to the bedroom and rapped lightly on the door.

"Mary, your brunch is ready."

There came no reply.

Keri slowly turned the handle and opened the door. The drapes were still drawn closed and the room lay still and dark. In the bed she could see the form lying motionless beneath the covers. Fear seized her. "Mary! Mary!" She ran to her side. "Mary!" She put her hand against the woman's cheek. Mary was warm and damp and breathing shallowly. Keri grabbed the telephone and called the hospital for an ambulance. She looked out the window. Steve's car was still in the driveway. She ran across the street and pounded on the door. Steve opened it, instantly seeing the urgency on Keri's face.

"Keri, what's wrong?"

"Steve! Come quick. Something is terribly wrong with Mary!"

Steve followed Keri back to the house and into the room where Mary lay delirious on the bed. Steve took her hand. "Mary, can you hear me?"

Mary raised a tired eyelid, but said nothing. Keri breathed a slight sigh of relief.

Outside, an ambulance siren wound down. Keri ran out to meet it and led the attendants down the dark hall to Mary's room. They lifted Mary into a gurney and carried her to the back of the vehicle. Keri grabbed Jenna and followed the ambulance to the hospital in Mary's car.

I met Keri and the doctor outside of Mary's hospital room. Keri had called me at work and I had rushed down as soon as I could.

"This is to be expected," the doctor said clinically. "She has been pretty fortunate up until today, but now the tumor has started to put pressure on vital parts of the brain. All we can do is try to keep her as comfortable as possible. I know that's not very reassuring, but it's reality."

I put my arm around Keri.

"Is she in much pain?" Keri asked.

"Surprisingly not. I would have expected more severe headaches. She has headaches, but not as acute as most. The headaches will continue to come and go, gradually becoming more constant. Coherency is about the same. She was talking this afternoon but there's no way of telling how long she'll remain coherent."

"How is she right now?" I asked.

"She's asleep. I gave her a sedative. The rush to the hospital was quite a strain on her."

"May I see her?" I asked.

"No, it's best that she sleep."

◆

That night the mansion seemed a vacuum without Mary's presence and, for the first time, we felt like strangers in somebody else's home. We ate a simple dinner, with little conversation, and then retired early, hoping to escape the strange atmosphere that had surrounded us. But even my strange dreams, to which I had grown accustomed, seemed to be affected. The music played for me again, but its tone had changed to a poignant new strain. Whether it had actually changed, or I, affected by the day's events, just perceived the alteration, I don't know, but like the siren's song, again it drew me to the Christmas Box and the next letter.

December 6, 1916

My Beloved One,

Another Christmas season has come. The time of joy and peace. Yet how great a void still remains in my heart. They say that time heals all wounds. But even as wounds heal they leave scars, token reminders of the pain. Remember me, my love. Remember my love.

◆

Sunday morning, Christmas Eve, the snow fell wet and heavy and had already piled up nearly four inches by afternoon when Steve met me near the mansion's front porch.

"How's Mary today?" he asked.

"About the same. She had a bad bout of nausea this morning but otherwise was in pretty good spirits. Keri and Jenna are still at the hospital with her now."

He nodded in genuine concern. "Well, let's go," he said sadly. "It will be good for you to see this."

We crossed the street and together climbed the steep drive to his home. Still unaware of our destination, I followed him around to his backyard. The yard was filled with large cottonwood trees and overgrown eucalyptus shrubs. It was well secluded by a high stone wall that concealed the cemetery I knew to be behind it.

"There's a wrought-iron gate behind those bushes over there," Steve said, motioning to a hedge near the wall. "About forty years ago the owner here planted that hedge to conceal the access to the cemetery. He was an older man and didn't like the idea of looking out into it each day. My family moved here when I was twelve years old. It didn't take us boys long to discover the secret gate. We hollowed out the hedge so that we could easily slip into the cemetery from it. We were frequently warned by the sexton never to play in the cemetery, but we did, every chance we got. We'd spend hours there," Steve confided. "It was the ideal place for hide-and-seek."

We reached the gate. The paint had chipped and cracked from the cold, rusted steel, but the gate remained strong and well secured. A padlock held it shut. Steve produced a key and unlocked the gate. It screeched as it swung open. We entered the cemetery.

"One winter day we were playing hide-and-seek about here. I was hiding from my friend when he saw me and started to chase. I ran though the snow up to the east end of the cemetery; it was an area where we never played. One of our friends swore he had heard the wailing of a ghost up there and we decided the place was haunted. You know how kids are."

I nodded knowingly as we trudged on through the deepening snow.

"I ran up through there," he said pointing to a clump of thick-stumped evergreens, "then up behind the mausoleum. There, as I crouched behind a tombstone, I heard the wailing. Even muffled in the snow it was heart-wrenching. I looked up over the stone. There was a statue of an angel about three feet high with outstretched wings. It was new at the time and freshly whitewashed. On the ground before it knelt a woman, her face buried in the snow. She was sobbing as if her heart were breaking. She clawed at the frozen ground as if it held her from something she wanted desperately—more than anything. It was snowing that day and my friend, following my tracks, soon caught up to me. I motioned to him to be quiet. For more than a half hour we sat there shivering and watching in silence as the snow completely enveloped her. Finally she was silent, stood up, and walked away. I'll never forget the pain in her face."

Just then I stopped abruptly. From a distance I could see the outspread wings of the weather-worn statue of an angel. "My angel," I muttered audibly. "My stone angel."

Steve glanced at me.

"Who was buried there?" I asked.

"Come see," he said, motioning me over.

I followed him over to the statue. We squatted down and I brushed the snow away from the base of the monument. Etched in the marble pedestal, above the birth and death dates, were just three words:

I studied the dates. "The child was only three years old," I said sadly. I closed my eyes and imagined the scene. I could see the woman, wet and cold, her hands red and snow bitten. And then I understood. "It was Mary, wasn't it?"

His response was slow and melancholy. "Yes. It was Mary."

The falling snow painted a dreamlike backdrop of solitude around us.

It seemed a long while before Steve broke the silence. "That night I told my mother what I had seen. I thought that I would probably get in trouble. Instead she pulled me close and kissed me. She said that I should never go back, that we should leave the woman alone. Until now, I never did go back. At least not to the grave. I did come close enough to hear her crying, though. It would tear me up inside. For over two years she came here every day, even in spring when the pouring rain turned the ground to mud."

I turned away from the angel, thrust my hands in my coat pockets, and started back in silence. We walked the entire distance to the house before either one of us spoke. Steve stopped at his back porch.

"The child was a little girl. Her name was Andrea. For many years Mary placed a wooden box on the grave. It resembles the boxes the wise men carry in Nativity scenes. My guess is it's the box you found with the letters."

I mumbled a thank you and headed for home alone. I unlocked the heavy front door and pushed it open. A dark silence permeated the mansion. I climbed the stairs to our quarters and then the attic, and for the first time I brought the Christmas Box out into the light. I set it on the hall floor and sat down beside it. In the light, I could see the truly exquisite craftsmanship of the box. The high polish reflected our surroundings and distorted the images, giving a graceful halo to the reflected objects. I removed the last letter.

December 6, 1920

My Beloved One,

How I wish that I might say these things to your gentle face and that this box might be found empty. Even as the mother of our

Lord found the tomb they placed Him in empty. And in this there is hope, my love. Hope of embracing you again and holding you to my breast. And this because of the great gift of Christmas. Because He came. The first Christmas offering from a parent to His children, because He loved them and wanted them back. I understand that in ways I never understood before, as my love for you has not waned with time, but has grown brighter with each Christmas season. How I look forward to that glorious day that I hold you again. I love you, my little angel.

Mother

CHAPTER SIX
THE
ANGEL

set the letter back in the box and pulled my knees into my chest, burying my head into my thighs. My mind reeled as if in a dream, where pieces of the day's puzzle are unraveled and rewoven into a new mosaic, defying the improbability of the cut edges fitting. Yet they did fit. The meaning of Mary's question was now clear to me. The first gift of Christmas. The true meaning of Christmas. My body and mind tingled with the revelations of the day. Downstairs I heard the rustling of Keri's return. I walked down and helped her in.

"I came back to get Jenna some dinner," she said, falling into my arms. "I am so exhausted," she cried. "And so sad."

I held her tightly. "How is she?"

"Not very good."

"Why don't you lie down, I'll put on some soup and get Jenna ready for bed."

Keri stretched out on the sofa while I dressed Jenna, fed her, then carried her downstairs to the den.

It was dark outside, and in absence of a fire, the room was bathed by the peaceful illumination of the Christmas tree lights. Strands flashed on and off in syncopation, casting shadows of different shapes and hues. I held Jenna in silence.

"Dad, is Mary coming home for Christmas?" she asked.

I ran a hand through my hair. "No, I don't think so. Mary is very sick."

"Is she going to die?"

I wondered what that meant to my little girl.

"Yes, honey. I think she will die."

"If she is going to die, I want to give her my present first."

She ran over to the tree and lifted a small, inexpertly wrapped package. "I made her an angel." With excitement she unveiled a petite cardboard angel constructed with tape, glue, and paper clips.

"Dad, I think Mary likes angels."

I started to sob quietly. "Yeah, I think she likes angels, too."

In the silence of the lights we faced the death of a friend.

In the outer hall I could hear the ringing of the telephone. Keri answered it, then found us downstairs.

"Rick, that was the hospital. Mary is dying."

I wrapped Jenna up warmly and set her in the car with Keri. We drove separately, so that one of us could bring Jenna home when the time came. We arrived at the hospital and together opened the door to Mary's room. The room was dimly illuminated by a single lamp. We could hear Mary's shallow breathing. Mary was awake and looked toward us.

Jenna rushed to the side of the reclining bed and, inserting her tiny hand through the side rails, pressed the little angel into Mary's hand.

"I brought you something, Mary. It's your Christmas present."

Mary slowly raised the ornament to her view, smiled, then squeezed the little hand tightly.

"Thank you, darling." She coughed heavily. "It's beautiful." Then she smiled into the little face. "You're so beautiful." She rubbed her hand across Jenna's cheek.

Painfully, she turned to her side and extended her hand to me.

I walked to her side and took it gently in mine.

"How do you feel, Mary?"

She forced a smile through the pain. "Do you know yet, Rick? Do you know what the first Christmas gift was?"

I squeezed her hand tightly.

"You do understand, don't you?"

"Yes. I understand now. I know what you were trying to tell me."

Tears started to fall down my cheeks. I took a deep breath to clear my throat.

"Thank you, Mary. Thank you for what you've given me."

"You found the letters in the Christmas Box?"

"Yes. I'm sorry that I read them."

"No, it's all right. I'm glad the letters were read. They were meant to be read." She fell silent for a moment.

"I'd like you to have the Christmas Box. It's my Christmas gift to you."

"Thank you. I will always treasure it."

The room was quiet.

"Andrea waits," she said suddenly.

I smiled. "She has been very close," I said.

She smiled at me again, then lifted her eyes to Keri.

"Thank you for your friendship, dear. It has meant a lot to me."

"Merry Christmas, Mary," Keri said.

"God bless you, child," she said back lovingly. "Take good care of your little family." She looked at Keri thoughtfully. "You'll do fine."

Mary closed her eyes and lay back into her pillow. Keri's eyes watered as she lifted Jenna and carried her out of the room. I stayed behind, caressing the smooth, warm hands for the last time.

"Merry Christmas, Mary," I whispered. "We'll miss you."

Mary's eyes opened again. She leaned forward toward the foot of the bed. A smile spread across her face as a single tear rolled down her cheek. She said something too soft to hear. I leaned my ear near to her mouth. "My angel," she repeated. I followed her gaze to the foot of the bed but saw only the green cotton hospital gown draped over the end rail. I looked back at her in sadness. She was leaving us, I thought. It was then that I heard the music. The gentle, sweet tines of the Christmas Box. Softly at first, then as if to fill the entire room, strong and bright and joyful. I looked again at the weary face. It was filled with peace. Her deep eyes sparkled and the smile grew. Then I understood and I too smiled. Andrea had come.

◆

By the time I reached home it was well past midnight. Mary's brother had arrived from London and in deference I had left them alone to share the last few minutes together. Jenna had been put to bed and Keri, not knowing when I would return, had sadly laid the Christmas packages under the tree. I sat down in the rocker in front of the illuminated Christmas tree and lay my head in my hands. Somewhere between the angel and Mary's house I had figured it out. The first gift of Christmas. It just came. It came to my heart. The first gift of Christmas was love. A parent's love. Pure as the first snows of Christmas. For God so loved His children that He sent His son, that we might someday return to Him. I understood what Mary had been trying to teach me. I stood up and walked up the stairs where my little girl lay sleeping. I picked up her warm little body and, cradling her tightly in my arms, brought her back down to the den. My tears fell on her hair. My little girl. My precious little girl. How foolish I'd been to let her childhood, her fleeting, precious childhood slip away. Forever. In my young mind everything was so permanent and lasting. My little girl would be my little girl forever. But time would prove me wrong. Someday she'd grow up. Someday she'd be gone and I would be left with the memory of giggles and secrets I might have known.

Jenna took a deep breath and snuggled close for warmth. I held her little body tightly against mine. This was what it meant to be a father, to know that one day I would turn around and my little girl would be gone. To look upon the sleeping little girl and to die a little inside. For one precious, fleeting moment, to hold the child in my arms, and would that time stood still.

But none of that mattered now. Not now. Not tonight. Tonight Jenna was mine and no one could take this Christmas Eve away from me but me. How wise Mary had been. Mary, who knew the pain of a father sending his son away on that first Christmas morn, knowing full well the path that lay ahead. Mary understood Christmas. The tears in the Bible showed that. Mary loved with the pure, sweet love of a mother, a love so deep that it becomes the allegory for all other love. She knew that in my quest for success in this world I had been trading diamonds for stones. She knew, and she loved me enough to help me see. Mary had given me the greatest gift of Christmas. My daughter's childhood.

EPILOGUE

t was around nine o'clock Christmas morning that Mary's brother called to tell us Mary was gone. The call found Keri and me holding each other on the couch in Mary's den, surrounded by the aftermath of Christmas giving. I lifted the Christmas Box down from the fireplace mantel where we had placed it in memory of Mary. I set the box near the hearth, then one by one, let the flames devour the letters as Keri watched in silent understanding. The Christmas Box was at last empty.

Mary was buried next to the small angel statue that she had so faithfully visited. In the course of our assisting in the burial arrangements, the funeral home had asked Keri what they should engrave on the headstone. "A loving mother," she said simply.

Every Christmas Eve, for as long as we lived in the valley, we returned to the grave and laid a white lily beneath the feet of the angel with outspread wings. Keri and I lived in the mansion for the space of several more Christmas seasons until the family decided to sell the estate, and we purchased a home in the southern end of the valley. In the years since, our family grew from three to six, and though the demands of providing for such a family oftentimes seemed endless, I never forgot the lessons I learned that Christmas with Mary.

And to this day, the Christmas Box remains a source of great joy to me. For though it appears empty, to me it contains all that Christmas is made of, the root of all wonder in a child's eyes, and the source of the magic of Christmases for centuries to come. More than giving, more than believing, for these are mere manifestations of the contents of that box. The sacred contents of that box are a parent's pure love for a child, manifested first by a Father's love for all His children, as He sacrificed that which He loved most and sent His son to earth on that Christmas day so long ago. And as long as the earth lives, and longer, that message will never die. Though the cold winds of life may put a frost on the heart of many, that message alone will shelter the heart from life's storms. And for me, as long as I live, the magic inside the Christmas Box will never die.

It never will.

Timepiece

CONTENTS

◆

The only promise of childhood is that it will end.

PROLOGUE

 find myself astonished at mankind's persistent yet vain attempts to escape the certainty of oblivion, expressed in nothing less than the ancient pyramids and by nothing more than a stick in a child's hand, etching a name into a freshly poured sidewalk. To leave our mark in the unset concrete of time—something to say we existed.

Perhaps this is what drives our species to diaries, that some unborn generation may know we once loved, hated, worried, and laughed. And what is there to this? Maybe nothing more than poetic gesture, for diaries die with their authors—or so I once believed. I have learned there is more to the exercise. For as we chronicle our lives and the circumstances that surround them, our perspectives and stretching rationales, what lies before us is our own reflection. It is the glance in the mirror that is of value. These are my words on the matter and I leave it at this—if we write but one book in life, let it be our autobiography.

◆

The most valuable of the keepsakes left in the attic of the Parkin mansion were thought worthless by the auctioneers of the estate. They were the leather-bound diaries of David Parkin. A lifetime of hopes and dreams, thought of no significance by those who value only what could bring cash at an auction block. The diaries came into my possession shortly after we took leave of the mansion, and it was within the pages of David's diary that I found the meaning of MaryAnne Parkin's last request. For this reason, I have shared his words throughout my narrative—for without them, the story would be incomplete.

And if it is nothing more than poetic gesture, then still I am justified.

For poetry, like life, is its own justification.

CHAPTER ONE
THE GRANDFATHER'S CLOCK

"Of all, clockmakers and morticians should bear the keenest sense of priority—their lives daily spent in observance of the unflagging procession of time . . . and the end thereof."

DAVID PARKIN'S DIARY. JANUARY 3, 1901

hen I was a boy, I lived in horror of a clock—a dark and foreboding specter that towered twice my height in the hardwood hallway of my childhood home and even larger in my imagination.

It was a mahogany clock, its hood rising in two wooden cues that curled like horns on a devil's head. It had a brass-embossed face, black, serpentine hands, and a flat, saucer-sized pendulum.

To this day, I can recall the simple and proud incantations of its metallic chime. At my youthful insistence, and to my father's dismay, the strike silent was never employed, which meant the clock chimed every fifteen minutes, night and day.

I believed then that this clock had a soul—a belief not much diminished through age or accumulated experience. This species of clock was properly called a longcase clock, until a popular music hall song of the nineteenth century immortalized one of its ilk and forever changed the name. The song was titled "My Grandfather's Clock," and during my childhood, more than a half century after the song was written, it was still a popular children's tune. By the age of five, I had memorized the song's lyrics.

> My grandfather's clock was too large for the shelf,
> so it stood ninety years on the floor,
> It was taller by half than the old man himself,
> tho' it weighed not a penny-weight more.
> It was bought on the morn of the day that he was born,
> and was always his treasure and pride,
> But it stopp'd short never to go again
> when the old man died.

My fear of the hallway clock had its roots in the song's final refrain.

But it stopp'd short never to go again
when the old man died.

When I was young, my mother was sickly and often bedridden with ailments I could neither pronounce nor comprehend. With the reasoning and imagination of childhood, I came to believe that if the clock stopped, my mother would die.

Often, as I played alone in our quiet house after my brothers had left for school, I would suddenly feel my heart grasped by the hand of panic and I would run to my mother's darkened bedroom. Peering through the doorway, I would wait for the rise and fall of her chest, or the first audible gasp of her breath. Sometimes, if she had had an especially bad day, I would lie awake at night listening for the clock's quarter-hour chime. Twice I ventured downstairs to the feared oracle to see if its pendulum was still alive.

To my young mind, the clock's most demonic feature was the hand-painted moon wheel set above its face in the clock's arch. Mystically, the wheel turned with the waning moon, giving the clock a wizardry that, as a child, transfixed and mystified me as if it somehow knew the mysterious workings of the universe. And the mind of God.

It is my experience that all childhoods have ghosts.

◆

Tonight, just outside my den stands a similar grandfather's clock—one of the few antiques my wife and I received from MaryAnne Parkin, a kind widow we shared a home with for a short while before her death nearly nineteen years ago. The clock had been a gift to her on her wedding day from her husband, David, and during our stay in the mansion it occupied the west wall of the marble-floored foyer.

David Parkin had been a wealthy Salt Lake City businessman and a collector of rare antiquities. Before his death, in 1934, he had accumulated an immense collection of rare furniture, Bibles, and, most of all, clocks. Time-marking devices of all kinds—from porcelain-encased pocket watches to hewn-stone sundials—filled the Parkin home. Of his vast collection of timekeepers, the grandfather's clock, which now stands outside my doorway, was the most valuable—a marvel of nineteenth-century art and engineering and the trophy of David's collection. Even still, there was one timepiece that he held in greater esteem. One that he, and MaryAnne, cherished above all: a beautiful rose-gold wristwatch.

Only eleven days before her death, MaryAnne Parkin had bequeathed the timepiece to my keeping.

"The day before you give Jenna away," she had said, her hands and voice trembling as she handed me the heirloom, "give this to her for the gift."

I was puzzled by her choice of words.

"Her wedding gift?" I asked.

She shook her head and I recognized her characteristic vagueness. She looked at me sadly, then forced a fragile smile. "You will know what I mean."

I wondered if she really believed that I would or had merely given the assurance for her own consolation.

It had been nineteen winters since Keri, Jenna, and I had shared the mansion with the kindly widow, and though I had often considered her words, their meaning eluded me still. It haunted me that I had missed something that she, who understood life so well, regarded with such gravity.

Tonight, upstairs in her bedroom, my daughter Jenna, now a young woman of twenty-two, is engaged in the last-minute chores of a bride-to-be. In the morning, I will give her hand to another man. A wave of melancholy washed over me as I thought of the place she would leave vacant in our home and in my heart.

The gift? What in the curriculum of fatherhood had I failed to learn?

I leaned back in my chair and admired the exquisite heirloom. MaryAnne had received the watch in 1918 and, even then, it was already old: crafted in a time when craftsmanship was akin to religion—before the soulless reproductions of today's mass-market assembly.

The timepiece was set in a finely polished rose-gold encasement. It had a perfectly round face with tiny numerals etched beneath a delicate, raised crystal. On each side of the face, intricately carved in gold, were scallopshell-shaped clasps connecting the casing to a matching rose-gold scissor watchband. I have never before, or since, seen a timepiece so beautiful.

From the dark hallway outside my den, the quarter-hour chime of the grandfather's clock disrupted my thoughts—as if beckoning for equal attention.

The massive clock had always been a curiosity to me. When we had first moved into the Parkin mansion, it sat idle in the upstairs parlor. On one occasion, I asked MaryAnne why she didn't have the clock repaired.

"Because," she replied, "it isn't broken."

◆

Treasured as it is, the clock has always seemed out of place in our home, like a relic of another age—a prop left behind after the players had finished their lines and taken their exits. In one of those exits is the tale of David and MaryAnne Parkin. And so, too, the riddle of the timepiece.

CHAPTER TWO
MARYANNE

SALT LAKE CITY, 1908

"A young woman came to my office today to apply for employment. She is a rather handsome woman, and, though simply dressed, exuded both warmth and grace, a pleasant diversion from the society women I too frequently encounter who exhibit the cold refinement of a sterling tea service. I proceeded to acquaint myself with her, offend her, and hire her all in the course of one half hour. Her name is MaryAnne Chandler and she is an Englishwoman.

"There is a curious chemistry between us."

DAVID PARKIN'S DIARY. APRIL 16, 1908

lectric sparks fell like fireworks from the suspended cables of a trolley car, as the brash clangor of its bell pierced the bustle of the wintry Salt Lake City streets. At its passing, MaryAnne glanced across the snow and the mud-churned road, lifted her skirt above her ankles, and crossed the street, stepping between the surreys and traps that lined the opposite stretch of the cement walk. Near the center of the block, she entered a doorway marked in arched, gold-leafed letters: PARKIN MACHIN-ERY CO. OFFICE.

As she pulled the door shut behind herself, the chill sounds of winter dissolved into the cacophony of human industry. Brushing the snow from her shoulders, she glanced around the enormous room.

Its high ceiling was upheld by dark wooden Corinthian columns from which projected the brass fittings of gaslights. Maplewood desks lined the hardwood floor, each with a small rug delineating the employee's work space.

An oak railing separated the work floor from the entryway, and the man who occupied the desk nearest the entrance acknowledged MaryAnne with clerk-like nonchalance. He was a balding man, attired in a wool suit and vest with a gold chain spanning his ample girth.

"I am here to see Mr. Parkin about a secretarial situation," MaryAnne announced. She pulled the kerchief back from her hair, revealing a gentle complexion and high, shapely cheekbones. Her beauty piqued the clerk's interest.

"Have you an appointment with Mr. Parkin?"

"Yes. He is expecting me at nine. I am a few minutes early."

Without explanation, the clerk stepped away from his desk and disappeared through an oak doorway near the back of the spacious room. A few minutes later he returned, followed by another individual, a well-groomed young man in his early thirties.

The man had a pleasant face with strong but not overbearing features. He was of medium height and well proportioned, with dark, coffee-colored hair, which had been parted and brushed back in the latest continental style. His eyes were azure blue and alive with interest in all that moved about him. He wore no jacket, revealing the pleated front of his wing-collared shirt and the garters that held his sleeves. He carried himself casually, yet with a confidence that bespoke his importance with the firm.

"Miss Chandler?"

"Yes."

He extended his hand. "Thank you for coming. If you will please follow me," he said, motioning to the door he had just emerged from. MaryAnne followed him through the doorway, then down an oak-paneled corridor to a staircase. She stopped her escort at the foot of the stairs.

"Sir, if I may inquire . . . ?"

He turned and faced her. "Yes. Of course."

"When I address Mr. Parkin, shall I call him 'Mr. Parkin' or 'sir'?"

The young man considered the question. "He likes to be called 'Your Majesty.'"

MaryAnne was dumbstruck.

"I am joking, Miss Chandler. I don't suppose it matters at all what you call him."

"I am not seeking to flatter him. I am just grateful to be able to meet with someone as prominent as Mr. Parkin. I hope to make a favorable impression."

"I am certain that you will do just that."

"Why so?"

"Because I am David Parkin."

MaryAnne flushed. She covered her mouth with her hand. "You are so young to . . ."

". . . Be a millionaire?"

MaryAnne turned a brighter shade of crimson, at which David chuckled. "I am sorry, Miss Chandler, I should have introduced myself properly. Please come up to my office."

They climbed the stairway to the second level and entered a corner office overlooking Second South and Main Street. The office was large and the cherrywood cabinets and shelves that lined the walls were cluttered with books and a score of mantel clocks, which were used as bookends and adornment. No fewer than a dozen other clocks—free standing cabinet or wag-on-the-wall clocks—garnished the room as well. Outside of a clock shop, MaryAnne had never seen such a congregation. They ticked loudly and she wondered how anyone could think in such a place.

In the center of the room was a beautiful hand-carved mahogany desk with a gold-embossed leather writing surface dyed in rich green and umber hues. To its side was a Dictaphone table with a large battery box underneath.

"May I assist you with your coat?" David offered, helping to slip the wet garment from her shoulders.

"Thank you."

MaryAnne settled into a wooden chair, straightened her dress and lay her hands in her lap, while David returned to his desk.

"You have many clocks."

He smiled pleasantly. "I collect them. At the top of the hour, there is quite a racket."

MaryAnne smiled. "I would think so."

David sat down at his desk. "Your accent betrays you. You are from England, are you not?"

She nodded.

"What part of England?"

"A borough of London. Camden Town."

"I was through there a few summers back. Just outside of Regent's Park. I occasionally spend time in England at the auctions."

She smiled. "I have fond memories of Regent's Park."

David leaned forward in his chair. "Your letter said that you are skilled in secretarial work."

"Yes. I have three years' experience on the typewriter, both a Hammond and a Remington. I know Pitman's shorthand and am a member of the Phonetic Society. I have used a Dictaphone," she replied, pointing to the heavy table a few feet from his desk. "An Edison model like this one. I have also kept a register for six months." Then, looking up at a row of clocks, she added, "And I am very punctual."

David smiled at her reference to the clocks.

MaryAnne reached into her purse and brought out a bundle of papers. "I brought letters."

David accepted the papers. "Where did you acquire your skills, Miss Chandler?"

"I worked with Marley and Sons Glaziers as Mr. Marley's assistant. When Mr. Marley took ill, I was given leave. He passed on shortly afterward. Then I went to work at Walker's stationery shop on Main Street. I typed invoices and recorded receipts. The shop closed on account of the death of Mr. Walker."

"This is not a good omen, Miss Chandler. Do all your employers release you through such somber means?"

"I prefer to think that they would rather die than release me."

David smiled at her quick reply. "So it would seem. How much did the position pay?"

She swallowed nervously. "I require twelve dollars a week."

David looked back down at her letters. "You were only two weeks at your last employment." He paused, inviting response.

She hesitated. "I could not meet my supervisor's expectations."

David was surprised by her honesty. "Exactly what was it that you found so challenging?"

"I would rather not say."

"I appreciate your hesitation, Miss Chandler, but if I am to hire you in good faith, it is quite essential that I know your limitations."

"Yes," she relented. She turned from her interrogator and took a deep breath. "Sitting on his lap."

David cocked his head.

MaryAnne blushed. "Sitting on his lap," she repeated. "My supervisor wanted me to sit on his lap."

"Oh," David replied. "You will find none of that in this office." He hurriedly changed the subject. "How is it that you came to live in Salt Lake City? It is not a place you accidentally arrive at."

"My father came from England in the hope of capitalizing on what was left of the gold rush. When we arrived at Ellis island, he heard that California was either panned out or the big finds were controlled by large interests, but that there had recently been a large silver strike in Salt Lake City. So my father brought his family out to settle. I was only seven years old at the time."

"Your father came to mine?"

"No. To sell goods to the miners. He said it is easier to pan gold from a purse than a river."

"A wise man, your father. I have never seen so many fools work so hard for easy money and end up with so little of it. How did he fare in the business?"

"Unfortunately, my father was not of good health. He died shortly after our arrival in the valley. The West is not an easy place for a man used to the comfortable life of nobility."

"Your father was a nobleman?"

"My father was the second son of a baron."

David studied her carefully, resting his chin on his hands. "And that makes you . . ."

"It makes me nothing, as I am an American."

David nodded. "It is just as well," he said. He leaned back, lacing his fingers behind his head. "A title is much too troublesome and high-minded."

MaryAnne glared back, certain that she or, at the very least, her ancestors had been offended. "Whatever do you mean?"

"I believe Your Grace was saying," David said, adopting an exaggerated British accent. "My Most Reverend, Most Noble, Right Honorable, Venerable, Duke, Duchess, Squire, Lord, Lady, Baron, Baroness, Viscount,

Marquess, Earl." He breathed out in feigned exasperation. "It is a business in itself and all too tiresome."

"You mock me!"

David waved a hand. "No. No. I am merely amused by the show."

MaryAnne sat back, her arms folded defensively across her chest. "America has its castes."

"True. But in America they are for sale."

MaryAnne glowered, then suddenly stood up, brushing down her skirt as she rose. "I think I shall go now, Mr. Parkin."

Her response surprised him and the smile left David's face.

"I have offended you."

"Not in the least," she replied, raising her chin indignantly.

"No, I have. I am sorry. Please don't go."

She said nothing.

"I apologize, Miss Chandler. I did not mean to be offensive. Attribute my rudeness to my crass upbringing as an American. Surely you cannot begrudge me of that."

"Pity you, perhaps."

"Touché," David said, grinning.

She retrieved her coat from the pole and put it on. David walked over to the doorway. "MaryAnne, I should like to work together. I will pay you eighteen dollars a week. If you choose to accept, you may begin immediately."

MaryAnne lifted her chin proudly, retaining an air of indignation. "I will see you Monday morning at five minutes to eight, Mr. Parkin."

David grinned. "It will be a pleasure, Miss Chandler."

CHAPTER THREE
DAVID

*"My new secretary manifests a peculiar confederation of
English ritual and American sensibility. I enjoy her company,
though she seems of a rather serious nature and I wish she were
not so formal."*

DAVID PARKIN'S DIARY. APRIL 29, 1908

n hour after the close of the business
week, Gibbs, the company's head clerk,
lumbered up the stairway sporting a tumbler in each chubby fist. When he reached David's
office, he was breathing heavily. He set the glasses on
the desk and announced, "I brought you some port."

David was standing behind his desk thumbing
through a leather-bound manual. He brought the volume to his desk and sat down.

"Ah, you are well trained, Gibbs. Or at least opportunistic. Thank you." He bowed back over the book.

Gibbs took a chair in front of the desk and claimed one of the drinks as his own. "The Salisbury mine is now in possession of a new ore crusher and our account runneth over."

"Well done, Gibbs. It is a strong year."

"They have all been strong years." Gibbs looked around the room. "Your girl is gone?"

"MaryAnne? Yes, she has left for the day."

"You have not said much of her."

David continued reading, acknowledging the observation with only a nod.

"Is she capable?"

David looked up from his register. "She is wonderful. In fact, I am growing quite fond of her."

Gibbs pushed back in his chair. "Fond? Why so?"

David closed the book. "She is a curiosity to me. She has the work ethic of a farm wife and the refinement of the well-bred." He took a drink. "Only better, for it is not an acquired grace, but a natural refinement."

"Refinement?" Gibbs laughed. "Wasted on the likes of you."

David grinned. "No doubt." He set down his tumbler. "Still, they use the pig to find truffle."

"A fitting analogy, I might say."

"You might not," David countered.

Gibbs laughed. "Her apparel is common enough."

"Mark me. She is a poor woman with nobility hidden beneath rags."

"And you a rich man with the common touch. How incongruous."

"How perfect."

"How so?"

David leaned back in his chair. "Two oddities make a normality. It works in mathematics, as in life."

"You are still just talking about a secretary?" Gibbs asked sardonically.

David studied his associate's expression with consternation.

"I have said more than I ought and you have clearly heard more than I have said." He lifted his glass to the light. "Is there much talk among the typists?"

"Some. They like a scandal and if they cannot find one, they invent one."

"Then I suppose I am doing them a service of sorts."

He leaned back over his register. "Still, I wish she were not so formal."

Just then, the first of the mantel clocks struck the seventh hour, immediately followed by a chorus of bells, gongs, and chimes, all counting out the hour in a different voice. Gibbs, accustomed to the hourly pandemonium, waited for it to settle before continuing. "I think you are asking for trouble, David. Love and business do not mix well."

"Gibbs, you surprise me. What do you know of love?"

The man licked the rim of his glass, then set it down on the desk. "Only that it is the worm that conceals the hook."

"You are cynical."

"And you are not?"

David frowned. "I should be."

Gibbs nodded knowingly. He had grown up with David in the California mining town of Grass Valley and knew of what David spoke. David's mother had abandoned him as a child and stolen from him as an adult.

Rosalyn "Rose" King, a music hall singer of mediocre ability, had married David's father, Jesse Parkin, believing he would someday strike the mother lode. Ten years later the two had managed to produce only a son and a miserly shaft mine called the Eureka.

The year David turned six, Rose abandoned the Midas dream and left everything, including David, behind. It wasn't until the lonely and celebrationless Christmas day of that year that David accepted that his mother wasn't coming back.

Thirteen years to the month of her departure, the Eureka lived up to its name. It was to be one of the largest gold strikes in California history.

Jesse ceded the mine to his son's care, built a sixteen-hundred-acre ranch in Santa Rosa, and settled about the life of a Western Gentleman. Not two years later, Jesse was thrown from a horse and died instantly of a broken neck.

Gibbs accompanied David as he buried his father in the foothills of Mount Saint Helena. David mourned greatly.

The following spring, David received a letter from a mother he no longer knew. Rose had come West to Salt Lake City and learning of her husband's fortune and recent demise, inquired into the will. Learning that David was the sole heir and not yet married, she invited him to come and live with her, with the urgent request that he send money ahead.

Against Gibbs's advice, David sold the mine. In a day when the average annual income was scarcely more than a thousand dollars, the Eureka fetched two million.

David wired twenty-five thousand dollars to his mother and purchased, sight unseen, an elaborate Salt Lake City mansion for them to reside in.

By the time he and Gibbs arrived in the Salt Lake Valley in spring of 1897, his mother had taken the money and moved to Chicago with a man she had met only three weeks previously, leaving only a penned regret that forever lies pressed between the pages of David's journal.

As powerful as David had become financially, in matters of the heart he was vulnerable and Gibbs brooded over him, protecting him from those who sought financial gain through romantic liaison. This role gave Gibbs no pleasure, however, for he knew his friend's loneliness. Despite David's unhappy experience, he desired the companionship marriage brings, but was not sure how to proceed, viewing women much as the novice card player who understands the rules, but not how the game is really played.

◆

David finished his drink, then set it down in front of him as his friend studied him sadly. Gibbs gathered the empty glasses and stood to leave. "Still, she is quite pretty."

After a moment, David looked up. "Yes. Quite."

CHAPTER FOUR
LAWRENCE

"The first mechanical clock was invented in the year A.D. 979 in Kaifeng, China. Commissioned by the boy emperor for the purpose of astrological fortune-telling, the clock took eight years to construct and weighed more than two tons. Though of monstrous dimensions, the device was remarkably efficient, striking a gong every fourteen minutes and twenty-four seconds, nearly identical to our modern-day standard, at the same time turning massive rings designed to replicate the celestial movements of the three luminaries: the sun, the moon, and selected stars, all of which were crucial to Chinese astrological divination.

"When the Tartars invaded China in 1108, they plundered the capital city and after disassembling the massive clock, carted it back to their own lands. Unable to put the precision piece back together, they melted it down for swords."

NOTE IN DAVID PARKIN'S DIARY

aryAnne knocked gently at David's door, then opened it enough to peer in. "Mr. Parkin, you have a visitor."

David glanced up. "Who is it?"

"He would not give his name. He says he is a close friend."

"I am not expecting anyone. What does he look like?"

"He is an older gentleman . . ."

David shrugged.

". . . and he is a Negro."

"A Negro? I do not want to see any Negroes."

"I am sorry, sir. He said he was a close friend."

Just then, the man appeared behind MaryAnne. He was a large man, dressed as a soldier in a navy cotton shirt and tan pants with a leather bullet belt clasped to a silver cavalry buckle. He smiled at David. "David, you givin' this nice lady a bad time."

David grinned. "I could not resist. Come in, Lawrence."

Surprised, MaryAnne stepped back and pulled open the door for him to enter.

"Sorry, ma'am. It's David's sense of humor."

"Or lack of," she replied.

Lawrence laughed jovially. "I like you, ma'am. Who is this lady, David?"

"Lawrence, meet Miss MaryAnne Chandler. She is my new secretary. Miss Chandler, this is Lawrence. He is the godfather to most of the clocks you see in this room."

"It is a pleasure meeting you, sir."

Lawrence bowed. "It's my pleasure, ma'am."

"Gentlemen, if I may be excused."

David nodded and MaryAnne stepped away, shutting the door behind her.

"Where's Miss Karen?" Lawrence asked.

"It has been a while since you have been around. Her mother took ill and she went back to Georgia."

"She was a nice gal."

"Yes. She did not think much of Negroes, though."

"Her upbringin'," Lawrence said in her defense.

"You are kinder than you ought to be," David said, reclining in his chair. "What have you brought to show me?"

Lawrence lifted a gold pocket watch by its bob and handed it to David, who examined it carefully, then held it out at arm's length. "Look at that," he said beneath his breath.

"It's a fine piece. Maybe the finest I seen. French made. Never even been engraved. Belonged to a Mr. Nathaniel Kearns."

"Gold plate?"

"Solid."

"How much does Kearns want for it?"

"Mr. Kearns don't want nothin'. He's dead. The auctioneers askin' seventy-five dollars."

"Is it worth it?"

"Sixty-seven dollars, I'd say."

"I will purchase it," David decided. "For sixty-seven." He stood up. "Would you care for something to drink?" He pulled a crystal decanter from a cabinet against the west wall.

"Shore I would."

David poured Lawrence a shot glass of rum. Lawrence took the glass, then leaned back while David walked back to his chair.

"How long this MaryAnne worked for you?"

"About six weeks." The corners of his mouth rose in a vague smile. "She is rather special."

"I can see that," he said. "Called me 'suh'."

David nodded, then glanced over to the door to be

certain it was closed. "I have a question for you, Lawrence."

Lawrence looked up intently over his glass.

"What do you think of me marrying?"

"You, David?"

"What would you say to that?"

"Now why you askin' me? I ain't ever been married."

"I value your opinion. You are a good judge of character."

Lawrence fidgeted uncomfortably.

"Come now, Lawrence. Speak freely."

Lawrence frowned. "It's my way of thinkin' that some folk shouldn' get themselves married."

David grinned. "Some folk? Folk like me?"

"I'm jus' sayin' someone shouldn' take a perfectly good life and go marryin' it. Seen it happen my whole life, someone has the good life. Plenty to eat. Plenty of time to jus' do nuthin', then a woman comes 'long and ruins it all."

David began to laugh. "Lawrence, you have a clarity of thought I envy."

"There someone you be thinkin' 'bout?"

"Yes. But I think she would be rather astonished to know of my intentions."

Lawrence glanced back toward the door and smiled knowingly.

"You do have a clarity of thought, my friend," David said.

Lawrence stood up. "Well, I best be off so you can be 'bout your business." His face stretched into a bright smile. "Whatever that business may be."

David grinned. "Thank you for bringing the timepiece by, Lawrence. I will come by this afternoon with the payment."

Lawrence stopped at the door. "Ain't no woman goin' to like all those clocks 'round her house."

"The right one will."

Lawrence opened the door and looked out at MaryAnne, who glanced up and smiled at him. He turned back toward David, who was examining his new timepiece. "You have an eye for finer things."

"So do you, Lawrence. So do you."

◆

Lawrence was a novelty in his neighborhood and the children of his street would wait patiently for his daily, slow-paced pilgrimage to the Brigham Street market, then scatter like birds at his appearance. No child could visit the area without hearing the boast from the indigenous children, "We got a Negro in our neighborhood."

His home was a ramshackle hut built behind a large brick cannery, and all in the neighborhood knew of its existence, despite the fact that it was well secluded and Lawrence was as inconspicuous as his skin allowed him to be.

Lawrence's last name was Flake, taken from the slave owners who had purchased his mother in eastern Louisiana in 1834. He had seen war twice, once in the South, and once in Cuba, and had grown old in the military, his black hair dusted silver with age.

He was tall, six foot, and broad-shouldered, and though he had a thick, powerful neck, his head hung slightly forward, a manifestation of a life of deference. His skin was patched and uneven from exposure to the elements, but his eyes were clear and quiet and said all that society would not allow spoken.

He walked with a limp, which increased with his age. The adult spectators of his daily march called it a Negro shuffle, ignorant of the Spanish bullet still lodged in his inner left thigh, a souvenir from the Spanish-American War.

Lawrence had belonged to the Negro Twenty-fourth

Cavalry, a "buffalo soldier" so named by the Indians who feared the black soldiers, convinced that their black, "woolly" hair and beards were evidence that they were mystical beings: half men, half buffalo. He had come to Utah when the Twenty-fourth was transferred to Fort Douglas, cradled on the east bench of the Salt Lake Valley, and remained behind when, four years later, the cavalry was restationed in the Philippines.

Lawrence's entry into clock repair was happenstance. He had been the army's supply and requisition clerk, and, naturally gifted with his hands, had a knack for repairing rifles, wagons, and whatever the post required fixing. On one occasion, he repaired a pocket watch for one of the officers, who, in appreciation, made Lawrence a present of a manual on clock repair and nicknamed him "the horologist," a title Lawrence clung to, as it made him feel scientific.

Salt Lake City had few horologists, and as word spread of Lawrence's expertise, civilians began bringing him their timepieces as well.

When he left the cavalry, his clientele followed him to his new shop. His clock-cleaning-and-repair business grew into a trading post of sorts, as people left notes of clocks they wanted to acquire or sell, and estate auctioneers found Lawrence to be a good wholesaler of their wares.

David met Lawrence through the purchase of a Black Forest cuckoo clock and instantly liked the man. There was a calmness in his motion, the temperament of one suited to repair the intricate. "Slow hands," David called it. But there was more. There was something comfortable in his manner that reminded David of earlier days. Growing up in the womb of the Eureka mine, David had worked and lived with black men, listened to their stories of injustices and enjoyed their company. In the depth of a mine, all men were black, and he had learned to appreciate people for their souls. The two men spent hours talking about clocks, California, and the cavalry.

Though both were fascinated by clocks, they were so for vastly different reasons. Where David saw immortality in the perpetual motion of the clocks' function, Lawrence was fascinated by the mechanism itself, and for hours on end, he would lose himself in a brass clockwork society—a perfect miniature world where all parts moved according to function. And every member had a place.

As the falling sun stretched the remnant shadows of the day, David rapped on the door of Lawrence's shack.

"Lawrence?"

A soft, husky voice beckoned him in.

David stepped inside. Lawrence sat on a cot in the corner of the darkened room, a single candle cast flickering slivers of light across the man's face. In his hand was a smoldering pipe, which glowed orange-red.

"Sit down," he said. "Sit down."

The dwelling consisted of one room divided by function: the living quarters toward the east and the shop toward the west, separated by a plethora of clocks and a heavy table covered with clockwork, candles, and dripped wax.

Lawrence was proud of his humble furnishings: a small, round-topped table, splintered and worn in parts with odd-lengthed legs to hold it steady on the shack's unlevel floor. Around the table were three chairs, each of different manufacture. His bed was a feather mattress set on a home-built wooden frame and covered with the thick wool army blankets and roll he had slept on for nearly forty years. In the corner of the room, a potbelly stove sat on a stone-and-concrete platform. Where the room wasn't illuminated by the stove, it was lit by kerosene army lamps that hung from the rafters.

There were no windows, though they would have been unusable, as Lawrence had stacked firewood across the outside wall of his home.

David sat down on one of the chairs near the round table. "I brought the money for the pocket watch." He laid a wad of bills on the table.

"Thank you."

"Who was that woman I passed on the way around?"

"Big woman? Tha's Miss Thurston. The preacher's wife."

"What did she want?"

"Same thing she always wants."

"Which is?"

"Wantin' to get me out to the colored church." Lawrence shook his head in wonder. "Woman gets talkin' and soon ain't talkin' to me no more, but like she preachin' to a congregation. Gets herself all riled up about sinners and heathens and their sorry souls. I think it must make her feel good. Like she talked some sense into me."

"Did she?"

Lawrence frowned. "Don't rightly know what to reckon of it all. S'pose there is a heaven, I wanna know what kinda heaven it be. Is it a heaven for white folks? Or is it a different heaven for colored folk and white folk? What you make of it?"

David shrugged. "I am not an expert. I have only been to church on a few occasions. It seems to me that people who spend their lives dreaming about the gold-paved streets and heavenly mansions of the next life are no different than those who waste their time dreaming about it in this life. Only with a poorer sense of timing."

Lawrence responded in low, rumbling laughter reserved for when he found something particularly amusing. He clenched down on his pipe. "Never thought of it that way," he replied.

"The way I see it, it's not about what you are going to get, it's about what you become. Divinity is doing what is right because your heart says it's right. And if that puts you on the wrong side of the pearly gates, seems you would be better off on the outside."

Lawrence took in a long draw on his pipe. "You could've been a philos'pher."

Just then, in the dancing radiance of the candles, David noticed something he had never seen before, despite his many visits. Across the room, amidst the squalor of metal springs, and the shells and corpses of clocks, was what appeared to be a shrouded sculpture slightly protruding from beneath a cloth sheet.

"What is that in the corner? Under the cloth?"

Lawrence lowered his pipe. "Tha's my angel. Jus' this mornin' had some help and we brought her up from the cellar."

"Angel?" David walked over to the piece.

"Real Italian marble," Lawrence said.

David pulled a floor clock back from the sculpture and lifted the drape, exposing a stone sculpture of a dove-winged angel. Its seraphic face turned upward and its arms were outstretched, raised as a child waiting to be lifted. David ran his fingers over its smooth surface.

"This is a very expensive piece. Probably worth a hundred dollars or more. Is it new?"

"Had it for nearly six years, jus' never take her out of the cellar."

David admired the sculpture. "How did you come by this?"

"Right after I left the cavalry, I did some work for a minister. Fixed his church's steeple clock. Took me 'bout the whole summer. Problem is, before I got done, the church treasurer run off with all their buildin' money. So the minister asks me if I won' take this angel for payment."

David stepped away from the statue, rubbing his hand along its surface once more.

"Why didn't you sell it?"

Lawrence shook his head. "Don't need nuthin'." "Nuthin' you can buy." He tapped his pipe against the table, looking suddenly thoughtful. "Way I figgur, black man got no r'spect in this life. So I was thinkin' when I die, they put this angel here on my grave. Somebody walks by, even white folks, see that fine angel. 'Looks like real Italian marble,' they say. 'Mighty fine. Mus' be someone real important has that kinda monument. Mus' be a rich man or a military officer,' and they go on like that." Lawrence's eyes reflected red from the smoldering pipe, but seemed to glow beneath their own power. "Black man don' get much r'spect in this life."

David looked at Lawrence and nodded slowly as the night's silence filled the humble shack.

CHAPTER FIVE

THE
PRESUMPTION

"MaryAnne came into the office today. I was surprised to see her, as it was her Sabbath. I was much too forward and I fear I have frightened her. I am clumsy with romance."

DAVID PARKIN'S DIARY. MAY 13, 1908

avid disliked suits and never wore them on Sunday when he came in to the office to work alone. He was intent over a stack of papers on his desk when MaryAnne's presence startled him.

"Miss Chandler. What brings you here?"

"I did not finish my letters."

David stood. "Monday is soon enough."

"I did not want to fall behind. You have been so very busy."

David smiled, pleased for her concern.

"I think I would be worried if you could keep up." He walked over to her. "Thank you, Miss Chandler, but go on home and rest. We have a full week ahead."

She put her hands in her coat pockets.

"Yes, sir."

Just then, a Westminster chime denoted a quarter of one. Both looked at the clock.

"I have not had supper, Miss Chandler. Would you care to join me? Perhaps at the Alta Club?"

MaryAnne smiled. "Thank you, Mr. Parkin, but if I am not needed, I should be off to church."

David nodded. "Yes. Of course. I suppose that I should go on home as well. Catherine is expecting me."

MaryAnne looked at him as if she had just been informed of some terrible news. She knew of no women in David's life. She tried to dismiss the thought and turned to leave, then paused at the doorway.

"May I ask you something, Mr. Parkin?"

"Of course."

"Who is Catherine?"

"Catherine is my housekeeper."

MaryAnne appeared relieved and turned to go, but David stopped her.

"Any other inquiries, Miss Chandler?"

She smiled playfully. "Now that you ask, I have wondered what makes a man collect clocks? And so many of them at that."

David studied her face, then leaned forward as if to reveal some great secret.

"It is because I need more time."

MaryAnne met his eyes and, for the first time in David's presence, laughed. It was a beautiful, warm laugh and David found it nourishing and laughed in turn.

"You have a wonderful laugh, Miss Chandler."

"Thank you."

"The truth is, I have wondered the same." He walked over to a cuckoo clock and lifted a brass pine-cone-shaped weight. "I am sure there are those who think me mad. As a boy, I had a penchant for collecting things. When I turned twenty-one, I received the first clock of my collection. It was my father's pocket watch." He suddenly stopped. "May I get you some tea? Peppermint?"

"Yes. Thank you." She started to rise. "I shall get it."

"Miss Chandler, please, sit down. I can manage." He brought the tea service over to his desk, poured two cups of tea, handed one to MaryAnne, then sat down on the arm of a nearby chair.

"I only drink peppermint tea. It's the one habit I borrowed from the English."

"Peppermint tea is an American concoction."

"Oh. Then I must just like it."

MaryAnne laughed again.

"I lived in Santa Rosa, California, at the time—when I turned twenty-one," he clarified. "It was the year my father died. It was also the same year that I first donned a pair of eyeglasses and acknowledged the creeping vines of age that entwine our lives."

MaryAnne nodded.

David looked back at a row of clocks. "I have wondered if I am deluding myself with these, that I am buying time—surrounding myself with man-made implements of immortality." He looked back at Mary-Anne. "Whatever the reason, my fascination has grown into a full-blown obsession. My home is besieged with them."

"I would like to see—" MaryAnne stopped herself midsentence at the realization that she had just invited herself to a man's home.

"I would like to show you," David answered. He sat back in his chair and slowly sipped his tea. "I am curious, Miss Chandler. Do you like it here?"

"Here?"

"At my company."

"Very much, I think. More so than my other employment."

"You do not seem to socialize much with the other secretaries on the floor."

"You do not employ me to socialize."

David smiled. "The proper answer," he replied. "You work hard for nobility."

MaryAnne gazed at him. "Are you teasing me?"

He quickly set down his cup, anxious that he might have offended her again. "No. Not at all."

She took a sip of tea to hide her smile, then cradled the cup in her hands.

"I have always had to work hard, Mr. Parkin. My father left England because he had been disinherited for marrying my mother—a common woman of whom my grandparents disapproved. We had little when we arrived in America and less when my father passed away. As soon as I was able, I had to assist in my family's support. My mother passed on two years ago. So I am alone now."

"Have you any siblings?"

"I have a brother. But he returned to England more than six years ago. He sent money for a while—when times were better."

David quietly digested the information, then rested his chin on the back of his clasped hands. "May I ask you something of a personal nature?"

She hesitated. ". . . Yes."

"Are there men in your life?"

"Men?"

"Suitors."

She hesitated again, embarrassed. "There are a few I cannot seem to discourage."

"That is your goal? With men?"

"With these men. I know them too well to marry them, Mr. Parkin."

David nodded, then set down his tea. "Miss Chandler, I would prefer that you not call me Mr. Parkin."

"What would you have me call you?"

"David. Please call me David."

She considered the request. "I do not think I would feel comfortable in front of my coworkers."

David sighed. "I would not want you to feel uncomfortable, Miss Parkin."

"Miss Parkin?"

His face turned bright crimson as he suddenly realized his slip. "Miss Chandler," he stammered.

Suddenly the amusement faded from MaryAnne's eyes. She turned from him and stood.

"I must go."

"Must you?"

"It would be best."

There was an uncomfortable lull.

"I am sorry, MaryAnne. Perhaps I seem like your last supervisor who wanted you to sit on his lap."

"No, I did not mean . . ."

"My intentions are honorable. I would never seek to take advantage. . . . It is just . . ."

MaryAnne stared at him with anticipation. He turned away from her gaze.

"I have never met anyone quite like you. I am nearly thirty-four and have no real lady friends. Not that there are not interested females. Unfortunately, there are too many." He frowned. "They are attracted to money and status and cannot see my faults for my wealth. Though I have no doubt that marriage would open their eyes. His voice softened. "I feel very comfortable in your presence."

MaryAnne glanced briefly into his eyes, but said nothing.

"I am very sorry, Miss Chandler, I have made you uncomfortable. Forgive me. I shall not broach the subject again."

MaryAnne looked down. "Mr. Parkin, there are just things that—" She stopped herself midphrase. "I think that I must go now."

She slowly walked over to the doorway, followed by David's sad stare. She stopped and looked back at him.

"Good day, Mr. Parkin."

"Good day, Miss Chandler."

◆

Catherine pushed the drawing room door open with her shoulder and entered carrying a silver tray with a sterling tea service. The drapes were drawn tight and David sat on a haircloth love seat, staring into the crackling fire that provided the room's only illumination.

For Catherine bringing tea to the drawing room was

a familiar ritual, established years before David had purchased the house; in a sense, Catherine had come with
the house. Her former employer, the mansion's previous
owner, fleeing the cold Salt Lake City winters for the
refuge of the southern Utah sun, had left behind
Catherine, his young housemaid, and Mark, his foot-
man, to consummate the sale of the property, then seek
employment elsewhere. When David arrived, he found
the house larger than he imagined and emptier than he
expected. As he was now alone, he entreated the two to
remain. They gladly accepted and quickly became part
of his family. The first year, David had tried to persuade
Catherine to call him by his first name, without success,
and he eventually abandoned the undertaking.

"Excuse me, Mr. Parkin, I brought some tea."

David turned, his trance seemingly broken. "Oh.
Thank you."

She left the service on a bird's-eye-maple parlor table
next to his chair.

"Mr. Flake brought the French clock. I had him leave
it in the parlor." She turned to leave, then stopped. "Are
you well, sir?"

He sighed. "I am well enough, I suppose. Thank you
for asking."

She turned again to leave.

"Catherine."

"Yes, sir."

"May I ask you something?"

"Certainly."

"As a woman . . . you being a woman . . ."

Catherine looked at him blankly.

"I meant . . . Oh, I sound foolish. How shall I ask this?" He appeared flustered with his inability to communicate his question. "What kind of man am I?"

Catherine looked confused. "I do not know how to answer that."

"I mean . . . do women, would a woman, find me attractive?"

"You are very handsome."

"I do not mean quite that. I mean . . . am I the kind of man a woman would want to marry? Or am I too long alone? Am I too rough? Do I say the wrong things?" His brow furled. "I need not ask that." David looked down. "I suppose it is no secret that I am fond of MaryAnne. Everyone seems to know it but her. Or perhaps she does not wish to know. Have you met MaryAnne?"

Catherine tilted her head thoughtfully. "I have only

seen her from a distance, though Mark tells me she is very pleasant."

"Yes. She is very pleasant. She always says the right thing—has the proper answer." He took a sip of tea. "A skill I obviously lack."

Catherine smiled kindly. "Mr. Parkin, you are a very good and kind man. Any woman would be fortunate to have you."

David looked up. "Thank you, Catherine."

"Good night, sir."

"Good night, Catherine."

She stopped at the threshold. "I spoke forthright, sir. Any woman would consider herself fortunate."

"Thank you," he repeated softly, then turned back toward the fire and lost himself in his thoughts.

◆

In the next nine weeks, as spring gave way to the oppression of summer, David noticed peculiarities in MaryAnne's behavior. It seemed to him that she was unusually preoccupied, and even her motion had taken on a peculiar deliberateness. At first, he had blamed himself for the change, attributing it to his "presumptuous blunder," until the peculiarities began to manifest themselves in more physical ways.

One afternoon, David heard her slowly climbing the stairway. She was winded when she reached the top of the stairs, and caught the railing, breathing heavily. Her face was flushed and she brushed her forehead with the back of her hand. David had watched her curiously from his doorway. When she saw him, she dropped her hand back to her side and walked quickly past him. David followed her. She sat down at her desk and began to type, ignoring his presence so deliberately as to acknowledge it.

David interrupted her. "Miss Chandler, are you well? You look peaked."

"I am fine," she replied. She did not look up, obviously avoiding his eyes. David continued to stare at her. "I'm concerned. You have not seemed yourself of late."

"Are you unsatisfied with my work?"

"No," he said firmly. "My concern is personal."

MaryAnne just bowed her head. Then, unexpectedly, she raised a hand to wipe a tear from her cheek.

The silence lengthened into an uncomfortable lull. David turned to leave.

MaryAnne took a deep breath. "David, may we speak?"

He stopped. It was the first time she had called him by his name and he knew that this was a matter of great significance.

"Of course. In my office."

Inside, he offered her a chair, then, after shutting the door, returned to his desk and leaned against its front edge.

She looked down, catching tears in a handkerchief, then swallowed and looked up into his face.

"There is a reason I have behaved so peculiarly." She paused to gain courage. "David, I am with child."

The words had a strange effect on him. He sat back on the desk, as if his legs would fail him, and slowly shook his head. "I am such a fool. I did not know you were married."

She lowered her head in shame. "I'm not. Nor will I be." She wiped her cheeks, then cradled her face in her hands. "I am so sorry. I should have told you sooner, but . . ." She stopped, unable to continue.

"Yes?" he gently coaxed.

She took a breath. "Shortly before I came to work

with you I was betrothed to be married. I was so foolish. He had pledged to me his love and I did not want to displease him. We were to be married this April." She looked up. "When he found out I was with child, he beat me."

The room was quiet except for the sound of the clocks.

"Why didn't you tell me before?"

"I was afraid."

"For your employment?"

She nodded, wiping away more tears. "I am all alone; I need the wages to care for my child. At first, I was afraid that you would not hire me if you knew. After I came to know you, I realized that it would not matter— that you would have hired me anyway. But by then I . . ."

David leaned forward.

". . . I was . . . Oh, this must sound so strange!"

"No," he said gently. "Go on, MaryAnne."

She looked away from him, then buried her head in her hands.

"I was beginning to have other feelings for you. I was afraid you would disapprove of me." She began to cry harder. The sound of the clocks seemed to increase in volume, interrupted by MaryAnne's occasional sobbing. Suddenly, David stepped forward and crouched down next to her chair. "There is a solution," he said gently.

MaryAnne lowered the handkerchief from her eyes.

"You could marry me."

She looked at him in disbelief, then covered her eyes with the handkerchief again. "Oh, David. Please do not play with me."

"No, I wouldn't."

She looked back up into his eyes. "You offer me yourself?"

"If it proves a bad bargain . . ."

"David? You would marry me with another man's child?"

David nodded, trying to coax a smile from her tear-streaked face.

For a moment, her eyes flashed brightly with hope, then extinguished almost as quickly. "It would be wrong for you, David. How could you?"

David took her hand in his. It was the first time that he had touched her in this way and it filled him with a strange electricity.

"In the wedding vow, they say for better or for worse. In sickness and in health. For richer or poorer. It would seem that the only thing certain about the alliance is a lot of uncertainty."

MaryAnne looked into his eyes. His gaze was direct and kind.

"I am not afraid of uncertainty or responsibility—it is what life is made of. But I am afraid that I will not meet another woman like you. And that you will not have me." The room fell silent except for the ticking of the clocks.

"David. I would be honored to be your wife."

David's eyes moistened. "I love you, MaryAnne." The words had come spontaneously, and he realized as he spoke them that it was the first time in his adult life that he had used the phrase. MaryAnne sensed the earnestness of his words and more tears welled up in her already moist eyes, then, before she could say anything, David pressed his lips against hers and gently kissed her.

MaryAnne pulled back suddenly and smiled. "I have a confession, David. Do you recall that Sunday when you accidentally called me Miss Parkin?"

David grinned, still embarrassed by the slip.

"Yes."

"It pleased me. I felt foolish, like a schoolgirl, but I

called myself MaryAnne Parkin all afternoon. I liked the sound of my name with yours."

"MaryAnne Parkin," David repeated. His face stretched into a broad smile. "Yes," he said, nodding his head. "There is something very natural about the confederacy of our names. . . . Perhaps it was meant to be."

CHAPTER SIX

THE ENGAGEMENT

"A conspiracy of florists, caterers, and clergy have done too well a job of shrouding the virtues of the elopement."

DAVID PARKIN'S DIARY. JULY 5, 1908

he many surreys and fewer motor coaches began arriving at the Parkin mansion at seven, dispensing their affluent cargo at the doorstep, then pulling off into the field alongside the house. The sudden engagement announcement had caused no small stir among the local society, and the party was considered an affair not to be missed.

Inside, David, dressed in black tails with a white, fish-scale vest and band tie, stood in the drawing room surrounded by a group of businessmen from the Alta Club, while Catherine scurried back and forth managing a bevy of servants and seeing to the details of the affair.

Meanwhile, Victoria Marie Piper, a woman of considerable social and physical presence, had taken it upon herself to find the bride-to-be and discovered MaryAnne in the parlor in the east wing, where she had been waiting for David. Victoria swept into the room in a high-necked peach gown, encircled by a pink feather boa. At first glance, the dress might have been mistaken for a wide-hooped crinoline, as it broadened out enough to obstruct the corridor. In reality, it was only the woman.

Crossing the room with a small plate piled with cake in one hand and a china tea cup in the other, she marched up to MaryAnne and formally introduced herself.

"Miss Chandler, I am Victoria Marie Piper, of the Boston Pipers," she prated. "I am embarrassed to admit that we have not yet been introduced at any of the functions. Are you new to the city?"

MaryAnne blushed. "No. I have just not been to any . . . functions."

"Oh," she said abruptly. "Then how were you introduced to David?"

MaryAnne smiled innocently. "I was David's secretary."

The woman made no attempt to conceal her horror. "Oh," she gasped. "An office girl." She took a step back. "There are such dreadful stories about the office, but I am sure they do not apply to you," she said, looking down at MaryAnne's slightly protruding stomach. "Myself, I do not think it a woman's place, but what do I know of such things? I am too old-fashioned and probably too sensible for my own good," she said, flourishing a corpulent hand in dramatic gesture.

MaryAnne glanced towards the door, hoping that David would soon appear and rescue her. The woman took another bite of cake, then chased it down with tea. "Do you know David well?" she pried.

"I met him last spring," MaryAnne answered. "I have not known him for very long."

Victoria's face contorted in pretense to some awful knowledge. "Well, I would be ill used to not warn you of David. He is a controversial sort."

"Controversial?"

"It is quite well known." She set her plate on the linen cloth of a buffet, then leaned close to MaryAnne. "He associates quite openly with the Negroes and makes absolutely no attempt to hide it. It is as if he is not ashamed of it."

MaryAnne felt her cheeks flush with indignation. Victoria continued.

"You should be apprised. Of course, I should be pleased if this was the worst of his vices. There is much more that you should know." She paused to fan herself. "But this is not the time or place. It is disloyal of me to eat his cake and poison his name."

"Yes," MaryAnne replied, "perhaps you should just poison his cake and be done with it."

The woman glared at MaryAnne. Just then, David entered the room. Victoria's mouth pursed in a garish smile. "Oh, David, how are you?"

"The state of my health cannot possibly be of any concern to you, Victoria. What gossip are you boring MaryAnne with?"

"Oh, David, you have such an imagination," she drawled, turning to MaryAnne. "We really must have tea sometime, dear. Before the wedding." Her words lifted in a cruel crescendo. "I have so much to tell you." She took her plate and strutted out of the room. MaryAnne breathed a sigh of relief.

David grinned. "So you met Victoria."

"I am afraid I have offended her."

"It speaks well of you to offend Victoria."

MaryAnne stifled a laugh.

"Though one should not be too hard on the woman. She cannot help but turn up her nose."

"And why is that?"

He pointed to his throat. "Her double chin."

"David, you are awful."

"Yes, but I am honest. Are you bored?"

"I feel a bit out of place."

"As do I. This affair reeks of pretension. It is like lard frosting without the cake. Of course, the truly criminal thing is that it is our affair!"

MaryAnne laughed heartily. "Oh, David, you make me happy." She sighed. "It is so good to laugh."

"I drink your laughter, MaryAnne. It intoxicates me." David took her hand and led her out onto the back patio overlooking the garden walkway. The July air was cool and the waning sickle of a moon dimly lit the cobblestone walkway below.

"So what did Victoria have to say?"

"Nothing worth repeating, I'm afraid."

"You should know that I love gossip about myself."

"Then I will tell you. She says that you are controversial and associate with the Negroes."

"If Victoria is nothing, she is honest. Have I lost you now?"

"She has endeared you to me. You should have seen her face when she learned I was your secretary. She kept looking down at my stomach."

"I would be disappointed in her if she had not noticed."

"Why does she act so?"

"Because Victoria is the worst kind of society. She is not old money or new money, but somewhere in between, so she is forever trying to prove that she belongs somewhere in society. You, my love, simply are not of their caste. Of course, neither am I, but as I am richer than they, and as money is their God, or at least their idol, they must bow. But they despise doing it." David smiled indulgently. "Money, as they say, is always chic."

MaryAnne suddenly looked down and leaned back against the railing. "David, how will marrying me affect your social standing?"

David laughed. "Very well, I think, now that I have

someone I care to socialize with." He paused, studying her sad countenance. "MaryAnne, you are thinking of your mother and father. It is similar in a way, is it not?"

MaryAnne nodded.

"Except our story has a happy ending. Besides, I believe the 'Victorias' of my world are happy for my decision. I am certain they believe a woman, if not able to civilize me, will at least round off the rough edges."

MaryAnne kissed his cheek. "How goes it downstairs?"

"Awful. When the mayor entered, he handed Lawrence his coat."

"Oh, my. What did you do?"

"I had just entered the foyer, so I greeted Lawrence as a war hero, flattered the coat he held, and asked if I could hang it for him."

"Oh, my," she repeated. "What did the mayor do?"

"He was florid. My only regret is that Victoria was not present. A good fainting is guaranteed to get a party into the social column."

MaryAnne laughed again.

"How was your first day off work?" David asked.

"I missed you." She sighed. ". . . But not Gibbs."

David smiled. "You know, he is to be my best man."

"As long as I get you at the end of the day, I do not much care." MaryAnne clasped her hands on her stomach and smiled dreamily. "Catherine and I found the most elegant wedding dress. It was quite expensive."

"Shall I sell the business?"

"Do not tease me. I feel awkward spending your money. It is improper of me to even speak of it."

"MaryAnne, it is wonderful having someone I care to spend it on. As your husband, I insist that you always allow me the luxury of spoiling you."

MaryAnne draped her arms around her fiancé. "What makes you think that I do not already have everything?"

"The proper answer," he replied. "Always the proper answer."

◆

"If the heavens were to open and a host of Angels descend, they could not have produced such an effect on my soul as MaryAnne descending the chapel staircase for our wedding."

DAVID PARKIN'S DIARY. AUGUST 11, 1908

It was common knowledge, if anything among the city's social elite was to be deemed common, that David

Parkin was not one for ostentatious display. So the extravagance of the wedding was a surprise to all, and even the most jaded admitted to being suitably impressed.

The preparation for the wedding had taken five weeks of daily attention from the time of the engagement announcement to the nuptial day, and Catherine, as instructed by David, saw to it all, conducting a symphony of florists, servants, and caterers. At one point, a florist wryly remarked, "Madam, I was told this was to be a wedding, not a coronation."

"This wedding will want for nothing," Catherine retorted. "Mr. Parkin expects an affair unlike one this city has ever witnessed. And nothing less."

The florist prudently apologized.

In the days leading up to the event, David considered MaryAnne's bridal gift with great care. Jewelry was customary, so in addition to the wedding ring, he had purchased a large diamond pendant, which, in afterthought, he found unsatisfying, as he thought gems generally cold, and the bauble's beauty easily outdone by MaryAnne's. Only two days before the wedding, the second gift arrived from a New York City brokerage and was promptly sequestered in the upstairs parlor behind a locked door. David was pleased by this gift most of all, and looked forward to its giving.

The morning of the wedding, Gibbs arrived early at the house to take David for breakfast. The florist and his assistants, under Catherine's watchful eye, were already busy wiring flowers to the chandeliers, railings, and brass hardware as David greeted Gibbs at the door. David was dressed in a high-necked, white linen shirt with a twelve-button silk vest. His tailcoat was pin-striped and cut at the waist. He wore charcoal trousers and a black silk top hat.

"Gibbs! Nice to see you, old man."

Gibbs embraced him in the open doorway. "'He was warned against the woman, She was warned against the man, And if that won't make a weddin', Why there's nothin' else that can!'"

"So there you have it, you are responsible for this affair."

"I do not take responsibility."

"It would be a good thing for you to do."

Gibbs smiled. "I am happy for you, David."

"I am happier for myself."

"I confess more than once I have been reminded of scripture about coveting a man's wife."

"You still have a few hours before it will be sin. Have you the license?"

Gibbs pulled the elaborate scrolled parchment from the breast pocket of his coat.

"Then you are an accomplice. And the ring?"

Gibbs nodded. "What a ring, David!" he exclaimed as he lifted the small box from his pocket. "Has MaryAnne seen it?"

David shook his head. "Not yet. It is one of the day's surprises."

Gibbs replaced the box and took two cigars from the breast pocket of his coat and offered one to David, as he turned looking out to his motorcar. "Well, David, we best be off. Your single carefree moments are fleeting." He grinned sardonically. "And with a new wife, perhaps your fortune as well."

◆

At the dictate of English custom, the wedding was scheduled for twelve noon. Ten minutes before the hour, David, with Gibbs by his side, entered the chapel and proceeded directly to the altar.

As the last noon strike of the steeple's clock resonated in a metallic echo, the church organ erupted in brilliant sforzando. MaryAnne appeared at the top of the circular staircase, and the entire congregation rose to their feet as much in collective awe as ceremony. She was radiant in a hand-embroidered ivory dress that laced down the front, corseting her narrow, though expanding, hourglass figure. Delicate lace gloves rose past her elbows and a cathedral-length veil cascaded down her back, held in place by a simple orchid wreath.

David could not take his eyes off his bride as she descended the stair, flanked by Catherine and preceded by Catherine's five-year-old niece, who dropped white rose petals before them as they passed beneath the great floral arches of white peonies and apple blossoms.

For the first time in his life, David truly felt fortunate. When MaryAnne reached the altar, he leaned close.

"You look stunning, my bride."

MaryAnne blushed as they knelt together before the clergyman on a silk pillow facing an altar of white-and-gold–leafed alderwood.

The organ ceased and MaryAnne handed the robed priest a prayer book. He thanked her, opened the book, and cleared his throat.

"Who giveth this woman to be married to this man?"

There was a sudden and uncomfortable silence. It had

been discussed previously that there was no one to give MaryAnne away. It was an error, born of habit, on the clergyman's part, and he instantly recognized his blunder.

MaryAnne looked up. "God does, Your Reverence."

The priest smiled as much at her cleverness as her sincerity.

"So he does, my dear."

He looked out over the congregation. "Dearly beloved, we are gathered here today to unite this couple in holy matrimony according to God's holy ordinance. Are there any who object to the union of this couple?"

There was no response, though Victoria Piper took the opportunity to cough. The priest turned to the bride. "My dear, if you will repeat after me."

MaryAnne looked at David affectionately as she repeated the words of the vow until the priest said "till death do us part."

David looked into her face as a tear rolled down her cheek. "MaryAnne?" he asked gently. At her name, MaryAnne looked up at David. "Not until death, my love, but forever."

David smiled and his eyes moistened. "Forever," he repeated.

Catherine wiped a tear from her cheek.

The priest smiled and continued. "And thereto I give thee my troth."

MaryAnne took a deep breath. "And thereto I give thee my troth."

The priest then turned to David, who followed him in the oath with the proper and extemporaneous alterations. When they had completed their vows, the priest nodded to Gibbs, who handed David the ring. MaryAnne removed the glove from her left hand and handed it to Catherine, who took it, and delicately folded it in half, then took MaryAnne's engagement ring and bouquet. MaryAnne offered David her hand.

David held out the ring. It was an exquisite diamond marquise of extraordinary cut and color, framed with sapphires, and set in a woven, white-gold band.

MaryAnne was breathless. "David!"

He smiled at her joy as he slid the ring onto her finger.

The priest bestowed a final blessing on the couple and the organ roared to life. David stood first, and offering his bride his right hand, helped her to her feet. She took his arm and, after Catherine had turned MaryAnne's train, they departed down the aisle. David shook a river of hands as they hurried out of the church to a flower-strewn carriage where a formally attired coachman sat waiting. At the couple's approach, the driver laid a step down and helped MaryAnne and then David into the carriage. He encouraged the horses with a flick of his whip and the carriage lurched forward.

When they were a distance from the church, David kissed his bride, then leaned back contentedly. "I would like to give you one of your wedding gifts now."

MaryAnne smiled. "One of?"

"Remember, my love, now that you are mine, it is my prerogative to spoil you." He handed her a small box wrapped in elegant white tissue. She tore back the paper, then lifted the lid. Inside lay the teardrop diamond pendant. It shone with exquisite brilliance, reflecting the afternoon sun.

"Oh, David," MaryAnne said softly. "You have made me a queen."

"No, MaryAnne. I have merely provided the proper accoutrements."

He raised the pendant, reached around her neck, and clasped its golden rope. It encircled her neck beautifully, falling just above her cleavage. She laid her head against his shoulder and looked down at her wedding ring. "I promise you that I will be a good wife."

"And, my love, I promise to be a good husband and friend. Your other present is back at our home."

"Our home," she repeated softly.

◆

The wedding-brunch arrangements had been made for the garden, and it had never seen such splendor. No expense was spared. Long-shafted oil lamps with ribbons and orange blossoms tied around their supports decorated the grounds. Peacocks strutted about the yard in full plume between the white-laced tables that dotted the estate. The wedding cake itself was an elegant feat of architecture, six-tiered and bedecked with freshly cut white and peach roses.

The food was served from the high-pitched, flower-laced gazebo. The menu had been especially selected and was abundant with cakes and bonbons, raw and fricasseed oysters, bouillon, cobblers, ices and coffee and entrées of crab, lobster, quail, and Cornish hens.

When the brunch had concluded, the caterers began the task of boxing and wrapping the wedding cake for the guests, and the couple moved inside to the elaborate drawing room, where white roses covered and concealed the room's chandeliers. Lilies and pink roses adorned the fireplace mantel and flowered vines encircled the mahogany pillars. David and MaryAnne stood before a backdrop of palms to meet their guests.

When the room's clocks struck five, David turned to his bride. "I would like to give you your wedding present now." Taking leave of their guests, he took her hand and led her upstairs to the parlor, where he removed a thin key from his vest and unlocked the door.

At his request, she closed her eyes, and taking his hand, followed him into the room.

"You may open your eyes."

MaryAnne opened her eyes. Before her stood a majestic grandfather's clock, larger and more magnificent than anything David had previously collected. It stood nearly eight feet in height, and the casing was ornately carved in floral renderings. Detailed pillars flanked the clock's hood, which rose in two swan-necked pieces of carved mahogany facing inward toward a central finial spire. The white-faced dial was hand-painted and bordered by ornately patterned brass spandrels, preserved beneath a lead-crystal door that locked with a skeleton key.

"David, it is the most beautiful clock."

David studied her face anxiously. "Do you like it?"

She stepped forward to her gift and ran her fingers

across its exquisite carvings. "It is so ornate. Yes. Very much."

David joined her. "I wanted the exterior to be as intricate as the interior clockwork. The chime is exquisite and unlike anything I have ever heard. It is angelic."

MaryAnne was enthralled. "I have never owned anything of such worth."

"May I tell you why I wanted to give you a clock?"

She turned to her groom. "There is greater significance than its beauty?"

David stared into the clock's face. "You once asked me why I collected clocks."

MaryAnne nodded.

"I have given this question a great deal of thought since then. A clock is a strange invention. A collection of cogs and gears that are always in motion, yet accomplish nothing. Not like a pump that provides water or a cotton gin that leaves something useful. A clock just moves without thought or meaning—worthless without interpretation." His eyes focused on the clock in condemnation. "It is just motion." He turned and looked into his new wife's eyes. "And so has been my life. I have moved, not with feeling, but because it is all that I could see to do. You have given my motion meaning."

MaryAnne looked into David's face. "I have given you my life, David."

"And in so doing, you have given me mine."

They embraced again, kissing at length. David smiled as they parted. "Let us be on our way!"

"Yes, my love."

◆

Gibbs was already outside with the hackney, loading the travel cases into the carriage. On the front step, MaryAnne hugged Catherine.

"Thank you, Catherine. You have made this day beautiful."

"I am so happy for you both. Take good care of him, MaryAnne. I love him dearly."

MaryAnne embraced her tighter. "How could you not, my sister."

After counting the cases, David took his bride by the hand and helped her up into the carriage.

Gibbs stood by the side of the carriage. "Good luck, David."

"Thank you, Gibbs. We will return in a fortnight. The company is in your hands."

CHAPTER SEVEN
ANDREA

"I had never supposed the cost women bear in the perpetuation of the species. Nor that such courage could be had in such a petite frame."

DAVID PARKIN'S DIARY. JANUARY 17, 1909

aryAnne's pains were still light when the hurry-up call went out to the midwife, one Eliza Huish. The woman was known as one of the most revered midwives in the city, and had given birth herself on eleven occasions.

Eliza arrived on horseback shortly before dusk. She was older than MaryAnne had expected; a stern, aged countenance worn into the matriarch's hard face. She was wide-hipped and buxom, her hair was streaked with gray and drawn back tightly in a bun with a few prodigal strands falling across her cheek. Her attire matched her manner. She was dressed austerely in a drab muslin dress partially concealed beneath a faded ivory apron, which carried the stains of previous deliveries. At her side was a worn carpetbag filled with the implements of her profession: herbs, ointments, tonics, and tattered rags.

"Waters not yet broke, Catherine?" she asked.

"No, ma'am."

The woman stopped at the room's threshold and surveyed the elaborate Victorian parlor, her eyes raised to the ornate frescoed ceiling. She was not likely to have seen such wealth before. The parlor was one of David's favorite rooms, and though he spent little time there, he endowed the room with his favorite collectibles, including MaryAnne's grandfather's clock. MaryAnne, at Catherine's suggestion, had chosen to birth in the parlor, as it was more convenient to the water closet and kept better temperature than the other upstairs rooms.

The woman sized up the room's occupants, then went to work with priggish fervor. Her first official act was to expel David from the room. In reluctant retreat, he left the parlor with his hands raised above his head and told Mark outside, "It is a time of female despotism."

"Why can't David be with me?" MaryAnne asked.

The question stunned the woman, who found the

very wish unnatural and could see no reason why a woman should desire a man's presence at such an occasion.

"It is not a man's place when a woman is in travail," she said. "Only a woman can know what a woman is suffering."

MaryAnne was in no condition to argue and relinquished herself to the woman's government. The midwife placed a hand on MaryAnne's forehead, then walked to the foot of the bed and lifted MaryAnne's gown up to the waist, singing hymns beneath her breath as she worked. She poured virgin olive oil into her hands and began rubbing it into MaryAnne's hips and abdominal muscles.

"This'll stretch you out, darlin'. Make it a whole lot easier. Also brought along some Lydia Pinkham's vegetable compound. Fetch that from my satchel, Catherine. And the spoon."

Catherine lifted a brown glass bottle filled with the tonic. She leveled a spoonful and offered it to Mary-Anne, who made a face at the bitter substance.

"Two spoonfuls, Catherine. Works miracles with all female ailments," the midwife said confidently, as she kneaded MaryAnne's thighs. After administering the dosage, Catherine pressed a cup of coffee to Mary-Anne's lips, which she gratefully received. The woman wiped the oil from her hands onto a rag.

"How long since labor started?"

"She had the first strong pain shortly after noon. She started regular several hours ago," Catherine said. Her voice rose hopefully, then fell in disappointment. ". . . But they stopped just before you arrived."

MaryAnne sighed.

The women sat and looked at each other quietly.

"Would you care for something to eat, Eliza?" Catherine offered.

The woman nodded. "Thank you." She looked over at MaryAnne. "Haven't had a bite since breakfast."

Catherine excused herself, returning fifteen minutes later with a silver tray stacked with cut cucumbers, honey candy, pine nuts, and cream cheese and walnut sandwiches. The woman snacked on the fare, eventually joined by Catherine, who ate only to pass time. A half hour later, MaryAnne suddenly began breathing heavily. The midwife set down a sandwich and placed both hands on MaryAnne's stomach, concentrating on the contractions with professional intensity. Three minutes later, MaryAnne started into another. "There, that's a good start. Long pains, close together."

MaryAnne grimaced. "It's taking so long."

"It is natural, the first birth always takes longer. We'll likely be here all night." As if to emphasize her words, she glanced over her shoulder at the grandfather's clock. "There's a fine clock . . . help us time these pains."

A minute later, MaryAnne tensed again, then groaned with another contraction.

"Just breathe easy, darlin'. No sense making it any harder than it need be. First always takes longer," she repeated. "Seen a first labor once go up on two days . . . but once the water broke."

MaryAnne was oblivious to the chatter, concentrating on the strange forces that had seized her body.

In the next ten minutes, MaryAnne had gone through five more cycles.

"How do you feel now, darlin'?"

"I want to push," MaryAnne panted.

"Good, good. It's moving along right quickly now. You go right ahead and push with the next pain."

The woman wiped her forehead with her wide

sleeves. Two minutes later, MaryAnne started into another contraction. As she began to push, her water broke. MaryAnne felt the sheet beneath her wet.

The midwife gasped. "Oh, dear." She stood looking at the bright red discharge. MaryAnne was bleeding heavily. The woman became suddenly grave. "Catherine, hurry now, get me some rags."

"What's wrong?" Catherine whispered.

"There may be separation of the afterbirth."

"What is wrong?" MaryAnne asked, her voice strained.

"A little bleeding, darlin'."

Catherine said nothing. MaryAnne was bleeding profusely.

MaryAnne looked up at the ceiling. "Is my baby all right?" She clenched for another contraction. Her voice pitched. "Catherine, where is David?"

"I don't know, MaryAnne."

"I want David," MaryAnne said between heavy breaths.

"It is not proper," the midwife returned, studying the continued flow of blood. MaryAnne sensed from the change in the woman's countenance that the crisis was greater than she confessed. Fifteen minutes passed beneath the clock's serpentine hands. The midwife's anxiety increased. MaryAnne began to feel light-headed.

"Is my baby still alive?" she asked again.

The woman did not answer. The blood continued to flow.

"Will I die?"

The midwife shook her head unconvincingly. "You will be well enough."

MaryAnne's breathing quickened with the onset of a new contraction. She did not believe the woman's reply. "Is there a chance that I will die?"

This time, the woman did not respond. MaryAnne exhaled, then clenched down with the pain. "If we are to die in travail it will be with David by my side."

The midwife looked up at Catherine. "Call the man."

At Catherine's summons, David quickly entered the dim room, his face bent in concern. He walked to the side of the bed and took MaryAnne's hand. It was impossibly cold. He glanced up at the midwife, who silenced him with a sharp shake of her head. His heart froze. She did not want to concern MaryAnne with the seriousness of her condition. How bad was it? He looked down at the foot of the bed and saw the pile of blood-soaked rags. He felt his stomach knot. MaryAnne was wet with perspiration. David held her hand as he blotted her forehead.

Oh, God, do not take her from me, he silently prayed. I will give anything. He rubbed her hand to warm it. "You can do this, Mary. It will be all right. Everything will be all right."

"I am so cold."

David bit back his fear. "It will be all right, my love."

Just then, the midwife walked to the side of the bed and bent over MaryAnne. Her forehead was beaded in perspiration and her face bore a solemn, dark expression. There was no more time to shield MaryAnne from the truth of the crisis. "MaryAnne, the baby needs to come now." Her words came slowly, each weighted with emphasis. "You need to give birth now."

"I don't know how to!" she cried.

"You can do it, MaryAnne," she replied firmly. "Go ahead and push. The baby must come."

"Is my baby alive?"

The midwife said nothing. Catherine began to cry and turned away.

"Is my baby alive?!" she screamed.

"I don't know. It is the baby's sack which is bleeding, so the baby is in the gravest danger. But it is still your blood, and if it does not stop soon . . ."

A chill ran up David's spine. "Can't you just take the baby?!"

"No," MaryAnne said. David turned to her pensively. Her face was pallid and though her eyes were dim they did not veil her determination. "No, David."

David clasped her hand in both of his.

"Oh, MaryAnne."

"I don't want to leave you."

"You're not leaving me, MaryAnne. I won't let you leave me."

Eliza walked back down between MaryAnne's legs as she started into another contraction. Just then, a cuckoo clock erupted in festive announcement of the second hour, followed by a gay, German melody accompanying tiny, brightly colored figurines waltzing in small circles on a wooden track.

"I feel the baby!" Eliza was certain that she would first feel the afterbirth, nearly assuring the infant's demise. "MaryAnne, push again!"

"I feel as if all my insides are coming out."

"You are doing wonderfully."

"Yes, you are doing wonderfully." David was seeing a whole new side of his wife, and of life, and it filled him equally with awe and terror.

"Push again, darlin'."

MaryAnne closed her eyes tightly and pushed.

"I have its head!" she exclaimed. "The baby is alive!"

MaryAnne cried out in pain and joy.

"One more push, Mary. Just one more."

MaryAnne obeyed and the child emerged, coated in blood and fluid. When she had taken the baby in her arms, the midwife looked up at David and MaryAnne, still breathing heavily. "You have a daughter." She severed and tied the umbilical cord, oiled off the baby, then laid her on MaryAnne's chest. MaryAnne took the infant in her arms and wept with joy. Eliza's stern, hazel eyes rested on David. "Now leave the room."

David beamed. "A daughter," he repeated. As he left the room, he paused at the threshold to smile at Mary-Anne, who, with tears streaming down her cheeks, smiled back at him, proud of the tiny daughter she held.

◆

In the dark hallway outside the parlor, David sat alone on a padded fruitwood bench, a wall separated from the muffled cry of the newborn infant. His heart and mind still raced—much as one who, narrowly avoiding an accident, finds his heart pounding and his breath stolen.

On a walnut whatnot at the far end of the hall, an antique French clock chimed delicately, denoting the half hour. He glanced down the hallway. His eyes were unable to discern the piece in the darkness. At one time, the clock had been the most valuable of his collection—an elaborate, gilded Louis XV mantel clock, signed by its long-dead creator. The clock's waist opened to expose a pendulum bob in the form of sun rays, and on its crown were two golden cherubs. In its base was set a musical box.

David had acquired the clock in the crowded Alfred H. King auction hall in Erie, Pennsylvania, a year after he had moved to Salt Lake City. He had paid nearly one thousand dollars more than he had intended to for the clock, the price escalating to match not its worth, but his desire. The day of the auction, he had visited the piece no fewer than a dozen times and obsessed over it, regarding all who came near it with wanton jealousy. He had never desired a piece so intensely and wanted the clock no matter the price.

That desire was a candle to the furnace he had just

felt at MaryAnne's side. What he had prayed in desperation, he meant just as fervently in the peace of resolution—that he would truly have given everything he owned to know that MaryAnne would be all right.

◆

"We have chosen for our daughter the name of MaryAnne's mother—Andrea. What a thing it is to be introduced to one's child. I find a new side to my being that even the gentility of MaryAnne could not produce from my brutal soul."

DAVID PARKIN'S DIARY. JANUARY 18, 1909

The birth of the child was greeted with great celebration by the thirty-four employees at the Parkin Machinery Company. Knitted booties and gowns came in from all quarters, each secretary, or clerk's wife, attempting to outdo the other.

Lawrence brought Andrea a homemade rattle that he had crafted by bending brass strips into a ball and covering it with sewed leather, concealing inside two miniature harness bells.

Once again, the Parkin home was adorned with flowers, many from neighbors and business associates, but most from David, who felt as if he had completed a great bargain in marrying one lady and only five months later found himself with two.

If the child's sireship was David and MaryAnne's secret, it seemed of little importance, as the child could not have been more his. It gave David great pleasure to be told that the child looked like her father, and, curiously, Andrea seemed to resemble him more than his wife. This fact was so frequently called to attention that David finally asked MaryAnne if he bore a resemblance to Andrea's real father.

"You are her real father," she answered. When he pressed her harder, she only replied, "He was not so handsome."

Andrea was a pretty child with large, piercing brown eyes that rested above sculptured rose cheeks. At first, her hair came in platinum wisps that curled on top until it grew long and fell to her shoulders in gilded chestnut coils. She had the delicate features of a porcelain doll, and whenever MaryAnne took her out in public, they were accosted by other women who strained to catch a glimpse of the infant, then squealed in delight that such a petite creation should cross their path.

In a strange ritual not fully understood even by its

practitioners, every acquaintance of the Parkins who possessed a male child staked their claim on Andrea for their son, which only served, if it were possible, to add to MaryAnne and David's pride.

◆

"In the year A.D. 69 the Roman emperor Vitellius paid the chief priest of Gaul, whose responsibility it was to determine the beginning and end of spring, a quarter of a billion dollars to extend spring by one minute. The emperor then boasted that he had purchased that which all man cannot. Time.

"Vitellius was a fool."

DAVID PARKIN'S DIARY. APRIL 18, 1909

With the birth of Andrea, David was born anew. If MaryAnne had given David's life meaning, Andrea gave meaning to his future. Since his own childhood had been spent in the blackness of mines and the company of adults, David had never been with children, and now he heralded each new stage of his daughter's development with the ecstasy of scientific discovery. The day Andrea first rolled over in her crib, he inwardly cursed the world that it had not stopped to acknowledge the marvel. It was as if he was finding the childhood he was denied, and, through Andrea, seized the wonder of it all—a child's world of stuffed dolls and menagerie animals sculpted in the clouds. The employees of the Parkin Machinery Company were informed on a daily basis of the baby's progress and were happily amused with this new side of their boss's personality. It was said at the office that David seemed happily distracted, though, in fact, he had just become more focused on the child, and, lest he miss her childhood, spent more time at home.

In late spring, necessity forced an extended business trip back East, which David returned home from a week early. Catherine met him at the door and took his coat and attaché case.

"Welcome home, sir."

"Thank you, Catherine. Where are MaryAnne and Andrea?"

"They are in the gazebo. May I take your shoulder bag?"

"Thank you, but no. These are gifts."

David passed through the house and out into the garden, where MaryAnne sat on the gazebo swing, gently rocking the baby she nursed at her breast. The yard was littered with the white popcorn blossoms of apricot trees, the crisp air filled with the perfume of the garden and the sounds of MaryAnne's hummed lullabies. MaryAnne, absorbed in a different world, looked up only when he was a few feet off.

"David!"

He smiled wide, laid down the heavy shoulder bag, kissed her, then, sitting down, pulled the blanket back, exposing the suckling child.

"What wonderful animals we are," he said. "It is so good to be home. You two have made my life very difficult. You have exposed me to the malady of homesickness."

"Then it is contagious," MaryAnne replied. "We have missed you so. How was the journey?"

"It is done." He leaned over and kissed Andrea on her head. "In my absence, I have thought a great deal about my business. I have decided that I miss my secretary."

"Yes?"

"I was hoping I could get her back."

"If you could accommodate two ladies for the position I may consider it."

He leaned back and breathed in the rich scent of lilac and apple blossom. "Spring breathes such life into this desert. I concluded the business faster than I, or they, planned."

"Was it productive?"

"Adequate." He suddenly smiled. "I have something to show you," he said excitedly. He released the straps of the shoulder bag, then extracted a gold-papered box from inside. He lifted the top of the box and parted the tissue. Inside lay a burgundy velvet dress with a black silk sash and white lace collar.

MaryAnne gasped. "It is beautiful!"

"I think we should try it on her," David suggested.

MaryAnne covered her mouth, then turned, trying to conceal her amusement.

"Why are you laughing?" he asked innocently.

"I am sorry." She chuckled. "David, it won't fit her for years!" With one hand, she lifted the dress out of the box.

He examined the garment then looked back down at the infant.

"Oh."

"It is a lovely dress. She will look beautiful in it." Her mouth lifted in a teasing smile. "When she is four or five." She laughed again.

"I am not much with sizes," he confessed. He reached

again into his bag. This time, he lifted out a miniature wooden crate, then carefully extracted from its cotton boll packing a small porcelain music box, a carousel, hand-painted in pastel-and-gold adornment. He wound the instrument then held it out in the palm of his hand. It plucked a simple carnival tune as the carousel revolved and its intricate horses rose and fell in clock-work mechanism. At the sound of the music, Andrea turned from MaryAnne's breast to see the toy. She cood happily, reaching out to touch the tiny, prancing horses.

"It is wonderful! Where did you find such a toy?!"

"At a clock shop in Pennsylvania. The proprietor, a Mr. Warland, creates the most intriguing inventions."

"You give good gifts, David."

"I have a gift for you, too."

"What is it?"

"It's heavy. And it is rather different, but I thought you might like it." He reached into the sack, lifting out a wooden box of dark, burled walnut. Leather straps ran across the top over an intricately carved Nativity and fastened into silver buckles. On the opposite side were two brass hinges skillfully forged in the shape of holly leaves.

"It is beautiful. Is it to hold Christmas things?"

"It is not empty." David set the box next to Mary-Anne. She unfastened its silver clasps and drew back the leather straps, then opened the box slowly. The interior of the box was lined with wine-colored velvet and occupied by an ancient leather Bible, its cover delicate with age and adorned with gold-leafed engravings.

"Oh, David . . ."

"I thought you would like it. It is at least two hundred years old. I bought the Bible at an auction. Then I saw the box and thought it a good match."

"Sir."

David turned. He had not seen Catherine approach. She stood outside the gazebo, holding a calling card in her outstretched hand.

"Gibbs has left a message."

"Thank you."

David took the card. MaryAnne looked up from the box. "What is it?"

"Gibbs wishes to meet with me tomorrow. From the tone of the note, I suspect he is concerned about business matters."

"Is there something wrong?"

"Nothing." He lifted the carousel again, then, winding it, held it out for Andrea. "All is well."

◆

"In Philadelphia I had such fortune to discover a most unusual piece, a sixteenth-century brass-and-gold sundial that duplicates the prophet Isaiah's biblical miracle of turning back time.

"'Behold, I will bring again the shadow of the degrees, which is gone down in the sun dial of Ahaz, ten degrees backward. So the sun returned ten degrees, by which degrees it was gone down.'

ISAIAH 38:8

"The gilded sundial is lipped to hold water and on one edge a figurine, a Moor, holds taut a line which extends from the center of the dial. The sun's rays, when reflecting from the water, bend the shadow and, for two hours each day, turns back time. Its possessor was unwilling to part with it."

DAVID PARKIN'S DIARY. APRIL 17, 1909

The next day, at Gibbs' behest, David came early to work and attacked a pile of paperwork and financial documents. Not an hour into the day, there was a knock on the door. A grim-faced Gibbs pushed the door open.

"David, may we have a moment?"

"Certainly."

"How was Philadelphia?"

"I was only able to negotiate a partial price concession, but it is acceptable."

Gibbs frowned. In all the years he had known David, he rarely did not get what he wanted—and never dismissed compromise so readily.

"You look concerned, Gibbs. I received your card. What is troubling you?"

"I am concerned. Our sales are down considerably."

"Yes. I have seen the ledgers."

Gibbs sighed. "It is difficult without you here. You are still our best salesman. When we meet with the larger accounts, they are offended that you are not present. One asked me if they had fallen in our esteem."

David frowned. "Are we still making a profit?"

"We could be making more. There is such growth in this city."

David walked across the room and looked out the window to the traffic below. For a full minute he said nothing, then, in a softened voice, began to speak.

"When is it enough, Gibbs?"

"I do not know what you mean."

David raised his hands, his back still turned to his manager. "When are we profitable enough? When do I have enough money? I could not possibly spend all that I have in two lifetimes. Not in twenty lifetimes."

Gibbs leaned back in exasperation. "There has been a great find of copper in the Oquirrh benches. There's talk of a large open pit mine to rival the world's largest. There are great opportunities. And we are missing them."

"You are right." David turned back around. "That is exactly what we are talking about. Lost opportunities. I can always make more money. But how shall I go about reclaiming a lost childhood? The only promise of childhood is that it will end." He paused in reflection. "And when it is gone, it is gone."

Gibbs sighed in frustration. "I am only trying to protect our interests."

"And I am not making it very easy for you to do your job." David walked over and put his hand on Gibbs's shoulder. "I appreciate you, and I will not let my business fail. Nor will I let you or any of my employees down. But right now I feel that I have finally found life. To leave it would be death. Do your best, Gibbs. But, for now, do it without me." His words trailed off in silence and Gibbs lowered his head in disappointment.

"Yes, David." He rose and walked from the room.

◆

"It would seem that my Andrea is growing so quickly, as if time were advancing at an unnatural pace. At times I wish it were within my power to reach forth my hand and stop the moment— but in this I err. To hold the note is to spoil the song."

DAVID PARKIN'S DIARY. OCTOBER 12, 1911

Two months before Andrea's third birthday, the cradle was taken up to the attic and an infant bed was brought in its place. The new bed was exciting to the small girl and represented freedom, which, to a child, is a poor requisite for sleep. David and MaryAnne found that it took more time to put her down each night.

One night, David finished reading a second story to Andrea, then, thinking himself successful in lulling her to sleep, leaned over and kissed her on the cheek.

"Good night," he whispered.

Andrea's eyes popped open. "Papa. You know what?"

David smiled in wonder at the child's persistence. "What?"

"The trees are my friends."

David grinned at the sudden observation. "Really?" He pulled the sheet up under her chin. "How do you know this?"

"They waved to me . . ."

David smiled.

". . . and I waved back."

David's smile broadened. He was astonished at the purity of the child's thought. "Andrea, do you know why I love you so much?"

"Yes," she replied.

"Why?" he asked, genuinely surprised that she had an explanation.

"Because I'm yours."

Strangely, Andrea's reply inflicted him with a sharp pang of dread. He forced a smile. "And you are right. Good night, little one."

"Good night, Papa," she replied sleepily and rolled over.

David did not return to his bedroom but retreated to the seclusion of the drawing room to think. After an hour, MaryAnne, dressed in her nightclothes, came for him. She quietly peered in. David sat in a richly brocaded green-and-gold chair. Several books lay next to him, though none was open. His head was bowed, resting in the palm of one hand. MaryAnne entered.

"David? Is business troubling you?"

He raised his head.

"No." His voice was laced with melancholy. "I have just been wondering."

MaryAnne came behind his chair and leaned over it, wrapping her arms around his neck.

"What have you been wondering, my love?"

"Shall we ever tell her?"

"Tell her?"

"That I am not her real father."

MaryAnne frowned. She came around and sat on the upholstered footstool before him. "You are her real father."

He shook his head. "No, I'm not. And I feel dishonest, as if I were hiding something from her."

"David, it isn't important."

"But shouldn't she be allowed the truth? I feel as if I am living a lie."

"Then it is the lesser of a much greater one."

"What is that?"

"Society's lie. The lie that claims that simply impregnating a woman makes a man a father." Her eyes glazed in loathsome recall. "The man who lay with me is not a father. He is not even a real man. I wonder that he is a member of our species."

David sat still, quietly weighing the intent of her words. "Have you seen him? Since our engagement?"

MaryAnne wondered why he had asked the question, but could not discern from his expression. "Once."

"You went to him?"

"David!" She took his hand. "That would be like emptying a cup of champagne to fill it with turned milk."

"You hate him?"

"I do not care enough about him to hate him. Nor pity him, as pitiful as he is. . . ."

David remained silent.

"He stopped me outside the company two days after you asked me to marry to tell me that he wanted me back. I told him that I had no desire to see him again. He called me a harlot and said that when I had the baby, it would be for the world to know, but that he knew of a way to take the child so that it would not interfere with our life together." MaryAnne grimaced as she turned away. "I have never wanted to hurt anyone in my life, but at that moment, I wanted to kill him. He just stared at me with this arrogant grin as if he had just rescued me from disrepute, as if I should fall to my knees in gratitude. I slapped him. I knew he would probably beat me again, even in public, but I didn't care.

"Just then, one of the clerks came around the corner. I suspect that he had observed the exchange, as he stopped and asked if he could be of assistance. Virgil was mad with rage, but he is a coward. He raised a finger to me, sneered, then stormed off. That is his name. Virgil. It leaves a putrid taste in my mouth to even speak it."

She looked into David's eyes.

"Once I thought I loved him, but now he is irrelevant, David. To me, he is nothing, but more especially to Andrea. I beg you, as her father, not to tell her. It has no chance of bringing her happiness and may bring her great pain."

Her voice cracked. "The only question we should reason is how it will affect her happiness, is it not?"

David silently contemplated the question. Then his mouth rose in a half smile. "I love you, MaryAnne. I truly love you."

CHAPTER EIGHT

THE
WIDOW'S GIFT

*"I find it most peculiar that these old women share their
deepest secrets with a man who, but a few months previous,
they would have shrunk from in terror had they encountered
him on a streetcar."*

DAVID PARKIN'S DIARY. AUGUST 1, 1911

n a strange twist of social convention,
Lawrence had become the toast of the
city's elite widowhood, and those who
sought its ranks would drop his name at teas and
brunches like a secret password. Initially, the elderly
women had begun the visits to Lawrence's shack
because it was perfectly scandalous and gave rise to
gossip, but through time, the visits had evolved and
now came more through loneliness than social preten-

sion. It was suspected that some widows would actually damage their clocks as an excuse to visit the horologist.

Though the widows rarely left their homes after dark, as summer stretched the day, the visits would sometimes intrude upon Lawrence's dinner. This particular evening, Lawrence was cutting carrots into a pan with a steel buck knife when there came a familiar, sharp wooden rap at his door. He lifted the blackened pan from the stove and greeted the widow. Maud Cannon, a gaunt, gray-haired woman, stood outside, leaning against a black, pearl-embedded cane. She wore a maroon poplin dress with a satin sash and a gold maple-leaf-shaped brooch clipped to its bodice. In her left hand, she clutched a beaded purse. She was flanked by a knickered boy who strained beneath the weight of a large, bronze-statued clock.

"Lemme take that," Lawrence said, quickly stepping outside to relieve the boy of the clock, who surrendered it gratefully. "You go right on in, Miss Maud."

"Thank you, Lawrence." She turned to the boy. "You wait outside," she said sternly, then stepped inside ahead of Lawrence, who set the clock on the worktable, then returned with a cloth and dusted off the chair she stood by. Its surface was already clean, but this was an expected ritual and one not to be neglected.

"Sit down, ma'am."

"Thank you, Lawrence." She straightened herself up in the chair. "I would like the clock cleaned."

Lawrence's brow furled. "Somethin' wrong with the work I done last week, ma'am?"

The woman looked back at the clock, as a confused expression blanketed her face. She cleared her throat. "No, Lawrence, you always do a fine job. It is just that I have visitors calling this week and I would like the clock ware to be especially nice."

Lawrence had known the woman long enough to discern the truth. She had forgotten which clock she had last brought.

"You shore know how to entertain your guests, Miss Maud. They must appreciate your hospitality."

She sighed. "I do not think they even notice." She brought out an elaborately embroidered handkerchief and patted her brow. "I think the bell on that one sounds flat."

"I'll be shore to check that, Miss Maud." He opened the crystal door and pushed the long hand to the half hour. The bell struck once in perfect pitch. "Shore is a luv'ly piece, it's a right honor to work on her." He stepped back and admired the clock. "Seth 'n' Thomas makes a right luv'ly piece."

It was a white-faced clock surrounded by a pot-metal sculpture of an angel pointing heavenward, as a young girl clasps her hands to pray.

"You'd think that angel gonna fly right off there."

The widow smiled, patted her brow again, then replaced the handkerchief in her purse. "I have a special request of you, Lawrence."

"Yes, ma'am?"

"I would like to call you Larry."

He looked back at the widow. "Larry?"

"Yes, we've known each other for some time. Would that be acceptable to you?"

Lawrence cared little for the name but had no desire to offend his client. "I s'pose so, ma'am. Ain't no one ever called me Larry before."

"If it's all the same."

"Yes, ma'am."

She sat back contentedly. "Larry, lately I have been given to much thought about you. Maybe it is because of you being a Negro and not having much, but it seems to me that you are one of the few people I know who truly appreciates the value of things. Like this clock here," she said, gesturing toward the table. "That is why I can take my clocks to you without anxiety."

"Thank you, ma'am."

"Back when my Rodney was alive, bless his soul, he appreciated things. Rodney would look at a sunset like he had discovered the thing. You would think it was God's gift just for him." She sighed and her voice softened in longing. "How life turns. The only family I have now is my miserable nephew."

"Your nephew appreciate things, ma'am?"

She frowned. "My nephew's a damn fool. I should not curse, but it is the gospel truth. I give him money and he spends it on liquor and gaming and I shudder to think what else." She leaned forward. "He thinks when I die he will have a pretty sizable inheritance, but that will be over my dead body!" she said indignantly. Suddenly, her mouth twisted into an amused grin. "I suppose all inheritances are over a dead body, Larry."

"Yes, ma'am, I s'pose they are at that."

"I'm sure it will come as a surprise, but I am leaving every dime to the church missionary fund."

"Now don't you go talkin' about no dyin', ma'am."

The old lady sighed. "Larry, I am not fooling anyone.

I haven't many sunrises left." Her voice suddenly turned tired and melancholy. "My friends are nearly all gone now. It's lonely here, Larry. I feel as if I am just waiting around." She leaned forward, shaking a willowy finger for emphasis. "Leave when they still want you, Rodney used to say." She looked down at the floor and her eyes blinked slowly. "I have stayed too long."

Lawrence could not help but feel sympathy for the old woman. "Don't no one know their time, Miss Maud. But it stops for all of us. Be right shore 'bout that."

She looked up. "You know, Larry, I enjoy our little visits. They are the sunshine of my week. When I go, I have a mind to leave you something." The idea brightened her face. "Yes. That rose-gold timepiece you think so much of."

"Ma'am, I can't go takin' no timepieces."

"It is a very special timepiece. It should go to someone who will appreciate it. I am sure it will cause a commotion, giving a piece of the family inheritance to a Negro, but I do not care. It feels kind of nice to be controversial at my age. I am going to have it written in my will."

"How 'bout your nephew?"

The woman humphed. "Damn fool. He'd pawn it for

liquor a half hour after it fell into his idle hands. Not another word, Larry, you must have it. I insist."

"S'pose I'd rather have your company, ma'am."

She smiled sadly and patted his hand. "That is not our choice, Larry. To be sure, I have not felt too well of late." She again produced the handkerchief from her purse and dabbed her cheeks. "I will be going now, Larry," she said feebly.

Lawrence rose first and helped the woman to her feet, handing her the ebony cane.

"Thank you, Larry."

"You're welcome, ma'am." Lawrence opened the door and gestured to the boy, who took the widow's arm and helped her back to her carriage.

◆

"It is a question worthy of the philosophers—do we have dreams or do dreams have us? Myself, I do not believe in the mystical or prophetic nature of dreams. But I may be mistaken."

DAVID PARKIN'S DIARY. MARCH 17, 1912

Two hours before sunrise, MaryAnne woke with a start and began sobbing heavily into the mattress. She was having difficulty catching her breath. David sat up alarmed. "What is it, MaryAnne?"

"Oh, David!" she exclaimed. "It all seemed so real! So horribly real!"

"What, Mary?"

She buried her head into his chest and began to cry. "I had the most awful dream."

David put his arms around her.

"I dreamt I was in bed nursing Andrea when an angel came in through the window, took her from my breast, then flew out with her."

David pulled her tight. "It was only a dream, Mary."

She wiped the tears from her face with the sleeve of her gown. "I must see her."

"I will go," David said. He climbed out of bed and walked the length of the hall to the nursery. Andrea lay motionless, her cheek painted in moonlit strokes. She suddenly rolled over to her side and David exhaled in relief. He quickly returned to the bedroom. "She is fine. She is sleeping fine." He wearily climbed back into the bed.

"Do you think it meant something?" MaryAnne asked.

"I don't think so. We always dream our greatest fears," David said reassuringly.

MaryAnne sniffed. "I'm sorry I woke you."

He kissed her forehead, then lay back with his arm around her and pulled her close. "Good night."

"Good night, David." MaryAnne cuddled up next to him and eventually fell back asleep. David stared sleeplessly at the ceiling.

◆

The following morning, MaryAnne walked into the nursery and pulled back the drapery, filling the room with virgin sunlight.

"Good morning, sweet Andrea," she sang lightly. She sat down on the bed. "Time to wake up." Andrea opened her eyes slowly. Her eyelids were heavy and swollen. Her lips were dry and cracked.

"Andrea?"

"Mama, my neck hurts."

MaryAnne lay her cheek across Andrea's forehead and instantly pulled back. She was hot with fever. She ran to the doorway and called for Catherine, who appeared almost instantly.

"Andrea is feverish, fetch me some wet rags and ice from the box. Send Mark with the carriage for Dr. Bouk."

"Yes, ma'am," she said, running off. MaryAnne knelt by the bed and stroked Andrea's forehead. A few moments later, Catherine, quite out of breath, returned with the articles.

MaryAnne took the cloth, wrapped it around the ice and held it up against Andrea's forehead. For the first time, she noticed the rash across her cheek. The night's dream echoed back to her in haunting remembrance. She quickly pushed it away.

Andrea had fallen back to sleep by the time Mark returned with the carriage. Catherine quickly led the doctor up to the nursery. Dr. Bouk had been David's personal physician ever since David first came to the city and was no stranger to the Parkin household. As he entered the room, MaryAnne moved to the opposite side of the bed. He was of a serious demeanor and acknowledged MaryAnne with a simple nod. "Mrs. Parkin."

"Doctor, she has a fever and a rash."

He set his leather bag on the ground and bent over the child. He placed his hands on the sides of Andrea's neck and lifted his forefingers beneath her jaw. "Does that hurt, sweetheart?" Andrea nodded lethargically. He frowned, then gently opened the child's mouth. Her tongue was white, with fine red marks.

"It is scarlatina," he said slowly. "The scarlet fever."

The pronouncement sent chills through MaryAnne. There had already been eighteen deaths in the city that year from the disease. She wrung her hands. Catherine moved next to her.

"What do I do?"

Doctor Bouk stood up and removed his bifocals. He was a tall, gangly man, emaciatingly thin, with an ironic pouch of a stomach. "She must stay in bed, of course. Within a few days, the rash may become dusky. I will administer an ointment that will help stop the spread of the disease. It should make her more comfortable." He reached into his bag, then lifted out a small vial. "This is biniodide of mercury. I will give her a half grain. It may arrest the fever and prevent the desquamation—the skin flaking off." He raised his hand to his mouth and coughed. "A daily hot salt or mustard bath may help. Glycerin and water will aid the throat. Catherine, you can get the glycerin from an apothecary. It should be administered directly to the inside of the throat."

"How long does the illness last?"

The doctor frowned. "Maybe forty days—with good fortune."

He did not need to explain. MaryAnne knew that death often occurred within the first two weeks.

"Be of good cheer, Mrs. Parkin. There have not been as many deaths from scarlet fever as there were before the century." He stood up and touched her shoulder, then stopped at the door. "I must notify the city health department. They will quarantine your home."

MaryAnne nodded. "Of course," she said. When he was gone, she sat down on the bed, fighting back the tears that gathered. Catherine put her arm around her.

"Where is David?"

"He is coming, MaryAnne. Mark went to fetch him."

MaryAnne looked down on her resting child. Catherine brushed back MaryAnne's hair.

"My brother got the fever two summers ago," she said, hoping to console her mistress. "He is fine now."

"What did you do?"

"My mama dipped bacon in coal oil and laid it on his head and throat."

MaryAnne wiped her eyes. "That is all?"

"We prayed over him."

"Your brother was healed?"

"He is weaker of constitution, but he is recovered."

She turned away from the child and spoke in hushed and desperate tones. "I will do anything, Catherine."

Catherine embraced her tighter.

"Anything, but lose her."

◆

That afternoon, the local health officer quarantined the home, posting on the doorway a large China-red placard that read QUARANTINE. The following weeks languished with MaryAnne sitting by Andrea's side. Each day was a carbon copy of the previous one, the one exception being MaryAnne, who appeared more haggard and frail with each passing day. By the end of the second week, she looked gaunt, her eyes encircled by dark rings, and her skin was waxen. She spoke infrequently and, to Catherine, seemed to be caught up in some fearful trance. David's concern for his wife grew until it equaled that which he felt for Andrea. Scarlet fever was uncommon in adults, but not unheard of, especially in someone as weakened as MaryAnne had become. David looked in on her with increasing frequency and anxiety until he could bear her vigil no longer. That night, he brought the dinners into the room himself. He set the tray down, then brushed the hair back from Andrea's forehead as she slept.

"MaryAnne, Catherine tells me you have not left Andrea's side all week."

She didn't reply, but took the bowl of clear soup. David observed that she moved slowly, as if her muscles had grown weak. He frowned. "Come, MaryAnne. Come out into the day. I will watch after Andrea."

She did not respond.

"MaryAnne!"

"I cannot leave her, David."

"You must!"

She shook her head.

David felt himself growing angry with her stubbornness. "This is madness, MaryAnne. Why can you not leave her?"

She looked up at him, her eyes filled with pain. She whispered, "What if I never got to say good-bye?"

David gazed back into MaryAnne's deep, fatigued eyes. "Will it come to that?"

She set the bowl down and leaned into him, looking down at her little girl. "It mustn't. It mustn't."

◆

"Is this life, to grasp joy only to fear its escape?
The price of happiness is the risk of losing it."

DAVID PARKIN'S DIARY. APRIL 3, 1912

It was a Wednesday morning that MaryAnne woke to the sound of laughter. Andrea was sitting up in her bed laughing at the mockingbird that pecked at the windowsill.

Doubting her senses, MaryAnne rose slowly and moved over to the child. She touched Andrea's forehead.

"Andrea. Are you well?"

The little girl beamed up at her mother. "Did you see the bird?" Her eyes, though still heavy from a month of sickness, were bright and color had returned to the previously ashen skin.

MaryAnne called for David, who, fearing the worst, quickly entered the room with Catherine following behind him. He was surprised to see the child sitting upright.

"I can't believe it."

Catherine clapped. "Oh, MaryAnne!"

"David, she is well! Andrea is well!"

David walked over to the bed.

"Hi, Papa. Did you see the bird?"

David looked to the window. "He has flown away. Did he say anything to you?"

"Birds don't talk."

"I forgot," he said whimsically.

He kissed her on the forehead, then turned back to MaryAnne and took her in his arms. "You did it, Mary. By sheer will, or love, you won."

◆

The next day, before the clocks of the Parkin home had proclaimed the tenth hour, Lawrence limped up the cobblestone drive to the mansion, his broad-rimmed felt hat bent against the morning sun. In one hand swung a book.

Catherine stood on the porch polishing the paned windows in curt, rectangular swipes. She turned around when she saw Lawrence's reflection.

"Good morning, Mr. Flake."

Lawrence tipped his hat. "Mornin', Miss Catherine. Is David or Miss MaryAnne 'bout?"

Just then MaryAnne, who had seen him approach, stepped outside. "Lawrence, welcome."

"Miss MaryAnne!" Lawrence's expression betrayed his surprise at how emaciated she had become.

MaryAnne blushed. "I'm sorry, I must look frightful."

"No, ma'am," Lawrence replied quickly, "you look as pretty as you always done."

MaryAnne smiled at the kind fib. "It's been a hard time, Lawrence."

"I know, ma'am. And you been a rock." Lawrence lowered his hat, relegating it to the same hand which held the book. He scratched his head. "I was thinkin' that maybe with the fever gone I could see Andrea. I brought her a book, thought maybe I could read to her."

"Of course you may. She would love that. Please come in." MaryAnne led him up to the nursery and announced the visitor to Andrea, who happily bounced up in bed, shedding the tied quilt that covered her legs.

"Hi, Lawrence!"

"How you feelin', missy?" Lawrence asked, stepping into the dusky room.

"You can come in. I'm not sick!"

"Your mama told me you feelin' much better."

MaryAnne smiled at the exchange, then excusing

herself, shut the door behind them. Lawrence sat down on the edge of the small bed next to her and displayed the book. "I came to read you a story."

"What's it about?"

"It's 'bout a rabbit."

"I know a story about a rabbit that got into a farmer's garden."

"Well, this, missy, is a story 'bout a rabbit made of velveteen. You know what velveteen is?"

She shook her head.

"Velveteen is somethin' real soft, like this blanket here. Feels good against your face." As he said this, he gently stroked her cheek with his forefinger. Andrea grinned accusingly.

"Your finger's not soft."

He held up his hands in easy surrender. "These hands done too much work to be soft."

She looked at the aged, scarred hands. "Lawrence, will I turn brown when I get old?"

Lawrence broke out in laughter. "No, missy, you won't be turnin' brown." He rubbed her head. "We best get us some more light if we gonna read." He drew back the curtains so that a beam of sunlight fell across the bed and climbed the opposite wall. He began the story, carefully holding the book so that Andrea could see its brightly illustrated pages. She was captivated by the tale and spoke only once: when he had committed the unpardonable crime of turning the page before she was done looking at the picture. A half hour later he announced the story's end and lay the book in his lap.

"That boy had what I had," Andrea said. "Scarlyfever."

"And you got better jus' like him."

She nodded. "I like that rabbit. Can we read it again?"

"I told your mama that I wouldn't be too long. Don't want to disturb your nap time."

The child frowned.

"I'll leave the book so you can look at the pictures," he said, holding the book out to her.

Andrea smiled as she accepted the offering. "I'm glad you turned brown, Lawrence."

"Why's that, missy?"

"Because I'll always know it's you."

Lawrence pulled the blanket up over her shoulders as she nestled up against his knee. He leaned over and kissed her on the forehead, then pulled the curtains tight as the room fell back into a silent infirmary.

As he left the home he noticed that someone had removed the red placard from the front porch.

◆

"The most consequential of life's episodes often begin with the simplest of events."

DAVID PARKIN'S DIARY. OCTOBER 15, 1913

Lawrence thought the widows peculiar about death. He learned of Maud Cannon's passing through another widow, who gossiped cavalierly about the small turnout at Maud's wake.

A few days later, there was a knock at Lawrence's door. A man, dressed in a brown-striped suit and carrying a leather valise, stood outside his shack. He was a pale man with oiled, combed-back hair and pocked skin. His left eye twitched nervously.

"Mr. Flake?"

"Yessuh."

"Mr. Lawrence Flake?"

Lawrence nodded.

He stared at the black man. "Do you have identification papers?"

"I know who I am," Lawrence said defiantly.

The lawyer rubbed his chin. "Yes." He set down his case, reached into his pocket and produced a small package. An aged jeweler's box with a vermilion crushed-velvet veneer. He handed Lawrence the box.

"Needs repairin'?"

"No. It belongs to you. Our client, the late Maud Cannon, specified in her will that this was to be endowed to you."

"You her nephew?"

"I am the executor of the will," he replied indignantly. "She wanted you to have this jewelry. Now, if you will please sign this paper, I will go."

Lawrence glanced up from the gift. He took the pen and signed the document, wherein the man disappeared as promised. Lawrence stepped back inside, extracted the watch from its case, and held it up to the light, smiling at the exquisite rose-gold timepiece. "Thank you, Miss Maud," he said aloud. He set the watch back in its case and went back to his paper.

◆

At first David thought the gunshot was the coughing backfire of his Pierce Arrow. He had concluded the day's business early and as Lawrence had recently received consignment of the estate of a former steel tycoon known for his eccentricities and remarkable antiques,

David thought to stop by to examine the former magnate's possessions.

He pulled his car up the dirt drive alongside the east brick wall of the cannery, parking beneath a large painted advertisement expounding the virtues of Schoals shoe black. The car coughed twice before the discharge of a firearm echoed loudly in the back lot, followed by a faint cry. It sounded as if it had come from Lawrence's shack.

Apprehensively, David sprinted around to the back of the building. He found the door to Lawrence's shack wide open. He cautiously peered inside. On the wood-planked floor a small man with a thick reddish beard lay on his back in a pool of dark liquid. The smell of whiskey reeked over the sharp stench of ignited gun powder.

On the wooden tabletop lay a Winchester rifle. Lawrence sat on the floor in the corner of the room, his eyes vacuous, as if waiting for something he was powerless to stop. He was moaning softly. "Oh Lordy, oh Lordy."

"Lawrence, what has happened here?"

Lawrence stared straight ahead.

"Lawrence?"

Lawrence slowly looked up. He extended a clenched

fist, then opened it to expose the delicate rose-gold wristwatch. The widow's gift.

"Man I ain't never see before pushed his way into my home screamin' no nigger gonna take his watch. Called me a thief, voodoo-witch doctor. Sez I put a spell on the widow to make her give it to me."

David looked down at the dead man.

"He was stinkin' drunk. Started a-shovin' me with his gun. I sez, 'You take the watch, I ain't never asked for no watch.' Made him crazier. Sez, 'You think this watch is yours to give, nigger? Think I need some nigger tell me what's rightfully mine?' Started into cryin', sez his aunt loves a nigger more than her own flesh. Tha's when he lifted his gun. I been in war. I know the look in a man's eyes when he's gonna kill."

Lawrence closed his hand around the timepiece. His face was hard, yet fearful, creased in deep flesh canyons. "Ain't no watch he wanted."

Just then, there was a sharp, metallic click behind them—the bolt action of a carbine. The door opened and a thin man with red cheeks and small puffy eyes stepped into the room. He wore a navy blue, double-breasted police uniform with gold buttons and a black velvet collar and a bell-shaped hat with a diminutive leather rim. He held a rifle chest-high and his eyes darted nervously between David, Lawrence, and the dead man.

"Stand up, Negro."

Lawrence pushed himself up against the wall. The officer knelt down and placed his fingers on the man's throat. "Everett, you jackass. So you finally got yours," he said to the corpse. He looked up.

"Who killed this man?"

"I did," David said.

The officer stood back up. He looked at the firearm on the table. "Whose gun is that?"

David gestured towards the lifeless body. "It's his. I killed him with his own gun."

The officer noted the look of astonishment on Lawrence's face. He pointed his rifle at David. "You come with me."

"You won't need the gun."

The sheriff turned towards Lawrence. "You come too."

"He doesn't have anything to do with this," David protested.

"This your home, Negro?"

"Yessuh."

"You see this man get shot?"

Lawrence glanced over at David. "Yessuh."

"Then you have something to do with this. Come along."

A crowd of onlookers had already gathered outside the shack as the two men were led to the horse-drawn paddy wagon and driven off to jail.

◆

The police captain stared at David over a desk cluttered with papers and a dinner of baked chicken, black beans, and Apple Brown Betty. He suddenly smiled. "Mr. Parkin, please sit down." He motioned to an austere wooden chair. "Please."

The sudden display of courtesy struck David as rather peculiar and he speculated that someone in authority had called on his behalf.

"Care for anything?" He gestured towards a platter. "Saratoga potatoes?"

David looked at the food and shook his head.

"I just heard from the mayor's office, Mr. Parkin. The mayor wishes to express his personal concern with this matter and hopes that you have been treated respectfully."

"I have no complaints."

"He personally vouches for your character and wishes to see you sent on your way. In light of Officer Brookes's report, and your reputation, I see no reason to further detain you."

David looked back at the door. "Then I am free to go?"

"Certainly. I am curious, though. Do you know the man that was killed?"

"No."

"Everett Hatt. He was a regular down here. Everyone in this building, including the domestics, knows him by sight." He leaned forward onto his thick hands. "This affair ought to be very clear, Mr. Parkin. Hatt was a brawler and a drunk. He was shot in someone else's residence. The only weapon that was discharged was his. What I don't understand is your testimony that you shot the man."

"Why is that difficult?"

He leaned back, picking his teeth with his thumb. "Witnesses claim they saw you enter the shack after the gunshot."

"They must be mistaken."

The police captain looked at him in disbelief. "Yes . . ."

His expression suddenly turned grave. "A word of caution, Mr. Parkin. In spite of your connections, these are serious matters. A man has been killed. There will be an inquest and no doubt a hearing." He pushed his chair back from his desk. "I don't know what this Negro has on you, but I hope to heaven it does not go bad. "

David ignored the warning. "May I go now?"

"You are free to leave." The Captain shook a brass desk bell and the officer reappeared at the doorway.

"Brookes, kindly take Mr. Parkin back to his automobile."

"What about my friend?" David asked.

He rubbed his nose. "And release the Negro."

"Yes, sir."

"And, Brookes, shut the door."

"Yes, sir."

When the door had shut, the captain leaned forward to a cold dinner and cursed the mayor for his interference in the affair.

◆

MaryAnne had just heard of David's arrest and was preparing to go to him when he entered the front door.

"David! Are you all right?"

David looked at her blankly. "I will be in my den," he said as he walked past her. Catherine smiled at Mary-Anne sympathetically. MaryAnne took her hand. "It will be all right," she said.

An hour later, she entered David's den carrying a silver-plated tea service. Two sconces lit the wall, teasing the darkness with flickering illumination. From outside, the din of crickets sang in syncopated harmony to the voices of the clocks in the room.

"I thought you might like some tea. And perhaps some company."

He looked up and smiled. "I am sorry. I did not mean to ignore you."

She handed him a cup, then set the tray on a buffet and sat on the love seat next to him. "Are you all right?"

"Yes. I am fine."

She hesitated, gathering courage for her question. "David. Why did you tell them that you shot the man?"

"You do not believe that I did?"

"I do not believe you are capable of killing a man."

David stared vacantly into space. The room was quiet and MaryAnne looked at him pensively.

"It seems unlikely to me that Lawrence would get a fair trial."

"Mark told me the police officer said that this was a very clear case of self-defense."

"Lawrence did not have the mayor vouching for him. If it was Lawrence on trial that clear case would suddenly become very murky." David frowned. "Even if he was acquitted, the man's family would likely lynch Lawrence for a miscarriage of justice, not because he was guilty, but because he is a Negro. The only way to protect Lawrence is to keep him out of it."

"What if they want to lynch you?"

David thought for a moment. He had not considered this possibility. "A man cannot live his life by the calculations of retribution. I did what I had to do and hope the consequences are kind."

"You are a good man, David. I pray that God will be good to us in this matter."

"I am disinclined to think God takes notice of such things."

MaryAnne took a sip of tea. "Then you believe it a mere coincidence that you arrived when you did?"

David found the query intriguing. "I had not considered it. I don't know, MaryAnne. I really do not know if God or fate meddles in our affairs."

"It seems to me that there is a 'divinity that shapes our ends.'"

David contemplated the assertion. "If this is true, then you must accept that this God, or fate, also besets our species with great calamities."

"It is our lot . . ." MaryAnne replied solemnly. She set down her cup. "I cannot answer for the whole of human suffering. I can only speak from my experience. But I have found that my pain is instructive. That through it I become more than I would otherwise."

David considered her argument. "To become . . ." He rubbed his forehead. "I think oftentimes that instruction is too hard to bear." He looked at his wife, then smiled in surrender. "I have become much too serious in my matrimonial state. And perhaps fatalistic. If that same divinity has brought you across the sea to me then it must be of some good."

"Or at least have good humor," she said, suddenly laughing at her husband. She kissed his cheek and laughed again.

David lay back in the plush seat. "Oh, MaryAnne, that laughter. How I need it."

"Then you shall have it." MaryAnne fell laughing into his arms as David covered her face with kisses.

◆

"I confess that I find it difficult to take this affair seriously, and were it not for MaryAnne's anxiety, I would, perhaps, not concern myself with it at all."

DAVID PARKIN'S DIARY. NOVEMBER 22, 1913

David received notice of the trial two weeks after his arrest and regarded it with little more concern than a coal bill. The trial had been set for the third of December and though it was not of any great interest to David, it provided ample fodder for the local tabloids, which increased circulation with sensational headlines: LOCAL MILLIONAIRE TRIED FOR MURDER.

The city became caught up in the scandal and nowhere more so than at the bar Everett Hatt had frequented with his soul mate and mentor, Cal Barker.

Everett Hatt's disposition could not be blamed entirely on Barker. Hatt was a self-made loser even before he met the man; a year after Hatt's parents died and he was taken in by his only living relative, the wealthy widow Maud Cannon. The widow learned with great distress of the shallowness of her nephew's character and, with Christian resolve, set about to reform the boy, leading to squabbles that increased daily in frequency and rancor. It was months before she began to learn the extent of his depravity. He readily took from her with no thought of gratitude or obligation, and when she finally refused to further finance his incessant drinking, valuables began to disappear from around the house. She confronted him with the losses, to which he responded so violently that she feared for her safety and never mentioned the subject again, quietly hiding the pieces with the greatest sentimental value. So when a few years later he begged a sizable stipend with the promise that he would leave her life forever, she gave him the money and considered it a small price to rid him from her life. Not surprisingly, he was not true to the arrangement and descended upon her at least twice a year for additional subsidy.

So it was for nearly a decade. Hatt had enjoyed a sense of celebrity among his friends as a relative of the rich, with an occasional allowance to prove it. As the widow's only relative, he, and Barker, erroneously assumed that Hatt would be the only heir of her estate and fantasized about the day when the old lady would die and they would live a glorious lifestyle of unlimited gratification. The fantasies filled the men briefly with delusions of wealth, but left them all the hungrier at the reality of their present circumstance.

Growing increasingly impatient with the woman's longevity, Barker had offered to hasten the happy occasion by helping the widow on her way. It was not a surprise to anyone that Barker would make such an offer. Cal Barker lived his life in darkness. As a miner, his days were spent in the belly of the earth and his nights on the darker parts of its surface.

He was married, though there was little evidence of his marital status, and he returned home just often enough to force himself on his wife, a plain-faced woman who feared the large man and tacitly accepted his abuse and neglect. She had borne four children which she provided the sustenance for through hiring herself out for domestic chores and occasionally from what was left of Barker's wages after the gambling and alcohol had taken its due.

Barker's life of darkness was more than one of locale. He lived his life in sole pursuit of its baser desires, discovering that pleasures diminish with indulgence and become harder to come by. And as those who chase the unattainable do, he grew meaner with age. Mean enough to kill a widow.

Hatt, on the other hand, though unfettered by moral turpitude, feared the possibility of a noose. "She's an old-enough bag of bones," he told Barker. "Ain't hardly got another year left in her. Let God do the dirty work."

◆

The day the widow died, there were two rounds of drinks on Hatt, which exhausted the last of his money, followed by another from Barker, who was sure to share in Hatt's good fortune. Not coincidentally, his register of friends swelled that day, and Hatt, who had never enjoyed such eminence, was just stupid enough to believe in his new-found popularity.

Six days later, at the reading of the widow's last will and testament, Hatt's dreams were shattered. It was fortunate for all present that Hatt had not brought a gun into the law office, as he would likely have killed all present, then turned the weapon on himself.

Once the initial shock of the reading wore off, the details of the will became of greater concern to the men. They found that the bulk of the estate was willed to a church—a faceless entity in which their only retribution lay in profaning God, something they had long before perfected. Then, a week later, Wallace Schoefield, one of the better readers of the group, stumbled onto the one individual who had received a personal gift. A golden timepiece had been bestowed upon a man by the name of Lawrence Flake. Upon further investigation, they discovered that the man was a Negro—a revelation that only added to their outrage.

In the twisted reasoning of the unjust (that all things which do not incur to their benefit are inherently unfair), the men decided that the timepiece was rightfully theirs and that they would claim it at any cost.

Hatt's motivations ran deeper. He was, as the widow ascertained, unable to derive gratification from anything of true value in life and, frustrated at his own character, despised all those who could. And this was Hatt's state of mind when he went after the delicate golden wristwatch, when in reality he wanted nothing more than to kill the man upon whom it was endowed.

◆

The trial began at exactly nine in the morning, presided over by the Honorable William G. Halloran—an old man rarely seen outside a courtroom, who dressed spartanly and viewed justice and wardrobe with the same idiosyncratic fervor.

Due to the sensationalism of the trial, the gallery was filled to capacity and spectators stood against the wall and outer doors. The press was well represented and had secured many of the better seats near the front of the courtroom or against the wall near the oak jury box, where hats were hung in a row.

The twelve-man jury wore stone faces throughout the ordeal, listening to the arguments dutifully. By six o'clock, it was over. The jury unanimously found Hatt guilty of trespassing with intent to kill and that David, a model citizen, had acted in self-defense.

Despite the tabloids' promise of a good show, by the end of the trial few were surprised at the reading of the verdict, and the only excitement of the day came when a juror, taking aim at a spittoon, inadvertently nailed a constable, who reacted by brandishing a billy club over the man.

At the conclusion of the reading, the judge thanked the jury for their service and dismissed them, while MaryAnne breathed a great sigh of relief and embraced Catherine, who sat next to her in the gallery. The four adult members of the Parkin household joined outside the courtroom and all seemed exceptionally relieved except David, who had never shared their anxiety.

"I had expected more of a show."

"I will not say I am disappointed," MaryAnne said. "I am just happy it is all over."

"I am happy that I have not lost all of the day," David replied, lifting a gold pocket watch from his vest pocket. "I need to meet with Gibbs. Mark, see the ladies on home. I will walk to the office."

"Shall I come for you later?"

"Gibbs will bring me home."

"Hurry back," MaryAnne urged.

"Always, my love."

David kissed her twice, once for Andrea, and they parted company. He entered the narrow alleyway next to the courthouse and hurried off to his office. As he neared the end of the passage, three men blocked his path. David recognized one of them from the court-room.

"Excuse me," he said, expecting and receiving little reaction from the men.

The largest of the men, Cal Barker, stepped forward and struck David across the face, knocking him backward. David rubbed his cheek, then, lowering his hand, noticed the blood on his fingers. Again, Barker sprang forward. This time, he grabbed David by the jacket and shoved him up against the yellow brick of the nearby building. His breath reeked of cheap whiskey.

"They say that you had nuthin' to do with Hatt's murder, that the nigger killed Hatt."

David said nothing.

"A white man coverin' for a nigger. Whatsa matter with you?"

David remained silent, staring at Barker dispassionately. The man's face turned crimson.

"You stinkin' rich, think you can buy anything. Well, you can't buy justice. We'll get our justice."

David's face showed no sign of intimidation, which only provoked Barker further. "Whatsa matter with you! You dumb?! Don't you know I could kill you right now?"

Confusing control with cowardice, Barker awkwardly recoiled to strike David again. David quickly swung around, slamming his fist against the bridge of Barker's nose and knocking him up against the opposite wall. Barker let out a small cry, then slumped to the ground. The two standing men moved toward David. David flashed a slim black ten-shooter from his waistcoat and leveled it at Barker.

"Back off! And you stay down or you will die like Hatt."

Barker motioned to the men with his eyes and they retreated. Barker wiped at the thin stream of blood that flowed from his nose.

"You are not the ass your appearance would suggest." He looked up at the two men, continuing to point the gun at Barker's head.

"Step aside."

The men moved to the wall. As David made his escape, Barker spat blood on the ground and scowled. "Justice will be served, Parker. We will have justice."

"Parker? It's Parkin, you ass."

◆

At David's arrival, Gibbs slid the bolt from the door and let him in, then barred it behind them. He noticed the blood on David's hands and chin.

"What happened?"

"Hatt's friends."

Without explanation, David went up to his office with Gibbs following closely behind. He set a lit candle on his desk, then reclined in his chair, rubbing his fist. Gibbs sat down in the chair before his desk.

"What are you going to do?"

"About what?"

"These hoodlums."

David shrugged. "Nothing. It's done."

Gibbs leaned forward toward the desk. "David, listen to me. There is much talk about these men. It's not going to end here. They are trouble."

David stared quietly at the candle burning on the table. A wax tear fell to its base. He looked up slowly. "What would you have me do? The trial is done."

"Go back. Turn Lawrence over to the law. Let him go to trial."

David looked at him levelly. "What kind of trial?"

"What does it matter! If they hang him, they hang him! He's an old man, a poor old man! He's got nothing, David, you've got your whole life ahead of you."

"What kind of life could that be knowing that I had betrayed a friend?"

"Betrayed?" His eyes squinted in disbelief. "He put himself in this situation, not you! David . . . he's a Negro!"

David looked at him sadly, then dropped his head in his hands. He felt weary. "Leave me, please."

Gibbs sighed, then reluctantly stood. "We have been through a lot together and you always seem to come out on top. But I have a bad feeling about this. I grant you that what you are doing is noble in its own way, but the cost of what you are doing is too great."

David shook his head. "No, Gibbs. Only the cost of doing nothing is ever too great."

◆

"All is ashes . . ."

DAVID PARKIN'S DIARY. DECEMBER 4, 1913

It was easy for the five hooded men to enter Lawrence's shack. The structure had been constructed by the cannery as a storage shed, so it could not be locked from the inside but only from the exterior by a rusted steel latch that had once run horizontally across the outside of the door. Lawrence had removed the latch the previous summer after some teens, in a schoolyard prank, had locked him in his own house. He had never considered moving the lock inside, thinking to himself, *Who would rob a shack?*

The men entered clumsily, growling in foul and guttural tones, drunk with whiskey and hatred. They hovered above the sleeping man only long enough to focus their assault. Lawrence was awakened by the rifle butt that smashed across his face. Panicked and bleary-eyed, he looked up at the hooded men who stood over him. Suddenly, one of them struck him across the face with a metal flask, then fell on him, thrashing wildly. With a powerful kick, Lawrence sent the man sprawling backward into a pile of clocks. In an instant, three men pounced on him, pummeling him with their fists, leaving his face a bloody mask. One clumsily tried to force a glass bottle into his mouth, which cut open his lip and cracked his front tooth, but slipped from the bumbling hands and bounded onto the floor and was lost in the darkness, followed by the man's cursing.

Lawrence managed to free one hand and, swinging wildly, knocked one of the men to the ground. His mind reeled in confusion. He did not know who was attacking him, nor what he could have done to warrant the assault.

As he struggled to raise himself, an ax handle caught him across the back of his head, knocking him off his cot and to the ground, unconscious. The men, growing increasingly sadistic in their violence, stripped him of his clothes, dragged him outside, and bound him to a tree, where they beat and kicked him until they thought him dead. Two of the men returned to the shack and, after taking what they had come for, smashed several clocks with the ax handle, then disappeared into the night.

◆

The fire spread quickly from the back porch, climbing upward to the second level, hungrily devouring all in its path. MaryAnne awoke to the baying of a mongrel dog and thought there was something peculiar about the dawn light shimmering through the bedroom window. Suddenly, there was a sharp crack, like the vaporous expansion of a log in the fireplace. She bolted up in bed as a thin stream of smoke snaked upward from beneath the bedroom door. "David! Our house is on fire!" She suddenly shrieked, "Andrea!"

David jumped up from the bed in horror. "Andrea! Dear God!"

David shot to the door and threw it open. A black pillow of smoke billowed into the room. The end of the hallway was completely engulfed in flames and from behind the wall of fire came a horrible sound. Andrea's cry.

MaryAnne screamed. "Andrea!"

"Mama!" Andrea wailed faintly from behind the flames.

David ran back to the bed and pulling a quilt over himself, pushed toward the inferno surrounding Andrea's room only to be repelled by the intense heat. He screamed out in frustration. The flames snapped fiercely, drowning out Andrea's pleas. Just then, another male voice hollered out. "David!" Mark raced up the stairs. "David!"

"Andrea is in the nursery! Alert the fire station!"

"Catherine has left to pull the alarm."

"Take MaryAnne out. I will climb the back railing to Andrea. Go!"

Outside, the pneumatic siren of a fire truck crescendoed as it entered the yard. A second fire vehicle, a large bell-shaped water drum drawn by horses, pulled into the yard behind it. The corps sprang to action. Two men began operating a pump hooked to the vehicle while a half dozen others, carrying leather fire buckets, streamed into the house, throwing water down the hallway.

In the yard below, Mark held MaryAnne back from her home. She sobbed and wrung her hands violently, each second weighing longer than the next. Where was David? Suddenly, he stumbled from the front doorway, coughing violently, his face streaked wet and blackened from smoke and soot. In his arms lay a motionless child.

CHAPTER NINE

THE
RELEASE

"I know not why I am compelled to write at this time except as those caught in a torrent seek the surer ground and those caught in life's tempests seek the familiar and the mundane."

DAVID PARKIN'S DIARY. DECEMBER 4, 1913

hrough the heroic efforts of the fire corps, the fire had been isolated to the east wing, though the stench of smoke permeated the entire mansion. The house itself had escaped serious structural damage, but the damage inflicted upon its occupants was of far greater consequence.

Night had fallen and the drawing room was illuminated by the yellow radiance of kerosene sconces. Usually by this hour Catherine would have extinguished the wicks and secured the downstairs. Tonight, however, there was company in the house. The police officer rose when David entered the room.

"Mr. Parkin, I am Officer Brookes. Perhaps you remember me from the other day."

David habitually nodded.

"How is your daughter?" he asked cautiously.

"She is badly burned," David replied, his eyes betraying the emotion within.

"I'm truly sorry. I have a little one at home scarcely older than yours." The policeman paused. Then he continued, "It is our belief that the fire was deliberately set."

David said nothing. Just then, Catherine entered the room. She walked up to David and whispered in his ear. David turned toward her, anticipating some change in Andrea's condition.

Catherine read his intent. "There is no change, sir."

"I am needed upstairs," David said. "The doctor . . ."

Brookes frowned. "I am terribly sorry and I will leave you shortly but, please, just two questions."

David looked at the officer impatiently.

"I understand that yesterday you were threatened by a man named Cal Barker."

"I don't know the man's name."

"I was alerted yesterday about the confrontation in the alley, but I arrived too late. I found Barker at a bar and questioned him. He had a broken nose and was raving like a lunatic, but denied the incident. What were his words to you?"

David breathed out. "He said something about getting his own justice."

The officer nodded. "Barker was a friend of Everett Hatt's. I will be arresting him this afternoon. I will keep you informed." He stood up to go. "I am heartfelt sorry to intrude on you now, but time is of the essence. God bless your little one."

David glanced over at Catherine, who was waiting anxiously.

"I will see you to the door, Officer Brookes," Catherine said.

"I would be obliged."

David mumbled a thank-you, then climbed the stairs to the parlor, where Andrea was being cared for. Dr. Bouk stood outside the door, grim-faced and fatigued.

"She has not stirred yet," he said directly, as if in answer to an unspoken question. "If I thought she could survive the move, I would transport her to the hospital." He took a deep breath, then looked David in the eyes. "The child cannot possibly live."

David turned from the doctor and peered in through the crack in the parlor door to where MaryAnne knelt at the side of the walnut-framed bed. It was the same bed and room where she had given birth to Andrea three and a half years previous. The moment seemed frozen, betrayed only by the faint sound of a mantel clock. David turned to the doctor again. His eyes pled for solace. "Is there nothing to be done?"

The doctor frowned, nodding his head slowly. "The burns are too severe. She is running a high fever from the wounds." He removed his bifocals and rubbed the bridge of his nose. "I am very sorry, David. I wish I could give you hope. If she were conscious, she would be in excruciating pain." He returned his glasses to his shirt pocket and untied his apron. "Frankly, I do not know what is keeping her alive."

David looked back in at MaryAnne, bowed fervently over the bed, her cheek pressed against the feather mattress with her forehead touching Andrea's motionless torso.

"I know what is keeping her alive," he said softly.

The doctor frowned again, then removed his vesture. "If there were anything else I could do." He shook his head helplessly. "I'm sorry, David."

David looked down and said nothing as the physician departed. A moment later, David took a deep breath, then grasped the handle and gently pushed the door open, wide enough to enter. MaryAnne did not stir or acknowledge his entrance.

Across the room, the mechanical operation of MaryAnne's grandfather's clock stirred, its hammer ground into position, then, once set, chimed the quarter hour. David walked to the bed and knelt down behind MaryAnne, wrapping his arms around her waist. He laid his head against her back.

"MaryAnne," he whispered softly.

She did not respond. Across the room, the clock allowed its serpentine hand to advance another minute.

"MaryAnne . . ."

"No, David." Her voice was hoarse. "Please . . ."

His eyes moistened. "You must let her go, Mary."

MaryAnne closed her eyes tightly and swallowed. Only the sound of the clock's oscillating pendulum tore at the silence.

"She is my baby, David."

"Andrea will always be your baby, my love." He took a deep breath. "She will forever be our baby."

MaryAnne raised her head and looked on her daughter. Andrea's hair was spread against the pillow, wet at the roots from fever.

With the back of her hand, MaryAnne caressed Andrea's ruddy cheek. She lifted her hand to her own breast, then buried her head back into the mattress and sobbed.

David lifted his hands from her waist to her shoulders. The long hand of the clock advanced three more paces.

MaryAnne raised her head and stared at Andrea, memorizing the delicate features of her face, the gentle contour of her florid cheeks, the smooth slope of her chin. Suddenly, the grandfather's clock struck eleven and the hammer rose and fell for an eternity, dividing the moment into agonizing compartments, as if challenging the fragile life to survive the day.

"Stop it. Please, David. Stop it."

David rose and walked to the clock. He opened its case and grasped the brass pendulum, ceasing its motion, then returned to his wife's side as the metallic echo of the chime died, leaving the room in an unearthly solitude.

MaryAnne suddenly leaned close to Andrea's ear. "I cannot keep you any longer, my love." She swallowed. "I will miss you so." She paused, wiping tears from her cheeks that were as quickly replaced. "Remember me, my love. Remember my love." She laid a hand against the velvet face and bowed her head back into the mattress. "I will remember for both of us."

David pressed the wet flesh of his cheek against MaryAnne's. She swallowed, nuzzled up against the warm, smooth cheek, then, through quivering lips, released her child.

"Go home, my little angel."

As if on command, Andrea suddenly opened her eyes and looked on her mother with no sign of pain or hope, but as one who falls from a cliff might focus their gaze on the ledge they leave behind. Her small chest rose and her lips parted slightly, drawing in breath, struggling against some invisible resistance. Then, in a sudden motion, her eyes turned upward, her tiny body expelled all breath, then no more.

For a moment, all was still. As if all nature had stopped to recognize the singular fall of a sparrow, until the silence was broken by a single, gasping sob, then another, then the unrestrained flood that poured from MaryAnne's convulsing body. David lifted the quilted cover up over Andrea's face, then pulled MaryAnne's head against his chest. She would not be comforted.

CHAPTER TEN

THE
WINTER
MOURNING

"How quickly the fabric of our lives unravels. We weave together protective tapestries of assumption and false belief that are torn to shreds beneath the malevolent claws of reality.

"Grief is a merciless schoolmarm."

DAVID PARKIN'S DIARY. DECEMBER 7, 1913

pon waking, MaryAnne's heart grasped on to the hope that the past few days might only have been a nightmare—then the first moment of recognition was seized by the horrid and breathless remembrance of reality. MaryAnne closed her eyes as the crushing weight of loss constricted her chest in agonizing pain. "No," she moaned.

David took her hand. "MaryAnne."

"I want my baby. Where is my baby?!"

"MaryAnne."

She looked at David through swollen eyes. "No," she moaned. "Where is she?"

"She is gone, my love."

"Bring her back, David. Can't you bring her back?"

David dropped his head in shame, but allowed himself no tears. "No, Mary. I could not even keep her safe."

◆

"In Hebrew, 'Mary' means 'bitter.'"

DAVID PARKIN'S DIARY. DECEMBER 8, 1913

The wagon from the cemetery arrived to bear the small coffin to the knoll—though the casket was small and could have been carried by one man and easily by two.

The noon sun was concealed by a dark tier of clouds as a somber crowd of more than one hundred assembled around the small grave, trampling the snow into a muddy slush.

The jovial greetings of long-unseen friends that usually marked such gatherings had been replaced by simple glances and nods of acknowledgment. Many were there from David's company, whose doors had been closed for the day. The mourners, apparently confused at the etiquette of such an occasion, were not sure how to dress. Some arrived in black and others in stark white.

A fine rain began to fall—a mist at first, which turned into a torrential downpour shortly before the ceremony. Few of the mourners held umbrellas or parasols, as rain in Utah was rare in December. David and MaryAnne stood uncovered, oblivious to the tempest. Mark raised his coat over MaryAnne and held it there the length of the service.

At the head of the cut patch of earth stood the same silver-haired priest who had presided at the wedding of David and MaryAnne four years previous, but his eyes reflected no memory of that happy day. An old man held an umbrella over him, shielding the clergyman from the rain. He raised a white book in his hands and the congregation bowed their heads. His breath froze before him.

"Oh Holy Father, whose blessed Son, in his love for little children, said, 'Suffer little children to come unto me, and forbid them not.' We thank thee for this merciful assurance of thy love, for we believe that thou hast been pleased to take unto thyself the soul of this thy child. Open thou our eyes, we beseech thee, that we may perceive that this child is in the everlasting arms of thine infinite love, and that thou wilt bestow upon her the blessings of thy gracious favor. Amen."

MaryAnne stepped forward and, kneeling, placed a simple white flower on Andrea's casket while David held her shoulders. She quaked as the small wooden box was slowly lowered into the earth's cavity. There was a brief moment of silence before the priest dismissed the proceedings and David helped his wife to her feet. With wordless embraces, the crowd somberly filed past David and MaryAnne to pay their respects, then returned to the forgetful sanctuary of their own homes.

◆

Officer Brookes sauntered into the bar, surrounded by the cold stares of contempt its patrons reserved for lawmen and bill collectors. Brookes was known in the tavern and, though not large of stature, had developed a reputation of being quick of gun and temper.

"Where's Cal Barker?" he shouted over the din. The room quieted, but there was no offer of the man's whereabouts. The officer walked over to a slovenly man nursing a tall brown bottle: Wallace Schoefield. He looked up at Brookes with a disdainful grin. His teeth were tobacco-stained and one front tooth was cracked sharp from a barroom brawl.

"Where is Barker, Wallace?"

The man leered at the policeman, then turned away, tapping his fingers on the slat counter. There were sudden footsteps behind him. Brookes spun around.

"Looking fer me?" Barker asked coolly.

"You're under arrest, Cal."

"Fer?"

"You know what for."

"Don't know nothin'." His thin lips pursed in a confident grin. "It's my right, ain't it? To know what I've supposed to have done before I'm arrested for doin' it."

"I'm arresting you for arson. And the murder of a child."

Through the corner of his eye, Brookes noticed the surprise on Wallace's face.

"What child?" Wallace asked.

Barker stepped in front of Wallace.

"The fire set at the Parkin estate trapped their three-year-old daughter," Brookes said venomously. "She is dead."

Wallace turned to Barker, who, in turn, glared back at him, then at the officer.

"You can't come in here makin' accusations without proof. We hain't done nothin'. Don't know nothin' about what you're talkin' about."

"You're under arrest," Brookes repeated stolidly.

"I hain't going. Didn't do nuthin'. I have witnesses."

Brookes lifted his gun to the man's chin, his eyes frosted with hate. "That's right, give me any reason, Barker. I have always wanted to kill you anyway."

Barker looked into the man's fierce eyes, scowled, then walked out of the tavern ahead of the officer.

◆

"There is an oft-misunderstood statement: 'Misery loves company.' To some, it implies that the miserable seek to make others like unto themselves. But it is not the meaning, rather there is a universality in grief, a family of sorrow clinging to each other on the brink of the abyss of despair. . . .

". . . I once heard it preached that pain is the currency of salvation. If it is so, surely we have bought heaven."

DAVID PARKIN'S DIARY. DECEMBER 17, 1913

Dark stratus clouds hung low and flat across the horizon in a gray, mournful pall. The naked and snow-gripped branches of the back estate bent in a frayed canopy to frame the barren winter landscape. Even the sentinel evergreens seemed shaded in a toneless, dusty hue.

The roof of the gazebo lay shrouded beneath thick snow and the dead vines of rose bushes intertwined through the latticework of the structure, frozen and coated in ice. MaryAnne, cloaked in a heavy black bombazine shawl, sat motionless on the suspended swing as still as the clinging icicles that encircled her.

Catherine wrapped herself in a heavy wool shawl and followed MaryAnne's path to the gazebo. She kicked the snow from her pointed, high-laced leather boots and sat down next to MaryAnne on the still bench, breathing the frigid air that froze the nostrils as well as the exhalation. The two women sat at length in silence. Finally, Catherine looked over.

"Are you warm enough, MaryAnne?"

MaryAnne diverted her gaze and nodded. Catherine looked ahead into the unending horizon of white, sniffed, then rubbed her nose. "I have tried to reason what to say that might be of comfort," she said, her voice weak from emotion. "It is too lofty an ambition for words." She fell silent again.

A solitary magpie lit on an ice-caked sundial, cried out into the gray winter air, then flew back into its cold grasp.

MaryAnne's eyes stared vacantly ahead.

"I have done the same," she said softly. "I tell myself that she will live in my memory. There should be comfort in this." She wiped her reddened eyes with her sleeve. "I should not say 'live.' 'Embalmed' is a better word. Each memory embalmed and dressed in grave clothes with a headstone marking the time and place as a reminder that I will never see my Andrea again."

Catherine said nothing, but looked somberly on, her eyes moistened with her friend's pain.

"There are things I do not understand about my pain, Catherine. If I had to choose never to have known Andrea or to have known her for one brief moment, I would have chosen to have known her and considered myself fortunate. Is it the unexpectedness that causes my grief?"

Catherine pulled her shawl up high enough to cover her chin. "How is David?"

MaryAnne swallowed. "I do not know how David feels, he says nothing. But I see the gray in his eyes and it frightens me. It is the gray of hate, not grief." She shook her head. "It is not just Andrea's life that was taken from us."

There was a moment of silence, then MaryAnne suddenly erupted in rage.

"Listen to me, Catherine! Our lives! My memories! My pain! It is all so selfish! One would think that it is I who had died! Am I so consumed with myself and my own agony that I do not even know if I am mourning for what my little girl has lost . . ." She stopped, her mouth quivering beyond her ability to speak, and lifted a hand to her face. "Or . . . or what I have lost?"

Catherine closed her eyes tightly.

"The wretched fool that I am. Such a selfish, pitiful . . ."

Catherine grabbed MaryAnne's shoulders and pulled her into her arms. Tears streaked down both women's cheeks. "MaryAnne, no! Do not speak such! In what have you done wrong? Did not the mother of our Lord weep at the foot of his cross?!" Catherine pulled MaryAnne's head into her breast and bowed over her, kissing the crown of her head. She wept as MaryAnne sobbed helplessly.

"Oh, Catherine, my arms feel so empty."

◆

"Such darkness besets me. I crave MaryAnne's laughter almost as the drunkard craves his bottle. And for much the same reasons."

DAVID PARKIN'S DIARY. DECEMBER 19, 1913

An hour before sunset, Officer Brookes knocked with the back of his hand on the engraved glass of the front door of the Parkin home. Catherine greeted him.

"Hello, Officer Brookes."

"Miss Catherine." He removed his hat and stepped into the house. Looking up, he noticed MaryAnne, who stood on the balcony above the foyer silently looking down. He turned away from her sad stare.

"I'll get Mr. Parkin," Catherine said without prompting.

David emerged from the hallway below. His face was tight and expressionless. He pointed to the parlor and

Brookes preceded him in. Once inside, David shut the door.

"Did you arrest Barker?"

"Yes, he's in jail. For now," he added.

David looked at him quizzically. The officer rubbed his chin. "I am convinced that it was Barker and his men who set the fire, but there is no proof. There are no witnesses to the crime. At least none who will admit it. Barker has a half-dozen witnesses who claim that he and Wallace were playing cards at the time the fire was set."

David fell silent for a moment as he digested the message. He leaned back against a cabinet.

"One thing more. Your Negro friend was severely beaten that same night—a couple of hours before the fire. Whoever did it left him for dead."

David's jaw clenched in indignation. "Where is Lawrence?"

"He's being cared for at that colored hotel on Second South. His face was swollen and it was difficult for him to speak, but he said something about a gold timepiece being taken. The one that belonged to Hatt's aunt."

Brookes walked across the room and looked out the window into the crimson twilight. "We've got Barker in jail, but we are going to have to release him."

"Can Lawrence identify who beat him?"

"The men were wearing hoods. But even if we could prove it was Barker and his friends, it still doesn't connect them to your fire. If someone don't come forward, there is nothing we can do."

David felt a sickening rage blacken his mind. "There is always something that can be done," he said half to himself.

A look of grave concern bent the policeman's brow. "I know you must feel the temptation real bad, Mr. Parkin, but don't you go taking matters into your own hands. Your wife needs you. It won't do anyone any good." The officer replaced his hat. "I'm sorry. I'll let you know if something happens. You never know. . . ." He walked to the doorway, then paused and looked back at David with a somber countenance. "Don't go doing something to make me have to arrest you. The injustice of this is already enough to make me vomit."

When he had seen him off, David returned to the room and pulled a Winchester carbine from his gun cabinet. He took a pouch from the shelf below and slid two bullets into its chamber. MaryAnne suddenly appeared in the doorway.

"David?"

He turned toward her.

"What did he say?"

"He said there is nothing they can do. . . ."

MaryAnne quietly looked down, cradling her forehead in her hands, then looked back up at David. "What are you doing?"

His eyes were granite. "What needs to be done."

MaryAnne walked over next to him. "David?"

He would not look at her.

MaryAnne knelt down before him and wrapped her arms around his legs and began to cry. A minute later, she looked up, her eyes filled with pleading.

"They killed our daughter," he said coldly.

"The men who killed our little girl were full of hate and vengeance and sickness. Will we become as they?"

David paused for a moment, then looked down at his wife.

"It is the price of justice."

"Such a price, David! How much more must we pay?!" She took a deep breath, her chin quivered. "Haven't we paid enough already?"

"You would have me forget what they have done?"

MaryAnne gasped. "How could we forget what they have done? We can never forget." She raised her head and as she did their eyes met. "But we can forgive. We must forgive. It is all that we have left of her."

"Forgive?" David asked softly. He broke her grasp and walked to the other side of the room. "Forgive?!" he shouted incredulously. "They murdered our daughter!"

MaryAnne sobbed into her hands, then, without looking up, spoke in a voice feeble with grief. "If this is life, exchanging hate for hate, it is not worth living. Vengeance will not bring her back to us. Forgiveness has nothing to do with them, David. It has to do with us. It has to do with who we are and who we will become." She looked up, her eyes drowned in tears. "It has to do with how we want to remember our daughter."

Her words trailed off in a pleading silence. David stared at his wife. "Who we will become," he repeated softly. He leaned the rifle against the cabinet, then returned and knelt by MaryAnne, wrapping his arms around her as she wept into his chest.

"David, I cannot imagine feeling any joy again in this life. It seems that all I can do is to ride the tide of the day's events. But I cannot bear to see any more hate. We must let it end here." She wiped her eyes with the palm of her hand. "I have already lost one of you to hate."

She placed her hand on his sleeve, gripping it tightly. David looked back over at the gun and as he did, she released her grasp. Her voice became soft, yet deliberate. "I cannot choose for you, David. It is your choice, not mine. But if you will be taken by it, I ask that you promise me just one thing."

David looked into her eyes. They were red and swollen, but beautiful still.

"What would you have me promise, Mary?"

"That you will save one bullet for my heart."

CHAPTER ELEVEN

THE SERAPH
AND
THE TIMEPIECE

"As a child, to visualize nobility was to conjure up images of kings and queens adorned in the majestic, scarlet robes of royalty. As a man, softened by the tutelage of life and time, I have learned a great truth—that true nobility is usually a silent and lonely affair, unaccompanied by the trumpeted fanfare of acclaim. And more times than not, it wears rags."

DAVID PARKIN'S DIARY. DECEMBER 19, 1913

 decrepit, wood-planked wagon drawn by a seasoned mule plodded up the cobble-stone drive to the Parkin home. When it neared the double-door entry, Lawrence tied back the reins and climbed down from the buckboard. David had seen the approaching wagon from an upstairs window and descended the stairs to meet it. When he reached the front doorway, Lawrence was already standing on the porch. His forehead was bandaged with white linen strips, and his right eye was nearly swollen shut. His left arm was suspended in a sling. He had removed his hat, and was holding it in his right hand over his chest. His eyes were moist.

"I'm sorry 'bout your little Andrea," he said solemnly.

David lowered his head. Both men were silent.

In the bed of the wagon, a canvas sheet concealed an awkward form. Lawrence wiped his eyes.

"I wanted to do somethin'. I want your Andrea to have my angel."

David said nothing for a moment, then frowned. "No, Lawrence. We couldn't."

"No use, David . . . I gave her up. Thought over it all night. Wha's the use havin' people thinkin' I was somethin' important. If I'm in heaven, it won't matter much, angels all 'bout and such. And if I'm burnin' in hell, shore won't bring much satisfaction. If I'm just cold dead I won' know no difference. No use," he said resolutely, "I said my good-byes. That Andrea, now she's somethin' pure. A child should have an angel." Lawrence glanced up the road, toward the cemetery. "I'll be takin' her up to the sexton's. People be goin' to the grave oughta have somethin' special." His voice choked as he wiped his cheek with his shoulder. "Real Italian marble. You tell MaryAnne there's be somethin' special."

David gazed at the man with quiet respect.

"Jus' somethin' I oughta do," he said solemnly. He put his hat back on his head and turned to leave.

"Lawrence."

"Yessuh."

"Thank you."

Lawrence nodded and with one hand pulled himself up into his rig and coaxed the mule toward the cemetery.

◆

"Today, someone, thinking themselves useful, said to me that it must be a relief to have this 'affair' over with. How indelicately we play each other's heartstrings! How willingly I would carry that pain again for but one glance of her angel face! How she nourished me with her innocence. She once confided in me that the trees are her friends. I asked her how she knew this. She said because they often waved to her. How clearly she saw things! To have such eyes! The trees, for her, shall ever wave to me.

"If I am ever to comfort someone, I will not try to palliate their

suffering through foolish reasoning. I will just embrace them and tell them I am heartfelt sorry for their loss."

DAVID PARKIN'S DIARY. DECEMBER 29, 1913

◆

"What prudery so ritualizes my grief as to press my letters with black sealing wax."

DAVID PARKIN'S DIARY. DECEMBER 31, 1913

As the last six hours of the waning year fell beneath the tireless sweep of the grandfather's clock's serpentine hands, Catherine found David in the drawing room sitting at the marble-topped writing nook, barefoot and dressed only in nightclothes and a crimson robe. He wrote with a quill pen, and a crystal well of India ink sat at the head of the stationery. In the background a wide-mouthed Victrola scratched out a Caruso solo of *La Forza del Destino*.

"Sir?"

David looked up from his letter. "Yes, Catherine."

"Officer Brookes is come."

David lifted a corner of the letter and blew the ink. "I will see him."

"I will let him know." She quickly stepped away. David set down the pen, tightening the sash on his robe, as he left the room. Brookes was not in the foyer as he expected but stood outside the home, twenty feet from the doorway. He had declined Catherine's invitation to enter. Just as peculiar, the police wagon was parked in the shadow of the home's gated entrance and Brookes had walked the length of the drive to the house. David walked out. He found the scene odd and the strange expression on the lawman's face offered no explanation.

"Last night Wallace Schoefield shot himself through the head," Brookes said bluntly.

David stared ahead coldly. He could not pretend sympathy.

"He couldn't live with what they'd done. Barker wanted you, and Wallace and four others went along with him. He said they didn't know about the child."

David looked past the officer toward his horse-drawn paddy wagon. "Who did he tell?"

"He left a letter. Barker started the fire by leaving a bottle of kerosene around the back of your home with gunpowder and a cigar to ignite it after they had left. That's why Barker wasn't there when the fire started."

Behind him, the horse whinnied and shook its head impatiently.

"The child was killed unintentionally." Officer Brookes suddenly squinted, then removed his revolver from his holster and handed it to David, who looked up quizzically. Brookes's eyes darted back and forth nervously. His voice dropped coldly.

"They'll send Barker to prison, but they won't be hanging him. He's getting off easy. He should die for what he's done. Barker's locked in the wagon. If you want to kill him, I'll say that I shot him in the taking."

David caressed the gun in his hand. It was evenly balanced and he ran his fingertips along the engraving that rose up its steel barrel. He stared at it for a moment, rubbed his forehead, then handed the gun back to the officer.

"No," he said softly. He turned and began to walk away.

The response surprised Brookes, who returned the firearm to its holster. "It's better than he deserves," he shouted after him.

David stopped and looked at the officer. "Yea. It probably is. But it is not better than Andrea deserves."

He looked back at the wagon and frowned. "Do your duty, Officer."

The officer tipped his hat. "Good evening, Mr. Parkin. To a new year."

"Good evening, Brookes."

◆

At Catherine's summons, MaryAnne came to David in the drawing room. She found him gazing silently out the tall twelve-paned windows that lined the north wall. She paused at the doorway, then slowly entered.

"David?"

He turned around. He was still wearing his robe and was unshaven, with several days' growth shading his lower face. His eyes were red-rimmed. For a brief moment, she felt a pang of apprehension, as though she were approaching a stranger, not her beloved.

"Remember, Mary? This is where we met our guests at our wedding. It looks so different to me now." He surveyed the surroundings as if the room held some new intrigue. "Of course, there were flowers . . . and that palm . . ."

MaryAnne clasped her hands behind her back. His

words seemed to float with no apparent destination. She suddenly felt afraid.

"I am sorry. I am babbling like an idiot." He ran a hand through his hair, then breathed heavily. He turned back toward her. "I do not know how I am to act, MaryAnne. How a man is to act."

MaryAnne stared back quietly.

"I walk around with this stone expression like some kind of statue. But I do not have a stone heart." His eyes moistened. "And I wonder if this wall I have built up is to protect me from further assault or to retain the last vestige of humanity within me. Are men not supposed to feel loss? Because I feel it, Mary. I feel it as heavy as a horse falling on me." He lowered his head. "And I miss my little girl and I don't even feel worthy to do so."

His voice began to crack.

"She was so small and needed someone to protect her." He raised a hand to his chest. "I was to protect her, Mary. Every instinct I was born with cries out that I must protect her!" His voice rose in an angry crescendo, then fell sharply in a despairing monotone. "And I failed. I have more than failed, I have caused her death." A tear fell down his cheek. His lips quivered.

"Oh, what I would give to hold her just once more. To hear her forgive me for failing her." He wiped his cheek, then lowered his head. MaryAnne walked across the room to him, then stopped abruptly. On the counter beside him lay two bullets. She looked up for an explanation. David glanced at the bullets, then back up into her face.

"You were right. It is all that I have left of her. All my feelings and love for Andrea were in my heart—" he rubbed his eyes—"and hate kills the heart. Even broken ones."

He took a deep breath, then, in anguish, dropped his head in his hands and began to weep. "I need you, Mary. I need you."

MaryAnne took him in her arms, then pulled his head to her breast as he fell to his knees and, for the first time since Andrea's death, wept uncontrollably.

◆

FIVE YEARS LATER. SALT LAKE CITY, 1918

"There are moments, it would seem, that were created in cosmic theater where we are given strange and fantastic tests. In these

times, we do not show who we are to God, for surely He must already know, but rather to ourselves."

DAVID PARKIN'S DIARY. DECEMBER 8, 1918

It was a chill night and the winter winds rolled in frozen gusts down the foothills of the Wasatch Range, drawing the valley in its crystalline breath. Two hours after the sun had fallen, a child, not suitably clad for such a December night, knocked on the front door of the Parkin home.

David was out of the state on business and as Catherine had been given leave for the evening, MaryAnne came to the foyer to greet the winter visitor. As she opened the door, a chill ran up her spine. Mary-Anne recognized the girl right away. She was the daughter of Cal Barker.

"What brings you here, child?" MaryAnne asked softly.

The little girl timidly raised her head. Her face was gaunt and her clothes were dirty and ill fit.

"I would like some food, ma'am," she replied humbly. Her breath froze before her.

MaryAnne stared for a moment, then slowly stepped away from the door. "Come in."

The girl stepped into the house. Her eyes were filled

with wonder at its richness and beauty. MaryAnne led her down the corridor, then into the dining room, where she pulled a chair away from the table.

"Sit down," she said.

The girl obeyed, dwarfed by the ornate, high-backed chair. MaryAnne left the room, then returned a few moments later with a plate of bread and curd cheese, a sliced pear, and a small bowl of broth. She watched in silence as the girl devoured the meal. When she had finished eating, the child leaned back from the table and looked around the room. Her eyes focused on a small gold-framed photograph of Andrea, clothed in a beautiful umber velvet dress with a lace-bibbed bodice. She smiled at MaryAnne.

"You have a little girl!"

MaryAnne stared at the child, then slowly shook her head. "No. Not anymore."

"Where is she?" The girl's brown eyes blinked quizzically, partially covered by the long, dirty strands that fell over her face. "She would be lucky to live in this house."

MaryAnne looked down at the Persian rug and blinked away the pooling tears. "She is gone. She had to go away." She took a deep breath. "How old are you, child?"

"I am nine years."

MaryAnne looked carefully into her face. She thought she appeared older than her nine years—aged as a child who has had the harsh realities of life thrust upon her. "What is your name?"

"Martha Ann Barker, ma'am."

MaryAnne stood and walked over to the window. The snow outside fell in scattered showers and in the distance snaked across the paved street in snow-blown skiffs. "My little girl would be nine this winter," MaryAnne said into the frosted windowpanes. She stared out into the black. ". . . This January." She suddenly turned toward her small guest. "It is late for you to be out."

"I was so hungry."

"Haven't your parents any food?"

She shook her head. "My father was in the jail. No one lets him work."

The child's directness surprised her. "Do you know why he was put in jail?"

She shook her head again. "The boys say that he killed a child. I asked my mama, but she just cries, mostly."

MaryAnne nodded her head slowly. "Why did you come here? To this house."

"I saw the fire from the street. It looked so warm and nice inside."

"The fire . . . ," MaryAnne repeated softly. She sat down at the table next to her guest, contemplating the strange circumstance that had befallen her. She had been given a gift. A terrible, wonderful gift. The chance to see her own soul. She sat motionless, her hands joined in her lap, as her mind reeled with emotions. Then a single tear fell down her cheek. The girl observed it curiously. MaryAnne leaned close to the child and took her face in her hands.

"You must remember this night, Martha. You are loved here. You must know this for the rest of your life."

The girl stared back blankly.

"You will understand someday." MaryAnne stood up. "Just a moment, dear." She left the room, then returned with a small bag of flour and a canister of salted bacon, as much as she thought the child could carry. In a kerchief, stowed in the canister, MaryAnne had wrapped three gold coins.

"Can you carry this?"

Martha shook her head. "Yes, ma'am. I am strong."

MaryAnne nodded sadly. "I can see that. Now you run home and take this to your mama." She escorted

Martha back out to the foyer and opened the door. A chill wind swept into the house. "Remember, Martha. You are always welcome. You are loved here."

The little girl stepped out the door, walked a few paces, then turned back. "Thank you, ma'am."

"You are welcome, child."

She looked at the woman gratefully. "Don't be sad. Your little girl will come home." The girl smiled innocently, then turned quickly and disappeared into the winter night. MaryAnne shut the door and fell against it weeping.

◆

The next morning, the first sheaths of dawn illuminated the windows of the downstairs parlor in iridescent brilliance, meeting MaryAnne, where it had daily for the past five years, before a fireplace reading her Bible. The Bible David had brought back with a wooden box, a porcelain music box, and an oversized dress that would never be worn. The book bore witness of her devotion to the daily ritual, marred with teardrops and wrinkled pages. MaryAnne had followed the routine every morning since she had lost Andrea, holding to the words as one who is drowning seizes a life ring.

At the conclusion of her reading, MaryAnne wiped her eyes, then replaced the Gothic book on the elaborately carved rosewood bookshelf. She donned her coat and scarf and started outside on her daily trek to the angel statue.

The winter air was damp and heavy, carrying moisture pilfered from the Great Salt Lake, which salt-saturated consistency kept it from freezing even in the severest of winters.

In the distance, MaryAnne could see the angel at the top of a knoll, its head and wings capped in a new-fallen shroud of snow. She walked solemnly, her head bowed. She need not look to find her way, she could have followed the trail without sight.

She suddenly stopped.

In the freshly fallen snow were tracks leading to the angel. Heavy tracks, clumsy, large-bodied footprints that had come, and departed, falling back on themselves, but leaving evidence of the visitor at the base of the grave. MaryAnne approached pensively. Someone, that very morning, had knelt at the foot of the angel.

As she neared, she could see that the snow had been wiped from the stone pedestal. On its surface, she saw a small parcel, a white flour sack bundle bound with jute.

She looked around her. The morning sun illuminated the grounds and the snow sparkled in a virgin, crystalline blanket. All was still and quiet and alone.

Noiselessly, she stooped down and lifted the offering. As she pulled back the cloth, the contents cast a gold reflection on the surrounding coarse material—a soft radiance from the treasure that lay within. There, without a note, on the marble step of the monument, had been laid a rose-gold timepiece.

CHAPTER TWELVE

THE ENDOWMENT

SALT LAKE CITY, 1967

stood outside Jenna's room holding the velveteen case in my hands. My throat was dry as I slid the box into my trouser pocket and knocked gently on the door. A soft voice answered.

"Come in."

I stepped into the room. Jenna sat on her bed writing in her diary. A bridal gown, sheathed in a transparent garment bag, hung from the closet door above a new pair of boxed white satin pumps.

"Hi, sweetheart."

Her face wore the unique blend of melancholy and excitement given rise on such an occasion. I sat down on the bed next to her.

"Are you ready for tomorrow?"

Jenna shrugged. "I don't think I will ever be ready."

"I was just thinking the same about myself," I said. "I once read a poem about the pain of a father sending his daughter to another village to be married. It was written four thousand years ago in China. Maybe things never really change."

Jenna bowed her head.

"I just remind myself that this is what I've always hoped for you. All I have ever wanted for you is to be happy."

She leaned over and hugged me.

"I have something I need to give you." I brought the box from my pocket and set it in her hands. Her eyes shone with delight as she opened the case.

"It's beautiful." She lifted the delicate timepiece from the case, dangling it admiringly from one end. "Thank you."

"It's not from me," I said. "But it is from someone who loved you very much." Jenna looked at me quizzically.

"It's from MaryAnne."

My words sounded strange even to me—a name on a grave near the stone angel we visited every Christmas, now resurrected in a single act of giving.

"MaryAnne," she repeated. She looked up into my eyes. "I don't really remember her," Jenna said sadly. "Not really. I remember her once holding me in a chair and reading to me. How good I felt around her."

"Then you remember her, Jenna. She loved you as if you were her own. In some ways, you were."

Jenna looked back down at the timepiece.

"Nineteen years ago, MaryAnne asked me to give this to you the night before your wedding. It was her most prized possession."

Jenna shook her head in astonishment. "She wanted me to have it?"

I nodded. "MaryAnne was a good giver of gifts," I said.

She draped the gold watch back in its case, set it on her nightstand, then sighed. "So are you, Dad."

I smiled.

"Dad?"

"Yes?"

She turned away and I noticed that her chin quivered as she struggled to speak. As she turned back, her tear-filled eyes met mine. "So, how do you thank someone for a life?"

I wiped a tear from my cheek as I stared back into my

daughter's beautiful eyes. Then, in that bittersweet moment, I understood MaryAnne's words of the gift. The great gift. The meaning of the timepiece.

"You give it back, Jenna. You give it back." I took my girl in my arms and held her tightly to my chest. My heart, bathed in fond memory, ached in the sweet pain of separation. This is what it meant to be a father—had always meant. To know that one day I would turn around and my little girl would be gone. Finally, reluctantly, I released her and leaned back, looking down into her angelic face. It was time. Time for the cycle to begin anew.

"It's late, sweetheart. You have a big day tomorrow." I leaned over and kissed her tenderly on the cheek. "Good-bye, honey."

It was good-bye. To an era. A time never to be returned to. Her eyes shone with sadness and love. "Good-bye, Daddy."

The silence of the snow-shrouded evening enveloped the moment and time seemed to stand still for just a moment. For just us.

I took a deep breath, rose from the side of her bed, and with one last embrace walked from her room. I descended the stairway with a new lightness of understanding. I understood what MaryAnne had meant by the gift. The gift Jenna had given me had been life. That the very breath I had once given to her had come back to me in an infinite return of joy and life and meaning.

In the dimly lit entrance below, the grandfather's clock struck once for the hour, and I paused momentarily at the base of the stairway to look into its time-faded face as, perhaps, MaryAnne and David had done so many years before.

This relic will outlive us all, I thought, just as it had outlived generations before us. For within its cotillion of levers and cogs and gears, there was still time. Time to outlive all things human. Yet, in my heart, something told me otherwise. For perhaps there was some quality about love that sprang eternal—that a love like MaryAnne's, and like mine, could last forever.

Not could. Would. This was the message of the time-piece. To let go of this world and aspire to something far nobler in a realm that regards no boundaries of time.

I glanced back upstairs as the light switched off in my little girl's room and I smiled. Twenty years after MaryAnne's death, she had bestowed upon me one last gift of understanding. I wondered if, in some unseen realm, MaryAnne was watching and was pleased that I had learned her lesson. That some things, like a parent's love, do last forever in a time and place where all broken hearts will forever be made whole. And if, in the silent vastness of a mysterious universe, or in the quietness of men's hearts, there is such a place as heaven, then it couldn't be anything more than that.

The Letter

CONTENTS

◆

. . . these dark days will be worth all they cost us if they teach us that our true destiny is not to be ministered unto but to minister to ourselves and our fellow men.

—FRANKLIN DELANO ROOSEVELT
FIRST INAUGURAL ADDRESS,
MARCH 4, 1933

PROLOGUE

It was with ardent horror that primitive man first witnessed a solar eclipse—the sun devoured by the predator moon until its light ceased and darkness fell upon the face of the land. The aborigine, too, fell upon the land, crying for the loss of heaven's fire and fear of everlasting night.

We, their more enlightened posterity, have also suffered eclipses. Some, as those in the Dark Ages, endure for centuries, while others pass in blessed brevity. I am not certain if it is the crisis or the uncertainty of its duration that causes the human spirit its greatest anguish, stirring men to cry out to the faceless heavens, *"How long, Lord? How long?"*

One such eclipse was the darkness that befell the world that black October of 1929 christened in the annals of history as the Great Depression. Commencing with the stock exchange's collapse in New York City, there was scarcely a corner of the globe that did not feel the tremor of that institution's great fall or the bleak chill of its darkness.

The bitterness of the era may only be fully known by those who felt its desperation as banks foreclosed, then folded themselves, leaving millions unemployed, homeless, and hopeless.

But among the tales of despair are also stories of quiet heroics; corner grocers extending credit they know will never be repaid, and landlords overlooking rent until finding themselves faced with destitution. It is often during the worst of times that we see the best of humanity—awakening within the most ordinary of us that which is most sublime.

I do not believe that it is circumstance that produces such greatness any more than it is the canvas that makes the artist. Adversity merely presents the surface on which we render our souls' most exacting likeness. It is in the darkest skies that stars are best seen.

During these days of darkness, in one small corner of the earth—a cemetery in the Salt Lake Valley—a letter was found at the snowy base of an angel monument that marked the grave of a little girl.

I discovered the letter in the winter of 1949 pressed between the pages of a diary that belonged to the child's father, and, at first glance, I regarded it of little consequence. It was only after I had read the diary that I learned of the letter's great significance and the events it set in motion.

The diary—the last volume of a series of leatherbound books which documented the lives of David and MaryAnne Parkin—came into my possession shortly after the death of MaryAnne. Her husband, David, had died fourteen years previous.

MaryAnne Chandler Parkin was a beautiful Englishwoman with the sad, clear eyes of one who has touched the flame of life and learned from its heat. Even in her autumn years she remained beautiful, though, in retrospect, I am not sure if her beauty was entirely physical or induced of the dignity and grace that permeated her being. Whatever the truth, MaryAnne personified compassion—and love makes all comely.

My wife, Keri, and I had, for a season, shared the mansion with the kindly widow up until her passing on the eve of Christmas of 1948. Those were winter days not to be forgotten.

From the soliloquies of David Parkin's diary, I learned a great truth about life—and all relationships—that even the greatest of loves may shudder beneath the shadow of eclipse. I believe that the story of David and MaryAnne is, simply, a love story, though not in the fanciful romanticism of poets and pulp novelists. I am not a believer in love at first sight. For love, in its truest form, is not the thing of starry-eyed or star-crossed lovers, it is far more organic, requiring nurturing and time to fully bloom, and, as such, seen best not in its callow youth but in its wrinkled maturity.

Like all living things, love, too, struggles against hardship, and in the process sheds its fatuous skin to expose one composed of more than just a storm of emotion—one of loyalty and divine friendship. Agape. And though it may be temporarily blinded by adversity, it never gives in or up, holding tight to lofty ideals that transcend this earth and time—while its counterfeit simply concludes it was mistaken and quickly runs off to find the next real thing.

◆

This is the story of David and MaryAnne Parkin's love.

CHAPTER ONE
THE GRAVEYARD ENCOUNTER

"The sexton is a peculiar man, enslaved by the dominion of ritual and constancy. His vocation is well chosen as nothing is so reliable as death."

DAVID PARKIN'S DIARY. JANUARY 29, 1934

SALT LAKE CITY CEMETERY, 1933

s the graveyard fell dark into the shiver of the canyon's breath, the sexton, with the arduous motion of arthritic hands, donned his coat, hat, and scarf, lit the wick of a candle-lantern, then emerged from his cottage into the snow-draped graveyard to chain the cemetery's gates against the threat of grave robbers. Only once, at the outset of his forty-seven-year tenure, had a grave in the cemetery been plundered, but he had decided then that his grounds were in peril and the sexton was a creature of habit in thought as well as observance.

The old man started northwards, up the snow-banked street, until, atop a moonlit knoll, the silhouette of an angel statue came into view against the velvet backdrop of night. The statue had been erected over the grave of a three-year-old girl, the only child of a wealthy Salt Lake City couple, David and MaryAnne Parkin. It had become a landmark in the cemetery and a signpost of the sexton's routine, who, two decades earlier, had changed his daily ritual in this one regard—to commence his morning tour of the grounds from east to west to avoid the child's mother weeping at the foot of the monument.

To his astonishment, as he mounted the knoll, he discovered the woman crouched at the base of the statue. He thought the scene peculiar, for as long as the site had graced his cemetery, the child's beautiful mother had never visited her grave past dusk.

He advanced more slowly, hoping his lantern's dim light or his crunching footfalls would divulge his presence without startling the woman, who, immersed in her grief, was ignorant of both. He stopped, five yards removed, as the snow fell silently around and between them. He impatiently lifted his pocket watch by its fob, dangling it within the light of the flickering lantern, replaced it, then, his routine threatened, loudly cleared his throat—his breath clouding before him in a fog.

The bowed head rose.

"Mrs. Parkin, I must be closin' the yard."

The form moved stiffly, struggling to her feet. To the sexton's surprise it was not the graceful, slender form of the child's mother, but instead the withered and heavy-set personage of a woman, older than himself. Her steel-hue hair, framed by a vermilion kerchief, was matted against her forehead, and the lantern's light reflected off the residue of tears which streaked her cheeks. Bewildered, she turned to look at him.

"Excuse me, ma'am. I thought you some other body . . ."

Her grey eyes widened.

". . . 'tis after dusk, I must be closin' up the grounds."

The woman nodded slowly, then wiped her cheeks with an open palm. "I'll go now," she said in a voice as haggard as her appearance. She turned again to the angel, and her hunched shoulders rose and fell with a deep sigh.

The sexton looked down at the monument's granite pedestal at the woman's offering: a single crimson rose atop an envelope.

"Will the trolley board again tonight?"

"Last run to the end of the line at nine forty-five." He glanced again to his pocket watch. "You've twenty minutes, yet."

"Thank you," she muttered, as she dropped her head and started off, shuffling through shin-deep snow, leaving a wide trail between the stone and wood grave markers, until she disappeared into the deeper shadows of a grove of mourning willows.

Without further consideration, the sexton continued his routine, reaching the north gates six minutes and thirteen seconds past his usual schedule.

◆

"Unlike myself, MaryAnne frequently visits our daughter's grave—oftentimes with weekly regularity.

"I do not know what she finds in the ritual, nor the particulars of its observance, but at her return her eyes are swollen and her

voice spent. It is a reminder of the grief I have unearthed in her life and so deeply buried in mine. I would say that each day the expanse between our hearts widens, except that I cannot be certain.

"At such great distance it is difficult to perceive the increase of a few extra yards."

DAVID PARKIN'S DIARY. OCTOBER 11, 1933

◆

MaryAnne Parkin stood before the marble angel nearly as still as the statue itself. Her laced, leather boots were buried past her ankles in a crystalline blanket of crusted snow as a light fall continued to descend. The dawning sun lit the statue in a burgeoning crescent, illuminating half its face and robe—leaving the sculpture divided as a waning moon. A cascade of foot marks, preserved from previous visits, flowed and ebbed from the statue, gathered at its base in a single depression. MaryAnne was aware that not all of the prints were hers, for as she entered the cemetery she had encountered the sexton who had told her of the elderly woman he had, two evenings prior, found kneeling at the angel and mistaken for her. She had not given the sexton's account much consideration, as

her mind was filled with thoughts of greater consequence.

She felt as if her heart would break.

"Good-bye, sweet Andrea," she whispered. "I do not
know if I shall ever return."

She shuddered at the finality of her words, then lifted
a gloved hand to brush back a fresh onset of tears. "I
have prayed and prayed for answers. I don't know why
God is so silent. I am sorry if I have failed you, but the
silence from the two I love most I cannot bear. I know of
no other way."

She lowered her head and sobbed until her body
shook.

MaryAnne could not recall when she had first considered leaving her home. The notion had, perhaps,
attended her daughter's funeral, waiting patiently
among the congregation of mourners. But it was not
until she had fully felt the estrangement of the man she
loved that the notion became real.

The sexes do not deal with tragedy in like manner,
and while woman and man may differ in response on
many of life's weightier issues, the disparity is far less
forgiving in this unhappy realm. Where MaryAnne

had outwardly worn her grief as she did its raiment—
the veils and cloaks of death's rituals—David had
buried his, secreted it away in dark recesses behind
stoic walls that widened daily. But walls, emotional or
otherwise, are not particular and hold out more than
just what they are erected for. In the construction of his
walls, David had sequestered more than his pain, but
also his love, MaryAnne.

MaryAnne had told no one of her planned escape,
as she had continually procrastinated the painful confession for an opportune moment. As the years had
relinquished to hours, she realized that there was no
opportune moment to share such tidings and now
reconsidered telling her husband, as he was certain to
entreat her to stay—a request she did not know if she
could deny. For the last three years, MaryAnne had
viewed herself as one helplessly stranded on the edge
of a towering precipice delaying the inevitable leap
until the wait had become more painful than the fall
she avoided. The event of her brother's wedding in
England had provided the ideal opportunity for her
departure. It was time to jump.

It was moments later, as she raised her eyes, that she

first noticed, on the snow-blanketed shelf of the monument's pedestal, a wilted green stem protruding from the snow. She slowly crouched forward, her petite, gloved hand grasped the flower, raising it to her nose—it was a rose, its bud closed tightly and encrusted in the frost that both killed and preserved. Looking down, she noticed that the flower was not the only occupant of the shelf. Something lay beneath it. She brushed back the snow, uncovering an envelope. The envelope's seal was pressed in burgundy wax, the embossed image of a rosebud, its thorny stem and leaves swirled about the icon in an elaborate flourish. Lifting it from the base, she slid back its flap, extracted its contents, and unfolded parchment as fragile snowflakes lit on the paper, melted, and joined the ink in constitution.

MaryAnne gasped.

Pressing the note to her breast, she glanced furtively around the silent yard, though it was evident that the letter had endured the freezing night and snowfall. The yard was, as it was always at dawn, vacant of all but its usual breathless inhabitants. She pulled her scarf tighter around her neck and chin, lay the rose at the angel's feet, then stowed the letter in the besom pocket of her fur-lined jacket.

She glanced one last time into the angel's face, then retraced her steps down the knoll and through the west bend of the cemetery where a small wooden gate, fastened between stone supports of weathered brick and mortar, opened to the road which ran in front of the home she prepared to flee.

CHAPTER TWO
LAWRENCE

"Lawrence has never spoken of the hardship of the Depression. Perhaps it is because, for the Negroes, the scenery hasn't much changed."

DAVID PARKIN'S DIARY. SEPTEMBER 10, 1933

s MaryAnne returned from the cemetery, in another part of town, the Parkins' housemaid, Catherine, called on the home of a friend of the Parkin family—an elderly black man named Lawrence Flake.

At the gentle rap, Lawrence turned towards the door though he was unable to see it. Lawrence was blind, his eyes fogged over, in part from age, but chiefly from a cruel December night, twenty years previous, when four men, wild with vengeance and alcohol, had entered the black man's shack and savagely beat him, leaving him for dead. Not an hour later, the same men, led by a brutish miner named Cal Barker, had set fire to the Parkin Mansion, resulting in the death of their three-year-old daughter Andrea. Lawrence had long outlived that tragic night, and two years earlier passed the milestone age of eighty. Had it been within his power, he would gladly have given his years to the little girl.

At the turn of the century, Lawrence Flake was a buffalo soldier serving with the twenty-fourth regiment of the Negro U.S. Cavalry; a commission he held until, at the age of fifty, he retired from the military and settled where it had left him, in the inclement bowl of the Salt Lake Valley.

Most of his years in the military had been spent as troop supply and requisitions clerk, a duty he acquired after demonstrating unusual proficiency in the repair of wagons and rifles. It was here where he had mastered the art of clock repair—the vocation he continued after his discharge. Although he could no longer repair or build clocks, his home was still full of them: some collected with great deliberation, while others he adopted after their owners, most of whom had died years earlier, had abandoned them.

In daily ritual, Lawrence wound the chime clocks, for if he could not see their faces he could still hear their voices, though the custom was practiced for habit, not necessity. At his age and station, he was emancipated of the clocks' tyranny—ate when he was hungry and slept when he was tired. The one exception to his hourless routine was the morning call of Catherine. She came to Lawrence's shack with such constancy that one could set a clock by her visit.

"Come in, darlin' girl," Lawrence shouted. "The ancient, ol' man is waitin' for you."

Catherine pushed open the warped door and entered, preceded by a rush of winter air. The chill braced the small shack, repelled only by the hissing fire in the cast iron belly of the Franklin stove. Her cheeks were rosy from the drive and from the crook of her arm hung a straw basket. She did not remove her coat.

"Good morning, old man. I have brought apple dumplings and ash-pone."

Lawrence sniffed the air, then expelled a loud sigh of pleasure. "Still hot from the oven. Got no reason to envy royalty, Miss Catherine. You take such fine care of me."

His benefactress smiled as she lay the basket on the table. She never doubted her service was appreciated.

"If you would stay at the house I could take better care of you."

"Like I always say, Miss Catherine, Parkins don't need an old, blind Negro sittin' around their place like some piece of broken furniture."

"You are the most stubborn man," Catherine replied, as she set about her morning routine. She extracted a wide-mouthed jar of buttermilk and a bottle of absinthe from her basket and set them both on the table. She unscrewed the cap from the bottle of green liqueur, then twisted the lid off the milk. "Here's your milk."

"That ain't from no bovine."

Catherine smiled. "Mr. Parkin thought you might need a little something."

"David's a right generous soul. You know President Roosevelt done a smart thing in re-peelin' Prohibition, just wish he'd done it 'fore the revenuers got to my stash. Had a whole crate saved for my weddin' or my funeral. Never intended to wet the ground with it."

Catherine emptied the rest of her basket then sat down across from Lawrence as he slowly felt around the table, familiarizing himself with the articles set before him.

"Both Mr. and Mrs. Parkin have said how nice it would be to have you stay at the house. I wish you would consider their invitation. There is plenty of room."

Lawrence's expression grew somber. "It's a hard thing, miss. No doubt David and MaryAnne be sincere in their askin'. No matter where I'm livin' they be takin' care of me. Sometimes I think it might be nice, too, 'specially the way I put you out comin' all the way to my house each day. Feel truly sorrowful 'bout that."

"It is no trouble, Lawrence."

"Just somethin' 'bout a man's castle. No matter how humble that castle be."

He reached for the bottle of absinthe, and Catherine pushed it within his grasp. He ran his fingers up the bottle's neck, then, discovering its cap absent, raised the bottle to his lips, swallowed, then wiped his mouth with his sleeve. "Truth is, won't be much longer when no one need fret over me."

"Don't talk that way."

"Didn't mean no offense by it. Just, man knows when his time's a comin'. Somethin' inside like a clock windin' down."

"I am not one to frequent cemeteries," Catherine rejoined. "In my mind or otherwise. Just foolishness, talking about death."

"I ain't got no problem with dyin', Miss Catherine, it's one of life's simpler things. Like nightfall, it don't require no decision." He paused for Catherine's reprimand, but she said nothing. "Just as well. What use's a horologist that can't see? Been my philosophy that if life ain't useful it ain't nothing. I met people still breathin' that been dead going on twenty years or more. Only difference between them and the stone-cold is a headstone and six feet of dirt." Lawrence paused again, sensing his benefactress's unusual quietness. "You all right this morning, Miss Catherine?"

"I am just a little sad. MaryAnne is leaving tomorrow for England and will be gone until Christmas. It's the first time she's been away so long."

"What's MaryAnne doing in England?"

"Her brother Ethan is getting married."

"Lord and butter. Ain't he a bit old to be settlin' down?"

"We're almost the same age. You'll make me feel like a spinster talking like that," Catherine mused.

Lawrence grimaced, embarrassed by the faux pas. "Sorry, Miss Catherine, didn't mean nothin' by it. Just makin' talk."

A clock chimed the quarter hour, reminding Catherine of the day's obligations. She stood, pushing her chair back by her motion. "I best get back to the house. I have much to do to prepare for MaryAnne's journey."

She gathered the containers back into her basket. "Is there anything else you need?"

Lawrence's voice lowered. "No thank you," he said. "Now don't you go worryin', I won't go talkin' 'bout death like that no more. Least not when you're 'round. Didn't mean to get you upset."

"It's all right, Lawrence." She stopped at the door. "I wrapped the ash-pone for your supper. I will see you tomorrow."

"Tomorrow," he echoed. "My thanks."

He waited for the door to shut before he cussed himself out for offending his day's only visitor.

◆

Through stained and embossed windows, the sweet light of the winter morning lit the mansion's capacious foyer, finding MaryAnne sitting on the second step of the curved stairway. In one hand she held the letter she had just discovered at the angel, her forehead in the other, deliberating the dilemma the letter presented. Catherine's return through the front entry momentarily startled her from her thoughts.

"Good morning, Mary."

"Good morning, Catherine."

Catherine set her basket on the marble floor and, after brushing the snow from her shoulders, commenced to unbutton the vestment. "I have brought out your cases. I left them in the hallway outside the boudoir. I thought I would consult you before I began your packing."

"Thank you, dear."

"What time does your train depart?"

"Tomorrow, before noon. I must be to the station by ten." She rose, concealing the letter at her side. "Were you home when David left?"

"I saw him off a few moments after you went out."

MaryAnne took Catherine's hand and led her to the adjacent drawing room where both women sat on the same velvet love seat, their knees touching. MaryAnne brushed back a threatening tear, removed the letter from its envelope, and handed it to Catherine.

"This morning I found this letter at Andrea's angel."

Catherine unfolded the letter and read it. A perplexed expression blanketed her face. "Is it from Cal Barker?"

MaryAnne hesitated. "I don't think so. It was left with a rose. I believe it is from David's mother."

Catherine gasped. What little she knew of David's mother was unpleasant. David's mother, Rosalyn King, had been a music hall singer when she met Jesse Parkin, a prospector in Grass Valley, California. When David was only six years of age, Rosalyn, having grown weary of the hard life, followed the sirens of celebrity and abandoned her small family to return East to pursue her career on the stage. Thirteen years after her departure, Jesse's dig, the Eureka mine, surrendered one of the richest veins in California history. Jesse Parkin died just two years after the find, leaving twenty-one-year-old David the sole heir of the fortune.

When Rosalyn learned of her former husband's death, she returned to David's life, urging him to send money and come to her in Salt Lake City. Alone, and covetous of family, David immediately forgave his mother, purchased, unseen, the Salt Lake City mansion for the two of them, and impetuously sent ahead twenty-five thousand dollars for the home's furnishings, which Rosalyn immediately absconded with, leaving only a note of her intention to return to Chicago to resurrect her career. She had not been heard from since.

Catherine was only seventeen when she had first met David. She had been left at the mansion by her former employer to watch over the house until its purchaser's arrival. She had nonchalantly delivered the message of Rose's departure, unaware of the pain her news would invoke. Even then, though just newly acquainted with the young David, she could not help but feel empathy for his pain and enmity towards his cruel mother. This morning's reference to the woman sounded peculiar, like a character from a history textbook.

"David's mother?" Catherine repeated. "She is still alive?"

"It is possible." MaryAnne took up the letter and slid it back into the envelope. "I do not want David to see this. I cannot bear that she hurt him again."

"She is an awful woman. It is incomprehensible that she would abandon him."

The words were not intended for MaryAnne, but pierced just as deeply.

"Its arrival at this time is so peculiar," MaryAnne said.

Catherine received her words unable to comprehend their full meaning. "Perhaps you should wait until your return to show him."

The suggestion evoked pain, and MaryAnne's gaze dropped back to the letter. "That is what I'll do." Her words hung in silence as she opened the drawer of a cherry-wood lamp table to hide the letter inside.

"Are you all right, MaryAnne?"

MaryAnne forced a smile. "Anxious for my journey I suppose."

Catherine leaned into her friend's shoulder. "I feel the same. I do not think we have been apart for more than a few days since you and David wed." She sat back. "I am being silly. It is only eight weeks. You will be home before Christmas." She looked into MaryAnne's face. ". . . it is just that you are my best friend."

MaryAnne pulled Catherine closer until her chin rested on the crown of her head, and gently stroked back her hair. "I am weary of good-byes" was all she said. MaryAnne could not believe that a heart that had been through as much as hers could still hurt so.

CHAPTER THREE

MARYANNE'S DEPARTURE

"At the train station I suddenly had the forceful impression that I would not see MaryAnne again. The premonitions that we so quickly dismiss are sometimes our truest glances of reality."

DAVID PARKIN'S DIARY. OCTOBER 31, 1933

aryAnne lay awake beneath the bed's comforter when David entered the darkened bedroom at a quarter hour past midnight. She was well aware of the time, as the dozen strikes of the mantelpiece clock had only served to heighten her anxiety of his return. For the past several hours she had awaited the moment in growing trepidation—rehearsed her announcement, anticipated his response, then rehearsed again.

He undressed in the darkness.

"David . . ."

MaryAnne's gentle voice drew his eyes to the bed as he searched for her silhouette.

"I am glad that you are still awake."

He lay his clothes across the back of a nearby chair, then sat on the edge of their bed. "I have been thinking all day about your leaving. I wish you were not traveling alone . . ."

"I will be all right."

"I noticed something peculiar about your tickets. The steamliner was only fifty-three dollars. A round-trip should be twice that. Are you certain your passage is booked correctly?"

"I thought I would not reserve the return trip until I was in England and certain of how long I need stay . . ."

He was appeased by the explanation, which further saddened her. There was a time when he would not have let her travel so far alone. David lay back next to her, pulling the sheets up to his chest.

"David . . . I . . ." Her voice, as her courage, faltered. David rolled over towards her.

"What is it, Mary?"

There was so much to say and nothing she could. She

leaned her head into his chest. "Could you just hold me tonight?"

◆

MaryAnne woke a full hour before the dawn. The room's drapes had not been drawn, and the moonfall's luminance cast the room in indigo hues, projecting shadows of the bedposts' spires against the opposite wall. She lay especially still, looking at her sleeping husband, and wondered at how extraordinary the ordinary is rendered when in its final expression. She lay close to him, feeling the warmth of his body and the soothing rise and fall of his chest. There were mornings when he left early for work that she would roll to his side of the bed to feel his lingering warmth pressed against her chest and face. She would never again wake to this man or share his bed. When she could bear the thought no longer she climbed from their berth, slipped off her nightgown, and drew a bath.

She bathed long, powdered and dressed slowly in an effort to fill each moment as full as she could to choke out the pain of the pending day. Not until she heard Catherine's movement downstairs did she descend.

In a daily ritual of more than twenty years, she was drawn to the den and her Bible. The room's fire blazed. It was Catherine's first obligation of the day, a self-appointed task, to start the fire for MaryAnne. MaryAnne took her Bible down from the cherry-wood bookshelf—an aged, Gothic book with an intricately embossed leather cover and gold-edged pages—the most beautiful of the rare Bibles that David had collected in the last several years. She carried the book to her chair, opened to the ribbon marker, then read and wept and read again. Forty minutes later she carried the book out to the kitchen where Catherine was chopping walnuts with a butcher's blade, rolling the wide steel blade in easy motion against a marble breadboard. At MaryAnne's entrance, she turned to pull the drape against the glare of the morning sun.

"Good morning, Catherine. It smells wonderful."

"I am making sweet bread for your journey."

MaryAnne touched her arm. "You are always so thoughtful."

Catherine sprinkled the nuts over the bread, then placed the pan in the oven while MaryAnne lay the Bible on the counter, poured herself a cup of peppermint tea, and carried it to the table.

"I hope you have good weather for your journey. Especially for the ocean liner."

"Especially the ocean liner," MaryAnne repeated. "I get queasy on the rowboats at Liberty Park."

"There is nothing worse."

David entered the kitchen soon after, barefooted and wearing a flannel robe. He was unshaven and his hair was tousled.

"You woke early," he said to MaryAnne.

"It must be the travel jitters."

"Then they are contagious. I tossed and turned all night." He glanced at the Bible, then over to Catherine. "What confection are you about, Catherine?"

"Sweet bread for MaryAnne's journey."

She brought his coffee over to the table. He lifted the cup and looked to MaryAnne.

"Are you all packed?"

MaryAnne answered softly. "I think I have everything."

"You didn't leave your Christmas list."

"It's only October."

He winked. ". . . I need time for these things."

"I will think about it on the train."

He took an envelope from his robe's pocket and set it

on the table in front of her. "I think you should carry more money. Just in case."

"I have ample."

". . . Just in case."

She acquiesced, leaving the envelope where it lay.

"How long has it been since you've seen Ethan? It has been nearly twenty years hasn't it?"

"Nearly twenty . . . since Andrea."

"He'll be an old man," David mused. He thoughtfully sipped at his coffee. "Did you recall what you wanted to tell me last night?"

"Last night?"

"You started to tell me something."

She gazed at him for a moment, then took a sip of her tea. "No."

Catherine spread a knife of apple butter across a slice of the hot bread, then brought it over to the table.

MaryAnne suddenly stood. "I had better check my trunks once more."

"Would you like some help?" Catherine offered.

"I am just looking them over." She took the envelope from the table, then slid it between the pages of the Bible and carried both out of the room.

"What time does Mary's train board?" David asked.

"Ten-ten."

David glanced at his watch, then quickly downed his coffee and rose. "I'd better dress."

◆

As the dawn sun stretched above the crest of the Wasatch range, David carried two leather cases from the foyer, followed out by MaryAnne, who paused to take a long look at the house, then silently walked out to the car. She was dressed in heavy winter clothing, a knit, gray wool dress beneath a sable coat that fell to her ankles. A wide-rimmed, felt hat covered the paisley kerchief that concealed her ears and tied beneath her chin. The strap of a leather bag draped across her shoulder.

Catherine emerged a moment later carrying a woven basket filled with sweet bread, sandwiches, and fruit, all bundled within a red, checkered cloth. They stood together a few feet from the automobile while David finished placing the trunks in the back. Catherine handed her the basket.

"I made you some snacks for the train. Walnut sandwiches and ladyfingers. And the sweet bread. I don't suppose the food will be like home."

"I don't suppose it could be."

"Would you like me to see you off at the station?"

MaryAnne shook her head. "Good-bye here is good. I would like to spend some moments alone with David."

Catherine nodded with understanding. MaryAnne set the basket on the ground and lifted from her handbag an ivory, linen envelope sealed with a gold wax imprint. Across its face was scrawled in her own hand, *"My heart."*

"Will you place this in the drawing room next to David's armchair?"

Catherine thought it curious that MaryAnne did not just deliver the letter to David herself, but took the envelope. "I'll deliver it as soon as you are off." She added, "You know, David will miss you dearly."

She smiled sadly. "I know he will."

"Will you write upon your arrival in England?"

"Of course." She looked into Catherine's eyes, and the emotion she had fought so well slowly began to release. The two women embraced for a full minute before MaryAnne pushed back, took a deep breath, and, with one final glance to Catherine, took up the basket and climbed into the front seat of the car. Catherine shut the door behind her as David turned over the engine. MaryAnne looked once more to the home as the automobile pulled away.

◆

The depot bustled with the usual cacophony of an arriving train. The Los Angeles Limited had completed its Salt Lake City disembarkment, and the last of the Salt Lake passengers were in process of boarding. David transported the bulky luggage to the east platform, relinquishing them to a burly, black porter who examined MaryAnne's ticket, then carried the bags on board.

David scratched his head. "I do not know why I feel so apprehensive about your journey. I am not one for premonition."

"I feel this way every time you leave," MaryAnne said truthfully. "You are just not used to seeing me off."

"I am sure you are right."

A blast of steam whistled from the train's engine.

"You have everything?"

She nodded, then glanced anxiously around the harried depot. "I should board," she said. David pulled her in close, engaging her in a long, ardent kiss. Suddenly he drew back.

"What is the matter?"

MaryAnne turned away. Just then the train released a hiss of steam, followed by the conductor's warning shout that echoed through the depot.

"MaryAnne . . ."

"You worry too much about me. I will manage."

He pulled her to him again, placing his cheek against hers. "Come home soon."

MaryAnne took a deep breath, desperately fighting back the emotions and the man she wished to succumb to.

"Good-bye, David."

She walked briskly to the moving train, beckoned by a porter who clung to the rail between the cars and helped her board. David watched as the train departed the station. As he returned to his automobile, a peculiar thought flashed across his mind which he just as quickly brushed aside—for there was no reason to believe that he would never see his wife again.

◆

When David returned from MaryAnne's departure, he found Gibbs, his company clerk, standing in the threshold of his office.

"Congratulations," Gibbs announced, "we now qualify as the state's largest private charity."

David stepped past him to his desk, casually examining the documents that had appeared on it overnight. He spoke without looking up. "How bad is it?"

"Wages in January exceed company profit. When next quarter's orders decrease, we'll be overstaffed by twelve men." He walked to the front of David's desk and reclined in a leather wing chair. "We cannot support this many employees without selling company holdings." He waited for David to advance the obvious remedy, then, deciding it was not forthcoming, proceeded with it himself. "We cannot delay the inevitable any longer . . . it is time we start laying off."

"How does our net look?"

"Happily, gold stocks continue to climb. When you told me ten years ago to start taking payment in stock from the gold mines I thought you were just being charitable. They've gone from forty-eight dollars a share to more than six hundred. My only regret is that we didn't take more."

"Never trusted banks," David said laconically.

"Wisely, apparently."

David sat down at his desk and pushed aside the clutter from its surface. "Where will they go?"

"Who?"

"The employees you would have me lay off. Sharecropping? Panhandling? Suicide?"

"It's not your concern what happens to them."

"Whose is it?"

The retort stumped Gibbs.

"The Depression won't last forever. I don't want to lose a single employee if possible."

"Profits can't support them all."

"Then we'll tighten our belts."

"We already have."

"Then we'll tighten them more," David said. "Cut salaries across the board—including administration."

"You mean you and me."

"Implicitly."

"It won't solve all of our problems. A pay cut will be a hardship on all the workers. There are already factions forming within the company."

"What kind of factions?"

"There is a group that thinks the Negroes should all be laid off. I hear that some of these men are with the Ku Klux Klan."

The news, though of little surprise, was of great concern. Propelled by the tide of economic austerity, the resentment of "Negroes taking white men's jobs" had washed across the continent in a burgeoning wave, leaving in its wake a spell of lynchings—for a dead black man not only told no tales but left a vacancy in the job market as well. The swell had finally crashed down on his company's doorstep.

"The balloon dips and everyone starts looking for ballast," David said caustically. "These are mean days."

"They will get meaner," Gibbs prophesied.

"Anything else we need to discuss?"

Gibbs stood, pushing himself up from his knees. "We could be profitable," he said as if the prospect had entirely eluded David. David grinned at his friend's tenacity. "What profiteth a man to gain the whole world and lose his soul . . ."

"I was not aware sainthood was one of our business objectives."

"It's not. I just prefer sleeping at night."

"At least someone can sleep," Gibbs said. Then, suddenly remembering, asked, ". . . the governor's Holiday Charity Ball at Saltair. It is still a few months away, but shall I RSVP for us?"

"I'll postal a contribution."

"I wasn't asking if you intended to contribute. Elaine and I hoped that you and MaryAnne would join us. If I might be presumptuous, it would be good for the two of you to dance."

"Dance?"

"People do it from time to time."

"It's been a lifetime."

"It is none of my affair, but with the hours and travel you impose on yourself, I cannot see how the two of you find the time to even see each other—let alone dance."

"I recall you once chiding me for not spending enough time at work."

"Things change."

David looked to the wall calendar and counted days. "I don't think MaryAnne will have returned yet from Britain. And you are right, Gibbs."

Gibbs was surprised at David's concession. "Really?"

"Yes. It is none of your affair."

Gibbs smiled in surrender as he walked out the door.

◆

Gibbs immediately informed the company of the pending pay cuts, and by late afternoon a small group of sullen-faced men congregated outside David's office. At David's behest, the men entered. There were nine men in all, staggered in height and width, their attire was worn and soiled from the mechanics they performed on the work floor below. David sat at his desk while Gibbs stood a few feet behind him, his hands clasped behind his back. Gibbs leered at the men, suspicious of their intentions.

"What may I do for you?" David asked.

The chosen mouthpiece of the delegation stepped forward, holding a felt fedora at his waist. He was a florid, balding man, a floor supervisor who oversaw the production of the iron-casted parts for ore cars, keeves, and kibbles.

"Mr. Parkin, the boys and I would like to speak our minds concerning the recent cut in wages."

Gibbs put his hands in his trouser pockets and leaned back against the window's perimeter, his demeanor perceptibly grown more vehement. Contrarily, David smiled, seeking to assuage the man's anxiety. "Please."

"We know things been slow of late and require a cutback—don't get us wrong, ain't a one of us complainin'. Fact I was just sayin' that most companies been through three or four pay cuts by now, wasn't I boys?" He nodded to the congregation who, on cue, bobbed and grunted in affirmation.

He hesitantly proceeded. ". . . But we thinkin' . . . rather than cause undue hardship . . . maybe the more decent thing be to just let the Negroes go. We knowed we could do just fine without 'em. Wouldn't slow production up. You can have our word on that."

Gibbs inhaled deeply, anticipating David's impassioned response. To his surprise, David merely reclined in his chair hearing the request with apparent interest.

"You are Mr. Boggs, am I correct?"

"Yes, sir. Judd Boggs."

"Mr. Boggs, how long have you been employed at my company?"

"Since I came to the valley. Goin' on nearly five years now."

"Before the Depression."

"Yes, sir."

"Do you feel that you have been treated fairly here?"

"Yes, sir. Been treated real good. Don't think many bossmen care as much to even ask such a question."

The men again bobbed and grunted in consensus.

"Five years. Are you aware that some of these Negroes you speak of have worked here for more than twenty years—a trifle longer than you. In fact a few of them are among my most productive workers."

"Didn't say they ain't good workers," he said unabashedly. "Just Negroes."

David raised a pen and began tapping it against the desk as he considered his response. His voice sounded weary. "It is not easy running a company. I am told by my advisor here that I should have already laid off a third of my workers—that all of my profits are being eaten up by wages of employees that do not have enough to do. What do you think of that?"

Judd clenched his hat. "You're right charitable, Mr. Parkin. Like I said, work been slow—Depression and all. That's why we thought maybe it'd be in your best interest to put out the Negroes."

"My best interest?" David's jaw tightened, the only indication of the emotion that brooded behind his controlled demeanor. He leaned forward across his desk. "Do you pretend to know my best interest, Mr. Boggs?"

The man's face twitched. "No, sir."

"You men are still working here at my expense and by my grace and you come to me to ask if I won't fire your coworkers? How should I respond to that?"

"But . . . we talkin' about just the darkies," he stammered in clarification.

"Of course—they're only darkies. Darkies don't suffer, do they? Their children don't feel hunger pangs like yours do. They don't know fear. Don't worry about taking care of their own." He shook his head incredulously. "They are just darkies."

The man replied nothing, while a few, near the rear of the congregation, squirmed uncomfortably, convicted by their own consciences.

"Mr. Boggs, if you, or any of your esteemed colleagues, value your employment, then I suggest you return to it and never speak of this matter on my grounds or my time again. If you cannot endure working side by side with the Negroes perhaps you should try standing beside them in the breadlines because there's already more than enough of them there. Is that perfectly clear?"

"Yes, sir."

David's voice rose. "I am not just addressing Mr. Boggs."

"Yes, sir," the group replied in staggered and startled response.

"Then return to your work. You should consider yourself fortunate that I am more merciful than you."

The men turned on their heels and quickly disappeared back into the cacophony of the workplace.

◆

An hour after the end of the workday, Gibbs poked his head into David's office. David sat at his desk studying several blue-ink plans that lay flat before him. To one side of the table, an opened leather valise had spilled its contents to the crowded surface.

"Eventful day," Gibbs said.

"It breaks the monotony, at least."

Gibbs leaned against the doorjamb. "I'm a clerk. I like monotony."

David smiled without looking up from his task.

"Elaine and I are going out for some dinner. Would you care to join us?"

"Thank you, but I think I'll stay and finish some of these quotes."

"You'll be a bachelor for a while. Maybe next week."

"I'll look forward to it. Give Elaine my love."

Gibbs gave David a mock salute and left him to his drawings.

CHAPTER FOUR

THE
SILENT PARLOR

"MaryAnne will neither enter the parlor nor acknowledge its existence. I cannot fault her for such, as we all have rooms we lock and daren't visit, lest they bring pain."

DAVID PARKIN'S DIARY. FEBRUARY 22, 1932

mongst the Victorian architecture of the Salt Lake City Avenues, the Parkin mansion was an edifice of singular grandeur. It had originally been constructed as the residence of Salt Lake City's second mayor, the honorable Thomas Nash. Nash was a federally appointed easterner who viewed the city's inhabitants as cretins and simpletons, and brazenly used his position to advance his financial situation. When the mayor made vulgar advances on one of the city's venerable widows he was run out of town on a rail. Three days later, sixty miles north of the city, he was recognized by an inebriated relative of the widow and was shot outside an Ogden saloon and left for the city undertaker for a pauper's burial. It was an era of great pragmatism in western politics.

The disreputed mayor had spared little expense in the creation and furnishing of the mansion, garnishing the home with all the fineries the city had to offer, and many that it didn't, requiring great shipments from the mills and factories of the East and beyond the Atlantic. Each of its thirteen rooms was rendered with unique resplendence—consistent only in extravagance.

Inlaid parquetry floors were dressed with beautiful rugs and tapestries, English Victorian chenilles or Oriental weaves, matched in opulent competition with the ceilings, bedecked with exquisite, intricate stencil works and fixtures—chandeliers of crystal and bronze, from Strasbourg and Lancashire, hung from elaborately carved ceiling rosettes painted pastel and gilt.

The home's windows were crowned with stained-glass designs of fruit or seraphs, while the designs of the door panes and the humbler windows—florals and rococo flourishes—were etched in the blue-tint glass.

David Parkin had purchased the mansion in 1902

and was joined by MaryAnne, in matrimony and home, six years later. In 1913 the home had undergone extensive renovation as a result of the fire that had taken their daughter's life. Ironically, the room most affected by the tragedy had never been touched by flames. The second-floor parlor. It was in the parlor where, one day after the fire, Andrea had died. Its threshold had not been trespassed since.

◆

It was past one o'clock in the morning when David returned home. Though he was accustomed to working late, with MaryAnne's absence he felt even less impetus to return at any seemly hour. Catherine had retired long before, leaving the house dark.

Despite the late hour, David went to the drawing room, switched on a single lamp, and poured himself a shot of brandy from a crystal decanter as he reclined into his Turkish armchair, propping his feet before him on a leather ottoman. It was then that he first noticed the envelope that Catherine, at MaryAnne's request, had left on the side table beside his chair. He recognized MaryAnne's script and seal, set down his drink, and took up the envelope. He could not recall the last time she had written him a letter, and he opened it with great curiosity.

◆

My beloved David,

No matter how I write, the words fall so cruel, I wish I could use them more sparingly. This is farewell, my love. I shall not return from London. I do not know anymore if my departure is right or wrong, I have reasoned until I can think no more—all I know is what I feel and what I can bear. Or cannot. I can no longer endure the pain of your alienation. Your love was my sun, David, and the walls you have built around your heart have deprived me of its warmth until my heart has wilted. My departure is only the final act of a separation that took place years ago and what we have prolonged has only mocked the beauty of what we once shared. It is with heartbreak that I admit that our marriage died with our daughter.

I know that you love me—as I do you. This is what has given wings to my flight, for love is a traitorous emotion. Never once did you hold it against me that you were not Andrea's birth father, yet it is thrown back at you daily as you cannot give me more children and you blame yourself for losing our only. You did not lose our daughter, David. Andrea's death was caused by the cruel actions of evil men. You were nothing but courageous *and compassionate. Shall we not stand up to evil because it threatens our personal situation? If we do not, evil will always prevail. You taught me this and although you may know that you did the right thing, you do not believe it. There is a difference, and in that difference I have lost my husband. I cannot change your heart, I can only break the cycle of our pain.*

Forgive me for my weakness—for bidding farewell in ink, not words. I could not face you. I was afraid that you would implore me to stay and I would not be able to resist. How could I deny the man I cherish more than all? I once gave you my life, David, but I had never imagined that I would steal away yours. I give it back to you. I beg you to not pursue me. Go and be free.

You are forever in my heart.

MARY

◆

David gaped at the writing as if awaiting the explanation to a vicious hoax—but the words held no hope of such blessed cruelty. As its truth settled, his mind reeled in a thousand thoughts and directions, all equally horrible. It was as if the great wall of protection with which he had surrounded his heart had been pierced, and his vulnerable heart, rendered all the more defenseless from years of shelter, felt that it would burst. He wanted to run to her, to stop her, to scream back the train that carried her away.

He grabbed the decanter and drank directly from it. The brandy burned his throat. He read the letter again, half hoping for some alteration of its message—some line that he may have overlooked—some reprieve from the pain that spread throughout his body, faster than the liquor that numbed it. He began to cry, wiping his tears with the same hand that held the bottle, following each bout with another drink until the bottle was nearly half drained.

Clutching the note and bottle in one hand, he staggered out of the room, inexplicably drawn up the darkened staircase. At the door of the upstairs parlor he extracted a skeleton passkey from his breast pocket, fumbled with the instrument, then, for the first time since their daughter's death, opened the door. He reached inside and switched on a lamp. It was as if he had stepped back into the past and the flood of memory that washed over him drew his thoughts from his pain. The room was a time capsule, perfectly preserved from twenty years previous—each article, once ardently sought and admired, now carried greater meaning because of its absence from his life.

The day Andrea had died in the parlor, the room had been pronounced dead and as if by mutual assent, life inside the room ground to a halt. The room's clocks fulfilled their obligations until springs unwound and pendulums faltered, wearing on their spandreled faces the hour of their death. Even the greater clockwork of the cosmos had been kept at bay behind drapes which grew moth-eaten and faded through time. Dust had settled in a singular sheet on the room in a grey, batting-like shroud. Spiders had woven the room in their silk tapestries as intricate as those wrought from Indian looms that lay on its floor.

In the corner of the room was the tiny bed. Its sheets remained in the same throw as when they had been peeled back and their daughter's lifeless body was carried out. David quickly looked past it to the far wall, where towered the grandfather's clock that he had given MaryAnne on their wedding night—and stopped at the moment of their daughter's death. He had given MaryAnne the prized clock as a symbol of the meaning she had brought to his life. Now it stood motionless. He threateningly raised the decanter to its glass-enclosed face, then turned and hurled the bottle against the opposite wall where it exploded into crystal shards. He leaned back against the wall next to the clock and slumped down until he rested on the floor, his knees pulled up to his chest.

The parlor lay only a few doors from Catherine's room, and she had hurried from her quarters, awakened by the crash. Astonished to find light coming from the parlor, she rushed to its threshold. She gasped when she found David on the floor against its far wall. The stench of alcohol wafted through the room. He looked up at her, his eyes lifeless, his face streaked with tears. Their eyes met. In all her years in his service she had never seen him drunk, and she awaited his actions with fearful anticipation. David was the first to speak, his voice heavy with emotion.

"MaryAnne never came in here. There were too many memories . . ."

"David. What has happened?"

He shook his head, as if unwilling to accept the news he bore. "She's not coming back," he cried incredulously. "MaryAnne's not coming back."

Catherine took two steps into the room. "Not coming back?"

With a trembling hand he offered the letter to her. Catherine walked to him and took the parchment.

"Dear Lord," she exclaimed, biting down on her lower lip.

David began to sob, burying his face into his knees. Catherine, equally fraught, knelt down by his side. He looked up at her. His face suddenly flashed to rage. "Did you know about this? About her plans to leave me?!"

"David!"

"Did you know?!" he demanded.

Her body, as well as her voice, began to tremble. "David, you are frightening me."

His harsh voice faltered, sublimating to pleading sobs ". . . did you know?"

Catherine struggled to speak, her own voice surrendering to emotion as well. "Of course I didn't know," she cried. "Oh, Mary, what have you done?"

David again began to cry and Catherine put her arms around him, maternally pulling his head into her breast. When his sobbing subsided he looked up into her eyes. "I have loved three women in my life, Catherine. And I have lost them all . . ."

Catherine brushed back a tear from her own cheek.

". . . But MaryAnne's abandonment is the only one I deserved."

◆

Morning found David in the sanctuary of his den recording his thoughts in his diary. The habit of his journal writing had a therapeutic effect, not that he had consciously determined this, rather, it was simply a natural act, as one might seek shelter from a storm. His head and heart ached from the previous night and his pen wandered slowly across the page.

◆

"I feel so lost.

"No. To be lost is to not know where one is—and I am all too sure. I am alone. My heart, my love, has been torn from me and I am consumed by the pain of that loss.

"Yet I feel MaryAnne around me as keenly as before. Maybe more so. For I see her absence in all the evidences of the home that she left behind.

"I am a fool. What selfishness so blinded my heart that I could not see that she still required its nourishment?

"My pen rambles with more foolishness. I mourn what I am missing and the pain that pierces my heart—not hers. This is the paradox that keeps MaryAnne from my reach—for to go after her, for my heart's sake, is to be unworthy of her. Could it be that

to truly love a thing is not to desire it, but to desire happiness for it? If so, I cannot have her back, to relieve my heart at the expense of hers. If I truly love her.

"And I do love her. More than my own life I love her.

"I can only hope that she might return. Yet hope is oftentimes the cruelest of virtues.

"How did I come to such a dark place? I don't know where my road now leads but I fear the shadowlands that lie ahead. But it is not the darkness of the path I fear. Just the loneliness of the trail."

DAVID PARKIN'S DIARY. OCTOBER 21, 1933

CHAPTER FIVE
VICTORIA'S INTRODUCTION

"Even as I withheld my love from MaryAnne, she had never stopped filling me with hers. I had never supposed how cold my world would be without her warmth."

DAVID PARKIN'S DIARY. NOVEMBER 2, 1933

t was nearly a fortnight before David returned to the office, an occurrence which proved to be a vicarious act mostly, for he spent the better part of the morning staring out the window of his second-story office, as oblivious to the activity of his company as he was to the street's activity which he blindly observed. Around noontime Gibbs entered his office. David did not greet him. Gibbs shut the door and walked to his side. "I am glad that you are returned, David."

"How have things been in my absence?"

"The month's orders have not declined as much as I had anticipated, so with the pay cuts we may actually come out ahead. The men you chastised have prudently taken your counsel and have not broached the Negro issue again. That is what I am told by those on the floor." Gibbs looked at David empathetically. He knew that he had lost him even before he had finished his response. "Go after her, David."

David raked a hand back through his hair. "I can't, Gibbs. I would carry her back in chains if I knew that it could be different . . ." His voice fell like the second refrain of an echo. ". . . If I could be different. I can't promise that. I don't even know where to start." He bowed his head. "She has buried me, Gibbs. My love has buried me. The dead should stay put."

For many years, Gibbs had counseled David on all his affairs, from the daily running of his plant to the rituals of courtship. He had never before felt so inadequate. He put his hand on David's back. "If anyone ever belonged together it was the two of you. It just doesn't seem right. If there is anything that I can do . . ."

"I would like for you to arrange with her brother a

financial settlement. I want her to live in the manner to which she is accustomed." He added, ". . . at least financially."

"I will wire him immediately."

At that moment, David's secretary peered through his door. "Mr. Parkin, Mrs. Piper is outside. She insists on seeing you."

David grimaced. "Word travels."

"I'll get rid of her," Gibbs said.

"No, I might as well see her. At least someone will derive joy from my misfortune."

Gibbs frowned as he left the room, passing on his exit Victoria Piper, a local socialite and flagship of the city's haute monde. She strut-waddled into the office, momentarily eclipsing the light from the doorway with her ever-widening girth.

"I will be brief, David. I know that you do not wish to speak with me."

David made no effort to deny the allegation. She sat down opposite his desk.

"Honestly, I do not know why you treat me so petulantly. I have only your best interests at heart."

David responded to the assertion with as cordial a

voice as he could intone. "And what interests of mine do you have in your heart today?"

She ignored his sarcasm. "I am the chairwoman of the governor's charity ball this Christmas. Will you and MaryAnne be attending?"

"MaryAnne will not be available."

"So I had heard," she said with particular relish. "I am sorry that she is indisposed."

David glowered.

Victoria said thoughtfully, "I think you should meet my niece, David. She is arriving from Chicago next Thursday for my cousin Lucy's bridal shower and will be staying with me through the holidays."

"You have never felt the inclination to acquaint me with your kin before now. Why would I want to meet your niece?"

Victoria smiled benignly. "Oh, David. All men want to meet my niece."

Her intent infuriated him.

"I am married, Victoria."

"Yes, I was there," Victoria replied with the banal drawl she usually reserved for bad theater. "And how is that marriage, David?"

David bit back his anger and turned to his work, bending over the stacks of carbon invoices that had piled up in his absence. "I am not interested."

Victoria was more amused by his response than dissuaded. She smiled easily as she stood to leave. "Oh, you will be, David. You will be."

CHAPTER SIX

THE
LETTER
REVEALED

*"Catherine delivered to me a letter today that she supposed was
written by my mother. I am uncertain whether it should be
celebrated or incinerated."*

DAVID PARKIN'S DIARY. NOVEMBER 9, 1933

n the quiet waning of a Sunday, Catherine
entered the drawing room bearing a sterling tea service, a large, pear-shaped server
bedecked by two, gold-rimmed cups with pink florals
baked into their porcelain enamel. David sat motionless,
embraced in the wide, tapestry cushions of his Turkish
chair, as a string ensemble of the *Messiah* from the *Ford
Sunday Evening Hour* filled the room. The radio was posi-
tioned just an arm's length from his side—an RCA cabi-

net with cathedral carvings on the face of the polished walnut console. David stared blankly into the fireplace at the orange-red embers from which clung the ebbing flames. The drapes had been drawn, and near the doorway a single lamp with an opaque, leather shade vaguely lit the room. Catherine pushed the door shut behind herself.

"I brought you some tea."

David looked over, noticing her entrance for the first time. "Thank you, Catherine," he said softly. He reached over and switched off the radio, which silenced with a death rattle of static. "Would you join me?"

"I would love to." She set the service on the parquet veneer of the lamp table, poured a cup to the brim, handed it to David, then turned and did the same for herself. She sat sideways on the ottoman before him.

"How is business?"

"Like trying to paddle a schooner up a dry riverbed."

Catherine smiled. "It is that bad?"

"I am afraid so. This drought has everyone on such edge. If we get through this without a lynching it will be a miracle."

Catherine's voice turned serious. "Is that what is troubling you?"

David sipped his tea, then sat back into the chair looking thoughtful. "No. Actually, I was thinking about my father."

Catherine cocked her head. "It has been many years since you have spoken of your father."

"He was a good man. And he was wise. I wish he was still around."

Catherine nodded sympathetically.

"You know, he never once complained about my mother leaving us. Even after I had grown. I guess maybe he thought it was inevitable. I never saw it—with her or MaryAnne."

"You can't compare MaryAnne with your mother."

"I know that it's different, but it feels the same." He gazed blankly at his cup while his thoughts coalesced. "I remember the morning that my mother left. I was curled up in the hallway as she packed her trunks. When she came out with her cases I asked her where she was going. She said Nevada City. It was true, in part. The train out of California rode through Nevada City."

An air pocket exploded in the nearly depleted log in the fireplace, and Catherine looked to see if any sparks had escaped the hearth.

"I didn't want to believe that she was gone. Even after

my father told me that she wasn't coming back, I didn't believe him. I held on to her for nearly a year—until Christmas. I am doing the same with MaryAnne. Just trying to hold on."

"It is only natural," Catherine said gently.

"My mother had this playbill on the wall of her bedroom—the only art in the house. It was a picture of a woman surrounded by black, demonic, winged creatures. It terrified me. When I realized that my mother wasn't coming back, I connected those demons with her disappearance and tore up the poster and threw dirt on it." David bowed his head and his voice grew in emotion. "There are just things that I don't understand. You know I would have given anything to have my Andrea back. Anything."

"Of course you would have . . ."

"Then how is it that my mother abandoned me? I wasn't taken from her, she gave me up. She willingly gave me up." His voice rose with indignation. "How could she do that?"

The question was as unanswerable to Catherine as it was to him, though she wondered for an instant if he truly spoke of his mother or MaryAnne.

"It is a ghost that has haunted me my whole life. It

was chased away for a season by Andrea, but it has returned. It would make all the difference in my life if I could only ask my mother why."

"If you had the chance you would talk to her?"

"If I had the chance I would ask her questions until every demon had left my soul." David rested his head in his palm. "I don't even know if she is still alive."

Catherine silently contemplated his words then set her china teacup next to the caddy. "David, I need to share something with you."

David looked up as she stood.

"I must retrieve it from my quarters."

She left the room, returning a few moments later with a wrinkled envelope. The parcel filled him with foreboding.

"Is it from Mary?"

"MaryAnne gave it to me before she left. But she didn't write it." She held out to him the envelope. The wrinkled paper bore the water-stains of the snow that had once blanketed it and run its ink. The rose seal was unfamiliar to him. He removed its contents.

◆

THE LETTER

Dearest Child,

That I did not know you, my loss is greatest.

Forgive me for the pain I have brought to those who love you.

So gladly would I trade my sad life for your realm.

Angel, watch over this little one.

◆

"Where did you get this?"

"MaryAnne found it at Andrea's grave. She didn't want you to see it."

"Why?"

"She thought it would bring you pain." Catherine hesitated. ". . . She feared that it was left by your mother."

"My mother?" David returned his gaze to the letter. Suddenly he set his cup on the tray, stood, and walked from the room. When Catherine caught up to him, he was standing on the middle rung of an oak book ladder facing a rosewood bookshelf that climbed to the ceiling. He was searching amidst a row of books six shelves above the library's parquet floor. Books of his own writing—his journals.

David extracted one of several leather-bound diaries

and brought it to a mahogany, Queen Anne writing desk. He leafed through its pages until discovering the insert he searched for—a brittle, folded parchment, no larger than his hand—folded once, then pressed flat between the pages. It was the penned regret he had received thirty-six years previous from his mother. He carefully lifted it from the book, unfolded it, and pressed it flat against the desk's surface, to the side of the note Catherine had delivered minutes earlier. Though it had been pressed in the book for more than three decades, it still showed evidence of David's first reaction to its message when he crumpled and threw it to the floor. He had retrieved the note a day later, preserving it in his journal.

◆

Dear David,

Such grand tidings I share. While awaiting your arrival in Salt Lake City, I met, by wonderful fate, a man from the Chicago theatre—a producer no less! I am returning tomorrow morning to Chicago to begin production of Bohemia, *where I shall play the role of Mimi. I shall send for you when the time is better.*

YOUR MOTHER,

ROSE

◆

Even now the note evoked pain. Pushing emotion aside, David meticulously scrutinized the documents, comparing the calligraphy letter by letter. There was a marked similarity in the penmanship of the two letters, though the scrawl of the more recent correspondence seemed frail and less disciplined.

David pointed out to Catherine the similarities.

"Note this letter . . . and here." His index finger rested on the page as his voice rose in excitement. "The scroll is nearly identical. But how would my mother know of Andrea? Or the angel?"

"It was in the papers—she could have learned of it. Who else could have left such a letter?"

"Why would she have come all this way and not come to see me?"

Catherine considered the question. "Perhaps she came to see but not to be seen. After all she has done to you she could hardly expect to be welcomed with open arms."

"No," David said almost to himself as he slowly turned back towards the letters. "She would not expect it." He slid the letters together and put them back between the pages of the journal. "Could you check with the local hotels to see if Rose King has registered with any of them in the last month."

"King?"

"It is my mother's maiden name."

The passion behind his request pleased her. "Of course. I will get right to it."

CHAPTER SEVEN

DIERDRE

"Despite plans to the contrary, I ended up meeting Victoria's niece. She was not at all like Victoria—that is to say, she was pleasant."

DAVID PARKIN'S DIARY. DECEMBER 15, 1933

he Saltair resort, erected on the salt-caked shores of the Great Salt Lake, was the pride of the great state of Utah and an oasis to some of the world's most popular bands and celebrities. Even Charles Lindbergh, on transcontinental tour with the craft that had carried him to celebrity, could not resist a dip in both the lake and its ballroom.

The last time David had been to Saltair was before the fire of twenty-five that had nearly burned the resort to the ground, and he only knew of the park's reconstruction from the local tabloids. Evidence of that fire still remained as an occasional charred wall or column lay concealed behind potted palms or fabric screens. The resort's main pavilion, a behemoth stucco-finished structure, was topped with Moorish domes, painted in vivid Mediterranean colors and patterns, purveying the romance of a story from the *Arabian Nights*. The ballroom, billed as the largest of its kind in the world, was elliptical in construction, its ceiling rising sixty feet above sprung floors of polished maple.

This evening, large painted banners proclaiming the holiday gala hung above each of the room's four, keyhole archways, two of which exited to the planked boardwalk that extended four hundred feet out over the lake, a necessity for the resort's bathers as the capricious lake rose and fell with maddening uncertainty.

The evening's philanthropists paraded the pavilion floor in dance or strut, dressed in the masquerades of the affluent: black, wool tuxedos with long tails, spats, and silk top hats, and the more gracious sex in exquisite gowns of chiffon and silk with the high-necked décolletage the times demanded. There were few such socials in Salt Lake City, and when they came, those in attendance adorned themselves with the unabashed garishness of a Christmas tree.

Jerry Kirkham and the Saltair orchestra had just

completed their sixth tune of the evening to the ardent reception of the dancers and lesser reaction by David who stood next to Gibbs, sipping white wine from a stemmed crystal wineglass, viewing the evening's proceedings with the dispassion of a spectator of the ballet. David had not participated in any social activity since MaryAnne's departure, and Gibbs, worried about David's increasing reclusiveness, had relentlessly insisted that he attend the event. When Gibbs's girl, Elaine, and Catherine joined in the campaign as well, David acquiesced, deciding it easier to go than to resist their entreatments.

Elaine emerged from the crowd, took Gibbs's hand, and pulled him towards the floor.

"C'mon, honey."

"Dancing is imminent," Gibbs said. "Take my drink, David?"

David took the glass with his own and walked to a nearby table and set them both down, then returned to his place at the edge of the human perimeter that marked the floor. As he followed their pirouette, his eye was suddenly attracted to a young woman, who, standing alone, likewise watched the dancers moving in sway to the brass tones of the band. She was arrestingly beautiful—as attractive as she was unique from those around her in both fashion and demeanor. She wore a tight-waisted dress of crepe de chine with a low waistline and scandalously high hemline. Her hair was deep brunette, styled in a pageboy bob, slightly longer than permitted by the understated vogue of the austere decade. Her hat, a peach cloche, raked back to frame a facial structure of exquisite composition and further complemented her cream complexion. She smiled contentedly as she moved to the tune, fondling the pearls that encircled her neck.

Elaine and Gibbs suddenly reappeared next to him.

"Why don't you take a spin?" Gibbs shouted. "It will do you good."

"Yes," Elaine agreed, abruptly releasing her partner. "I would like a dance."

"You don't know what you are asking," David said. He obligingly took her hand and moved out to the crowded floor.

After a few steps David asked, "Is this why it is called a charity ball?"

"Oh, David. We love you."

". . . and pity me?"

Elaine smiled. "A little."

They had circled the floor just once when Gibbs tapped David's shoulder.

"I don't expect David and I will win the dance cup," Elaine announced.

"Ah," Gibbs replied, "but David is handsome and rich, which, in most decks, will beat a two-step. Precisely why I must cut back in."

"How sweet," Elaine cried, relinquishing David's hand for her lover's. "My man is jealous."

They immediately resumed their promenade. As David stepped back from the floor, he noticed that the young lady who had caught his eye was gone. He walked to a crystal punch bowl, ladled himself another drink, then stepped aside to resume his role as spectator. A petite, lace-gloved hand gently touched his sleeve.

"Would you care to dance?"

The question had been asked in a pleasant feminine voice with a hint of southern accent, and David turned to see the young woman he had noticed across the floor standing beside him.

"Dance?" she repeated. The woman gazed on him with piercing peacock blue eyes, nearly as lustrous as the bird's feathers. She smiled confidently. "I am sorry. I probably seem a bit forward."

"No, I just didn't expect to be dancing tonight."

"That is usually why one comes to a ball."

"Usually."

"Well," she said, the word drawn out for aesthetic effect, "as long as you are here . . ."

David smiled. "Why not." He abandoned his drink on a banister, took her arm, and led her to the floor, joining the dancers who gracefully spun to the Champagne Waltz.

"I have already been told tonight that I am not much of a dancer."

"You are doing fine," she said kindly. "I bet you are wicked with the Charleston."

"If wicked implies murderous, I am sure you are right."

The woman laughed and David smiled, worrying more about his step and marveling at hers. There was a simple grace to her motion—a carelessness free of the decade's burden.

"Are you new to the valley?"

"You mean Salt Lake City? No, my home is in Chicago. I am here just for a few weeks visiting with my aunt."

"Your aunt?"

"Yes, I came for a wedding."

David suddenly realized who she was. "You are Victoria's niece."

"You know Aunt Victoria?"

"She told me of your arrival," David replied. He glanced around the crowded room, suspect that Victoria had put the young woman up to the proposal. "Where is your aunt now?"

Dierdre followed his glance, then looked up into his face, her eyes sparkling with her offense. "It took some doing, but I lost her."

David chuckled at her candor. "Now why would you run out on your aunt?" he asked, perfectly willing to offer a hundred reasons himself.

"Tonight, she is a little too gregarious for my taste— that and her incessant nagging about coupling me with some man whose wife has just deserted him. Apparently he is rich, handsome, and pining—'a perfect combination,'" she said, mimicking her aunt's enunciation. "I told her that maybe the man's wife knows something that she doesn't." She read David's expression. "Oh, dear. He is not a friend of yours?"

David stopped dancing. "I believe your aunt was referring to me."

Dierdre flushed a deep crimson. "I am so embarrassed." She released his hand to go, but David took it up again. "I don't offend easily. And you are right. My wife does know something about me that Victoria doesn't."

They continued their promenade, the silence dragging on in agonizing minutes, with Dierdre turning away each time he ventured to look into her face. When the waltz concluded, she hastily thanked him and turned to leave.

"Just a moment," David said firmly.

She paused, awaiting a deserved rebuke.

"I hate to end a dance with the wrong step as much as I hate starting it with one." He grinned. "Though I realize, with my dancing, it is hard to tell the difference."

She smiled.

". . . besides, I was cheated of a whole dance. It may be my only of the night."

The band's silent lull gave way to the opening refrain of the next song, "Two Cigarettes in the Dark."

She gently replied, "Then perhaps another dance would be in order."

David took her hand, and she returned hers to his shoulder and back. David tried to ease her discomfort with conversation.

"What do you think of our city?"

Her voice fell humbly, still reeling from the pain of her faux pas. "Quaint, but lovely. The moon on the lake is beautiful tonight."

"Have you taken a plunge?"

One corner of her mouth rose in a crooked smile. "Is this a threat?"

David grinned. "The Great Salt Lake is an oddity. Its concentration of salt is more than ten times that of the ocean. It is almost impossible to sink."

"No wonder my aunt finds this resort of such great amusement." Her mouth bent in an impish grin. "Though I am certain that she would be difficult to sink no matter the liquid."

At this David laughed loudly along with Dierdre who, pleased that she had made such an impression, momentarily forgot her earlier gaffe. As the dance progressed, she pressed her body, rich in the perfume of youth and femininity, tightly against his. She lay her head against his shoulder, and David began to feel emotions rise up inside not felt since he first met MaryAnne. When the band concluded the number, she made no effort to start from her position. David slowly began to draw away. At his movement, she stepped back.

"I hope I did not step on you too many times," David said.

"An occasional trampling keeps one alert," she jested. Her voice turned more sincere. "I am still very embarrassed by what I said. Sometimes I think I was born with a silver foot in my mouth."

"It is already forgotten."

"My aunt was right about you being very handsome. She failed to tell me that you are also very nice."

Their eyes met, and there was a discernible and mutual spark of attraction. David felt confused by the flux of emotions that suddenly overwhelmed him.

"Are you always so forthright?"

"Yes." Her face relaxed into an easy smile. "Well, almost always."

The noise and motion of the burgeoning crowd vanished into the moment's enchantment. Just then, Victoria stepped towards them, attired in a gaudy, flowing gown, layered in excessive yards of cream-colored fabric—flesh and cloth restrained by an overworked gold chenille sash. Her garb was outdone only by the wide grin on her overly rouged face.

"There you are, Dierdre," she blared, her arms outspread in lavish greeting. She said to David, "I should have suspected that you would be involved with my niece's abduction."

Dierdre rolled her eyes.

"I have been regaling the governor with your anecdotes, and he insists upon meeting you." She turned again to David. "He is waiting . . ."

Dierdre smiled shyly. "It was a pleasure making your acquaintance, David."

"Likewise," he replied clumsily.

Victoria observed David's awkwardness and smiled. She had anticipated this moment for the better part of the month and received his reaction with great satisfaction. David and Dierdre's chance encounter could not have gone better if she had orchestrated it herself. Dierdre offered David her hand. "Will I have the pleasure of seeing you again?"

"Of course you will, my dear," Victoria interjected, "I will see to it."

"Good night, David," she said softly.

"Good night," he returned.

"And good night to you, David," Victoria said with a triumphant smile, then took her niece by the arm and whisked her away to her next social imperative.

CHAPTER EIGHT
THE
MORNING
AFTER

"A broken heart is always looking for a mend."

DAVID PARKIN'S DIARY. DECEMBER 15, 1933

ou were out late last night," Catherine observed as she stretched a pale, linen shirt over a fabric-sheathed clothes board. She dipped her hand in a bowl of water and sprinkled it over the material's surface. To her side, an iron poised vertically on its wide hips. David sat at the kitchen table, dressed for the day except for the absence of shirt and tie, his suspenders crossing his bare torso.

"I believe Elaine mistook the affair for a dance

marathon. I ended up waiting alone out on the beach. There is something about a body of water that stirs the mind."

"It's been years since I have been to Saltair," Catherine reminisced. "Or cut a rug." She pushed the iron across the shirt. "Did you dance?"

"I would never be convicted of it."

"With whom did you dance?"

"Once with Elaine."

With her closed hand she flattened down the shirt's collar. "Anyone else?"

David smiled at her surreptitiously.

"I was not prying. I was only curious."

"Pray tell the difference."

Catherine shook her head. "Since you are obviously uncomfortable with the question, I will withdraw it."

"I danced with Victoria's niece."

Catherine pretended to be disinterested. "I did not know she had a niece in the area."

"She doesn't. Dierdre is from Chicago."

"Dierdre." Catherine repeated the name slowly, committing it to memory. "Is she anything like her aunt?"

David sipped his coffee as if he hadn't heard the

question, and Catherine knew when to change the topic.

"You haven't mentioned the Christmas pine. Don't you like it?"

"I'm sorry. I haven't felt festive of late. It's beautiful. Are the ornaments new?"

"No." She smiled. "Same ones we've used for the last ten years." Her voice softened. ". . . About Christmas. My aunt in Park City has invited me up for Christmas dinner. I have yet to accept." She studied David's reaction.

"Why not?"

"I thought maybe you would join us."

"I appreciate your sympathy, Catherine. But I will be fine. It will be nice for you to spend some time with your family. It's been a long while since you spent Christmas with family."

"What about you?"

"Gibbs and Elaine have invited me to dine with them on Christmas Eve. That is about all the festivities I'm up to."

She went back to her ironing. "Then I will go," she said reticently. She lifted his shirt. "I am sorry that you have nothing to wear. Yesterday was ironing day, and I was out checking on the hotels you asked me to."

"I am in no particular hurry this morning. How did your search go?"

"The hotels weren't very helpful. Only two of them would check back to last month's registers. None of them show a Rosalyn King, or Parkin, as a guest. If she was in town, she isn't anymore."

David's brow furrowed. "I wonder if she has returned to Chicago?"

"If she didn't plan on seeing you I see no reason she would stay."

"Did you, perchance, visit with the sexton? I am told that he never leaves the cemetery. He might have noticed someone at the angel."

Catherine brought him the freshly pressed shirt, then returned to her bloated laundry basket. "I had not considered that. I would be happy to speak with him."

"Perhaps on your way back from Lawrence's this morning."

Catherine draped a pleated skirt across the board. "Speaking of Lawrence, I am worried about him. He is acting very peculiar."

"I saw him only four days ago. He was in reasonably high spirits."

"When I visited him yesterday, he had not eaten any of his food from the day before. I asked him why, and he replied rather sharply that he did not care to discuss it."

"Lawrence said that?"

"It is peculiar."

"Did he say anything else?"

"He kept talking about dying."

"That is standard fare. He has talked of dying for the last decade."

"It is different now. It is more than conversation. He said something about wanting to be buried next to a woman named Margaret. In fact, he mentioned her several times. Do you know who she is?"

"Margaret? He has never spoken of her to me. Any woman for that matter." He set down his empty cup. "I will drop by Lawrence's tonight, I am due a visit." His voice softened as if either embarrassed by the question he asked or the response he feared. "Have you heard from MaryAnne?"

"No. Not yet."

He nodded gently, walked to the doorway, then stopped. ". . . Dierdre is nothing like her aunt."

Victoria and Dierdre settled for brunch in high-backed wicker chairs in the sunroom of the Piper mansion, surrounded by the maids and butlers who were decking the home in the gold and silver tinsel of holiday attire. A centerpiece of pine cones and mistletoe adorned the table they sat at. Victoria's garish laughter resounded throughout the wing as the two women ruminated on the previous evening's escapades.

"So, now that you have met the man, what do you think of our Mr. Parkin?"

"I find him charming." A smile of amusement curled her lips. "He seems unsure of himself around women. It is a trait I am especially fond of in men."

Victoria chortled. "Why do I not find that surprising?"

Dierdre asked seriously, "Do you suppose I was too forward?"

"Forward is what forward does," Victoria proffered. "Truthfully, I think David was quite taken with you. He was behaving so peculiarly." She raised a colorful, long-stemmed glass to her lips.

Dierdre smiled. "I like his peculiar. There is a certain . . . virility."

"Perhaps you mean vulgarity. It is a standard of the

nouveau riche." Victoria read the displeasure on Dierdre's face and quickly repented. "But he does have a certain charm."

"I find him *very* charming," Dierdre asserted in defiance of her aunt's observations. "And very handsome."

"He is that. And clever. While other men lost their fortunes in the crash, he quadrupled his. You should witness the plebeians lined up outside his company each morning scavenging for work. I have the misfortune of having to pass it daily on way to the club. It is so odious."

Dierdre ignored the overt callousness of her aunt's remarks. "What of his wife? Has she granted him a divorce?"

"I don't believe so."

"Does he still love her?"

"He seems devoted to her, though I suspected fissures in the union even before her flight. Men hide behind their employment when the company at home becomes disagreeable, and David travels unceasingly. I wonder that he ever goes home." She rested her glass on a squat, wicker table and pointed a stout finger at her niece.

"Someone would be doing him a service to free him of such drudgery."

"You believe then that his marriage is imperiled?"

Victoria again broke into ostentatious laughter. "My dear, all marriages are imperiled. That is precisely why one must marry right. To ensure a comfortable solitude."

"You *are* dreary today."

"And you are romantic," Victoria retorted. "Though I will not seek to dissuade you from your illusions. They will shatter soon enough. And if I am dreary, it is this blasted climate. I do not know why I stay in this miserable desert." She held out a corpulent wrist. "Look how dry my skin is. I would have fled east decades ago had I not been so lazy." At this she yawned.

"Aunt, you will never leave Salt Lake City. Utah society would collapse without a puppeteer of your dexterity."

Victoria beamed.

"Do you suppose that David will call on me?"

"I would think so, but who could know? I have long stopped trying to foretell the man's ways."

"I hope that he does," Dierdre said wistfully. She

held up a sprig of mistletoe and smiled. "I hope that he visits on Christmas Eve." She sat back in her chair and picked at a plate of winter melon and pears, momentarily abdicating all conversation to the servants in the outer corridors.

CHAPTER NINE
A
GLASS
SLIVER

"I stopped by Lawrence's this evening and, in the course of our visit, he hinted at something I had never before imagined—that he had once been married. It is a peculiar thing to believe that you know someone intimately only to find that you really do not. It is like finishing a book only to discover that you have missed several key chapters."

DAVID PARKIN'S DIARY. DECEMBER 17, 1933

s dusk blanketed the city in its tenebrous shadow, David drove his Packard down the steep and darkened alleyway of the now vacant cannery building and turned off the concrete path at the dirt front entryway of Lawrence's shanty. He clutched a paper sack from the seat beside him, stepped from the car, then rapped on Lawrence's door with his free hand.

"Come in, David."

David slowly opened the door. Except for the amber radiance of the coal fire, obscured beneath the thick grate of the potbelly stove, the room was pitch black—of little consequence to a blind man.

"One of these times I will change my knock."

"Ain't your knock, it's your automobile's. If I still had my eyes I'd get under your hood."

"I have been meaning to get to it," David replied. "Maybe now with MaryAnne gone." It was a foolish excuse, and he felt foolish for thinking it. David took up a box of matches and lit the charred wick of the kerosene army lantern that hung from the rafter above the cot, taking mental note of its diminishing store of fuel. The pungent smell of sulphur wafted throughout the chamber. David squatted to open the stove's grate and fed the waning fire from a scuttle of coal. He reached over to an adjacent washbasin, then rose, lifting with him two shot glasses. He sat down to the table across from his friend.

"I brought you a Christmas present." He pushed an unwrapped box his way.

Lawrence felt the box, lifted its lid, and felt the cast image inside. "It's an angel. Is it brass?"

"It is sterling silver. Merry Christmas, my friend."

"Thank you, David."

He pulled the bottle from his bag. "And I brought some scotch."

"What's the occasion?"

"None's as good as any." David poured the first glass and pushed it across the table to Lawrence, who followed its motion by sound. Lawrence lifted the glass but did not drink.

"'Bout what hour it gettin' to be?"

It was an odd question to hear from Lawrence, and David glanced around the room at the gathered clocks. For the first time in thirty years they were silent.

"Around nine. Maybe ten minutes past." His forehead condensed. "Catherine says you haven't been eating."

"Ain't much been hungry." David sensed his uneasiness.

"Just things a happenin'." The old man shifted the conversation from himself. "How you been since your lady gone?"

David sighed. "Lost. And so lonely I could bust."

"I am sorry, David. Truly sorry."

"These are strange days. I have been having crazy thoughts lately."

"What kind of thoughts?"

"About my mother. I believe she is still alive."

"Miss Catherine told me 'bout the letter MaryAnne found at the angel."

"I have considered going to Chicago to find her. There are just so many unanswered questions."

Lawrence nodded understandingly. "We all got things under our skin. Everybody does. Like a glass sliver. Can't see nothin' there, but it works its way in deeper until it gets to festerin' and hurts so that we're ready to just cut the whole thing out."

David poured himself another glass.

"Comes a time that everyone needs to find their answers. Need to connect with their past. You ain't crazy, David, you just filled with the spirit of Elijah."

"What is that?"

"Like the Bible talk 'bout. Turnin' of the children's hearts to the parents'."

David looked down and frowned. "Then I get to thinking that I should let it go—maybe there is nothing to be gained. Maybe my mother was like MaryAnne— she fell out of love."

Lawrence groaned incredulously. "MaryAnne never stopped lovin' you. Lord, David, you talk 'bout love like it a hole. Somethin' you can fall in and out of."

"Isn't it?"

His aged face further wrinkled in indignation. "That ain't love at all, just squirrel fever. Just a storm of emotions." Lawrence grimaced. "Man sees a pretty skirt and calls it love. Most women folk ain't much smarter. Give more credence to butterflies than friendship. Real love's ain't that way. It's more like a tree or plant or somethin'."

"How is that?"

"Grows if you take mind of it. But it takes work and sacrifices. No one stand back of a neglected tree and watch it die and say, 'Guess that tree just ain't suppose to live.' Only a fool would talk like that. But people do it all the time with their loves."

David turned the ideology over in his mind, then abetted its acceptance with another drink. "What of you, Lawrence? How is it that you never loved a woman?"

"Never said I didn't love no woman." His voice suddenly took on a faraway quality. "Loved just one woman my whole life." He lowered his head in sadness. ". . . loved me too."

David stared at his friend in astonishment. "You have never spoken of a woman before."

The name fell reverentially from his lips. "Margaret."

"Margaret," David echoed. "Catherine said that you spoke of her."

Lawrence didn't look up.

"Who was this woman?"

"My greatest love."

"Why weren't you married?"

"Maybe we was."

David could scarcely believe the course of the conversation, and were it not for Lawrence's somber demeanor, he would have believed that Lawrence was fooling with him. Lawrence continued without prompting.

"Margaret was the daughter of a cavalry officer."

David's brow creased. "What is so wrong with an enlisted man marrying an officer's daughter? It must happen all the time."

Lawrence shook his head. "No, it don't happen."

"Why doesn't it?"

Lawrence's voice suddenly flared with annoyance. "Ain't no Negro officers in the U.S. military, David."

David felt foolish for his flawed assumption. "I am sorry, Lawrence."

Lawrence's voice softened. "If I'd of loved her less I'd be with her now. Fine, beautiful woman."

David replied nothing and the conversation withered, supplanted by the lapping of the declining fire in the stove and the chorus of crickets that serenaded the sun's interment. After a few moments, Lawrence broke the silence. His voice was drawn out as if moving along a slower, more weary course. The lantern's orange tongue reflected off the wet streak on Lawrence's cheek.

"There was two women I loved for most my life."

"There is another?"

"There is Sophia," he said, his voice cracking with emotion. He fumbled for his glass, and the conversation again lulled. "I need ask you a favor, David."

"Of course. Anything."

"I don't know how much life this old body of mine has left in it. After I'm gone, if Sophia ever come 'round, I have somethin' for her. Got it put away in the munitions box under my bed."

David glanced over at the cot but could not see the small crate concealed beneath it.

"What is in the box?" David asked.

Lawrence sat quietly for a moment, then said in a trembling voice, "Her answers."

David poured another shot for both men and no more was said of the women.

CHAPTER TEN
CHRISTMAS

"There is nothing so healing to oneself as to heal another."

DAVID PARKIN'S DIARY. DECEMBER 26, 1933

n Christmas Eve, the Parkin Machinery Company closed its doors at noon, and, in festive spirits, the employees fled home to their holiday revelry. Only David remained in the quiet building, alone except for the loneliness that darkened his mood as well as his countenance. He returned home in time to see Catherine off, and when her taxi arrived she boarded with great reluctance. Her concern for David was such that she could scarcely bid him farewell.

The winter sun, rendered succinct by the season, had already set when he dressed for the evening's dinner party, and he arrived at Gibbs and Elaine's tardy of the appointed hour. They were joined for dinner by three other couples, making him painfully aware of his own solitude. Gibbs and Elaine tried to cheer him, which made the evening more difficult as there is nothing so certain to exacerbate melancholy as to call attention to it. Three hours after his arrival, he excused himself and made his way home, alone, to the darkened and vacant mansion. Prior to his departure, a rare winter rain had commenced, and the encroaching clouds had blackened out the moon's reflection and wet the landscape. To David, the drenched city had never seemed so dark.

To his wonderment, as he unlocked the front door to his house, he heard the sweet, muted strains of a piano. He gently shut the door behind himself and followed the music down the darkened corridor to the conservatory and peered through the open doorway. Catherine sat at the ebony grand piano, partially visible through its raised hood. Her eyes were closed as she moved to the swells of the music—the repercussions filled the room, bathing it in gentle and healing waves. The room was lit only by a cluster of thick-stemmed candles, their bases encircled by holly leaves. David quietly sat down just inside the doorway while Catherine continued to play, moved only by the music's pull. She gently touched the song's last note and held down the key, relishing the tone as a taste.

"Rachmaninoff was MaryAnne's favorite," David said softly.

At his voice, Catherine let out a small gasp.

"David, how long have you sat there?"

"I didn't mean to startle you," he said. "Just a few moments."

She covered the keys. "I couldn't begin to count the number of times I've played that song for her . . . whenever she was sad." She felt bad for the observation. "What are you doing home?"

"I should ask you the same."

She walked around the piano and sat down next to him. "I didn't want to spend Christmas anywhere else. Or with anyone else." Her countenance lightened. "And don't think that I am pitying you. My motives are entirely selfish."

"Of course they are," David replied in jest.

"Then you would not be averse to joining me in a cup of wassail?"

"Not at all."

She returned with two teacups, handed one to David, then sat back down next to him. The fragrance of cloves filled the air.

"Are you feeling any better?"

"I feel lonely. No offense, Catherine."

"I understand. I feel homesick for MaryAnne, too. Loneliness is always worse at Christmastime." She sipped the hot drink. "Is this your worst Christmas ever?"

David frowned. "No. The year my mother left was the worst. All I asked for that Christmas was to have my mother back. I don't know if I thought St. Nick would bring her back . . ." He smiled sadly. "I truly believed that she would come back." He suddenly looked up, his face showing the pain of the day. "It's still early. Ask me tomorrow."

Catherine moved the conversation to something more cheerful. "What was your best Christmas?"

"My last Christmas with MaryAnne and Andrea. Andrea was at that age that she could sense the spirit of the holiday. Everything was tinsel and magic. Every bauble was for her. I felt it through her. That is the amazing gift of childhood." His words floated reminiscently. "How about you? What was your best Christmas?"

Catherine smiled thoughtfully. "The Christmas when I was nine. My family never had much. That Christmas I got a rag doll my mother had made from scraps she had saved from her sewing. My oldest brother had brought home a pine, and we made our own decorations—painted walnut shells and paper snowflakes. I was so excited you would have thought that I had spent Christmas at the Vanderbilts'. Later on that day, my uncle, who lived just down the road from us, came to the house. He told my mother about a family whose father had been killed only two weeks earlier, leaving them destitute. My mother asked us children if we would be willing to share our Christmas. We all knew what that meant as we only had one present." She smiled. "There was a little, flaxen-haired girl about my age. I'll never forget the look in her eyes as I gave her my doll."

David's eyes moistened as he considered the child's sacrifice. "That is truly remarkable, Catherine. What was your worst Christmas?"

A wry grin stole across her face. "Same one."

David laughed heartily until his laughter died in a pleased sigh. "Are you going to mass?"

"I think we're too late," Catherine replied. "St. Marks is usually filled by ten."

David glanced at his watch. "I didn't realize the hour was so late."

Catherine just smiled lovingly. She held up her teacup. "To Christmas, David."

David lifted his. "To Christmases past. At least some of them."

Catherine's smile fell as David's toast evoked a pang of sadness.

"Thank you for coming back."

"You're welcome." She kissed him on the cheek, then stood. "I better finish my rum sauce." She stopped at the door's threshold. "You were wrong when you said I hadn't spent Christmas with my family for too long. You and Mary are my family. And I hope she comes back soon."

"Me, too, Catherine."

"Good night, David."

◆

Christmas morning arrived in cheerful declaration by the bells of the Cathedral of the Madeleine and the pleasing fragrance of Christmas sweet breads still hot from the oven—stollen and "Julekake"—filled the downstairs of the Parkin house and could not help but sweeten the home's disposition. The night's rain had turned to snow, and the city was covered in flawless white sheets as smooth as the blue skies above. Catherine smiled as David entered the room.

"Merry Christmas."

"Merry Christmas," he replied jovially.

The kitchen's counters were lined with fluted pies, mincemeat and gooseberry, that awaited the roast goose for their turns in the oven. Two tins of Parker House rolls rose under dishcloths, and a small pan of rum sauce boiled on the stove for the plum pudding which Catherine was preparing to steam.

"So what congregation are you feeding today?"

"Just you, Lawrence, and me."

David sat down at the table. "It is almost a shame to go to so much work for so few people."

"Not when they are people I care about."

David smiled gratefully. "Can I help you with something?"

"You can pick up Lawrence."

"I had already planned on it. I thought I would bring

him here early and listen to some records or read to him."

"Well, be sure to eat something. Dinner won't be ready until two."

David snatched a pepparkaker from the counter, placed the cookie in his palm, and struck it with his knuckle. It broke in a half dozen pieces.

"You're hitting it too hard," Catherine said. "Here." She placed a cookie in her palm, made a silent wish, then struck it. It broke in three pieces. She handed the largest of the pieces to David. "You always give the largest piece to someone you love. Then your wish will come true."

"What did you wish for?"

"I think you could guess." She handed a small stack of the cookies to David. "Here. Take these for Lawrence and you to snack on."

◆

David was gone much longer than Catherine had anticipated, and, for a moment, she worried that perhaps something was wrong with Lawrence. When David finally returned it was with great commotion. He walked into the kitchen.

"Catherine, we have some unexpected guests."

Just then a mop-haired boy in tattered dungarees stuck his head into the room. He was followed by a thin, balding man who pulled the boy back by his denim straps. The stranger looked up at Catherine.

"Good Christmas, ma'am."

"Catherine, this is Frank Cobb. The Cobbs are passing through the city and had nowhere to spend Christmas."

"Sorry to impose, Mrs. Parkin. We got stranded in town yesterday. I asked Mr. Parkin if he might have a little work—somethin' to help feed the kids. He offered us to come and spend Christmas dinner with you. We're all mighty grateful."

Catherine smiled. "You are welcome here, Mr. Cobb. And I am Catherine, Mr. Parkin's housekeeper. Mrs. Parkin is out of the country."

"I apologize, ma'am."

"Not at all. How many are there of you?"

"Eight of us. With the baby."

A plain-faced woman came around and stood behind her man. She had desolate eyes that confessed the family's hardship and the burden she bore. She was dressed in a worn gingham dress slipped down over her shoulder as she nursed an infant at her breast. Catherine could not help but feel compassion for the woman.

"This is my wife, Bette."

The woman stooped. "Ma'am."

"Welcome, Bette. It is a pleasure having your family join us. In fact, Mr. Parkin was saying only this morning what a shame it was that we didn't have someone to share this meal with."

"Thank you, ma'am." She glanced around the cluttered kitchen. "Is there somethin' I can do to help in the kitchen? Been a while since I really got to preparin' somethin' more than fry dough or baked beans."

"I could use a good hand. I haven't mashed the turnips yet and the rolls still need basting."

The woman smiled at the invitation to help. ". . . be kind of nice to be in a real kitchen again."

Five children stood quietly out in the large foyer, captivated by the wealth that surrounded them, and the older of the clan kept close eye on the younger, slapping them if they dared touch anything or looked like they were thinking about it. David went out to them carrying a tin canister of pepparkaker. He handed the container to the second oldest. "Would you children like to listen to the radio while you eat these cookies? I think it's about time for *Death Valley Days.*"

The children's faces lit with delight, and the chamber echoed a chorus of "thanks, mister" and "much obliged." While the children happily congregated at the foot of the instrument, cookies in both hands, the men— David, Lawrence, Frank, and his oldest son, Leroy— resigned themselves to the parlor. The young man surveyed the room with wide eyes.

"Gee, mister. You got more than one radio set?" he asked with astonishment. "Ain't that the Ritz. Just listen anywhere you please. I'm gonna have me a place like this one day."

Frank Cobb scowled. "You hush up or you can go sit with the children. Ain't you learned a single manner."

The boy flushed. "Sorry, mister."

David smiled. "It's okay, Leroy."

Frank leaned forward. "Now this here Negro. He your help man?"

Lawrence chuckled. "If I am, he shorely could do much better."

"Lawrence is my friend," David said. He leaned forward and opened a decanter of whiskey. "Care for something to drink?"

"Well, don't mind if I do."

David poured a drink for all four of them, and Leroy looked especially proud to be drinking with the men.

"So what brings you through Salt Lake City?"

"Truth is, we headed to California, but we run out of fare for the train and couldn't buy tickets for all of us. So we thought we'd find a place for the missus and the kids, and Leroy and I'd go on and send back for them. Hear there's always something need'n to be picked in California. Hate to split up the family, but you gotta do what you gotta."

David frowned. He knew the way of the plantations and the greed that ran them.

"Have you had any luck finding anything here for your wife?"

"We've only been in town a day, but we thinkin' somethin'll turn up. Just gotta."

David looked suddenly thoughtful. "You know, splitting up a family is a hard thing. It would be better if you stayed together."

"If you ain't got three dollars for a ticket then you ain't got three dollars."

"Perhaps there is something I could do."

A look of distress flashed across Frank's hard, sun-baked face. "Don't mean to be ungrateful, Mr. Parkin, but no Cobb has ever taken charity, and I don't mean to be the first. We're hard workers and respectable folk. Always have been. If we hadn't lost our land to the bankers we'd still be plowin' it."

"I'm not offering charity, Frank. I'm offering a business proposition. That's the way things work in the world of high finance."

The man stared at him without comprehension.

"It's like betting on hog bellies or corn futures. I'm betting that you're going to do well in California. All I'm saying is that any business needs a little seed money. So I'll give you enough to get your family there and a little to settle with. Say, two hundred dollars."

The man looked astonished.

"Then, when things are comfortable I expect you to pay me back. With interest."

"How you know I wouldn't just run off with your money?"

"I can tell what kind of man you are, Frank. I've made my living reading people."

"Well, what if things don't work out. I mean they're a gonna, but what if . . ."

"That's business, Frank. No one has ever given me a guarantee. Certainly is no more risky than the stock market."

"Well, I can't argue that."

Leroy watched his father with great interest. "You gonna do it, ain't you, Pap?"

"Well, I'll give it a thought."

"You give it a thought," David said. "My investment portfolio could use a little diversification."

"Don't know what that means, but I'll give it a thought. You got a contract? I know them bankers in the finance world got contracts."

"What's paper if people aren't honorable? I do business with a handshake."

Frank leaned back, and Leroy looked at him anxiously. "I like the way you do business, Mister Parkin. I think we can make a deal. How much interest you thinkin'?"

"I don't know. I'm not giving any handouts, now. I want at least two percent."

Lawrence said, "David's no fool. He's gonna get two percent somewhere."

Frank thought some more. "Okay. Two percent. As soon as we got a roof over our head."

David hid his smile behind his glass. "Couldn't ask for more than that."

Bette Cobb came into the foyer and called the family to supper. When they had all gathered around the table Catherine said, "Would you mind if I blessed the food, David?"

"Not at all."

They all bowed their heads.

"Father, for this bounty we thank you. And for this day and the gift of your Son. Bless MaryAnne while she is away. Bless the Cobb family with health and safety and in all their travels. In the name of our Lord. Amen."

The room resounded with "Amens."

"Much obliged," Frank said.

The family loaded their plates as the platters moved around the large table—creamed turnips, carrots with glaze, lutefisk and limpa bread, and hot Parker House rolls. The children's eyes were wide as they anxiously awaited permission to start in.

"Go on," Catherine said. "We've said grace. No reason to hold back."

"Shore's some fancy food," Frank said, raising a fork.

"Catherine's family is from Scandinavia," Bette explained. "Brought lots of traditions with them."

"Best meal of the year," Lawrence said. "Start lookin' forward to it the day the first snow flies."

Catherine blushed. "Bette helped me," she said.

The family ate ravenously, and David and Catherine watched them happily. When they had been through several helpings, Catherine and Bette brought out the pies to the mutual acclaim of the diners, and they were cut and placed on small plates and, along with the sweet breads, were handed around the table. As they ate, David leaned over and whispered something to Catherine. She smiled as David excused himself from the table and disappeared from the room. When he returned he had a large box in his hands.

"St. Nick must have known you would all be here because he left these toys, and I don't have anyone to play with them. Let's see. We have a pretty doll here. Just right for . . . Amanda. And another for Sharon."

The two girls squealed. Catherine's eyes moistened as she watched David hand out Andrea's toys.

"Here's a stuffed bear." David looked into the child's eager face. "I believe this is for Phillip. Let's see. There is one present left. A monkey. Anyone here need a monkey?"

"Is it for me?" Thomas asked.

"I'm certain it must be." He handed the gift to the boy.

"Thank you, mister," he said as he clutched the animal tightly.

As the women cleared off the table, the children ran off to play with their new treasures, and David led Lawrence to the parlor to nap in front of the fireplace on the large sofa. David then went to his den and chair and turned on the radio. There was a soft knock at his door.

"Mister Parkin?"

David looked up. Leroy stood in the doorway. A grave look of anxiety blanketed his face.

"Hello, Leroy."

"Need to talk with you," he said tensely.

David motioned to a chair. "Of course. Sit down."

Leroy walked to the chair but stood behind it, nervously swaying from foot to foot.

"'Bout what you said earlier. 'Bout the two percent and all. We may be Okies, but I been around some. That's just hooey."

David leaned back in his seat, carefully studying the boy's expression.

"I want to know why you'd go givin' us two hunderd dollars we both know you ain't never gonna see again."

"Why do you think?"

"Don't know what to think. My pap's just a farmer. He don't know 'bout finance and stuff. He still don't know how it was them bankers came and took our land. I gotta tell him like it is, Mister Parkin. Gotta tell him somethin' ain't right."

"I don't think you should do that, Leroy."

Leroy answered defensively, "Why shouldn't I?"

"People like your father are the mortar that holds this world together. And it's their dignity that holds them together. Say you go on and tell him that it's really just charity I'm offering. Then, if he takes the money he loses himself. Or, if he decides to decline the money, he loses his family. Either way a good man loses. You take his dignity from him and you're as damned a fool as the bankers."

Leroy could not reply.

"Your father's not *just* a farmer. He's not *just* anything. A man's worth isn't measured by a bank register or a diploma, Leroy. It's about integrity. You remember that."

The boy looked embarrassed. "I'm sorry, Mister Parkin."

"It's all right, Leroy. You just care about your folks. There's not a thing wrong with that."

Leroy nodded thoughtfully as he quietly walked out of the room.

◆

As night fell David found Catherine on the landing.

"I have been looking for you. Why is your dress wet?"

"Bette and I bathed the children, then washed their clothes. She had never seen an electric washing machine."

"You look exhausted."

"I don't think I have ever worked so hard on a Christmas."

"I'm sorry. I'll make it up to you."

"No you won't. I wouldn't trade today for anything. That was kind of you to invite the Cobbs to spend the night."

"Are they all down?"

"The children are asleep. Leroy is still in the parlor listening to the radio. Frank and Bette are in the east guest room."

"Frank wants to leave at sunup."

"I'll make sure they have a good breakfast. And I'll pack something for the train. Bette told me about the 'business deal.' That was really good of you, David. You have made a difference."

"It's only one family. There are millions of Cobbs out there. It is silly to think it made a difference."

"It made a difference to them."

David nodded slowly.

"Where is Lawrence?" Catherine asked.

"I took him home."

"I thought he was going to spend the night."

"He wouldn't. He just complained that he gets lost in a big house like this and knocks everything over. He's really afraid that we're conspiring to move him out of his shanty."

"MaryAnne would have been so pleased with today," Catherine said. She suddenly sighed. "I'm sorry. I shouldn't have spoken of her."

"You don't need to be afraid to speak of MaryAnne. Besides, today was your doing, really."

"How so?"

"The story you told me last night—about the rag doll. You reminded me that sometimes the best remedy for a broken heart is to use it."

"I don't think you ever forgot."

David looked down. "Yes, I did."

"You said you were looking for me."

"I want to give you your Christmas present." He

reached into his pocket and brought out a small crushed-velvet box. The sight of the box made Catherine's heart skip. She felt uncomfortable taking it from him.

"Open it."

She carefully lifted its lid. Inside was a petite, brilliant, sapphire and diamond brooch. She gasped. "David."

"Merry Christmas."

A tear rolled down her cheek, and for several minutes she was unable to speak. "I have never owned a diamond."

"No woman, especially you, Catherine, should go through life without a diamond."

She could not take her eyes from it. "What will I wear it with? Oh, David. Is it really for me?"

"Thank you for Christmas, Catherine." He kissed her on the cheek, then went off to his room.

CHAPTER ELEVEN
THE TOMMY KNOCKERS

"It is a peculiar domain the mind enters when one is asleep. Why it chooses one landscape over another, or horror over joy, is the most baffling of mysteries. My nightmares have returned."

DAVID PARKIN'S DIARY. DECEMBER 27, 1933

t was not the first time that the same nightmare had plagued David's sleep. The nightmare was staged two hundred feet below the earth's surface and always with the same performers: a small boy, his face soiled from the mine's clay walls, and an elderly Cornishman, his oily face gleaming from the amber radiance of the kerosene lanterns that hung from the shaft's shoring timbers. The small boy stared anxiously into the foreigner's squint eyes as the flickering lanterns danced their shadows against the earthen walls in demonic contortions. The musty odor of dirt filled the nostrils, and the only sound was the distant crying of men and the slight, incessant tapping echo that rose from somewhere below. From the black.

The boy's expression asked the question without voice.

"It's the Tommy knockers, lad. Poundin' their pick-axes."

"What's a Tommy knocker?"

". . . souls of miners swallowed in the shafts."

The boy looked fearfully at the man. "What does it mean?"

The old man's lips pursed in a cruel smile. "Why, it means there's gonna be a cave-in." The jaundiced face suddenly erupted in laughter. "Run, lad! . . . Run!"

The boy bolted, frantically pumping his twig legs between the vacant steel tracks of the ore cars. Behind him, from the depths of the mine, a low rumble emerged, rising in growing intensity like an approaching avalanche. The hysterical laughter of the Englishman was drowned out by the mounting roar, and the subterranean walls trembled beneath its groan.

Ahead, the child could see the distant light of the mine's mouth, partially eclipsed by a form that stood at the entrance. It was his mother's form, her arms outstretched to catch her son. "Run, David! Run!"

Suddenly, thirty yards ahead, a thick, wooden rafter collapsed, and a wall of rock and dirt cascaded before him, followed by a river of muddy sludge that surfed over the splintered timber's back, flooding downward into the pit.

"Mama!"

All light vanished and David fell in the torrential mud, grasping for a handhold in the craggy walls, lest the current sweep him into the earth's bowels.

"Mama!" he screamed again. But there was no answer. And even the suffocating walls of the cavern returned no echo.

◆

David jolted up in bed. His heart raced as he gasped for breath. At the sound of his cry, Catherine had come to his room, her distress manifest across her face. "David . . ."

He looked towards her, and Catherine felt a pang of apprehension. His eyes were wild and his chest continued to heave. She walked to the side of his bed. "Are you all right?"

He exhaled. "It was just another bad dream."

". . . you were calling for your mother."

David stared at her as if the revelation was beyond his comprehension, then, recounting the vision, groaned as he rolled back into his pillow.

"When did the nightmares return?"

David hesitantly replied. "When you gave me the letter."

Catherine sat down at the foot of his bed with one leg crossed beneath her. In the eight years she had lived in the mansion before David had married, Catherine had come to expect the nightmares and the regularity of David's scream echoing throughout the house's dark hallways. She had come to dread the night terrors almost as much as did David. Almost miraculously, the nightmares had ceased with MaryAnne's arrival, and, after twenty years, Catherine had forgotten about the once nightly phenomenon. She did not welcome its return. She rested her head in her hand.

"Then MaryAnne was right. I should not have shared the letter."

David gently took her hand. "No, you did right. No

matter how painful, the truth is rarely a disservice."

Neither spoke, and the room's only sound was the clock. Suddenly Catherine looked up.

"Do you remember when I told you about the hobos that come to the house almost every day to ask for food?"

David looked at her quizzically, unable to guess what the anecdote had to do with the moment.

"Yes."

"The Monday last, another one came by. I made him a jam sandwich, and he asked if he could eat it out on the porch. A few minutes later my curiosity got the better of me, and I went back out and asked him why it was that he, like the others, walked past three other homes and came directly to our place to ask for food." A vague smile surfaced on Catherine's lips. "He pointed to the large sycamore at the corner of Fifth Avenue and said, 'See that tree yonder? There's a sign that someone nailed to it says the fourth house on this street will feed you.'"

"A sign?"

"One of those hobos must have put it up for those that came after," Catherine said. Her modest smile receded. "My point is, there is always a reason that things happen. When MaryAnne showed me your mother's letter she said its arrival at this time was rather peculiar. I didn't know what she meant at the time. But I think that I do now. I think there is a reason that the letter came when it did."

"And what might that be?"

"Maybe that it's time that you come to peace with her."

David considered her theory.

"I stopped by the cemetery to see the sexton as you requested. About a month back, as he was closing the yard, he came across an old woman crying at Andrea's angel. She left a letter and a flower."

An astonished look crept over his face. "Then it was my mother."

"Perhaps. As I grow older I find that I become more fatalistic. Looking back over my life, I believe that it has been guided by unseen forces. And that I have been showered with clues to direct my path."

"What kind of forces?"

"I'm not certain. God. His angels. Maybe just some great universal force of truth. Whatever you call it, there is something that shapes and directs our lives. I am certain of it. We can ignore the clues, we all do from time to time, sometimes we don't even see them. But I don't think that we, or our lives, will be complete without them."

David spoke seriously. "That is exactly how I have felt. Incomplete. Like an unfinished puzzle with a piece of me out there waiting to be found." A look of pain crossed his face. "And yet, with all my heart, I fear it."

"You fear that you won't find your answer?"

"No, I fear its discovery. To come face to face with my mother and learn who I really am."

"David, what your mother is, or was, has nothing to do with who you are."

David shook his head. "It has everything to do with who I am. Especially now. My mother's leaving is the reason I cannot forgive myself for losing my own daughter." He hung his head. "And it is why I fear to go after MaryAnne."

Catherine squeezed David's hand. "Then you must search out your mother. If for no other reason than to exorcise your demons."

"How could I hope to find her?"

Catherine spoke with uncharacteristic assuredness. "If it is to be, you will find her."

David looked up at the dim ceiling as the night's weariness enveloped the room. Catherine's countenance glowed with empathy as she gazed into his darkened face. When David spoke again it was with resolution.

"After the new year I will go to Chicago."

CHAPTER TWELVE

ROSE

"I do not remember much of my mother, but that she left me. And that, perhaps, is too much."

DAVID PARKIN'S DIARY. DECEMBER 28, 1933

FORTY-EIGHT YEARS PREVIOUS.
1885, GRASS VALLEY, CALIFORNIA

osalyn Parkin folded in the leg-of-mutton sleeves of a threadbare satin dress, creased the garment in thirds, then pressed it tightly against the print interior of the Saratoga trunk. She need not be so efficient. She had come to northern California a decade earlier with three cases of wardrobe—the costumes of her trade—velvet and satin dance hall dresses, tight-waisted and full-bodied with the risqué necklines of the burlesque, teased by boas of swansdown and fur: lynx and chinchilla. In the last decade, the garments had frayed and faded, were used as rags, or converted into a child's clothing. What remained of the wardrobe now fit too comfortably in the lone trunk.

She surveyed the room a final time for anything she could not part with from the last decade. The pre-dawn darkness concealed nothing. There was nothing to hide.

The room consisted of a few pieces of scavenged furniture, a chest of drawers, and a steel-banded cedar chest, both jettisoned with unfulfilled dreams by miners who had abandoned the small town, cured of their gold lust by austerity's stark tutorial.

The abode's slat walls were bare except for two faded playbills set in place and adored quietly with the reverence afforded religious icons: a color lithograph of the Kiralfy Brothers' performance of *Black Crook*, of which she had attended, and a parchment letterpress of *Macbeth*, where she had represented the role of Fleance.

She closed and buckled the trunk, then lifted it from the bed's stuffed, meadow grass mattress. There was not a thing she could not leave behind.

As she emerged from the dim room into the corridor, a cry, thin-voiced and undulating, emanated from the shadows. It froze her.

"Mama."

Through the pre-dawn blackness, Rose could make out the outline of her six-year-old son curled up in the corner of the hallway. The boy was feminine in form, petite and dark, his skin tanned from a life spent beneath the torrid California sun.

The child was created in her image. His eyes, like hers, were almond-shaped and azure blue, resting upon high, sculptured cheeks. His coffee-colored hair, matching hers to the tint, fell long to his shoulders, and, to the boy's shame, curled at the ends in sienna ringlets.

"I thought you were at the mine with your father, David."

The boy stared malevolently at the trunk, as if it were taking his mother away, instead of the inverse.

"Where are you going, Mama?"

She set the trunk down and approached her child, crouching before him.

"To Nevada City," she answered in partial truth. She would hire a hack the four miles to the Nevada City depot, board the Central Pacific to Colfax, where the tracks would change direction, conveying her through a myriad of mining towns before assaulting the great hewn stone terraces of the Sierra Nevadas—the last great obstacle to her escape from California.

The boy's forehead wrinkled. In the instinctual premonitions of survival—as animals flee before natural calamities—children, too, perceive when their world is threatened. He pushed at a tear which crept down his cheek. "When will you come home?"

Rose gazed at the boy solemnly.

"I don't know," she finally said, and it was quiet except for the babbling of the creek that fell behind their shanty home.

The boy sniffed, then rubbed his nose on the arm of the tattered cotton shirt he wore, then, inexplicably, relinquished his fear, as if in acceptance of an unknown fate.

"Will you bring me a molasses stick?"

"I will bring you two."

A hopeful smile stretched across the boy's face. "You won't be gone so long, will you?"

She brushed back the hair from the boy's forehead, but did not answer. David lifted the small toy he held. A music box carousel, carved in wood and hand-painted in oil pigments that had begun their desertion of the wood. The boy's treasure.

"Take my horses, Mama. To keep company."

The magnanimity of the gesture was not lost on her. She hesitated, then received the toy from his outstretched hand, avoiding the ardent gaze of his pleading eyes.

"Be sure to bring it back, Mama. Don't lose it."

She took a deep breath, then rose to her feet. Taking up her bag, she walked out of the home. Suddenly, David became frightened and cried out after her, "Mama."

But she did not return, and the child never considered that he might not see her again.

CHAPTER THIRTEEN
A
CHANCE
ENCOUNTER

"*Chicago boasts a profusion of theaters and cabarets—myriads more than I had presumed. One often does not realize the bulk of the haystack or the meagerness of the needle until one has sorted the first bale.*"

DAVID PARKIN'S DIARY. JANUARY 6, 1934

he five-hundred-and-thirty-ton San Francisco Zephyr crawled beneath a flat, grey ceiling of stratus clouds into the Chicago Union depot thirty-seven hours from its Salt Lake City departure, heralding its arrival with the fanfare of its hydraulic brakes.

The bedouin cast of porters heaved trunks and cases to the wood-planked platform where bags were claimed, hands extended, and tips bestowed, pocketed by the performers who disappeared back onto their moving stage for the next act. David, lugging his only case, emerged from the train into the brace of the cold Chicago air.

A forest of paper has been inked on the Chicago of the early century when America's second city was its first—as much an ideology as a locale—a symbol of a country's tenacity. Even the city's name was canonized in the vernacular of the era. If someone or -thing looked hard or tough it was deemed "Chicago."

David had not been to the sprawling metropolis for nearly a decade and was astonished by its burgeoning growth, in population as well as architecture. Wide grilled automobiles filled the tar roads or parked at their curbs, where they served as bleachers for the unemployed and vagabond who watched the city's motion with quiet, hungry eyes. Others, more resigned to their situation, gathered in small quorums to play hands of tattered cards or patient, endless games of bottle-cap checkers on chalked concrete sidewalks.

It was a city of paradox, from the sidewalks, where apples were sold by the hungry to the well fed, to the rising skyscrapers that optimistically stretched heavenward, casting their shadows on the homeless below.

Out of the depot crowd broke a small boy, mop-haired, angular in form, preceded by the wood-crate cart he pushed. His speed was fueled by the competition of dozens of other men and boys who raced to the trains like a flashing tide of piranha.

"Carry your bag, mister?"

David judged the child ten or eleven, nearly outweighed by the bag he proposed to carry.

"Can you lift it?"

"Yes, sir," the boy replied, raising his small frame—his protruded chest made absurd by the depression it left of his stomach.

"Just to the curb, then."

"Swell."

When he had traveled the distance to the street, the boy, left breathless by his journey, held out his hand. David produced a silver dollar. "For your trouble."

For a moment the boy stared at the sterling orb in disbelief, then, with the wariness of a sparrow pecking a morsel of bread from an open palm, he snatched the coin.

"Thank you, sir!" he shouted, fleeing with his fortune.

David smiled as he watched the boy disappear into the amorphous crowd, then turned back to the street and lifted his hand to a yellow cab for a ride to the Drake Hotel.

◆

Of the city's grand hotels, the world's for that matter, few shone with the refulgence of the Drake on Chicago's gold coast, a limestone edifice rising thirteen floors above the lapping waves of Lake Michigan. Since the munificent fanfare of its opening in 1920, the hotel had been the favorite of the city's visiting dignitaries— the kings and presidents, queens and first ladies—as well as the celebrities of the era. The hotel's plush ballrooms served as forums for the country's great bands, broadcast to the rest of the world from WGN radio, located on the upper level of the H-shaped building.

David's cab sided up to the hotel's front curb, shadowed beneath an iron canopy which hung from chains over the hotel's attendant bronze sentinels—lanterns of winged dragons, borrowed from the crest of the brothers Drake. A top-hatted doorman in a black uniform with bright crimson leg-striping attended to the curbside door, slightly bowing. "Welcome to the Drake, sir."

David paid the driver, then stepped from the car to the pavement. While the driver surrendered David's trunk to the awaiting bell captain, David climbed the steps into the luxuriant, crowded lobby of the hotel, amidst the aristocratic swoon of the perfumed gentry, attired in the costumes and furs of their status. The Depression did not exist inside the Drake, in decor or humanity, and as the world groaned beneath the weight of financial distress, the Drake's gilded walls rendered its suffering imperceptible.

The interior walls of the lobbyway were marble or wood-paneled in rich oak with burled parquet insets, set between intricate alabaster moldings. The floor was a collage of swirling Tennessee marble, accented by ebony inlays, overlaid, in the winter, by thick, vermilion carpets. Two crystal chandeliers, each a man's length in breadth, hung from high ceilings above twin, round-topped tables, each sustaining a sterling flute with a large spray of dried florals. The chandeliers hung thirteen feet above the floor—eye-level to the lobby's terraced sitting room, where guests would take tea and look down upon the high-hatted registrants in hopes of a celebrity sighting.

A clerk, tall, capped with a shock of brilliant red hair, greeted him. "At your service, sir."

"The name is David Parkin. I have a reservation."

"Welcome to the Drake, Mr. Parkin." The clerk stepped back from the counter as he shuffled through a register, then retrieved a set of brass keys stowed in the pigeonholed wall behind him. "You are reserved a suite, Mr. Parkin. Your accommodations are prepared. I took the liberty of having a fruit basket delivered to your room."

"Thank you."

"You will be staying in suite seven twenty-nine." The clerk handed David the key. "You have an extraordinary view of the lake. The elevator is just south of the lobby."

At the clerk's summons a bellboy approached.

"May I assist with your bag, sir?"

The clerk answered for him. "Please see Mr. Parkin to suite seven twenty-nine."

"Right away, sir."

David handed the man a quarter with the instruction to just leave the bag inside his room, then sauntered over to the concierge's counter. The concierge set down his telephone.

"Good evening, sir. How may I serve you?"

"I need a list of the city's theaters."

"That would be quite a listing, sir. Perhaps there is a specific production you are interested in."

"I am trying to find someone. I may have to visit every theater in the area."

"I see," he replied with a smile. "You have your work cut out for you. The most complete listing would be the telephone directory. I believe that I have an extra copy." He crouched below the counter, then rose, clutching a thick book in his hands, thumbed through the pages until he found the designation of theaters. "Here you are, sir."

David examined the directory. The theater listing was nearly three pages in length.

"As I stated, it is quite extensive. However, many of the theaters are now used exclusively for moving picture shows."

"It appears as though I'll be a guest of your hotel longer than I had anticipated." David tucked the directory under his arm. "Thank you for your help."

"My pleasure, sir."

"Is there a nearby restaurant you would recommend?"

"The Charlie Whiting band is performing in the Gold Coast dining room."

"Perhaps something more intimate."

"I would recommend the French Room. Just past the palm court and to the right of the mezzanine."

"Thank you."

David made his way through the crowded corridors to the restaurant. The French Room was smaller than most of the Drake's other dining rooms, dimly lit and partitioned by large columns accented with white moldings and flourishes. Windows, divided in small, abundant panes, revealed the lakeshore beach rendered vacant by the season. French doors opened to an outer terrace where dancing was held in the warmer months. It was sparsely occupied for a weekend evening.

David ordered his meal, then laid out a map of the city and on the back of a cloth napkin began the work of dividing the theaters by city regions. When his meal arrived, he closed the directory. He ate slowly as he looked out over the dying day—the dusk obscuring the lake's dark waters, visible only in the outline of the bleached swells. He wondered about MaryAnne; where she was and if she thought of him as frequently as he thought of her. And if her heart hurt too. He finished his meal, ordered black coffee and cherries

THE LETTER

jubilee, and only departed the dining room after a boisterous crowd entered the tranquil restaurant, occupying two nearby tables.

The hallway outside the French Room reverberated from the blare of the Gold Coast Room's brass band. The ballroom was the Drake's, as well as the city's, premier dance floor, and the biggest bands in America aspired to its venue. The spacious ballroom, currently dressed in gold and cream, changed its name twice yearly as it was repainted for the season. In the warmer months it was the Silver Forest Room as its winter hues yielded to cooler tones of silver and blue.

The ballroom's double doors were open to allow circulation of both air and guests, and the hallway outside was crowded with flushed dancers and the more sedate, who came to see and hear the famous bands without investing their own activity. As David pressed his way through the crowd, a woman brushed past him, then spun around.

"David!"

"Dierdre?"

She shouted over the din, "What in the world are you doing here?"

"I am a guest at the hotel. What are you doing here?"

"All the great bands come to the Drake. I come here every Friday."

Suddenly, a man, tall and well-built, with flaxen hair curled in carefully manicured swells, stepped forward and took Dierdre's arm, asserting his claim on the woman. He was immaculately dressed in a striped suit with cuffed, baggy trousers and a jacket with sharp, thin lapels.

"Robert, this is my friend David. He is from Salt Lake City."

"A real pleasure," the man lied, obviously more annoyed than pleased. "I only went to get you a drink. I didn't expect you would be absent upon my return."

Dierdre smiled. "Relax, Robert, I just went for some air. It was getting too hot in there." She straightened his lapel, and her drawl thickened. "Come on, let's go back inside." She glanced back at David. "How long are you in town, David?"

"Maybe a week. Possibly longer."

"We must get together. I will ring you."

The man glared at David before offering his arm to Dierdre.

David waved her off. "Go dance."

Dierdre smiled. "Toodleoo," she replied, then let her rankled date lead her back to the ballroom.

◆

"Within a few hours of my arrival in Chicago I chanced to meet Dierdre. I can only wonder how this fits into Catherine's theory."

DAVID PARKIN'S DIARY. JANUARY 6, 1934

◆

Early the next morning, David began the first of his calls to the theaters. His first dozen attempts taught him that those who answered the phones at theaters and those nearer the stage were of two different breeds. Those who greeted him often knew little more than the price of a ticket and their stage's current inhabitants, and sometimes not even that. Around noon, he went out and visited several theaters closest to the Drake. The only useful bit of information he garnered was discouraging. He learned that there was such turnover in the business that a performance just a decade earlier might as well been of a different century.

When he returned to the hotel at around six, he found a message waiting for him. Dierdre had invited him to dinner, assumed the engagement for seven that very evening, and requested no confirmation. He went up to his room and changed his shirt.

At a quarter of the hour, Dierdre arrived in the hotel's lobby dressed with her usual panache. She wore a form-fitting, black velvet dress with an ivory, lace collar, and an Empress Eugénie was strategically dipped over her left brow. She clutched a red-sequined handbag with both hands. When she did not find David, she patiently sat down at the end of a tucked, red velvet love seat, seemingly content in her examination of the passing guests—most of whom were very content to examine her back. When David arrived five minutes later, she hailed him from across the room.

"David!" she called. She rose as David approached. "It is so nice seeing you again," she said jubilantly. "It was such a surprise bumping into you last evening."

"I was surprised that you recognized me. It was only one dance."

"One and a half." She smiled. "And you are not as forgettable as you think."

David smiled bashfully. "I feel a little embarrassed."

"Whatever for?"

"I wasn't sure if . . ." He paused, feeling suddenly awkward. "Well, perhaps you had expected me to call."

"I had hoped," she replied candidly. "I am just glad you would meet me for dinner. So where would you like to go?"

"It's your city."

"Do you care for German cuisine? There is a superb restaurant and brewery just a few miles from here, on Adams."

"Do they serve sauerbraten?"

"With spaetzle and sauerkraut."

"Perfect."

"Swell." She took his arm. "Bennie is parked out front."

"Bennie?"

"My chauffeur."

At the front curb of the hotel idled a hunter green, chrome-grilled Duesenberg sedan, a full fourteen feet in length. The Duesenberg was the rare and luxurious automobile of czars and presidents and, as such, procured its own celebrity status which it lavished upon all who occupied its coach. David had admired the vehicle, as did all who knew automobiles, but had never before set foot in one. At their approach, a uniformed chauffeur, a black man of medium build, scrambled to their door. David followed Dierdre inside.

The automobile's coachwork was of the finest leather with adornments of polished hardwood and ivory inset with sterling silver. The rear side of the driver's seat had instrumented panels duplicating the driver's dashboard.

"A Duesenberg?"

"It's Daddy's car. You expected a DeSoto?"

"No. It's perfectly you."

Dierdre smiled wryly. "I will take that as a compliment."

The chauffeur closed the door behind them.

◆

The Berghoff was a Chicago landmark and boasted a heritage as rich as the ale it brewed. The restaurant's interior was attired in the dress and spirit of the Oktoberfest, and trophies of boars heads and wide-antlered hart hung from the walls of ocher wood. When they had settled in, ordered, and discussed the glory and pitfalls of the cuisine, Dierdre turned the conversation more intimate.

"How was your Christmas?"

"Mostly lonely."

"I'm sorry to hear that. You should have come to Chicago. During the holidays there are just hordes of people downtown. I don't know where they all come from."

"Sometimes there is nothing so lonely as a crowd."

Dierdre understood and smiled.

"Fortunately, I did have Catherine."

"Is Catherine your sister?"

"Catherine is my housekeeper."

Dierdre lit a cigarette and took a drag. "So what business brings you to Chicago?"

"Not business. I came for personal reasons."

She turned her head to expel a cloud of smoke. "Even better."

David grinned. "I came to find my mother."

Dierdre made no effort to conceal her disappointment. "Your mother lives in Chicago?"

"Perhaps."

Dierdre leaned her elbows on the table, her chin resting on her clasped fingers, awaiting an explanation. A thin stream of smoke snaked up across her face.

"My mother abandoned my father and me when I was

still a child. The last correspondence I received from her said that she had received an offer to perform in Chicago."

The waiter returned with steaming platters and heavy glass steins filled with dark lager.

Dierdre lifted her stein. "To the search for your mother."

David tipped his glass against hers.

"I confess that I had hoped your visit was really just pretense to see me again. I am disappointed to learn that you have another motive."

"I am sorry to disappoint you."

"You can still make it up to me," she replied. She cut into a medallion of veal. "Have you given any thought as to how you will find her?"

"Hopefully someone at a theater will remember her and know where she is. I had planned to telephone the local playhouses, but it hasn't proved as fruitful as I hoped. I may have to visit them all."

"This isn't Salt Lake City. There are scores of theaters."

"So I have discovered."

"You could well use the assistance of someone who knows their way around."

"Is that an offer?"

"Yes."

"It's a generous offer . . ."

"But . . ."

"But I feel I ought to do this alone."

Dierdre smiled defiantly. "It is just as well, David. All the longer I will have you in my city."

Just then, from outside the restaurant came a commotion. Across the street, two men engaged in fisticuffs over the contents of the restaurant's garbage can. Dierdre turned away.

"These incidents are becoming commonplace. These men act like wild animals."

"It is hunger."

"I shouldn't think they would be hungry. There are ample breadlines in the city."

"There are other ways to be hungry," David said.

"Six weeks ago a truck delivering baked goods to the Drake was stopped near one of the breadlines and more than a thousand men mobbed the truck and made off with all the bread. Fortunately no one was hurt . . . except the bakery."

David turned back. "I hadn't heard that."

"It was in the *Sun*. After that the Drake insisted their

vendors change their routes to avoid breadlines and parks." She ground out her cigarette. "You know, Mary Pickford and Amelia Earhart have both stayed at the Drake. I am a great admirer of both."

"That does not surprise me."

"That they stay at the Drake or that I am an admirer?"

"Neither surprises me. They are women like you, strong-willed and independent. Admirable qualities."

Dierdre blushed. "Thank you."

"In truth, I really do not know much about you. Except that you are quite different from your aunt."

"For which we are equally grateful. My family is fourth-generation Chicagoan. Back in the twenties, my father was mayor. He was, and still is, a very controversial figure. He did much to ease Prohibition's great thirsts, making him loved by some, hated by others, and distrusted by all. He is retired now, though he still keeps a hand in things—brings home an occasional governor or gangster."

"Governor or gangster?"

"Well, they both run the city." She smiled mischievously. "Actually there is not a great difference between the two, except the gangsters are much more amusing."

A smile spread across David's face. "And your mother?"

"Mother bides her time with crusades."

"What kind of crusades?"

"Oh, they change monthly. Mother chooses her causes with the same criteria that she selects her wardrobe."

Again, David smiled. "So what do you do?"

"The answer to that question is what keeps my father up at night. Vassar graduate, class of thirty-one. Now I just play, avoid marriage, and pretty much disappoint everyone." She lifted her glass to her chin. "And what does David Parkin do with his life?"

"Work. Though I also have a talent for disappointing."

"Aunt Victoria told me that you are a shrewd businessman."

"The truth be told, I am more lucky than shrewd. My father was a miner in Grass Valley, California. Thirteen years after my mother left we struck the mother lode. My father died two years later, and I ran the mine for a while before I sold it and moved to Salt Lake City to start the machinery company."

"It is better to be lucky than good."

"So I have heard."

"Why Salt Lake City?"

"My mother was going to meet me there. When I arrived she was gone."

"But you did meet your wife."

David's demeanor turned suddenly somber.

"I am sorry, I didn't mean to make you uncomfortable."

David wiped the corners of his mouth with his napkin. "Yes. That is where I met MaryAnne."

"My aunt told me some about her."

"Victoria never cared much for MaryAnne."

Dierdre sensed his agitation and quickly changed the topic, the conversation evolving to easy chatter. As the evening waned, David noticed Dierdre's necklace timepiece. It was a silver-cased pendant, its bevel inlaid with chips of diamonds and rubies.

"That is a beautiful timepiece."

"Are you bored of my company or are you really interested in timepieces?"

"You are easily the most candid woman I have ever met."

"Thank you. So which is it?"

"I collect timepieces. At least I used to. I'd hoard pretty much anything that kept time—even sundials."

She lifted it away from her breast. "My mother and father gave it to me for my graduation from college." She suddenly yawned, then laughed at herself. "It is late. You are probably exhausted. Are you ready to leave?"

"I am tired."

David laid down his napkin, and they both pushed back from the table. The ride back to the Drake was mostly silent. When the car stopped at the curb, Dierdre took David's hand.

"Thank you for dinner, David. I am very pleased that you are here."

"It was my pleasure."

She leaned over and kissed him on the cheek.

"As it was mine. May I see you again?"

The hotel's attendant opened the curb-side door and greeted David. David looked back.

"Perhaps we could have dinner again Tuesday evening?"

Dierdre beamed. "Swell. If you like we can have dinner at the Cape Cod Room inside the Drake. They have some of the best seafood in Chicago. You can update me on your search."

"I'll look forward to it." David stepped from the car to the pavement. "Good night, Dierdre. Thank you for your company."

"Good fortune finding your mother."

David smiled as he shut the door, bewildered that a woman as beautiful and sought after as she found him of such interest.

◆

The night Dierdre met David in the Saltair ballroom, she had felt something magnificent—the same intangible quality that MaryAnne and a thousand other women had instinctively felt in his presence. Included on that list was her aunt Victoria, who took perverse satisfaction in living vicariously through her niece's exploits.

Surrounded by the flux of society that pulsed through the Williamses' home, Dierdre had observed all types of men and found David a rare specimen. He was strong yet gentle, cunning yet harmless, rich yet unaffected by wealth's toxin.

MaryAnne presented no real concern to Dierdre, for while she did not care for the label "home wrecker," she ascribed no demonical significance to it either. Dierdre was accustomed to getting what she wanted, sometimes impeded by social mores and less frequently by conscience, but, in David's case, neither. His wife had deserted him and like a land title, when a claim is abandoned, it is open to the first to secure it. A mining man like David Parkin would understand that.

A
SECOND
DATE

Will Rogers: "Now everybody has got a scheme to relieve unemployment. There is just one way to do it and that's for everybody to go to work. Where? Why, right where you are, look around and you will see a lot of things to do, weeds to cut, fences to be fixed, lawns to be mowed, filling stations to be robbed, gangsters to be catered to . . ."

FROM A NEWSPAPER CLIPPING FOUND IN
DAVID PARKIN'S DIARY

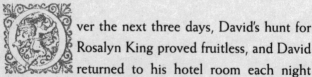ver the next three days, David's hunt for Rosalyn King proved fruitless, and David returned to his hotel room each night fighting mounting discouragement. He had experienced a brief glint of hope when a flamboyant, elderly

actress at the Haymarket Theater recalled performing with Rose, and, with halting diction, divulged her fondest memories of the woman's exploits and her present situation and whereabouts. It was not until twenty minutes into her oration that David realized that the Rose she spoke of was a black woman from Kentucky. For the first time, he began to consider that his mother might never have really come to Chicago or, perhaps, had moved on as quickly as she came.

His lack of success also allowed time to think of MaryAnne, and the weight of her absence grew heavier with each passing day. Catherine had agreed to contact David at first word from MaryAnne, but he returned to his room each night with hope of that message only to be disappointed anew.

◆

Tuesday evening David met Dierdre in the Cape Cod Room—a small eatery annexed through a street-level corridor to the Drake Hotel. The restaurant was dark, mostly lit by the hurricane lanterns atop its red-checker-clothed tables. Their table was crowded with large platters of blushed spiny crab legs with glass dishes of butter, porcelain bowls of soup, and deep glasses of beer and juice. The bar was the restaurant's most prominent fixture, and it was always well-stocked, and occupied, and in its countertop were engraved the names of celebrities who had visited the establishment. And there were many.

Dierdre held her spoon out to him. "Try this."

"What is it?"

"Bookbinder soup. With a touch of sherry. It's a specialty here."

David sampled her offering. "That's good."

"I tried it without the sherry once. Didn't like it. Must be the southern girl in me."

"I have been meaning to ask you how a Chicago girl came to have a southern accent."

Dierdre stifled a laugh. She had worked hard to perfect her mother's southern drawl and deftly slipped in and out of it as benefited the situation.

"It is my mother's," she answered. "And, speaking of mothers, how goes the search for yours?"

"Twenty-one theaters, one job offer, and no one knows her."

"A job offer, that is impressive. I am a little hesitant to ask, but is it possible that your mother never settled in Chicago?"

"I am beginning to wonder."

Dierdre worked the meat from the crab leg's hollow with a crab fork. "You have come a long ways on faith."

"Faith or fate."

"You do not strike me as the fatalistic type."

"I am beginning to wonder. Are you a believer in fate?"

"You mean, like our chance encounter outside the ballroom?"

"That would count."

"Well, I don't believe in coincidence."

David wiped his mouth with a napkin. "A few days before MaryAnne left, she discovered a letter at our daughter's grave. It appears to be written by my mother. Catherine believes that it came at this time to lead me somewhere."

"Catherine, your housekeeper?"

"Right."

"It sounds very peculiar."

"I wonder."

"One thing I don't understand is why, after all this time, it is so important that you find her."

David looked at her thoughtfully. "I feel like I am trying to put together a puzzle of myself. To know why she left might help me understand who I am."

"Do you think she could answer that?"

"I don't know."

Dierdre set down her utensils. "May I ask you something very personal?"

David looked at her warily and his gaze made her reluctant.

". . . I would like to ask you about MaryAnne."

David turned the request over in his mind. "All right."

"Do you still love her?"

He hesitated. "She broke my heart when she left me."

Dierdre wondered if he had intentionally not answered her question. "Why did she leave?"

David stared listlessly at the lantern's candle as he deliberated on his response.

". . . If you would rather not talk about it."

David shook his head. "When our daughter died, I buried much of my heart with her." His voice wavered. "MaryAnne just grew tired of being alone."

"I don't mean to sound simplistic, but had you considered having more children?"

"We tried for years. But I couldn't give her children."

"Curious that you blame yourself. How do you know that she's not at fault?"

He paused, considering how much he desired to share. "Andrea wasn't really my daughter. MaryAnne was pregnant with another man's child when I met her."

Dierdre tried to conceal her astonishment. "And still you married her?"

David nodded.

"David, that is the most beautiful thing I have ever heard."

David did not reply.

"Tell me about Andrea."

He smiled sadly. "She was joy. It was as though she healed everything in my life that was amiss."

"I bet you were a wonderful father."

David again grew quiet. Dierdre moved to change the subject.

"You mentioned that you collect clocks. I find that fascinating."

"I once had an extensive collection, but I've sold most of them now. I stopped collecting them after Andrea died. I collect other things now."

"What are you after these days?"

"Antiquities. Wooden boxes. Bibles."

"Bibles? How peculiar. Are you religious?"

"MaryAnne is quite pious, but I have never been accused of it."

Dierdre looked suddenly thoughtful. "Sometimes I wish that I were more religious. I frequently think about God, but I do not often attend church. I just want to go for the right reason—because I really believe it, not because it is socially advantageous." She suddenly grinned. "Of course that's another check on my father's blacklist."

"I think you are more religious than you give yourself credit for."

"How so?"

"There is integrity to your belief. I have to believe that pleases God."

"I don't think so. I think God wants blind observance."

"I find it difficult to accept that God created rational beings and would want them to be marionettes."

"Then what about faith?"

"Faith is misunderstood. It is treated as an end when, in fact, it is really a beginning."

"What do you mean?"

"It is a state we cultivate to get us somewhere—a principle of action. Every gold mine ever dug was dug by faith."

"But not all gold mines have gold."

"True, but you don't know that until you turn a shovel. It is only foolish, if one keeps panning when there is nothing there."

"I don't understand why faith is required at all. Why doesn't God just appear to everyone and tell them what He wants them to do?"

"Then we *would* become marionettes. We would do things because of the promise of reward or the threat of punishment, not because they are intrinsically good or noble. Our actions would change, but our hearts wouldn't. The truth is, in this life, cause and effect are often disjointed. Sometimes very bad things happen to very good people—sometimes for doing the right thing." At the statement David paused. ". . . like with Andrea."

"Still, there is too much confusion. I think it would make sense for God to appeal more to the senses."

"I have come to the conclusion that if the one universal truth of existence is the unknowing, then there must be something in the unknowing. I believe that's what life is about—to learn what it is about. And, to the level we apply ourselves to learning this, we evolve."

"Evolve to what?"

"Hopefully, to a state closer to God."

"How does religion fit into your theory?"

"It is part of that evolution. Religion, in a way, is like a clock. I used to have more than a hundred of them. I could tell you where every one of them came from, what company made them, sometimes even how. Yet, I am the first to admit that I do not comprehend time. The things that this German scientist, Einstein, talks about may only be the first real glimpse of our understanding of time." He lifted his pocket watch and unclasped the shell that protected its crystal. "But I can read a clock. In the same way I cannot comprehend God or the magnitude of power that could create an infinite universe, let alone the human mind. So if religion can help me to understand that being, then I am better off. As long as I do not confuse the clock for the time."

"That is profound, David."

"It just makes sense to me," David said. He yawned unexpectedly.

"Another long day?"

"They have all been long days. Or at least short nights."

"How about we call it an evening and have dinner again on Friday? If that's okay, I don't mean to distract you . . ."

David laughed. "You're a positive distraction. Our visits are the only things keeping me sane."

Dierdre's face animated. "Then why don't you take tomorrow off and let me really show you the city. You could use the break."

David thought over the proposition.

"You have me for the day."

She smiled broadly. "Swell. I have some things I need to do in the morning. How about I come for you just before noon?"

David nodded. "I'll meet you at the curb." David signed the tab, then walked her out to the Duesenberg and a very patient Bennie.

◆

Back in Salt Lake City, the weather had again turned inclement. Large snowflakes fell and stuck to the roads. Traffic slowed. Children went inside their houses and waited for enough of it to fall to be of use. After the close of business, Gibbs knocked at the door of the Parkin house and was met by Catherine.

"Hello, Gibbs."

Gibbs removed his hat and tilted the snow off of it before brushing the snow from his shoulders and sleeves, then stepped inside the temperate foyer. "Catherine, have you heard from David recently?"

"Not a word since he left." She read the concern on his face. "Is something the matter?"

"Last night, there was a fire in the back lot of the building."

She raised a hand to her breast. "Oh my! Was anyone hurt?"

"No, and thankfully there wasn't damage to the building. The snow hindered it."

"Thank goodness."

"I wish that was all there was to it."

"What do you mean?"

"It wasn't an accident. The fire was started by a burning cross."

Catherine turned pale. "But why the machinery company?"

"Because David employs Negroes." A shadow of apprehension dimmed his countenance. "This isn't an isolated instance. I have read that some stores back East have been looted for doing the same."

"What are we going to do?"

Gibbs thought for a moment. "The police already know about it. There is nothing else to do." He replaced his hat and turned to leave. "If you hear from David, don't tell him. He already has enough on his mind."

RIVERVIEW

"Dierdre is a woman endowed with the rare quality of contentment—the ability to find the joy possessed in each circumstance as mysteriously as the desert aborigine finds water in the parched desert . . ."

DAVID PARKIN'S DIARY. JANUARY 11, 1934

ennie stood at the Drake's front curbway, oblivious to the biting wind which funneled down the corridor of buildings, whistling through open doorways and alleys. When he saw David approach, he started for the rear passenger door and David quickly released him of the duty with an upraised hand and opened his door himself. Inside, Dierdre sat with her legs crossed and an open compact flat in one hand and a puff in the other. She was dressed in a long skirt and wore a thick mink coat. She looked up from the mirror.

"Good morning, David. I hope you brought a warm coat."

David pulled the door tight. "I brought my only coat. Where are we going?"

"That is a surprise."

She closed the compact, then examined his jacket. "I brought a blanket just in case."

As Bennie pulled away from the curb, David noticed the deferential glances of other drivers as they followed the car with covetous eyes. As they rounded the block, David asked Dierdre, "Have you ever driven this car?"

"My father won't let me. I would love to, though. The manufacturer claims it will go more than a hundred miles per hour. I would like to see if that is true."

Bennie glanced nervously into the rearview mirror.

"I am surprised," David said.

"That a Duesie can go that fast?"

"That your father can stop you from doing anything."

Dierdre laughed. "He has a little help. Watch," she whispered to David before leaning forward against the front seat.

"What do you say, Bennie? How about I drive today?"

Bennie's response was well rehearsed. "No, ma'am. I

would lose my job. Your father gave me explicit instructions."

"You mean an explicit threat." She leaned in close. "He didn't say anything about David driving."

Bennie looked more anxious. "Please, ma'am. Your father would not like it."

She patted his shoulder gently, then leaned back into the seat. "Relax, Bennie. I am only kidding."

The extravagant automobile quietly moved forward, driving northward along the Chicago River until the terrain leveled to a broad area more than one hundred acres square. The wooden latticework peaks of rollercoasters rose above towering groves of sycamore and elm. As they neared the park, a large, circular sign read: RIVERVIEW AMUSEMENT PARK—JUST FOR FUN. Bennie pulled into the large, empty parking lot, drove up to the spacious front gate, and stopped the car.

"Riverview," announced Dierdre. "Home of two-ton Baker and the largest amusement park in the world."

David glanced around. "It looks to be the most unpopular amusement park in the world—that or it's closed."

Dierdre shuffled through the contents of her purse. "Of course it's closed, darling. It's winter."

Her reply produced more questions than it answered. Bennie opened Dierdre's door.

"We're here for a picnic," she said, and stepped out of the car. Bennie opened the car's trunk and brought out a straw picnic basket, which he handed to David. Bennie took his instructions from Dierdre, then returned to the car, and the automobile whisked away. David looked at the barred turnstiles beneath the large, twin-domed entrance and thought it looked a little like Saltair.

"How do we get in?"

"Through the front door."

She walked to the side of the turnstiles to a discreet door painted in the same rust pigment as the surrounding walls. She pushed it open to an austere, cement-bricked room. A doorway in the opposite wall entered into the park.

"It's the service entryway. The watchman is too lazy to come up front to let maintenance people in, so he just leaves it unlocked."

"How do you know that?"

She smiled. "I just do."

They walked out into the park, and at the entrance of the midway David stopped to take in the deserted landscape.

"Do you come here often?"

"During the summer I do. The boys always take me here. I think coming here makes them feel manly."

"How so?"

"It's the unwritten law of the sexes. I scream on the coasters, lose at skeeball, and wait excitedly as they spend two dollars assaulting innocent milk bottles to win a ten-cent stuffed animal for me. Not that I am averse to this. I think there is something very primal about it—like when cavemen dragged back a saber-toothed tiger to their women. Only they're throwing softballs, not spears." She gestured with one hand. "Who am I to flout evolution?"

"And so you play along."

"Of course." She smiled innocently. "I do want to show them a good time."

David started walking again. "Why are you revealing your secrets to me?"

"Because you are not a boy, and you see right through me."

She took his hand as they continued down the deserted midway towards the skeeball and the grotesque artwork of the freak shows.

She pointed to a large structure. "I love that ride. It's

called the Flying Turns. It's a great ride." She suddenly chuckled. "I was on it once when my date pulled a Daniel Boone."

The phrase threw him. "A Daniel Boone?"

"Sorry. College jargon. It means that he shot his dinner."

David grinned. "Slang is the true line of demarcation between the generations."

"Are you saying that you are a lot older than me?"

"I am a lot older than you."

"Well, it's not like that's a bad thing. I like older men. At least I like you, and you're older." Somewhere a distant radio played "It's Only a Paper Moon," reminding David that they were not alone.

"The watchman's shanty is over there. But the codger never comes out," she said matter-of-factly. Dierdre reached into her bag and pulled out a box of cigarettes, offered one to David, who declined, then lit her own. A half mile into the park they stood across a row of boarded-up concessions.

"The summer before last, I had an interesting experience here. I was leaning against that rail eating an ice cream cone when this little waif of a boy came and stood in front of me, just watching me. Didn't say a thing. He just stood there looking like his eyes were going to pop out of his head. I asked him if he liked ice cream, and he nodded. So I bought him a cone and he ran off. A few minutes later this woman came up to me mad as a yellow jacket. She was dragging the little boy by one hand and holding the cone in the other. She said, 'What'ya think you're doin' buying him things his mama can't afford. How 'bout the other ones, huh? What am I gonna tell the other ones?' The poor little boy just stood there sobbing his eyes out. She gave me the cone back and dragged the boy off. I just threw it away. What was I supposed to do with it? It was just an ice cream cone."

"To her it was self-respect. These are hard times. It's all most can do to hang on to their dignity."

"I still say it's just ice cream." She suddenly pointed east to a small parkway dotted with picnic tables beneath covered pavilions.

"There's the picnic grove."

They digressed off towards the hedged terrace.

"Does Salt Lake City have an amusement park?"

"Yes. In fact you have been to one of them. Saltair."

"Oh yeah. I noticed the roller-coaster. It wasn't very big for an amusement park."

"It's nothing like this. There's also a park called the Lagoon. It's twenty miles north of Salt Lake. It also has a roller-coaster."

"Riverview has seven."

She ground out her cigarette and threw it into the snow around the table. They sat down and Dierdre opened the basket.

"I brought grapes—in multiple incarnations." She brought out a cluster of Concord grapes and a bottle of wine, then reached back in and brought out a loaf of flatbread and cheese. She reached in once more. "And my favorite part of any meal—chocolate. Do you like chocolate?"

David nodded.

"I am addicted to it. My life has been much happier since I admitted that all I really want to eat is chocolate."

"I would say that it's hard on the body—but you couldn't tell by looking at you."

"Thank you. I was starting to wonder if you had noticed."

Dierdre broke apart the bread and spread a piece with cheese and handed it to David. David poured Dierdre a glass of wine, then held up the bottle.

"This is good wine."

"Good wine is all my mother would allow in the house."

He poured his own glass.

"Did you see the Ferris wheel?"

"Which one?"

"Doesn't matter. I was going to tell you that it was invented by the mayor of Chicago—George Ferris."

"I had heard something like that. It's fortunate that his last name wasn't Schmetzel. Somehow the Schmetzel wheel lacks romance."

Dierdre laughed. "What is your favorite amusement ride?"

"Probably the carousel."

She lit another cigarette. "Carousels are boring."

"There is not much to the ride, but there is something pleasant about the motion and the art of the menagerie. I have always been fond of carousels. They are a literal manifestation of peace—the turning of swords to ploughshares."

"Now that's an interesting take on an otherwise banal experience. Please explain yourself."

"Carousels were invented in the seventeenth century to train for jousting tournaments. French noblemen would mount barrels on a revolving platform and try to put their lances through hanging rings as they went around. Hence, the idiom 'to catch the brass ring.' Through time it evolved into a thing of pleasure and childhood—moving pieces of art."

"That's almost poetic."

"And you?"

"I like coasters. They say the Bobs is the fastest in the world, except for maybe the one at Coney Island. You a coaster fan?"

"Not much. I end up more dizzy than amused."

"Who doesn't?" She exhaled a careful stream of smoke through pursed lips. "The trick, David, is to enjoy the ride."

"And when the ride is over?"

She smiled. "You get back in line."

When they had finished eating, Dierdre stuffed everything back into the basket, laced her arm through its handles, and stood. "Let's go."

"Where are we off to now?"

She began to walk away. "The Tunnel of Love."

A hundred yards from the grove, the amusement came into view—a broad, flat facade, painted white with red hearts and cupids like an oversized valentine. The ride's boats were inverted and dry-docked to the side of the empty cement troughs that in the open season held water. Dierdre set down the basket, and they both climbed over a short fence.

"This ride used to be called the Thousand Islands. They changed the name to Tunnel of Love and doubled their take. Image is everything."

"I have never walked through a Tunnel of Love."

She glanced towards the tunnel. "Me neither. But I have paddled through it. A century ago, I dated one of the owner's sons. When the ride is open, a paddle wheel creates currents that take you through the tunnels at its own pace, so lovers wanting to spoon would sometimes climb off the boats in the tunnel until an attendant came by and kicked them out. This guy used to bring girls after hours, pull out a canoe, and just paddle through. That way he could stop wherever he wanted. He tipped the canoe over more than once."

"With you in it?"

She smiled and did not answer. Suddenly, a barrel-chested man wearing the top half of a navy-blue uniform appeared outside the gate. On his chest was the shield of the Riverview Police. His face was florid. "Hey. What are you doing in there?"

They both looked over.

"I'll talk to him," David said. Dierdre smiled helplessly as David climbed over the fence and began talking to the man, who grew only more vehement as the discussion progressed. After a few minutes, Dierdre calmly approached. She put her hand on David's shoulder.

"Just a minute, David," she said, gesturing for him to step back. She turned towards the watchman, and though David could not hear what she said, the man's demeanor quickly changed from rage to impotence. He turned and sauntered away.

"What did you say to him?"

"Like I said, I dated the owner's son. C'mon."

They climbed back over the fence.

"You are used to getting your way."

"What do you mean by that?"

"It was just an observation."

"I was born into a wealthy and prominent family. I can't help that. But I don't flaunt it, and I don't abuse it. It is important to me to make it on my own."

"I didn't mean to imply otherwise."

David slid down into the concrete trough, then held up his hand to Dierdre, who took it, then slid down next to him.

"The truth is, I can never truly be fully independent,

because I know there is always a safety net. Like that guard incident. I was curious to see how you handled him, but I knew in the end that we would get our way. It's debilitating in a way."

"It's just the way it is."

"Maybe that's why I find you so interesting."

"Why is that?"

"You're not a sure thing."

They walked on through the empty troughs into the tunnel and beyond until Dierdre complained of being cold, and David lay the blanket across her shoulders.

"What time will Bennie return?"

"Oh, he's been parked out front for hours. He only left because I had a few errands for him in the city."

"What does he do when he's out there?"

"Just reads, I think. Though he's more likely to read Captain Whizbang than Hemingway. He says he likes it. People would die for his job."

"People would die for any job."

"A while back we almost had to let him go."

"Why?"

"You know, the Negro thing—coloreds taking good jobs while white men are out of work. My father was getting hassled by some of his colleagues. He usually succumbs to such things, but he drew the line at Bennie."

"That's commendable."

"Oh, he's hardly noble. It's just that good chauffeurs are hard to find." Her face suddenly brightened. "Would you like to see the house? I could fix dinner."

"Sounds unusually domestic."

"I can be domestic."

On their way out of the park, David caught sight of the shamed watchman as he darted behind a structure to avoid further humiliation.

◆

The Williamses resided in the Lake Forest district of Chicago, not far from the Drake or the street called Millionaires' Row. At their arrival, the Duesenberg passed between two brick pilasters topped with cement platforms which supported brass cupids, their arms extended to hold aloft electric globes. The Williams's mansion was not set back far from the street, but was well secluded by trees and foliage—an arboretum of red oak, red maple, elm, beech, and cottonwood. As they cleared the landscape, the mansion came into view. It was a large, three-story structure, surrounded on all sides by groves of trees. Its facade was blanketed by ivy with ocher-hued stucco exposed in rare patches.

"Have you lived here long?"

"Always."

"It is beautiful," he noted.

Bennie stopped the car at the side of the house and attended to their doors. As they entered the home, they were met by a handsome woman with greying hair and almond-shaped eyes climaxed by dark, swooping eyebrows. She appeared to be not much older than David, who, without introduction, immediately knew who she was for, though much more svelte, she showed a remarkable resemblance to her sister Victoria. The woman eyed David furtively.

"Dierdre, I thought you were out for the evening," she said with a prominent southern drawl.

"Hello, Mother. I wanted to show my friend our home." She turned to David. "This is David Parkin. He is the man I met in Salt Lake City. He is a friend of Aunt Victoria's."

Her expression relaxed, and she gracefully extended her hand. "It is a pleasure, Mr. Parkin. I am Samantha. Dierdre has spoken of you."

David noticed Dierdre's blush.

"It is my pleasure, ma'am."

"You came all this way to see our Dierdre?"

"Actually, I was in town on other matters, and we happened to run into each other at the Drake Hotel."

"What an odd coincidence," she said, raising her eyebrows. "All the same it is a pleasure having you in our home."

"Thank you."

"Will you be staying for dinner?"

Dierdre interjected. "I told David that I would fix him something."

"Nonsense, Dierdre, you'll poison the man. We will be dining in a half hour. I'll have Claire lay a few more settings. Why don't you all just retire to the billiards room until we are called?"

Dierdre relented, though she was clearly annoyed by her mother's insistence on interfering with her evening.

"Come, David."

◆

The bricked patio was visible from the spacious room, encircled by the garden and a pond lined by a wrought iron fence and weathered garden statuary. Dierdre walked up beside him.

"Most of my parents' social functions are held out on the patio. There used to be swans."

"What happened to them?"

"My mother was hosting a campaign fund raiser for an alderman and was standing by the pond when one of the birds took after her. You wouldn't think a woman could move so quickly in a long gown and heels. The bird only stopped chase when one of the guests headed it off with a pair of salad tongs. Everyone who is any-one was there, and to my mother's mortification, at every social function since then someone has recalled the incident."

David laughed. "What became of the swan?"

"Mother would have had the thing roasted if my father had allowed it. He sent them off to a park some-where in the city. Mean birds, swans. Beautiful things are often mean."

Outside the room a bell rang.

"That would be dinner," Dierdre drawled unenthusi-astically.

◆

The oak-paneled dining room was immense, yet so garishly lavished with bric-a-brac as to render the room cramped. The three of them sat down to one end of an elongated table, with Samantha at the head and Dierdre across from David. A servant came to David's side with a platter.

"Do you like mutton, David?" Samantha asked.

"Mutton? Yes. Very much."

The servant forked a piece of meat on his plate.

"Not everyone cares for mutton."

Dierdre said, "Personally, I prefer swan."

Samantha glared at Dierdre, then turned back towards David.

"How long have you known Victoria?"

"Since I moved to the Salt Lake Valley."

"Then you are not a native."

"No. I was born in a small mining town in northern California. I moved to Salt Lake City around the turn of the century. I met Victoria shortly after my arrival—at some affair."

"That is where one would meet Victoria. Frankly, I am surprised that she ever allowed her husband to locate in the West. But business is business, I suppose. I was sure she would come back after his death, but she hasn't. My theory is she likes to complain about living there, and if she moved she would have nothing to whine about."

David smiled knowingly. "You underestimate her ability to whine."

Samantha laughed heartily, covering her mouth with a linen napkin. "You do know her well." She lowered the cloth. "Personally, I find your city charming. The mountains are spectacular. I was there once in the fall, and the autumn leaves made the mountains look like an artist's drop cloth."

"It is beautiful." He took a fork of baked sweet potato, followed with a drink. "Dierdre tells me that you are involved in many causes."

"It is how I bide my time. Seems there is always something." She daintily raised a spoon of soup to her mouth, sipped it, then just as delicately returned it to the dish. She suddenly asked, "Are you wealthy?" She asked the question with the candor one might have used to inquire of one's health. Dierdre glared at her.

"I have sufficient means," David said.

"I find it hard to believe that a man of your looks and station has not yet married."

Dierdre interjected. "David *was* married, Mother."

David wasn't sure which comment he found more disturbing. He had no idea how to respond to either.

"You are a widower?" Samantha asked.

David looked embarrassed. "No. My wife left me."

There was an uncomfortable silence, and Dierdre again glared at her mother.

When they had finished their entrées Dierdre looked down at her watch. "I better get David back to his hotel."

"It is getting late," David said. He set his napkin on the table. "Thank you for dinner."

Samantha stood. "It was a pleasure having you in our home, Mr. Parkin. Victoria is fortunate to have such handsome friends."

Dierdre walked to the doorway and hollered for Bennie, then returned to escort David out to the car. When they were out of the drive, Dierdre said, "I thought we would never get out of there. My mother liked you."

"How could you tell?"

"If she stays in the room long enough to learn your name she's intrigued. The dinner invitation was unprecedented."

"Maybe it is because I am nearly her age."

"Bennie is nearly her age."

The chauffeur glanced up in the mirror.

"Maybe it's because you are handsome." David wondered if she was jealous of her own mother. Dierdre leaned into David's shoulder. He lifted his arm and put it around her. A half hour later they stopped in front of the hotel.

"It was a wonderful day," Dierdre said in a lilting voice. "Even with my mother's contribution. Thank you for sharing it with me."

"It was nice to escape."

"Sometimes it's necessary to escape." She sighed. "I do have one regret . . . Besides my mother."

"Oh?"

"The Tunnel of Love was a perfectly good waste of dark," she said playfully. "Are we still on for Friday?"

"Seven o'clock?"

"Swell."

There was another lull, and Dierdre looked away. Finally she said, "This is where you kiss me good night, David."

David grinned sheepishly, then pensively leaned forward to kiss her. A broad smile blanketed her face.

"Night night, sweetie."

"Good night, Dierdre." David stepped out of the car, and Bennie shut the door behind him.

"Good evening, sir."

"Good night, Bennie."

David stood at the curb as the Duesenberg slowly pulled away. Something inside of him ached. Since he had married, MaryAnne was the only woman he had ever kissed.

◆

"This world ain't going to be saved by nobody's scheme. It's fellows with schemes that got us into this mess. Plans can get you into things but you got to work your way out."

WILL ROGERS

◆

Early Friday morning, Dierdre knocked on the door of David's hotel room unannounced. When he finally answered, he wore only a robe, his hair was tousled, and his face, partially concealed beneath a shadow of unshaven stubble, still held the creases of his aborted slumber.

"Good morning, sunshine," she said brightly.

"I thought you meant seven P.M."

"I did. I'm just twelve hours early."

She stalked past him into the room, dressed in a bright print with matching shoes, the ensemble capped by a light green turban, as effervescent as the colors she wore beneath. She systematically set about opening the room's blinds while David watched drowsily.

"You look adorable, all rumpled and unshaven."

"You are fairly glowing. What is Chicago's most refulgent debutante doing out at this hour?"

"I am a woman on a mission." She glanced around the room. "Do you have coffee?"

"Not yet."

"Here. I brought you something." She walked over and handed him a single sheet of paper.

David glanced at it curiously. "Another listing of theaters?"

"Not just any old listing."

He sat down on the sitting room couch to examine the sheet. He noticed a date printed in its text. It read 1902.

"This listing is old."

"Ancient. You will notice that I marked a particular theater. The Gaiety."

The theater's name had been circled in ink.

"What is significant about the Gaiety?"

Dierdre sat down next to him, pausing for emphasis. "It is the theater where your mother performed."

David's face animated from disbelief to excitement. "You found her?"

"I told you that I have connections. An actor friend of mine found her. Congratulations, David, your mother really was here."

"Dierdre, thank you." He put his arms around her. Dierdre felt rhapsodic in his embrace, and her face moved closer to his, brushing up against his rough cheek. She suddenly pressed her lips against his, then put her hands behind his head and pulled his face tighter against hers, moving her body into his. Her turban fell off with the motion. To her surprise, David suddenly pulled back.

"No."

Her eyes flashed an emotion somewhere between bewilderment and anger.

"What is wrong?!"

"I am still married."

His reason enraged her. "Perhaps you should inform your wife, wherever she is, because she seems to have forgotten."

". . . and I still love her."

Dierdre took up her turban, stood, then brushed

down her dress. She exhaled slowly, and her voice softened.

"I'm sorry. I'm just frustrated. Your wife didn't even have the civility to tell you that she was leaving you. I don't see why she should deserve such devotion and I such pain."

"She's still my wife. A deal's a deal."

"She reneged on the deal."

"It is my fault that MaryAnne left. I am not ready to give her up." He looked down. "No matter how attracted I am to you."

His confession surprised both of them. Dierdre walked to the door and opened it. "I admire your loyalty almost as much as I despise it. We felt something, David. Something real."

When the door closed, David shook his head and sighed. After a while he lifted Dierdre's list and looked again at the denoted theater. Somewhere through the years his mother's existence had developed a mythlike quality, and now seeing the theater where she had actually performed filled him with a strange sensation. The Gaiety Theater.

Still unshaven and unkempt, David quickly dressed and descended to the lobby. He returned to the concierge's counter. Despite his appearance, the concierge recognized him from before. "How goes the hunt?"

"I have a theater name, but it is not listed in the directory that you gave me."

"The phone directory is the most current city listing available. What is the name of your theater?"

"The Gaiety." David held up the outdated listing. "It is an older theater."

He examined the list, then returned it.

"Some of these smaller theaters change names and ownerships nearly as often as their productions. Your theater is probably long gone."

David groaned. "Then I am back to where I started."

"I am sorry, sir. I would be happy to check with a few managers of some of the older theaters to see if they know anything about the Gaiety."

"That would be helpful."

"If I find something I will leave a message in your room."

Disheartened, David thanked him, then stepped away from the counter. Just then a young bell captain, corpulent and ruddy-faced, tapped him on the shoulder.

"Excuse me, sir, but I overheard you speaking of the Gaiety Theater."

"Yes. I am looking for it."

"I know a man who worked at the Gaiety. Up until they shut it down."

"Do you know Rose King?"

"I don't know anything about the place except this guy. He worked in the Drake's kitchen for a couple weeks. But he was always stinko. They caught him filching from the liquor shelf and fired him."

"Do you know where I would find him?"

"I still run into him every now and then out front of the hotel. He walks past here to get to an old gin mill about a mile from here. It's called Barleys, or something like that. It's a grey, cinder-block building with no windows, just a door—right across the street from the Rookery on LaSalle."

"What is your friend's name?"

"Fellow's name is Hill. Hill Simons. I don't know how much good he'll be to you. You can bet he'll be loaded for bear."

David handed him a bill. "You don't know how helpful you've been."

The young man pocketed the paper.

"I don't recommend you go down there after dark. It's down near a hobo jungle they call the Hoover Hotel. They'll roll a man down there for a plug nickel."

"Thanks for the tip."

"Anytime, sir." He patted his trouser pocket. "Thank you for yours."

JOHN BARLEYCORN'S TAVERN

"It is folly of our species that we reserve the greatest bouquets for our dead."

DAVID PARKIN'S DIARY. JANUARY 12, 1934

he grey, windowless tavern was nearly as obscure as it was during Prohibition when it was a blind pig, its bootlegging concealed behind the sedate facade of a tobacco shop. Only a crudely hand-painted sign that read JOHN BARLEYCORN'S TAVERN betrayed its locale. A cab released David at the sidewalk fronting the bar, and he walked uneasily into the building, barely acknowledged by the dozen or so denizens who were scattered throughout. The main room was dim and smoke-filled, lit by the weak, yellow incandescence of low-wattage globes and the ocher glow of cigarettes. A barrel-chested, aproned barkeep stood behind a counter polishing a glass with a grey and threadbare dishcloth. A smoldering cigar dangled from one side of his mouth.

"I am looking for Hill Simons."

The barkeep continued his motion as his eyes scrutinized the disheveled newcomer.

"You got money?"

"I do."

He gestured with a toss of his head. "Over there."

At a round table in the corner of the room sat the man—elfish in stature and feature, his bald head framed from rear to temple by tenacious sprigs of hair and long sideburns that fell to his sharp jaw in a scraggly mass. He wore a soiled green shirt and denim jeans, his attire matching his persona—disheveled and sloven. He suckled the rim of an empty glass as he stared blankly ahead. The table was bedecked with several other glass mugs and bottles, all drained except for the foam.

David approached the table.

"Hill Simons?"

The elf looked at him suspiciously, his glassy eyes tinged in the florid markings of inebriation. His mouth was covered by the upper rim of the glass.

"I don't know you," he said flatly, the words echoing in the glass he spoke into.

"I am looking for a woman named Rosalyn King. I was told that you might know where she is."

"Where she is?" he chuckled with a drunken laugh. "Feedin' fish."

David squinted at the cryptic reply, then extended his hand. "David Parkin."

The man made no effort to reciprocate. David lowered his hand.

"What interest you got in Rosie?"

"It's personal."

A smirk crossed the man's face. "Not likely to be professional . . . 'less she owed you money. What kind of personal?"

"My personal," David replied tersely.

The man grunted and turned back to his empty glass, still mourning its demise. "Your personal ain't worth my time."

David looked at the table strewn with dead soldiers, then took two bills from his vest and waved them beneath the man's nose. The man's quick eyes darted back and forth between David and his bribe.

"I will buy drinks as you talk."

The man cautiously reached up and, at David's nod, slipped the bills from his hand. Money pressed in his fist, he raised his hand to the bartender, who turned back to a wooden casket and filled a glass mug. The man looked decidedly relieved. "What you want to know about Rosie? I know it all."

"How did you know her?"

"I was working gas at a burlesque show on the lakeside with her. The Folly. Mostly hoofers. Not much talent but lots of shaking." He smiled weakly. "Folly went out least fifteen years before the Gaiety. Though it never really was in business—not the moneymaking kind. When it went under Rosie swapped to the Gaiety."

"I've never heard of the Folly."

"It ain't around no more. That's how these things are. Life span of a tsetse fly."

"Where do you work now?"

He chortled. "This here's my job. Help 'em clean out their bottles. Haven't worked theater for years."

"Why?"

"What's that got to do with Rosie?"

"Nothing. Just curious."

He wiped at his nose. "Innovations. What's a gas man got to do when there's electric lights?"

"Were you close to Rose?"

"With Rose? Nah. Nobody got close with Rosie. More thorn than flower to that one."

"How do you know so much about her?"

"Hang 'round Rosie long enough, and you'd hear it all—whether you want to or not. Woman was a walking ballad. Though I never suspected much of it was true."

"What was true?"

"Her stories . . . claimed she was the penniless widow of a millionaire gold miner someplace out West in California. Hit it big just after she divorced him. And, there's the boy she left behind and was always cryin' about. Way I see it, if the woman walked, then she ain't got no claim on none of it anyhow. But like I said, don't suspect any of it was true. No one did. Woman just wasn't singing from a full hymnal."

"Both of you came over from the Folly?"

"Yeah, but not at first. When the Folly went under she left town. Said she was going back to her man in Californy. Truth was she was past her prime, and she knew it. Then she came back a month later with a boat-load of money. Crazy amount, more than twenty thousand dollars I heard. Told everyone her son gave her the jake. Some said it proved her story about the millionaire husband, but I didn't give it much credence. She probably put the bite on some fool politician or something. Rose was always catchin' trouble with high-hats. Had the right bait for it."

"What did she do after she got the money?"

"When she was out West she met a guy named Adam Mason. Mason was a has-been stage producer turned charlatan. His ruse was that he was gonna make Rose a big star in his new production. After she was all excited, Mason just happened to lose his financing. He was smooth all right. Real oil merchant. Rosie thought it was her own idea to invest her money in the show. The day she relinquished the jake, Mason run off with two calico skirts and Rosie's last nickel."

David grimaced.

"Just the way it goes in this business. Woman wanted too much too bad, and the devil took her soul without ever deliverin' the goods."

"Then what happened to her?"

"Went on the skids. Next time I saw her she looked to have drunk on fifty pounds or more." He looked at his glass as if talking about her drinking had made him thirsty. "Funny thing, her voice wasn't that bad after that." The man pointed to his throat. "Fat improves the vocals. Just like all those bohunk opera singers. Fat, all of 'em."

"What happened to her?"

"She got her break. They gave her a billing at the Gaiety. Poor Rose," he lamented, shaking his head in mock sympathy. "Ship finally came in, and it sank in the harbor. Show stunk. The Gaiety was already hanging by a prayer. Place went belly-up. Papers blamed it on Rose cuz it was her name on the marquee. Said she had the kind of talent that could darken a stage permanently. Rosie couldn't buy a job after that. She was too fat for the burlesque. So she dropped her own curtain."

"Dropped her curtain?"

The man ran a finger across his throat. "Croaked herself."

David stepped back as if he had received an electrical shock.

"She is dead?"

"More than ten years cold." He gestured with a shaky hand. "It's practically lore. She jumped from a bridge the day they chained the theater doors." An anemic smile crossed his face. "There's a limerick about it. It's kind of catchy."

He spat into one of the drained glasses.

". . . 'once was a woman named King, Who feigned had the talent to sing, But the crowds disagreed, and her failure decreed, So King, from a bridge, took a fling.'"

David just stared at the man.

"She left a letter at the theater tellin' them she was gonna jump. It made all the papers. Not that anyone would remember. Wasn't exactly front page news." He grinned noxiously. "'ronic, ain't it. She wanted to be famous and finally got it. Just wasn't around to enjoy it." He took a drink. ". . . or whatever you do with fame."

David's rage rose against the little man. The man sensed his growing hostility.

"What's this Rose to you?"

"Where's the letter?"

"The theater's new owners got it. Cuthbert and Sinclair. Cuthbert was there when it was found."

"Where do I find this theater?"

"Six, seven miles from here. Down off Burley. It's not the Gaiety no more. It's the Thalia."

David threw a final bill on the table and turned to leave. The man smiled and raised his mug. "Thanks for the sap, sport."

As David walked out of the tavern the elf hailed another round.

CHAPTER SEVENTEEN
THE
GAIETY

"There is no more constant companion than the specter of regret."

DAVID PARKIN'S DIARY. JANUARY 12, 1934

he day the Gaiety Theater closed, the Chicago tabloids eulogized its demise with such eloquent and strident prose that one would never suspect their contribution to its murder—poisoning it with malicious ink. The paper had proclaimed the theater company's swan song, a pirated performance of Gilbert & Sullivan's *H.M.S. Pinafore*, as "the worst tragedy in Chicago theater since the Iroquois Theatre fire."

Like the Iroquois Theatre, the Gaiety's stage was darkened. The bankers added their own toxic ink to the title's default, and the theater's pulse ceased. The marquee was stripped, doors locked and boarded, while Rosalyn King observed in silence as her name fell from the marquee to a jumbled pile of wooden letters, then hobbled twelve blocks to her residence in the lightless tenement houses of Whiskey Row. In the damp, hopeless confines of the tenement, she wrote three letters, left two on the tobacco-stained counter where she had penned them, then, an hour past dusk, slid the third beneath the door of the now vacant theater, and was never heard from again.

The letter, like the theater, was unopened for nearly a decade, until new money breathed life into its vacant halls and galleries. The deed was transferred, carpets pulled up, and the gas lamps replaced by incandescent globes. The lobby, once embellished with gaudy, faux Raphaels, had been overpainted in the streamlined graphics of the art deco style, which was popular at that time. It was during the theater's resurrection that Rose's letter was discovered by a laborer, who immediately surrendered it to his employer—Theodore Cuthbert III.

The entrance to the Thalia was obstructed by an

iron-caged ticket window, shadowed beneath a large marquee that protruded out over the sidewalk, arrayed with large, gilt letters, and a flashing border of electric globes. The outer doors were unlocked, and David entered, glancing around the empty lobby for any indication of occupancy.

The walls and carpeting were cardinal red, and large murals were aligned along the back walls, framed in English walnut borders. To the left of the concessions was a narrow, red door with the word "Office" engraved on a brass plate. David knocked on the door, then, finding it unlocked, twisted the knob and entered.

The room was occupied by the theater's owners: Theodore Cuthbert and Alma F. Sinclair. A rotund, aging gentleman with receding, grey hair sat at a pine writing table cluttered with more trash than the receptacle that lay next to it. His wooden chair, as his demeanor, was casually reclined. The other man, only a few years his junior, was lanky and of autumn complexion. He leaned against the back paneled wall, his umber hair concealed beneath the bowl of a derby. They both took the intruder to be a vagabond.

David guessed at the identity of the seated man. "Mr. Sinclair?"

Surprised to hear his name, the standing man responded. "You have the advantage, sir. I am Sinclair."

"My name is David Parkin. I was told that you are in possession of a letter left by a woman who once performed at this theater. Rosalyn King."

"You a newspaper man?"

"No."

"Newspapers want to see that letter from time to time," said Sinclair.

"Why?"

The seated man spoke. "The legend, of course."

"I don't know anything about a legend."

"Why, then, are you here?" Cuthbert asked with obvious annoyance.

"I was hoping to see the letter."

The husky man leaned forward. "Regrettably, we haven't the time to satisfy every curiosity seeker who lands in here off the street. But if you would like to buy a ticket to tonight's performance, we will gladly see to it."

David stood dormant. He looked at the two men for a moment, then said softly, "I have greater interest in the letter than mere curiosity. Rosalyn King was my mother."

His words seemed to hang in the air, affecting the men with a gravity David could not have anticipated. The two men exchanged glances of astonishment.

"You are Rose King's son?" Sinclair asked.

"King was my mother's maiden name. Her stage name as well. She abandoned my father and me."

"Good Lord, it is just like the letter!" Cuthbert gasped.

"I would like to see the letter," David repeated.

"We have it locked away in the vault," Cuthbert said. "It is valuable."

". . . valuable?"

"The business that has been generated from that one letter probably accounts for a quarter of our take. Maybe more," Sinclair said.

Cuthbert leaned forward. "A little more than twenty years ago, for one week, your mother was the star performer here. Her show failed and the theater with it. The theater used to be called the Gaiety. It was teetering on the brink of financial ruin for several years, in fact, nothing short of a miracle would have saved it.

But Rose was blamed for the failure. The day they closed the house, your mother slid a letter between the front doors. Just before she took her life. When we purchased the theater back in eighteen, a worker found the letter on the lobby floor. I was there at the time and witnessed its opening."

Sinclair stood from the wall. "There were actually three letters. We possess only one of them. One was written to her landlady. The other, presumably, was for you. She lived in a tenement a mile or two from here, down on Whiskey Row. Her landlady brought them by, thinking she could get us to pay some of Rose's old debts. Seems her rent was in arrears. Everyone's is these days, but back then it was criminal."

"What of this legend? And what does my mother's letter have to do with it?"

"Your mother . . ." Sinclair paused to glance over to Cuthbert, as if seeking his approval to proceed. ". . . your mother is considered, by some, to be a ghost."

David looked at Sinclair incredulously. He continued. "The letter was a suicide note. She cursed the previous owners and wrote about haunting them."

David's face stiffened. "Haunting?"

". . . and she mentioned you," Cuthbert added.

"What did she say of me?"

"She spoke of your return. In fact there has been verse written about it."

"I've heard the limerick."

Cuthbert pulled on his fingers until the joints popped. ". . . 'so King, from a bridge, took a fling.' That is not the one I was referring to. There is another."

"I didn't know."

"There is a ritual that occurs before each performance," Sinclair interjected. "It is followed religiously. The performers gather around a vase and drop in a coin. Then they chant, 'A penny for Rose—a prayer for her son—that the take may be vast—and her child will come.'"

David did not respond but looked down thoughtfully. The partners joined his solitude.

"And I came."

"Yes you did." Cuthbert rubbed his chin. "Yes, you certainly did. I am not the superstitious type, mind you, but I do find this all rather odd."

David was unsure of what to think. It was certainly not the end he believed he would meet. "Does my mother haunt the halls?"

"If there is an apparition, I have never seen it," said

Sinclair. "Though it is no surprise to me that they imagine the thing. These are thespians. They fancy a shadow
into a phantom."

"They also believe the world will someday throw
daisies at their feet," Cuthbert mocked. "You tell me
which is more likely."

"May I see the letter?"

Cuthbert took from his desk's side drawer a key
attached to a heavy brass ring and tossed it to his partner. Sinclair left the office, then returned a moment later
with the letter and handed it to David. David extracted
the well-creased parchment from the envelope and carefully unfolded the paper. The scrawl looked similar to
that in the letters he had scrutinized in his den.

◆

March 17, 1912

To the proprietors of the Gaiety.

Messrs.

*With the closure of the Gaiety, you have effectively ended my
career, as my life, for they are the same. Tonight, I shall throw
myself from the Troop Street bridge. May my demise haunt your
despicable lives and the curtain fall on all of your ambitions, as
they have mine. I regret having been enslaved by the bonds of my*

ambitions. But I confess a greater regret, that I mistook this pantomime for something real—a life that might have brought lasting joy instead of the vaporous illusion of fame and fortune. My husband died in my absence. I have not seen my son since he was but six. I once fantasized that one day he would come to the theater to see me perform, and that our reunion would be grand. I am now certain that he should only know the bitterness of betrayal. Adieu.

ROSALYN KING

◆

There ensued a moment of thoughtful solitude. Finally Cuthbert cleared his throat. "Gaston Leroux has made the haunted theater of popular consequence, as well as financial. I do not suppose that we shall tell anyone of your appearance. You are much more useful as lore."

"No," David replied stoically. "I don't suppose you will."

"Are you staying in town?"

"At the Drake Hotel."

The men were surprised at the answer, as his state of dishevelment would not even qualify him as kitchen help at the luxurious inn.

"Then we may surmise that you are affluent," Sinclair said.

David nodded matter-of-factly. Cuthbert drew out several printed passes, offering them to David. "If you would please, they are vouchers for tonight's show."

David accepted the tickets.

"May I walk through your theater? I would like to see where my mother once performed."

"As you please. It has all been refurbished since she was here, but the main stage and fascia are principally the same. Take as much time as you wish. You can leave the way you entered."

"Thank you."

David left the men's company and entered the theater beneath the overhang of a balcony which shadowed a third of the main floor and, at each side of the auditorium, protruded in a single thrust of stepped, box seats. The floor gradually declined to a modest-sized, elliptical stage, its foot dressed in jet-black fabric. Massive red curtains, gold-ribbed and fringed, were pulled open and gathered to the stage's extremities, tied back in great, gilt ropes. Gold-leafed statues of demon-faced Greek gods and nymphs were carved into the large arch facade that encircled the stage. The stage was occupied with the sets and props of the current production—a southern scene with white picket fences and facades of homes propped up by obscured wooden beams.

He scanned the room, advanced slowly to the stage's perimeter, climbed the dais, then walked out to center stage, where his mother had once performed. The floorboards groaned beneath him, and each step confessed the platform's longevity. From the back of the stage, he heard the gentle fall of footsteps. David followed the sound, stepping to the side of the bound curtain into the shadow of the wings. He suddenly shook his head in wry amusement. At his feet lay an earthen jar nearly filled to its brim with copper pennies. More footfalls. He took a deep breath and looked around the dark, seemingly vacant stage back. To his own surprise, he suddenly whispered in a hushed, forced voice, "Mother?" He took a few more steps in the direction of the footfalls. "Mother?"

"Mr. Parkin?"

David spun to his side. Cuthbert stood alone at the backstage doorway wearing a perplexed countenance.

"I am sorry if I startled you. I thought this would be of interest to you."

He handed David a torn piece of paper with an address scrawled across it.

"It is the address of the tenement house where your mother boarded. It is about a dozen blocks north, just over the Troop Street bridge she jumped from. I don't know if they are still standing, but I suspect they are. Cost more to demolish them than they are worth."

"Thank you. Do these doors exit to the street?"

"Out to Fifty-third."

David folded the paper into his pocket and left the building. He walked nearly a mile before he remembered the night's engagement and hailed a cab back to the hotel to meet Dierdre for dinner. He had no idea whether she would come or not, but after the morning's incident he expected to be dining alone.

CHAPTER EIGHTEEN

DIERDRE'S PROPOSITION

"Still no word from MaryAnne. My feelings cannot be far distant from those of the dustbowl farmer who, looking out over his withered fields to the blanched sky above, wonders why it will not rain."

DAVID PARKIN'S DIARY. JANUARY 11, 1934

t ten minutes past the top of the hour, Dierdre sauntered into the dining room followed, as usual, by the ardent gaze of the waiters and male patrons and the indignant or envious gazes of the womenfolk. She was dressed casually in a pleated salmon crepe skirt with a cap of matching fabric. She wore a sheer silk blouse. David rose and pulled back her chair.

"I'm sorry I'm late," she said, smiling sheepishly.

"You look very nice," David said.

"It is a little daring. I thought that you might like it." Her smile receded. "Thank you for being here. I need to say this first. I want to apologize for this morning."

"There is no need."

"Yes there is. I had no right to be angry. There should be more men like you. I just wished it was me you were loyal to."

David smiled, but had no idea what to say.

"Did the lead I brought you help?"

David nodded, and Dierdre's face animated in genuine excitement.

"You found your mother?"

"In a sense." His voice lowered. "My mother is dead. She committed suicide thirteen years ago."

Dierdre covered her mouth. "Oh, David. I am so sorry."

"I cannot believe that I have come all this way to leave without answers."

His words filled her with dread.

"Then you will be leaving soon?"

"Not until the day after tomorrow. I still need to visit the tenement house she once lived in. I was told that she left a letter for me there."

Her demeanor grew more somber. "I will be sorry to see you go," she said softly. Neither spoke for a moment. "David. Remember the other day, when you asked me if I believed in fate?"

He nodded.

"I believe that you were meant to come to Chicago. But not necessarily for the reasons you think." She looked at him seriously. "These last few days have been very special. I have learned a lot about myself and life that I didn't know before. I have experienced feelings that are new to me. There is an inexplicable chemistry between us."

David gazed at her intently.

"What is left for you in Salt Lake City but pain?"

"My home."

"This would be a better home. We belong together, David. We would be very happy." She smiled. "We would be the toast of society. The Fitzgeralds of Chicago—Scott and Zelda. It would be a magnificent life we would share. And I would be proud to be seen on your arm." She took his hand. "I know this is a confusing time. But you care for me, David. And I care deeply for you. There is nothing complicated about that."

David looked down.

"Please tell me that you care for me."

David said nothing, and Dierdre's eyes began to moisten.

"Then tell me that you don't. Tell me that you have no feelings for me, and I will leave you alone."

Again David could not respond.

She touched the corner of her eye. "You do have feelings for me, David. Deny it if it soothes your conscience, but they are there."

David finally blurted out, "Of course they are there. How could they not be? Do you think that I don't notice that you are beautiful? Everywhere we go every eye is on you. Yet that desire is impotent compared to my other feelings. You are like ether. You waltz through life on a cloud while I carry the world on my shoulders. You offer to relieve Atlas of his burden, how could I resist?"

"You seem to be doing quite well."

"You don't believe that."

She paused. "No. I know that you aren't." Her voice rose. "So let someone else carry the world for a while. You cannot change the past or rectify the world's ills. And it will only kill you trying. I am yours, David, and all my world. It is time you are given the love you deserve."

"I have always been given the love I deserve. It is I who have shut out that love and brought such pain to MaryAnne."

"Then release her from it and let her get on with her life. From all that you have told me she is wonderful. I cannot imagine that you would marry less. Free her to find love. And free yourself."

"You use my words against me."

"For you. You are good to everyone but yourself. You have whipped yourself with guilt for so long that you don't know how to behave otherwise. You are not responsible for your daughter's death, and whatever twisted satisfaction you derive from blaming yourself won't make it so. Do you know what I think?"

David made no motion to respond, though he was clearly listening.

"I think that you are trying to run yourself to death. You are more gaunt each time I see you. You look like you haven't slept in a week. Someone has to save you from yourself. And it ought to be me, because I love you."

Her words pierced him as deeply as her gaze.

"I have never loved anyone so madly or desperately before. All the good in you, your loyalty, your kindness.

I want you for my own, and I know that you feel the same way."

David sat quietly for a moment. "I need to think this over."

She leaned over the table and kissed him. "I will make you very happy, David. I promise you."

Then she kissed him on the lips, and this time David did not resist. She withdrew, then stood from the table, her gaze still fixed on his. "I'll be waiting for your call."

WHISKEY ROW

"It is strange to me that two women could share such close proximity in my mind, yet be worlds apart. And only one of them cares to be there."

DAVID PARKIN'S DIARY. JANUARY 12, 1934

he perpetual noise of the metropolis wove through David's broken sleep, and at four twenty-seven he woke and lay on the rigid bed thinking about MaryAnne and Dierdre. MaryAnne had never before seemed so far away. He had never felt so alone. When the blinds glowed beneath the dawn light, he shaved, dressed, then lay back on the bed, and, without intending to, fell back asleep. When he finally woke, he checked his wristwatch and found it nearly eleven. He splashed water in his face, grabbed his jacket, then hurried down to the lobby. It was a cold day, and the bellboy rubbed his hands together as David approached.

"Taxi, sir?"

David nodded, and the man stepped out into the street and, placing a silver whistle to his lips, hailed the first of the line of cabs that awaited the hotel's patrons. He opened the door for David, who handed him a quarter. The driver looked up into his rearview mirror.

"Where to, fella?"

"Do you know this place?" David handed the driver the paper with the tenement's address. The driver confirmed the destination, then handed it back.

"You sure you want to go there, fella? It's a rough spot of town."

"I am sure."

"All right, then."

He put the motorcar in gear and started off towards the "back of the yards" and the tenements of Whiskey Row. The city's landscape and architecture became increasingly miserable as they approached the blight of the meatpacking district and its surrounding fertilizer mills and dumps, all divulging their presence with their putrid contributions to the local air. Smoke rose from squat stacks atop the myriad buildings, concealed behind high fences where each morning faceless men, women, and children of destitution lined up for daily wages amid the greenbackers and socialists who prose-lytized in their ranks. Though they came from all lands, they were but one nationality and one tongue—they were the impoverished, and their dialect was the voice of desperation. Even still, they, too, embraced the local mores of selective racism and shunned the Negroes who competed with them for work. Even the unionists, who espoused fiscal equality, shunned the blacks on the grounds that they were used as scabs—strikebreakers—only to be discarded by the plant owners after their objectives were met. There were no politics to the Negroes, only hunger.

Further south, David rolled up the taxi's window as the rank smell had reached intolerable levels and the driver pointed out the fetid waters of Bubbly Creek, where the blood and carcasses of the slaughtered ani-mals were discarded and the stench was born.

At the mouth of the Troop Street bridge, he could see the jagged rooftops of the tenements huddled tightly together, as a mouth of crooked teeth—as crowded in structure as they were in inhabitants of their damp and

sullen rooms. The streets outside the tenements were litter strewn and desolate, except for a few vagrants, who
walked with vacant eyes and spoke loudly to unseen
companions, and the smallest of children of Slav or
Lithuanian descent, who played, barefoot, in the
unpaved streets of the slums—as they were too young
to be of value to the packing houses.

The cab stopped in front of a stone-slab entryway,
and David examined the frame house. Its windows—
those exposed to the street—were clouded by dirt or
replaced with wood panels where glass had broken. A
yard toilet was visible at the side of the residence, surrounded by the litter that seemed to accumulate everywhere in the slums and piled up in drifts against the
houses' foundations like windswept snow. He confirmed the address, then ascended the tenement's short
steps and pounded on the door. About a minute later
he heard the approach of hobbling footsteps. The
door swung open to a hard and surly woman dressed in
soiled clothing that hung from the obese body in
crumpled drapes. She was old, and her face appeared
even more ancient than her advanced years—pocked
and blemished by the sun.

"Whad'ya want?" she asked harshly.

"I am looking for a Mrs. Talbot," David replied.

The woman gazed on, cupping a hand to her ear. "Whad'ya say?"

David raised his voice. "I am looking for Mrs. Talbot."

"Whad'ya want her fer?"

"Do you know her?"

"Whad'ya want her fer?" she repeated.

"I was told that she knew my mother—Rosalyn King."

She stared at him for a moment, then replied in a hoarse, but calmer, voice, "That's a name I never thought I'd hear again."

She glanced suspiciously at the taxi. "Who's that with you?"

"The cab driver."

The woman stared at him dubiously, but decided him harmless.

David gestured towards the lobby. "May I come in?"

"Ya want to come inside?"

"Please."

She stepped away from the door, and David followed her tedious motion as she hobbled up a short flight of stairs to an open room. The building reeked of rotting wood and other stenches from undistinguishable sources. The room was dingy and as battered as its absent boarders. Holes were broken through the lath and plaster walls, and the tobacco-stained floor was littered with whiskey bottles and food cans, infested with cockroaches. A bare mattress lay in one corner of the room next to a small coal stove. Beneath the room's only window, a single water faucet emptied into a stained washbasin. The woman motioned to a dilapidated wooden chair.

"This is where she lived?" David asked in repulsion.

"More'n three years." She sniffed, then wiped her nose with her sleeve. "Rose owed me money, you know."

David continued to survey the room. "I will pay some of her debt."

The woman's face twisted into a ghastly and toothless expression only vaguely definable as a smile.

"How'd you find the place?"

"The owners of the Thalia Theater . . ."

"Screws!" she screamed, her cheeks flushed. "Niggardly, stingy, tightwad, penny-pinchin' screws!"

She was left scowling and breathless by the tirade, and David waited for her to calm.

"You said my mother lived here for three years."

"Least three years."

"Can you tell me what she was like?"

"Rose was just Rose. Hungry for somethin' like it just ate at her. Some folk just ain't ever gonna be content. Grew kinda peculiar in the end. Spoke her name like someone might recognize it. R–ose K–ing," the woman mocked, holding the vowels of both names. "Talked 'bout herself like she was another person. Rose King did this. Rose King don't like that."

"I was told that you might have a letter that she left for me."

"A letter? Who told you that?"

David avoided the trap. "Just heard."

"Don't know about no letter," she said, dismissing the query. She suddenly cackled. "Paranoid too, Rose was. Always was the conspiracies. Blamed her failure on the damned Trust. She never said 'the Trust,' always said, 'damned Trust,' like it was its name." She interrupted herself, "You know, I think I might got something of hers." She stood up and walked over to a closet. As she searched through its rubble, David examined an ancient playbill still tacked to the wall.

"Is this my mother?"

The woman laughed and turned from her search. "What are ya, a rube? That's famous ol' Minnie Fisk, the actress. Your mother idolized Minnie. Had her playbills all stuck up to the walls, while she labored as a scrubwoman. She used to say that Minnie Fisk was made famous for the part of a scrubwoman, and she did a more convincing job of it every day. Cleaned a good toilet, Rose. Like to see someone get Minnie Fisk to do that."

David sat back down.

"She was tough as shoe leather. Hard to believe she did herself in. Just before, she kept saying that she oughta pack up and go to California. They make movies in California. It's easy work, the movies. But she never went." She said as if it had just occurred to her, "Maybe she should've went."

"You were looking for something," David reminded her.

"Oh, yeah, that box. Rose left a box of her stuff." She buried her head back into the closet. "Tripped over that thing for years. Damned if I don't know where it is now." After another minute she concluded her search. "Guess I musta just thrown it out."

David frowned in disappointment. "You're sure it's not somewhere else?"

"Ain't no place else." She pointed to the closet. "You're welcome to look yourself."

David stood, no longer able to bear the woman's or the room's repulsiveness.

"How much did my mother owe you?"

"Well, it been a long time. She didn't pay for nearly six months. Maybe twenty dollars."

David handed her thirty in three bills. "There's interest included with that."

Her eyes lit at the sight of money. "That's jake I never thought I'd see." She snatched the money, afraid that he might change his mind.

David reached into his pocket. "Here's my calling card. If you do find something, I am staying at the Drake Hotel."

As he walked from the building, she dropped the card to the floor with the other refuse.

David climbed back into the car.

"Back to the Drake," he said.

The driver happily obliged.

◆

As they crossed a steel-girdered bridge just a few blocks from the tenement, David asked, "What bridge is this?"

"The Troop Street."

"Hold up a moment," he said. "Just pull up to the side of the road past the bridge."

"Your dime. Meter's still running."

David climbed out of the car. Near the entrance to the bridge a ragged peddler, buffeted by the cold winds, stood next to a flower cart filled with a hodgepodge of jugs and kettles, make-do receptacles for his cut flowers—a potpourri of tulips, snapdragons and mums, and heather, gerber daisies, and roses.

David approached the peddler.

"I would like a rose. A red one."

The man spoke with a heavy, Lithuanian accent. "Don't sell 'em as one. Sell a bunch. Two bits a bunch."

David handed the man a coin, which the decrepit man exchanged for a bouquet, then drew out one stem, and let the rest fall to the ground. He advanced along the pedestrian walkway onto the bridge.

A quarter way up the expanse, he stopped and climbed atop an iron girder of the bridge's trestlework, then, clinging to a weathered cable, stared out over the water. His mother's last sight. More than sixty feet below, the azure, windswept river churned into meringue crests, sometimes obscured beneath a frozen mist. The banks of the river were steep and sharply cut. If one survived a fall from the bridge, they would be paralyzed by hypothermia and unable to climb the steep embankment—even if they had the Herculean strength required to cross the river's icy torrent. He stood only five inches from his own death, and the simplicity of that fact was not lost on him. Where was his MaryAnne? Not what continent, or even where her heart laid, but, rather, where was she in his own heart? He remembered a day when he had knelt before her and, on bended knee, held her shaking hand and proposed their marriage. Her eyes were wet, tears born anew in celebration of his love instead of the agony she felt just moments before as she spoke of her wretched circumstance and her shameful pregnancy. His love had rescued her, she had said, and now he wondered if it would rescue him. He gazed out over the deadly waters for many minutes. Then, an astonishing thought came to him—an insight that had eluded him since his daughter's death. In view of the murky waters he began to see things very clearly.

He released the rose and watched it fall, dancing on the strings of the wind's caprices until it disappeared from sight into the turbid water. He tarried in the spot for a few more minutes, then, with purpose, stepped down from the ledge and walked back to the idling cab. At his return, the driver looked relieved.

He said after David had climbed back in, "Thought for a moment you might be thinkin' of jumpin'."

"You didn't lose your fare," David answered. "Take me back to the Drake."

CHAPTER TWENTY
CATHERINE'S TELEGRAM

"It is of little consolation to learn of my mother's wretched past. For as miserable as it was she still chose it over me."

DAVID PARKIN'S DIARY. JANUARY 12, 1934

s David reentered the hotel, he was mistaken for a vagrant and accosted by the Drake's security. To his misfortune, he carried nothing to identify himself, except a suspiciously large wad of money and his room key, which, once revealed, produced the unfortunate effect of convincing the guard that the vagabond had fallen on one of the hotel's guests, emptied his purse, and now sought to further capitalize on his felony by cleaning out his room as well. The Chicago police were summoned, and such commotion ensued that it was noticed by one of the hotel's bellboys—a recipient of David's generosity—who rushed to David's defense and identification. A mortified and contrite guard followed David into the hotel and showered him with fervent apologies until David assured the man that he would not complain to the hotel management of the incident if he would just leave him alone. As David crossed the crowded lobby, he was flagged by the concierge.

"How are you today, Mr. Parkin?"

"I am fine," David replied tersely, still agitated from his brief detention.

He held out an envelope. "You have just received an urgent telegram."

David took the note.

MR. DAVID PARKIN.
DRAKE HOTEL. CHICAGO, ILLINOIS.
LAWRENCE SUFFERED STROKE. TAKEN TO HOUSE.
RETURN IMMEDIATELY. CATHERINE.

David turned to the concierge. "Do you have a train schedule?"

"Yes, sir," he replied, reaching for the timetable.

"When does the next train depart for Salt Lake?"

He ran his finger down the page. "Ten minutes past five. A little over two hours from now."

"Thank you." David handed him a five-dollar bill. "Thank you for all of your assistance."

"It has been my pleasure, Mr. Parkin. Would you like me to call the train depot."

"Please. If you would."

As he turned to go, the concierge stopped him again. "Mr. Parkin. Pardon my oversight. This parcel arrived for you as well."

He set a large beige envelope, stamped with a Chicago address, on the edge of the counter. It was from the Thalia Theater. David tore back its flap as he walked to the elevator. Inside was a letter written on embossed stationery, a playbill, a pair of silver-rimmed eyeglasses, and a skeleton key tied with a saffron ribbon.

◆

Mr. Parkin,

Your visit of yesterday was so unanticipated, we fear we behaved rather crassly. Please accept our sincerest apologies. We neglected to present to you these articles that once belonged to your mother. Also, Mr. Sinclair came across this playbill and thought it might be of interest. Please receive them with our kindest regards.

At your service,

THEODORE CUTHBERT AND ALMA F. SINCLAIR

◆

David guessed the key belonged to the tenement house, examined the glasses, then extracted the playbill. Its cover was graced by the rotund and buxom form of a woman. A wide-brimmed hat partially shadowed her face yet failed to conceal the beauty of her haunting eyes. He looked at it briefly, then returned it to the envelope and went to his room to pack.

◆

"It has been a mistake living my life in the past. One cannot ride a horse backwards and still hold its reins."

DAVID PARKIN'S DIARY. JANUARY 13, 1934

◆

David lay on the sleeping berth of the westbound train—his mind filled with emotions as converse as the direction itself. The playbill's picture of his mother haunted him, and when he slept he slept fitfully, revealed in the dark shadows of his eyes.

In his sudden departure he had left unfinished business, for he had not had the opportunity to speak with Dierdre, and his thoughts now revolved in a kaleidoscope of four women: MaryAnne, Andrea, Dierdre, and Rose—a very different image than the one he had carried with him to Chicago. On the bridge's expanse he had experienced a quiet epiphany, and though the identity of the author who had left the letter at the angel was now a greater mystery than ever, it was no longer of any import. Whether he had received Catherine's telegram or not, he was ready to go home.

The lumbering train entered the Salt Lake depot late Thursday afternoon beneath affable, cloud-pocked skies. He reclaimed his automobile from a dirt lot south of the station and drove home. At the opening of the front door, Catherine rushed down the stairs to greet him.

"Welcome home, David!"

She threw her arms around him. He had lost weight and his complexion was wan, his eyes revealing the succession of sleepless nights. She scolded him.

"You have not taken care of yourself."

"No worse than usual. How is Lawrence faring?"

"He is doing a little better. I have put him up in the east guest room."

"Good. We have much to talk about."

Catherine looked distressed by the remark.

"David, that won't be possible."

He looked at her quizzically.

"The stroke left him unable to speak. He is responding now, a little, but I do not know if he recalls anything from before. I am not even certain that he knows who I am."

David's face fell, and he grasped the stairs' banister.

"Oh, my friend," he said. He started up the stairway, followed by Catherine. As he entered the dimly lit room he could see Lawrence's husky form shrouded by thick quilts. He walked to his side.

"Lawrence?"

At first there was no motion, then Lawrence slowly turned towards him, mumbling incoherently. David took his hand. "How are you, my friend?"

Lawrence said nothing. David's eyes moistened.

"How long has he been like this?"

"I found him unconscious Monday morning last. He is doing a little better since then, but the doctor does not anticipate any more improvement."

David took her arm and led her out of Lawrence's hearing.

"What else has the doctor said?"

"There is grave danger of another stroke or heart attack." Catherine could see in David's eyes the sadness her news produced. She embraced him again. "You must be exhausted. Let me get you some supper."

David looked back at his silent friend. "Thank you for all that you have done, Catherine. I will sit with him awhile."

"If I had known you would be returning today, I would have prepared a more fitting meal. I have only made bread and soup."

"After the train's cuisine, that is feast enough."

She left the room as David returned to the quiet bed-side. David sat still for a moment, then suddenly began to speak with Lawrence as it had been before—as if they sat around the warped table of Lawrence's shanty and Lawrence's deep eyes reflected the glow of his pipe while words of deep consideration filled the air.

"I just arrived back from Chicago . . . I don't know if you remember . . . I was going to go look for my mother . . . because I found that letter and thought she was still alive." David pulled a slipped corner of a blanket up over Lawrence's muscular shoulder. "It didn't go quite how I expected it would, but I got my answers. Turns out that my mother never amounted to anything, and she ended up jumping from a bridge. My whole life I have felt like I needed to talk to her, to ask her why she left me. But I realized that what I really wanted to know is why I wasn't worthy of her love. That is something she couldn't have answered, because I was worthy of her love, whether she gave it to me or not. Every child is worthy of love." David sniffed, then rubbed his nose. "In a way, she was also looking for love. She thought she could find it in the applause of an audience. But what good is the love of strangers if your life is of no value to your own child?"

David paused.

"I met this other woman. Her name is Dierdre. You would like her—she's a firebrand. How would you say it . . ." He smiled. ". . . hotter than July jam. Anyway, something stuck her good. I don't know what she saw in me, she could do much better. The man part of me didn't have any objections, just the husband part. I have to admit that it felt good to be cared for by her. Made me feel young again. But she wasn't MaryAnne. You were right about that tree thing, the love tree, or whatever you called it. I am not ready to let the tree die. MaryAnne and I have given each other the best of ourselves and maybe the worst, too, but either way, we both own a significant portion of each other. That's not something you can just walk away from. When you are feeling better I am going to go to England to bring her back. What do you think of that?"

Lawrence did not make a sound, and David sighed.

"Where have you gone to, my friend?" He sat back in the darkness and, once again, was joined by the too familiar companionship of loss.

◆

"It is an awkward thing for a loved one to retain their breath but lose their faculties. I feel as though my heart has been cheated, as I have lost a friend and am not allowed to grieve his passing."

DAVID PARKIN'S DIARY. JANUARY 16, 1934

◆

Later that same evening, as the city was cloaked beneath a blackened curtain pierced by the pinpricks of a million stars, a tall, dark-haired woman stepped from a taxi that had parked out front of the Parkin mansion. She carried only a bag, its strap parting her breast over a grey wool coat. She ascended the home's driveway and pounded the great brass knocker on the front door. Catherine met the stranger, then, after a brief exchange, invited her in. A few moments later Catherine entered Lawrence's infirmary. With animated motion she gestured to David, and he came to the doorway.

"There is a woman in the foyer that has come to see Lawrence," Catherine whispered.

"Who is she?"

"Her name is Sophia. Do you know her?"

David remembered the name from an earlier conversation.

"No. But Lawrence has spoken of her. Who does she say she is?"

Catherine's eyes widened. "She says she is Lawrence's daughter."

CHAPTER TWENTY-ONE
SOPHIA

"Sophia's arrival at this time is too fantastic for mere coincidence . . . the fact that Lawrence had a daughter explains many things, but most of all why he held our daughter Andrea so dear."

DAVID PARKIN'S DIARY. JANUARY 15, 1934

avid stood on the parapet overlooking the foyer. Down below, a woman, slightly older than himself, sat on a walnut side chair, quietly looking down at the marble floor. He descended the stairway, and when she saw him, she rose, apprehensively following his descent with her eyes. Her skin was a fair mahogany, and though her features were dark, they were also sharp and hinted of European descent, giving her a Mediterranean appearance. Still, in her deep-set, umber eyes and the gentle slope of her jaw, he could see her father's endowments.

"Mr. Parkin, I am Sophia Disera," she said in beautiful diction.

David extended his hand. "Please call me David."

"Thank you. I was told that my father is being cared for here. I have come a long way to see him."

David extended his hand. "Allow me to take your coat."

She slipped the garment off, and he hung it on the room's walnut hall tree.

"How did you know that your father was here?"

"I didn't. I came to inquire if you knew of his whereabouts. A man with a fruit cart over on Brigham Street said that you and my father were friends. Your housekeeper told me that he is here."

"Are you aware of his condition?"

Her countenance turned more anxious. "His condition? Your housekeeper said that you have been caring for him. Is he ill?"

"Lawrence has had a stroke. He can no longer speak. We have no way of knowing if he even recognizes our voices."

"Your voices?"

"Your father is blind."

In shock, she lifted a hand to her breast. "Then I am

too late," she said, sitting back down and clasping her hands in her lap. After a moment she said, "I should still like to see him."

"Of course." David held out his hand and helped her rise. "He is upstairs." David led her to the corridor outside the guest room and opened its door, revealing Lawrence's silhouette. She walked in alone, shutting the door behind herself. David sat down outside the door. From time to time he could hear her gentle voice, but always to no response. Fifteen minutes later she came from the room. She sobbed heavily. As he approached her, she collapsed. David called for Catherine, who rushed upstairs from the kitchen. She opened the door of the adjoining guest room for David, who carried in the woman and laid her on the bed. Catherine returned with a damp cloth which she laid across the woman's forehead. Only a few minutes later Sophia's eyes fluttered, then opened. A confused expression blanketed her face.

"You have fainted, Sophia," David said softly.

She closed her eyes. "It was such a shock."

She looked again at the two strangers who stood over her. "I am sorry to cause such trouble. I should return to my hotel."

"Nonsense," Catherine said. "You will stay here tonight."

"You will remain with us," David concurred. "Just rest."

A few moments after Catherine had left to care for Lawrence, Sophia said to David, "I only learned that my father was alive two months ago. When my mother died. The last words on her lips were for Lawrence."

"What is your mother's name?"

"Margaret."

He nodded. "Of course. That is why he was behaving so strangely. He must have known of her death. How did you learn of him?"

"After my mother died I began to go through her things. I came across a large trunk filled with correspondence. There were more than a thousand letters, dated as far back as 1874. All of them were from Lawrence. I spent the next three weeks piecing together their story through their letters. My father met my mother when he was a soldier in the tenth cavalry my grandfather commanded. Over several years they fell in love and were married. Not legally, of course. It was unthinkable for a white woman to marry a Negro—even if no one

else wanted her. So they decided that they would perform their own ceremony.

"They took their own vows and hid their love behind
secret rendezvous. Every few weeks my mother would
supposedly go off to visit a college friend, and he would
take leave. In public he traveled as her valet, and no one
ever suspected. The arrangement worked fine until she
got pregnant. As she started to show, they got scared.
My mother knew her father would have Lawrence
lynched if he found out. So they fabricated an alibi that
she had eloped with a Cuban soldier. They had a falsi-
fied wedding document. She even pretended to receive
letters from him for a while. Then one day she informed
her parents that her husband had been killed in combat.
It was a lie I lived with my whole life.

"Despite their love they took a vow that they would
never see each other again." Her eyes filled with tears.
"I used to try to imagine what my father looked like. In
my imagination he was always a tall, beautiful
Spaniard, with flowing hair and the statuesque
physique of a warrior."

"Your father was a great man, Sophia."

Sophia looked down. "I want to believe that."

"What did you mean by 'no one else wanted your mother'?"

"No one, except Lawrence, ever called my mother beautiful. My mother was a beautiful woman, David, but not because society would bestow the title. She was beautiful because her spirit was beautiful. The world shunned her as disfigured and hideous. Most of my mother's face was covered with a cruel birthmark. I don't think Lawrence could see the blemish. In a way he was the same as her, they were both victims of their skin."

"What a shock this must all be to you."

"My mother didn't want anyone to know that I was half Negro—she even hid it from me. She prayed that I would be fair-skinned. A 'pe-ola.' She straightened my hair with pomade and a curling iron." She smiled sadly. "Imagine my surprise when I found out that my father was a Negro—that I am a Negro. Every belief that I accepted from society I now have to atone for with my own self-perspective. I do not feel any different than I did yesterday. I do not look or speak or think differently. But today I am a Negro. Am I to think less of myself?

"Mama worked hard to teach me that people are people and not to be judged by their appearances. I once thought that she taught me this because of her own flesh, her own mark. It wasn't so. It was to save me. She taught me so that I would not hate myself someday."

"Your mother was wise."

Sophia reflected on her mother and smiled distantly. "She was a good woman. She always knew the right thing to say."

"That is what I always said of MaryAnne."

"MaryAnne is your housekeeper?"

"No. That is Catherine. MaryAnne is my wife."

"She is out tonight?"

David hesitated. "No. She is away."

Sophia sensed that there was more to his answer and did not pursue it further. After a moment she said, "You know he mentioned you in his letters. He wrote of you as if you walked on water."

"He lied. I have trouble swimming."

She smiled. "In one of the letters he wrote about you claiming to have shot a man that he killed in self-defense. And he told her about your daughter. I feel like I know you, David."

David took her hand. "I am truly sorry that you cannot speak with your father. For both of you." He glanced over at the mantelpiece clock. "You better get some rest. I have to go into work early, but I will be back in the afternoon. What hotel holds your things?"

"The Beehive Room."

"If you do not object, I will pick up your things for you on my way back from work. Until then I am sure that we have whatever you may need at the house. Catherine will see to you."

She smiled gratefully. "Thank you, David. For everything."

BOGGS'S DISMISSAL

"The winds of depression have blown the dust from the horsewhip, noose, and hood . . ."

A NEWSPAPER CLIPPING

FOUND IN DAVID PARKIN'S DIARY,

BELIEVED GIVEN TO HIM BY GIBBS

avid departed early for work in anticipation of the mountain of documents that was certain to have piled up in his absence. As the red-bricked edifice of the Parkin Machinery Company came to view on the corner of second south, he noticed a crowd of considerable size gathered at the west end of his building. It was not unusual for a crowd of indigents to be gathered near his business to inquire for daily work, only this morning their ranks had swelled, joined by men and women dressed in business attire, drawn as spectators to the same site by some mutual force of fascination.

David could not see what held such interest until he parked his car and stepped to the curb. Hanging from his building's awning, from a rope around his neck, was a black man's lifeless body. David knew the man as Carville, an employee of nearly twenty years. He was a good man with a cheerful disposition. He had well earned his position as the company's night foreman, and only three years previous David had recommended the promotion himself. David angrily shoved his way to the front of the throng, removed his coat, and began swinging it angrily at the crowd.

"Get out of here, you vultures! Get away from my building!"

Slowly, the crowd began to dissipate. Taking a pocket knife from his trousers, he cut the rope and, despite his effort, the body fell heavily to the concrete sidewalk. The man's hands had been tied behind his back, then lashed again to his feet. David covered the body with his jacket, then recognizing one of the spectators as an employee, ordered the man to assist him in carrying the body inside before the other employees arrived.

◆

Gibbs entered David's office with a grave disposition. He could not read David's face.

"Is it true?"

"Would that it wasn't," he replied, his voice laced with disgust. "I don't even know if he had children."

"He did," Gibbs said. "His wife brought dinner down at night. Sometimes she'd have a little one hanging from her leg."

"You tell his wife to keep coming to collect his payroll," David said. He shook his head. "Why didn't you tell me about the fire in the yard?"

"I intended to. I just thought it would be best to wait until you returned. I couldn't see the point in telling you while you were still in Chicago."

David replied nothing.

"I am sorry. I thought I was doing the right thing."

"You did, Gibbs. There was nothing I could have done but given in. And that wasn't an option." David leaned back in his chair, held back by the one foot resting on the edge of the desk. "This was done by my employees. How else would they have known Carville's hours or his position? Wasn't that the point? If I won't fire the Negroes, they will frighten them into leaving."

"You don't know that."

"I am not sure that I don't." He lowered the front legs of his chair back to the floor. "Get me Judd Boggs. I want to see what he knows of the affair."

"You think he will tell you?"

"In not so many words."

David was more correct than he could have hoped for. When Boggs arrived at his office, he was clearly agitated, his movements tight and quick, as if at any moment he might bolt from the room. Gibbs stood near the doorway behind Boggs, which seemed to add to the man's anxiety, as every few minutes he would glance back around. Before David could question him about the lynching, Boggs blurted out in a tremorous voice, "You ain't thinkin' that I done hung the nigger?"

David glanced over to Gibbs. "I couldn't imagine such a thing."

"I didn't hang him. Didn't even tie his hands."

David looked sharply at Boggs.

"Did you see Carville this morning?"

"I ain't seen nothin'. Not a thing."

"I never mentioned that his hands were tied. How did you know that?"

Panic flashed across Boggs's face. "Buck nigger like that, you'd hafta tie 'em back."

"You seem to know a good deal about lynching."

Boggs turned paler. "I'd like to go now, Mr. Parkin."

David stared at him, his emotion raging beneath a dispassionate veneer. "You can go. Your services are no longer required at my company."

The words fell like a death sentence, and, during the Depression, often held the same weight.

"I am fired?"

"Despite Carville's unfortunate departure, we still have too many employees. I was sure that you would have no objection because you are concerned with my best interest. Aren't you, Mr. Boggs?"

The man turned from white to crimson, yet remained frozen beneath David's cool gaze.

"Payday was Saturday, you have two days' wages coming. Pay him up, Gibbs, and get him out of my building."

Gibbs approached the shaken man and escorted him out of the office.

A
SURPRISE
RETURN

". . . I would have sooner expected Hoover's re-election than what awaited me tonight."

DAVID PARKIN'S DIARY. JANUARY 16, 1934

t was twilight when David returned home, and the mountains were cast in the salmon hue of the sun's departure. On his entrance, he was passed by a wide-fendered taxi leaving his driveway, occupied only by the driver. He parked his car and entered the side door through the kitchen. As he walked into the foyer, he beheld a leather trunk at the foot of the stairway. And then MaryAnne.

She gazed at him apprehensively, and he looked back at her in quiet surprise—as if he had encountered an apparition, and, in truth, he considered a specter's appearance more likely.

MaryAnne spoke first. "Hello, David."

David just stared, unsure of his own feelings and less of hers. He wanted to run to her, to embrace her, but there was no assurance that she would not turn from him or even that she had come to stay. MaryAnne turned away from his gaze.

"Catherine wired me about Lawrence . . ." she said.

His heart fell.

"I am glad that you could come back for him."

"If it is permissible, I would like to stay in the east guest room."

"No. You take our . . ." He corrected himself, ". . . the bedroom."

"Thank you."

"Someone is already staying in the east guest room."

She looked at him quizzically.

". . . Sophia."

MaryAnne was surprised and upset by David's answer.

"Who is Sophia?"

"She is Lawrence's daughter."

MaryAnne lifted a hand to her breast. "Oh, my . . . a daughter?"

Catherine suddenly appeared at the crest of the stairway, was momentarily baffled by what she saw, then squealed when she realized the woman at the foot of the stairs was MaryAnne.

"MaryAnne. You have returned."

"Just for a while," David said curtly.

MaryAnne glanced towards him and frowned. Catherine descended the stairway to embrace MaryAnne.

"It is so good to see you again."

"I came as soon as I received your letter about Lawrence."

Catherine glaced anxiously at David, then lifted the bag at MaryAnne's feet. "Let's get you settled."

Without a word, David watched them ascend the stairway, then went to his den.

Upstairs, in the master bedchamber, Catherine began to unpack MaryAnne's trunk into the drawers of the armoire, while MaryAnne, at Catherine's insistence, sat idle on the bed, tempted to ask a thousand questions.

"How is Lawrence?"

"I am afraid that he is not doing well."

MaryAnne sighed. "Is it true that he has a daughter?"

"Apparently. She arrived late last night. Not even David knew of her."

As Catherine continued her dispersal of the trunk's articles she grew more quiet, and MaryAnne could not bear the mounting tension. "Catherine, please don't be angry with me."

She looked up. "I'm sorry, MaryAnne. I don't mean to be angry. I just feel so betrayed. I have gone over in my mind what you said the morning before you left, relived every word you said, and it drives me mad knowing that you knew and you didn't tell me. I guess it was presumptuous to believe myself your best friend."

"You are, Catherine. I just couldn't bear to tell David, and it wouldn't be right to tell you and not him." She looked towards the open door. "He is being so cold. He hates me now."

"I have never seen him in such pain—even when Andrea died. You broke his heart, Mary. But you misunderstand him. He fears you, but he doesn't hate you."

"Fears me? Why?"

"Who else can inflict on him such pain?"

MaryAnne bowed her head into her open palms. "This was a mistake. I never should have come back."

At this, Catherine came over and sat on the bed next to MaryAnne, taking MaryAnne's hands in hers. "I'm sorry. You had to expect it would be difficult. But it wasn't a mistake. I am so happy to see you again. Even if it is for a brief time."

"Bless you, Catherine," MaryAnne said, and the two women fell into each other's embrace.

◆

"I came home to find that MaryAnne had returned. She promptly made it clear that she does not intend to stay. My heart, of necessity, has become acrobatic."

DAVID PARKIN'S DIARY. JANUARY 16, 1934

◆

Sophia spent the better part of the next week sitting at Lawrence's side, sometimes talking, sometimes just staring with wet eyes, and never ceasing to hope for some sign—some acknowledgment that he understood who she was.

She had not planned to stay in Salt Lake City for this length of time, and she knew that her husband and family would soon require her return. As Lawrence's condition neither improved nor declined, she decided that it was nearing the time that she would return home. Friday night, the eve before her scheduled departure, she did not leave his side. Around midnight she slid her hand into his.

"I don't know what you understand. But I must say this, as much for me as you. I want you to know that Mother loved you with all of her heart. It was your name on her lips when she died."

Lawrence's eyes showed no sign of comprehension, but his breath seemed more shallow and halting.

"She never told me about you. I learned of you through the letters you wrote to her." She paused, and her voice was suddenly charged by emotion. "Why did you never come to me? Were you so afraid of being discovered that you wouldn't come to your own daughter?" She began to tear up and laid her head against his chest. "I am sorry. I am only thinking of myself. This is so unfair. Lord, let him know it's me. Please remove the clouds from his mind."

Lawrence's dark, brooding eyes looked steadily ahead.

She took a deep breath, forcing herself to regain her

composure. "You have three grandchildren, one boy and two girls. You would be proud of them, they are all good children. The youngest is a little mischievous. He is now sixteen years of age. He was named after you. I didn't know it, but he was. Mother was adamant we name him Lawrence. We call him little Larry most of the time." She caressed the rough hand again, then, overwhelmed by sadness, again lowered her head and said softly, "Father."

Suddenly, the hand squeezed tightly around hers. She looked up into his granite face and could see where a single tear had fallen down his cheek.

"You know."

She leaned close to him as tears began to streak down her own cheeks. "You know."

The great hand rose to the back of her head, pulling her closer, and Sophia wept into her father's chest.

◆

Sophia was at Lawrence's side when he died Sunday afternoon. His passing was not a peaceful one. A massive heart attack clutched Lawrence, and Sophia cried out for David. By the time David arrived, Lawrence lay gasping his last breaths.

THE LETTER

Sophia trembled, her hands raised to her cheeks. "I don't know what has happened."

Catherine and MaryAnne both entered the room, and Catherine had called for the doctor. David propped a pillow under Lawrence's head and held the big man from the bed's edge. When the doctor arrived, he parted Lawrence's flannel top and placed the steel orb of his stethoscope on his chest.

"He has had a heart attack."

Sophia cupped her mouth with her hands.

"What can be done?" David asked.

"Nothing to save him. I can give ether for the pain."

"Do it," David said. When the doctor had administered the vial's dosage, David herded everyone but Sophia from the room. Sophia held her father's hand as he lay dying. When he took his final breath, she bowed her head over him and said, "I love you, Papa."

THE
FUNERAL

"When we bury someone we love, we must also bury a part of our heart. But we should not bemoan this loss. Our hearts, perhaps, are all they can take with them."

DAVID PARKIN'S DIARY. JANUARY 28, 1934

our father wanted to be buried next to your mother," David said.

"It would be the right thing—but it isn't possible," Sophia said. "Mother was entombed in the family sepulchre. The family would never allow it."

"Then, with your blessing, we will have him buried in our family's plot, near his stone angel."

She looked at him gratefully. "I am sure he would have wanted it that way."

"I will see to it."

◆

The sexton of the Salt Lake City cemetery was an olive-skinned man of Italian descent, succinct of stature—a head shorter than most of his gender—with silver, wiry hair that grew vertical as if in compensation for the height nature had slighted him. He had come to work at the cemetery as a youth when his father, a driller at the Oquirrh copper mines, had been killed in the pit and the cemetery's previous sexton felt pity on the poor family and offered him, the oldest male of the clan, an apprenticeship. He had been there since.

The sexton's home was a weathered cottage of ginger-tinted stucco mostly concealed by the vines and ivy that climbed its walls and chimney and smothered its paned windows.

The sexton pulled his suspenders up over his shoulders and greeted David at the door.

"Mr. Parkin, isn't it?"

"Yes. I need to arrange for a burial."

The man's thick eyebrows knitted in consolation. He had long before mastered the art of mixing business with condolence.

"You considering any particular part of the cemetery?"

"Up near our daughter."

The man nodded knowingly. "The angel monument." He grasped the curved handle of a black cane and then his jacket. "Nice part of the yard. Let's go on up and take a look. My cart is near."

The old man's cart, drawn by a single, aged palomino, pulled them slowly to the center of the cemetery. The snow on the knoll was crystallized beneath the winter sun and pristine, as it had not been visited since MaryAnne's departure. As the seraph came into view, David's chest grew heavy. Unlike his wife, David did not often visit the angel, as it did not bring him condolence. The sexton pulled back on the reins lightly and, requiring little persuasion, the horse stopped, lowering its head to feed on the scant greenery that poked through the crusted snow. They both climbed down from the buckboard.

"Them your plots right there," the sexton said. He walked them off, delineating their circumference in the snow with his cane. He paused at the upper slope of the knoll. "How about this one? Just a little north of yours."

David glanced around the yard. A northern breeze whistled through the webbed canopy of the naked trees overhead. It was the season of the place. His gaze settled back on the plot. "It will do. What is the tallest monument in your cemetery?"

The sexton cast his eyes southward. "Over there. The Mormon prophet's."

From their vantage point they could see the pinnacle of the granite spire above the rest.

"It should be one inch taller than that."

The sexton was astonished. "Gonna cost a small fortune. Must've been one important gentleman."

David nodded.

"Politician or businessman?"

"He was a war hero."

The man squinted. "Didn't read about no hero's death. Usually there'll be something in the *Tribune* or *Deseret News*."

"There was no mention of his death. He is a Negro."

The sexton's face turned ashen at the revelation. "Mr. Parkin, you can't go buryin' a Negro up in this part of the cemetery."

"Why not?"

"It's against the law burying a Negro with white folk. Coloreds have their own place."

"Where?"

"In the colored section. On the south side."

David knew the place, a crowded, overgrown weed patch contained by a black spear fence.

"This is the city cemetery. He should be buried here."

The sexton's face twisted. "There'll be complaints."

David glanced around the graveyard. "You get complaints from them in here?"

"Well, no, but . . ." he stammered, "the folks that come."

"It's not their home."

"Maybe not, but it's against the law."

David pondered the dilemma. "Where does the law actually take offense in burying a Negro near a white man?"

"Don't follow ya."

"What part of the Negro is offensive?"

"What part?"

"It couldn't be the hair, my hair is as dark. In fact, my hair is darker than Lawrence's since he greyed. Couldn't be his eyes. Is it just the skin? Having black flesh?"

"Stands to reason. That's what makes a Negro, ain't it?"

"Is it?"

The old man didn't answer.

"Tell me, how long before the skin starts to decay?"

The macabre question surprised the man. "How long? Get 'm in the ground, suppose five weeks. Let 'm sit around in the sun a few days and might only be three."

"Then these folks buried here aren't really white."

"Well, most of 'em . . ."

"I don't see where we have a problem here." David counted out bills from a stack of currency and handed it to the man. "See to my request."

The man eyed the bills lustfully, then took them. Still shaking his head, he climbed back into the carriage. "You a' comin'?"

"No. I'll walk home from here. The body has been embalmed, I will expect you to come for it tomorrow. We will plan the funeral for the twenty-eighth."

"Frankly, I don't know why you'd want to go to such trouble for a Negro buryin'. It's not like black folk got a soul."

David glared back at the man incredulously, but was more filled with sadness than anger.

"It is not their souls I worry about."

The sexton pulled the horse's head back, and the horse plodded forward. When David was alone, he slowly approached the stone monument. He glanced at its inscription. Our Little Angel. He knelt down on one knee before it. In a serene voice he said, "I've got to tell you something, honey. I am letting you go. I once thought that to release the pain was a type of betrayal. I now know that the opposite is true—that the greatest gift I can give to you is to free you from the burden of my grief. If life is so precious that I mourned the loss of yours, how wrong to throw away mine. I wonder if the loss of my life has caused you the same pain that the loss of yours caused me." He stopped, glanced up to the angel, then dropped his head again. "I know how much you loved your mother. I promise you that I will not close my heart to her again." He looked around the cemetery, and the glare of the yard forced him to squint. "That's all I wanted to say." He closed his eyes for a moment, then rose and walked home.

◆

Only nine were in attendance at Lawrence's interment, including the white, southern, Baptist minister who would perform the rites. At the sexton's insistence, a black minister was not allowed, as the risk of discovery and subsequent controversy was far too great. The sexton's foreboding was not in vain. Two of Lawrence's mourners, fellow soldiers of the Negro 24th cavalry, had arrived early for the funeral and had been noticed by a group that congregated over another service. One of that party confronted the sexton about the Negroes' presence and was told they were grave diggers. The news appeased the inquirer, who expected little more of the race, and would somehow sleep better knowing that the Negroes still knew their place.

The preacher stood at the head of the casket and MaryAnne, flanked by Catherine and Gibbs, stood to one side, opposite of David, Sophia, and the two soldiers. At the conclusion of the preacher's blessing, David stepped forward.

"I am honored to say a few words about my friend, though I fear I will not do him justice. I don't know that anyone could. Lawrence Flake was a good man. He gave more than he had and expected less than he deserved. In so doing, he left this world a better place. I feel honored that he called me his friend and fortunate to call him mine."

David began to tear up as he looked over to the angel statue that viewed the proceedings with its usual stoicism.

"His giving of his angel statue to our little girl was

one of the noblest gestures I have ever beheld. He had hoped that it might someday mark his grave and passersby would know that here lay someone worthy of such a monument. Worthy of common respect. As I said, Lawrence expected less than he deserved. The Bible says that no greater love is there than to lay down your life for another. But I think that would not be difficult for Lawrence, as his life was bitter and not to be envied by any. What he did with his angel was to lay down his hope for the hereafter. I have only seen greatness a few times in my life. I saw it in Lawrence." He raised his head. "That's all I have to say."

MaryAnne looked up at David lovingly, but he turned from her soft eyes. Wiping back her tears, she stepped forward and laid a flower atop the casket. Sophia took David's hand and he put his arm around her. She leaned into him.

"Your words were beautiful. Thank you."

"It was my honor."

When Sophia was ready to leave, the remaining mourners walked back to the automobiles parked to the shoulder of the dirt road. Catherine, MaryAnne, and Elaine had all ridden with Gibbs, as Sophia's luggage filled the backseat of David's automobile, she had planned to catch the train back to Birmingham that very afternoon. David glanced over as Gibbs offered the door to MaryAnne and she thanked him and climbed inside. As Gibbs's car pulled away, MaryAnne glanced back to David, and for a brief moment their eyes met. David turned over the Packard's motor and drove off from the gravesite in a different direction.

CHAPTER TWENTY-FIVE
THE SECOND DEPARTURE

"I have heard it preached that on Judgment Day our sins will be shouted from the rooftops. I have come to believe that if this is so, it will not be by some heavenly tribunal or something loathsome that crawls beneath, but from our own countenance screaming out to the world who we really are—when the kind and the good, no matter how plain in this life, will shine forth like suns, while the loathsome and dark will cower from their light."

"If Heaven is a place where there are no secrets, it would, for some, also be Hell."

DAVID PARKIN'S DIARY. JANUARY 29, 1934

don't mourn for my father," Sophia said as they left the cemetery. She wiped her eyes with a moist handkerchief. "I believe that my parents are finally together in a place where love knows no color . . . nor deformity. But there are things I regret not being able to ask him. I understand the danger that his relationship with my mother posed. But his abandonment was so complete. I will always wonder why he never came to me."

"I can't understand it," David replied. "He was so close to our little girl. I am still astonished that after all these years he never told me he had a daughter."

"I know this will sound terrible, but I have wondered if his fear of being discovered was just greater than his love for me."

David turned from the road, glancing sternly into Sophia's eyes. "Lawrence was no coward. It's just not so."

"I would almost rather hear that he was. Then, at least, I would know why. The unknowing is worse than any truth."

David's countenance relaxed. "You and I have much in common, Sophia. In a sense, your journey is the same as mine. My own mother abandoned me when I was a child. I also went out to find my mother in search of answers. But she had already died."

"What did you hope to find?"

"Understanding of why I was not worthy of her."

"Then your journey was also a failure."

"Not at all. I brought back what I needed."

"What did you learn?"

"To leave the past behind. The answers are not in the past. Healing comes from purpose and purpose resides in our hope of the future." David suddenly pounded the steering wheel with his fist.

"I just remembered a request your father made. He said that if you were to ever come around that he had something for you he kept in a box. I asked him what it was, and he said, 'Your answers.'"

"Where is it?!"

"He kept it under his bed." David glanced at his watch. "Your train doesn't leave for an hour yet. We'll have time if we hurry."

David turned north at Brigham Street and drove to the defunct cannery that supported Lawrence's shanty. The Packard lurched around the side of the building, stopping in front of the black man's former residence. The shanty's door was wide open. They both stepped from the automobile, and David surveyed the back lot with caution before entering the decrepit shack. The room had been ravaged. Its once-full tables were now empty and turned over, and its floor littered with numerous beer and whiskey bottles and piles of cigarette butts. The clocks were gone, except for the ones that underwent repair—set in various stages of permanent dissection. Sophia quietly examined the humble room, and David wondered if it was a similar experience to the one he underwent at his mother's tenement.

"Someone has ransacked the place," David said. "They have stolen his things."

"Did they take my box?"

David knelt at the side of the cot and reached beneath it. The humble wooden munitions box, undetected by the home's intruders, was still there. He lifted it out and placed it on the cot. The box was held shut by a rusted padlock. David looked under the bed for a key, then, not finding one, forced his pocket knife's squat blade beneath the lock's casing and the aged wood it was mounted to and pried it free. He presented the box to Sophia, and she opened its lid, then lifted out an envelope.

For Sophia. 1893

"I was thirteen years old . . ." She put a hand over her mouth, then reached back into the box and pulled out an aged photograph—an image of an infant dressed in a long, embroidered silk gown.

"Oh, my." She turned it towards David. "This is my christening picture."

She set the photograph down and anxiously tore open the envelope. A smaller sheet was folded in half, then wrapped around the letter. She removed its accompanying typewritten note, and read it aloud.

◆

To whom it may concern.

For the price of ten cents I have transcribed this letter for a mister Lawrence (his family name has been withheld from me), a Negro, previously unknown to me, serving with the U.S. cavalry. The diction is my own. Mr. Lawrence requested that I include this memorandum as well as endeavor to make Mr. Lawrence's diction a trifle clearer for ease of reading. I accept no responsibility for any scurrilous message, mistruths, or fraud this letter may purport. I have merely acted as scribe in Mr. Lawrence's behalf.

—MR. CHARLES H. JENNINGS, ESQ.,
ALAMOGORDO, NEW MEXICO, 1877.

◆

Sophia set the note aside and opened the letter. It too was typewritten, and she commenced to read it out loud as well, but stopped after the first sentence. Tears fell down her cheeks. She handed the letter to David, then sat back in her chair, wiping back the still falling tears. David read the letter out loud.

◆

My dearest Sophia,

I do not hope that you will ever read this letter. For if you do, your mama and papa have failed in our duty to protect you from my identity. But as you have learned of me, there are things you must now know. You should know how much I love you. A child should know their father's love. You may ask why I was not in your life—why it was so important to us to hide myself from you. It is because we loved you that I gave you up—that people would not hurt you. You know, by now, that your papa is a Negro. Your mama and I didn't want you to know that you had mixed blood. We wanted you to have a life my skin color could not offer. The world has taken you away from me, but they cannot take you from my heart. I did see you once. I came and stood alongside the road where you walked from school. Even though I had come across half the country, when I saw you near I felt afraid of how you might treat a strange Negro and I wanted to turn back. You stopped and asked me kindly if I was a stranger in town and needed some help to find my way. Do you recall? I thanked you and said I knew just where I needed to go. Back home. My heart was so proud I thought it would burst.

I never got the chance to say it to your face, but I love you my darling.

YOUR PAPA

◆

Sophia was unable to speak. David handed her back the letter, then glanced down at his watch.

"You have a train to catch," he said gently. "I guess you got your answer."

◆

Together they waited on the platform for the train's arrival. When Sophia had completed the formalities of her boarding, David handed her a leather satchel.

"What is this?"

"Some of your father's things from his cavalry days."

She peeled back the bag's flap. Inside was a cavalry

belt rolled up to a brass rectangular buckle that read "US"; an ammunition pouch; a currycomb; Lawrence's troop manual; and his unit insignia—a blue and gold ensign with the words SEMPER PARATUS inscribed across a banner.

Sophia closed the bag and put it under her arm. "They sacrificed their love for me."

"Your father was a noble man."

Sophia looked at David thoughtfully. "There are people with fair complexions and beautiful faces with spirits as twisted and gnarled as a burr oak. My parents were the comely ones. The ones with the beautiful souls."

She leaned forward and kissed David on the cheek. "I will never be able to repay you for all that you have done for me and my father."

"It is I who am in debt."

As she boarded the train, she stopped and turned back and said, "Good luck with MaryAnne. I have faith that everything will work out. You've too good a heart for it not to."

◆

At David's return to the house, he was awakened to a great sadness as he encountered MaryAnne's trunks stacked on the front porch. She had packed two additional cases of things that she was previously unable to escape with without divulging her flight. Upon entering the home, David went directly to his den and, sequestering himself inside, turned on his radio, seeking refuge in its broadcast. The Boston Symphony played Tchaikovsky's *"Pathétique,"* and, alone with his pain, David hung on each murmuring refrain, and each cry of the violin was his own. Not thirty minutes later, Mary-Anne gently knocked on the door of his den, then entered. David turned off the set.

"I see you have packed your things."

She nodded humbly.

"What time is your train?"

She walked over to the world globe and ran her fingers across its surface, her back turned towards David.

"Not until morning. I thought I would spend tonight at the Hotel Utah."

David did not ask her why, and an uncomfortable silence filled the room.

"I wanted to say good-bye this time."

David dropped his head into his hand and sighed. It was more than a minute before he spoke. "You know, this is right where I was when I found your letter—found out that you were leaving. What a night that was—first time Catherine ever saw me drunk." He laughed cynically. "I don't know. Maybe it's good to get the wind knocked out of you from time to time."

MaryAnne's eyes moistened.

"Much has transpired since that night. Catherine gave me the letter you found at Andrea's grave. It got me to thinking that I needed to figure some things out. So I went to Chicago to find my mother. It turns out that my mother committed suicide twenty-two years ago."

"Catherine told me," MaryAnne replied softly. "I am so sorry, David."

"I have no idea who wrote the letter . . . but it's not important. I learned what I needed to learn—that it doesn't really matter what happened back then. There is nothing anyone can do with the past, except let it fade." He swallowed. "As I stood looking out over the bridge my mother jumped from, I had this remarkable moment of clarity. Do you know what I realized?"

MaryAnne began to tremble and did not turn, for she did not want David to see her tears.

"I realized how much I missed you. And that all that really matters in my life is earning your trust and getting you back. And then I thought, I will never get that chance, because you will never return. I understood the hopelessness my mother felt. Because when you lose something that precious, you have really lost. And I, too, wanted to jump."

MaryAnne began to sob quietly.

"And then I had the strangest thought. What if I jumped? And then in some other realm I encountered Andrea and she asked me what I had done with my life since she left. And I had to tell her that I had thrown away everything that I loved. That was my great epiphany, when I realized that what I had been doing was really no different than what my mother had done. That I had also abandoned myself and those that depended on me. I didn't get on a train to do it, but it was just as real." David cleared his throat. "I haven't been the same since. I don't know how to tell you this, because it just sounds like I am trying to get you to stay." His voice cracked. "And more than anything I want you to stay . . ." He dropped his head. "No, that's wrong. More than anything I want you to want to stay."

MaryAnne suddenly turned to him, no longer able to suppress her feelings. "David, I thought you wanted me to leave. I came to see if you would take me back. I don't want to live without you." She walked to his chair and knelt down at its side. "I am sorry I broke the promise of my wedding vow—my promise to you. I was just so alone."

David put his hand under her chin and tilted it up until her eyes looked into his, and a smile grew across his face, and then hers. David embraced her, and the two fell to the floor in each other's arms. It was at this moment that Catherine walked in to inform MaryAnne that her taxi had arrived. Instead, she quietly closed the door, paid the taxi his pick-up fee, and then tipped the man to carry MaryAnne's trunks back inside the house. Her face shone with such joy that the cab driver almost felt guilty begrudging his lost fare.

CHAPTER TWENTY-SIX
THE REUNION

"There is no confection so sweet as joyful reunion."

DAVID PARKIN'S DIARY. FEBRUARY 2, 1934

hen morning came, David stirred and MaryAnne nestled tightly into his chest. "Oh, don't go, darling."

David strained to see the clock, then pulled her closer and kissed her forehead. "I told Gibbs I would meet him downtown for breakfast."

"Why?"

"He says that he has important news that he must share with me in person."

MaryAnne sighed sleepily and laced her fingers behind David's head. "What do you think it is?"

"Well, either he's quitting or he's getting married."

"He's certainly not quitting."

"Gibbs has such fear of matrimony. Could Elaine have finally persuaded him?"

"We women have our ways."

"I won't argue that." He kissed her again, then climbed out of bed. As he left the room, MaryAnne abandoned her own pillow and embraced his tightly.

◆

As the sleepy city awaited its usual wakening of street vendors and storefronts, David found Gibbs seated at a small oak table near the back of the Temple Square coffee shop, reading the *Salt Lake Tribune*. A doughnut, a thick strip of grilled bacon, and a cup of coffee sat before him. When he saw David, he set the paper aside.

"Have you followed this trial in Detroit—those two men who murdered their landlord because he was about to evict their families?"

"I have heard talk about it."

"The jury acquitted them. They ruled it was self-defense."

"I'm not surprised. Survival is always the first law of the land."

A grey-haired waitress emerged from the kitchen, wiping her hands on her apron. She came to the table.

"What can I get for you?"

"Oatmeal and coffee." He looked at Gibbs's meal. "And a sinker."

She returned to the kitchen.

"So what is the big news?"

Gibbs paused for emphasis. "Elaine and I are getting married."

"Congratulations."

"I admit I am a little surprised at how happy I am about all this."

"Why is that? You're crazy about Elaine."

"It is just the commitment. It unnerves me."

"Then why are you taking the plunge?"

"I don't know. I guess it's about time."

"You mean she gave you an ultimatum."

"In so many words. We were outside the ZCMI department store when she said, 'You can only window-shop for so long before someone else comes along and buys the display.'"

David laughed. "Subtle."

"She's a clever gal," Gibbs said. "I'll have my hands full." A wry smile stretched across his face. "Not a bad thought, really."

"You are smitten. Didn't you once warn me that love is the worm that conceals the hook?"

"I guess if the bait is sweet enough, you don't worry about the barb."

"I always thought it was inevitable. Have you set a date?"

"Soon. Early April. Elaine wants to hasten it."

"The weather would be better in May."

"She's claiming grounds of superstition—'marry in May, rue the day.' I think the truth is she's afraid that I might change my mind."

"Have you planned where you will hold the ceremony?"

"Not yet."

"Why not have it at the house?"

"We'd hate to be such an imposition—especially with MaryAnne just back."

"We'll be offended if you don't. Besides, Catherine loves these things. She turns into a little tyrant, bossing around the florists and caterers. She'll be thrilled."

"I'll talk to Elaine about it this evening." He glanced at his wristwatch. "It's almost nine. I best unlock the company doors." He laid down a dollar bill and stood. "I almost forgot the most important thing. I would like for you to be my best man."

"I would be honored."

Gibbs smiled. "Swell. I'll see you at work." He saluted David and walked out of the cafe.

◆

On the dawn of Gibbs and Elaine's nuptial day, David fled the flurry of the mansion's final preparations and picked Gibbs up for breakfast, taking him to the nearby Alta Club, where the two men laughed and spoke of everything except the day, and Gibbs puffed cigars with the anxiousness befitting a bridegroom. They returned to the house twenty minutes before the scheduled event.

Spring, in Utah, more times than not, arrives in winter dress, and the wedding day was not excepted. The morning was clear and chill, and in preparation of the reception, the home's fires were all stoked and small heaps of firewood were raised near each hearth.

The house had been consigned as Catherine's canvas, and she spared no stroke in bringing forth her masterpiece. Every pillar on the main floor was wrapped in long foliage garnishes and vines, and the chandeliers were so adorned with flowers that they looked more bouquet than fixture.

The bride herself was not outdone by the surroundings, and it was remarked, in compliment, that Elaine resembled a Gibson girl. She wore an ivory satin and lace bridal gown of her mother's, with a high-necked bodice, full puff sleeves, and a long flared skirt with a tightly fitted waistline. As natural as the apparel took to Elaine, or she to it, Gibbs was conversely out of his element; his black cotton pants hung long, and his jacket was wrinkled from repeated fidgeting and removal.

The ceremony was held in the drawing room, and the double doors were opened to the vestibule for additional guests. The justice of the peace began the service at the strike of noon, and it proceeded quickly and unspectacularly, which suited everyone, and before the hour waned the couple was joined in matrimony. When the two were declared as one, MaryAnne dabbed her eyes with a lace handkerchief, and David squeezed her hand.

"I have never understood why it is that women cry at weddings."

"I have seen men cry, too."

"Yes. But only the grooms."

MaryAnne laughed. It had been a long time since David had teased her about anything. "You're terrible," she said happily.

At the conclusion of the service, the party moved into the foyer and downstairs parlor while tables were brought in and lunch was served.

When lunch was eaten and all had paid their respects to the newlyweds, the couple drove off beneath a hail of rice, and Catherine returned to her relentless tyranny of the caterers. The food was boxed and stored in the pantry, while several boxes of cake, sliced meats, and breadstuffs were sent to the breadlines for the homeless.

When the last of the guests had departed, David and MaryAnne walked up the stairs hand in hand.

"Honestly, are you surprised to see them married?" MaryAnne asked.

"No. In fact I wonder that it didn't happen sooner." David kissed her. "It brings back fond memories, doesn't it?"

"This day has been healing. I feel as if I had been reliving our own wedding day."

Suddenly, MaryAnne paused. She stood outside the parlor and looked at the door. David watched her. Hoping. Wondering if she would enter to see the clock he had given her on their wedding day.

"What is it, Mary?"

She turned away. "Nothing."

At the entrance of their bedroom, David stopped her.

"Wait here. I want to show you something."

He entered the darkened room, then returned with a small, wrapped package and handed it to her.

"What is this?"

"I never gave you a Christmas present."

MaryAnne smiled. "But it's April, David." She curiously weighed the box in her hands, as it felt empty. As she tore back the paper, David switched on the room's lights. To the side of the turned-down bed were two trunks. She glanced at them, then back into David's face.

"Why are the trunks out?"

"Finish opening your present and you'll know."

She opened the package to reveal two card tickets. David slipped his arms around her waist. "It has been too long since we have been away together. I thought a holiday to San Francisco was in order."

"David." She pressed against him.

"Catherine has packed for you. I have reserved seats on an airplane flight for tomorrow morning."

"An airplane flight? How exciting."

"I thought we'd stay at the Palace Hotel and spend a few days on the Barbary Coast. Perhaps sail to Tiburon for lunch at Sam's."

"Oh, David. It will be wonderful. We could see Grass Valley again."

David's demeanor fell at the suggestion. He looked at her gravely. "No, MaryAnne. There is nothing left for me there."

Still encircled in his arms, she leaned back to look into his face.

"Nothing?"

"I have wasted too much time in Grass Valley."

"But you haven't been there in twenty-five years."

"A part of me had never left it. It's time to move on."

She lay her head against his chest. "You really are back, my love."

"With all of my vulnerable heart. Do with it as you will."

She held him tighter and knew that she would never let him go.

"I will hold it tightly next to mine."

◆

David sat alone at a table on the wood-planked pier, drinking orange juice and reading from the *San Francisco Examiner*. A glass bowl of fruit—oranges and pomegranates—stood centerpiece on the white wrought-iron table next to a book and a folded cardigan. The wharf stretched out beneath the dawn California sun over the kelp-strewn beach of Sausalito Bay. The barking of sea lions resounded from a distant rock, above the seagulls' desperate screech—the ocean's cacophony carried on the breeze that swept in from the bay and ruffled MaryAnne's wraparound skirt as she walked from their room towards David.

David tilted the paper to watch his beautiful wife approach. MaryAnne looked younger than she had in years—the weight of his remorse lifted. She smiled demurely at his glance as she pulled back the strands of hair that the wind blew in her face.

"Good morning, my dear," David said.

"This is glorious, David." She sat down next to him. "I just love the smell of the ocean."

He leaned over and kissed her. "What can I order you for breakfast?"

"I'll just have fruit." She took an orange from the bowl. "This is just like our honeymoon."

"With much in common. It is a whole new life we have ahead of us." He set aside the paper and looked at MaryAnne with peculiar gravity. "Maybe we should start our new life here in California."

She laid a piece of rind on the table. "What are you saying, David?"

"I have been thinking. There is really no reason to go back to Salt Lake. Lawrence is gone. Gibbs is starting his family. He can certainly run the business without me."

"You are serious?"

"Why not? The snow seems a little higher and colder each year. Maybe it's time to retire to someplace more temperate."

"But our home . . . and Catherine."

"Catherine could come with us."

"We couldn't ask her to come."

"Of course we could. And she would. We're as much family to her as she is to us."

"But our home . . ."

"Mary." David smiled as he looked into her eyes. "Wherever you are is home."

MaryAnne was suddenly quiet. A line of pelicans flew by, and MaryAnne's eyes followed their roller-coaster flight.

"Are you worried about leaving Andrea?" David asked.

"No. Not anymore. It doesn't matter where we go. I carry her with me always."

"If you don't like the idea . . ."

"The idea of change is always hard. But I have always wanted to live by the coast. Perhaps a beach home in Monterey." She suddenly smiled with new excitement. "I think we should, David. Maybe this summer."

"I wonder what Gibbs will say?"

"He'll be heartbroken. The two of you are like brothers."

"Closer than brothers. He's the only one who has

seen me through it all." David suddenly smiled. "Of course it's Victoria I really worry about."

MaryAnne laughed heartily, and David reflected on how sweet that laughter sounded and could not imagine that he had lived without it for so long.

"Oh, David. What will the woman do without you?"

THE
SEXTON'S
CALL

"The noble causes of life have always seemed foolish to the uninspired. But this is of small concern. I worry less about the crucified than those who pounded the nails."

DAVID PARKIN'S DIARY. MARCH 4, 1934

aryAnne felt David's forehead for the fifth time. "It's the change in climate, David. Last week you were swimming in the ocean and today you are out shoveling snow." She sighed. "I had better stay," she decided.

David caught her hand. "I'll be fine. This is the troupe's last performance. I want you to go with Gibbs and Elaine."

Catherine entered the room. "Gibbs just arrived. Shall I tell him to go on without you?"

"No," David said adamantly, "Mary is going."

MaryAnne looked vexed. "I did want to see this opera."

"There is no sense in you missing it because I have a cold."

The sound of a brass knocker reverberated through the house, followed by that of the opening door.

David coughed. "Now go on. You know how impatient Gibbs gets."

MaryAnne kissed David's forehead. "You stay in bed. Catherine, we will be at the Capitol Theater. We should be back no later than midnight."

"Enjoy yourself," Catherine said. "Everything will be fine."

Gibbs stalked into the room, and his eyes fell on David. "What are you doing in bed?"

"David is ill," Catherine said. "Now go, Mary. You're making everyone late."

"Thank you, Catherine." She kissed David. "Good night, darling."

Gibbs slapped David's knee. "I tried to get out of it myself."

David smiled. "I am sure you will tell me all about it."

When they had left the room, Catherine smiled at David. "May I get you anything?"

"Hot tea would be nice."

"I found some Jeelung at the store." She descended to the kitchen, returning a quarter hour later with the tea service. She set it at the side of the bed.

"Is it true that oranges and avocados grow alongside the roads in California?"

David smiled at Catherine's childlike wonderment. "It is. Though most of them have high fences around them. Haven't you ever been to California?"

"I have never been outside of Utah."

"We are so happy that you are going with us. In truth, we would not have gone without you."

Catherine smiled. "Nor would I have let you."

"The three of us should go look for a home later this month."

Catherine's face showed her excitement. "I have always wanted to see San Francisco."

She sighed happily as she stood. "I told MaryAnne that you would rest. Would you like the light off?"

"No. I'll read."

Catherine went back downstairs to the laundry.

Two hours later the telephone rang. Catherine answered, then, a few moments later, peered in to see if David was awake.

"David, it is for you. It is the sexton of the city cemetery."

David lifted the receiver. "Hello."

The man's excited voice resonated from the earpiece, and David's countenance turned grave. Catherine tried to ascertain the crisis from David's contribution to the conversation.

"How did they know of it? . . . And the police?"

There was a long pause, and the concern on David's face was more manifest. "I will be right there."

David moved the phone from his ear, and Catherine took the handset from him to hang it up.

"You will be right where?"

"A group of men have gathered at the cemetery to dig up Lawrence's grave."

"Good Lord."

David swung his legs over the side of the bed. "I need to get up there."

Catherine lifted the handset. "I'll call the police."

"No," David said. He suddenly doubled over in a fit of coughing. Then, straightening up, he walked to the wardrobe and pulled on a pair of trousers, tucking his nightshirt into the waist. "The grave is illegal. The police won't stop the men."

"Illegal?"

"It's against the law to bury a Negro in the cemetery. I knew it when I purchased the plot."

David continued to dress.

"Please do not go."

"I can't let them do this."

Catherine wrung her hands. "Are you going to take your gun?"

"That would be foolishness."

"Then please wait for Gibbs to return."

"It will be over by the time he returns." He finished lacing his boots. "I am just going to see if I can talk them out of it." He took a wad of bills from the nightstand drawer and stashed it in a trouser pocket. "And, if that doesn't work, bribe them out of it. It will be all right."

He walked out of the room and descended the stairway with Catherine at his heels. "You shouldn't be out in this cold. Your cough . . ."

"I will only be a few minutes."

She brought out his long coat from the hall closet. "Take your good coat."

He slipped on the coat and buttoned it down, then opened the front door, ushering in a rush of freezing air. Catherine shuddered.

"What will I tell MaryAnne?"

"MaryAnne needn't know. I'll be back long before she is."

"David, I am afraid. What if something goes wrong?" Their eyes met. "Aren't you afraid?"

He thought momentarily, then said, "I am afraid of many things."

◆

David climbed the snow-capped western hill of the cemetery, creeping unseen through the shadows cast by the great canopies of oak. From a distance he could hear the excited sounds of the men, occasional laughter, and the rhythmic hit of shovels. He increased his gait. When he arrived, above the knoll, the grave had already been dug down three feet past ground level. There were no more than a dozen men gathered on the trampled snow, and the knoll was lit by two kerosene lanterns resting on the base of Andrea's grave. Two men, perspiration dripping down their faces despite the cold, flung dirt out of the cavity while the others shouted their encouragement. The shovelers' jackets were draped over the angel statue's head and outstretched arms. Despite the frigid climate, it was fast digging, for the dirt was still loose from the recent burial, and three men leaned idly against their pickaxes while the shovels did the work, heaping dirt on both sides of the grave. As the hole grew, so did their delirium, and they mocked the buried man and made plans of what they would do with his corpse once it was exhumed. The guttural talk turned David's stomach. He shouted into the commotion.

"Stop!"

The voices abated. His voice took on a calmer resonance.

"Please, stop."

A burly, barrel-chested man in a leather jacket and worker boots stepped forward. "Who are you?"

David didn't reply. Just then a small ruddy-faced man stepped from the crowd.

"It's Parkin. He's the nigger-lover who buried this here jig."

David faced his accuser, and the man cowered back into the shadows.

"Judd?"

"There are niggers takin' white men's wages, and it ain't right. Man's got a right to protect his family."

"How does a buried man threaten your families?"

The behemoth scowled. "This is what's the problem, right here. A bunch of high-hat nigger lovers giving the darkies our families' bread. Real high and mighty sermon preachin' comin' from a cake eater. I spit at you." At that the man spat in David's direction, then wiped the spittle from his mouth with his coat sleeve. "When the last time your children cried themselves asleep a hungered?"

The question evoked more feeling than the inquirer could have imagined. David held his silence.

"I say we show this high hat how we feels about darky-lovers."

David stood motionless as several of the men advanced.

"I have no quarrel with any of you. The man buried here was my friend."

"Maybe you got the wrong friends."

"Yeah," chimed another, "in low places."

The men chortled, then a cry went up. "Get him!"

David was quickly set upon by more than a half

dozen of the brood. Two held his arms while another struck him across the face and then in the abdomen. When they released David from their grasp, he fell to his side on the icy ground, clutching his ribs and gasping for breath. A trickle of blood gathered at the base of his chin and dyed the snow crimson. One of the men who had held his arms spit on him.

"Hey. No use soilin' that fancy coat. Coat like that fetch a dollar or two."

Two of his assailants pulled the coat from his back, while another pushed his face in the snow with his boot.

"Look at this pantywaist, wearin' a nightgown underneath."

The man holding the coat suddenly shouted. "Hey, there's money here. Drinks tonight." In celebration, he kicked David in the side. At that moment another swaggered up to him, carrying a decapitated pick handle, which he unceremoniously swung down on David's head. Unconscious and face forward in the snow, the men were no longer entertained by his presence. They left him and returned to the grave and their original designs. David was still unconscious when the triumphant shout went up as the first shovel struck the wooden top of the casket. He never saw the imbeciles haul the coffin from the pit or load it into the wood-planked bed of a battered pickup truck and cart it away.

◆

The foyer clock had struck midnight nearly a half hour earlier when MaryAnne, Elaine, and Gibbs returned. It had been more than two hours since David had left the home. Catherine rushed out to meet them.

"David went up to the cemetery to stop some men from digging up Lawrence's grave. He left hours ago and he hasn't returned."

"Dear God," MaryAnne exclaimed.

Gibbs shoved the car back into gear while MaryAnne shouted for Catherine to call Dr. Twede and then the police. They raced up to the cemetery. The cemetery gates were still open from the men's hasty departure, and a broken chain lay coiled against the curbway. Gibbs careened between the black, narrow cemetery trails. When the angel came into view, they could see the muddy, trampled snow of the knoll and the gaping hole in the earth where Lawrence had once lain. Near the top of the knoll the car's head-lights exposed a small heap. As they neared, MaryAnne gasped. "It is David."

Gibbs braked to a stop, and MaryAnne threw her door open. She ran to her husband's body.

"He is still breathing."

"Where is his coat?" Elaine screamed. Gibbs lifted David and carried him to the car, nearly dropping him into the backseat. MaryAnne covered David's frigid body with hers as they sped back to the house. MaryAnne did not stop praying the whole way.

◆

Around noon the next day, Dr. Twede stood in the door-way of the bedchamber rubbing his neck. His awkward, lanky frame seemed dwarfed in the white smock he wore, and a stethoscope fell to his buckle. MaryAnne left David's side to speak with him.

"He was beaten quite severely. He has a concussion from a blow to his head. I am surprised that I haven't found any broken bones."

"Will he be all right?"

"His wounds from the beating will be all right. The

exposure is what concerns me. He is running a very high fever. He was already ill. I am afraid it has turned to pneumonia."

MaryAnne shuddered at the pronouncement. "What can we do?"

"Just what we are," he replied. "And pray."

Despite MaryAnne's prayers, David's condition continued to worsen, and though he was lucid, by nightfall his fever had risen another two degrees. Gibbs walked into David's room holding his hat to his waist.

"David, Captain Brookes himself has come. Your overcoat has been recovered. He needs your help to identify the men who beat you."

David looked up thoughtfully, then slowly nodded. His words were slurred and spoken slowly. "No, Gibbs."

"But why not, David?"

"What could come of it but to spawn more hatred?"

Gibbs was incredulous. "Justice will come of it. David, it was you that spoke of justice."

David nodded. "I have said too much on the topic." He looked at his friend seriously. "Let the anger go, Gibbs. There will be justice."

Gibbs sighed at David's obstinance.

"What became of Lawrence's grave?"

"They took the coffin to a field and set it afire." Gibbs had shared only half of what he knew. He could no longer restrain himself. "Why did you put yourself in such danger for the Negroes?"

David took a deep, troubled breath. "I didn't do it for the Negroes. What happened that night is imperceptible on the pile of injustices heaped upon the Negroes. I do it for my own race, not theirs."

"For what purpose? You couldn't have stopped them."

"Perhaps not. But to not try would make me seem absurd in my own eyes."

The conversation collapsed into silence. After a minute David spoke again. "The papers were signed long ago for you to take over the business. We haven't always seen eye to eye, Gibbs. But you have always been a loyal friend." He was interrupted by a fit of coughing. He took a breath, then a drink from a tumbler from the nearby nightstand. "I have deeded half the business to you, the other half to MaryAnne. Promise me that you will always take care of Mary."

Gibbs looked frantic. "What are you insinuating?"

"Just promise me, Gibbs."

Gibbs's chin began to quiver. "I give you my word."

"Then I will worry no more of the matter."

The two men embraced, and as Gibbs walked to the doorway, David stopped him. "Gibbs."

"Yes, David."

"You are my brother."

Gibbs lowered his head and walked out of the room.

◆

By nightfall of the second day, a fatigued and greatly distressed doctor spoke with MaryAnne and Catherine in the hallway outside David's room.

"His lips have started to turn blue. He is not getting the oxygen he needs. The severity of his chest pain has increased as well. We can try chlorine gas, but, in honesty, I have not seen any evidence of it helping."

"Are you saying that my husband is dying?"

The doctor frowned. "I am not certain of that. I just want you to be prepared. If there is anything you need to say, it might be a good time."

MaryAnne suddenly began to hyperventilate. Catherine quickly led her to a chair. The doctor waited for her to gain her composure. "I am sorry, MaryAnne. I will be back in the morning." The doctor stopped once more in the room. He laid his hand on David's forehead.

His own forehead creased, and he said under his breath, "Good-bye, old sport."

When she had regained her composure, MaryAnne returned to David's bedside. The bedchamber's fire crackled and hissed, lighting the room with its dancing radiance. David's lips were covered with fever blisters, and to MaryAnne's dismay grew more discolored by the hour. His skin grew wan and transparent. At a half hour past two o'clock in the morning, Catherine entered the room. She spoke in hushed tones.

"MaryAnne, you must get some rest. I will come for you if he wakes. Even for a moment."

MaryAnne glanced up wearily, too tired to resist, and Catherine helped her up and out to another room, then took her place in the oak chair beside the bed. She thumbed through the pages of a book, turning pages without garnishing a thought. David's voice startled her.

"Catherine." The voice was slurred and gurgled.

"Yes?"

"Where's Mary?"

"I sent her to rest. I will wake her."

"No . . ." He succumbed to a tortured coughing fit, and Catherine grimaced with each fierce bark. ". . . I want to talk to you first."

She leaned close, her torso overhanging the bed.

"I want to say good-bye."

Catherine recoiled at his words. "No. It is not come to that."

"Catherine."

She began to shake and cupped her face in her hands.

"Catherine . . . ," he said still harder, the outburst causing him to again erupt in a fit of coughing. She looked back up at him.

". . . it has come to that."

Catherine could say nothing as tears began to fall.

"I want to thank you for the years of love and service."

"I should never have let you go out," she cried.

"Don't you blame yourself." Again he coughed, this time for nearly a full minute. When he could talk again, he spoke meekly. "You couldn't have stopped me."

She bowed her head again.

"You once spoke of angels guiding us. I believe that you have been my guardian angel."

Her whimpering grew into uncontrollable sobs. "What will I do without you, David?"

He motioned for her to draw near, and he leaned forward and kissed her forehead. The motion caused his head to spin, and he fell back into his pillow.

"Wake Mary."

Catherine nodded, stood, wiping back her tears with her sleeve. She paused at the doorway. "David . . ."

"Good-bye."

She tried to return his farewell, but the attempt was abandoned by her faltering voice. She dropped her head and walked from the room. A moment later MaryAnne entered, dressed in the cotton gown she had worn the day before, though it was crinkled as she had lain in it, and she pushed it down to lessen its severity. She clutched a crumpled handkerchief in her hand. Her skin was wan, a pallid white accented by her red-rimmed nostrils and eyes—further darkened by her drought of sleep. She walked to the side of his bed and sat down wearily beside him. He forced a smile when he saw her. For reasons she could not explain, she turned away from his gaze. Still looking down she asked, "How do you feel, love?"

He coughed again, and purposely did not answer.

"Shall I stoke the fire?"

He modestly shook his head. "No."

"Ethan has wired. He is coming from London. He is bringing Charlotta . . ."

David just continued to gaze on her, catching the rise

and fall of each word and tasting her voice. MaryAnne shuddered, then fell to her knees and cried, "Why, when I would pour out my whole heart, am I babbling of such trivial matters?"

David's voice was full of consolation. "The moment speaks for itself."

MaryAnne braved to look into his eyes. Then, suddenly, the moment flooded into her like a torrential current filling her entire soul to the extent of her heart's capacity.

"You cannot leave me, David. You cannot. I just got you back." She broke down in desperate sobs. "Please don't leave me."

David put his hand around the back of her head and pulled it into his waist, and he, too, cried.

"Not just yet."

He began choking, and MaryAnne looked up helplessly, squeezing his hand. He suddenly breathed in again, and his body relaxed. MaryAnne's heart pounded.

"David. Take me with you."

"It's not your time, Mary. Andrea and I will await you. I am convinced of that."

"And what if not? What if there is nothing after?"

He gazed silently into MaryAnne's pained eyes, then answered, "With you, I would do it again."

"Oh, David," she sobbed. Clinging desperately to the man she loved, she buried her head into his body and wept until the bed's wooden frame rocked with her convulsions. David held her hand. His grip gradually relaxed as the relentless pull of fatigue seduced him. MaryAnne's weeping also began to still, her murmuring softened until the only motion of her body was the gentle rise and fall of her breathing. He coughed hard, and her head rose.

"I am sorry, David. I am so tired."

He touched her hair and wanted nothing more than to spare her the pain of his leaving. "Rest, Mary. It is late."

"What if . . ." The words froze in her throat.

"I will be here in the dawn." He closed his eyes, and MaryAnne laid her head on his body and also closed hers.

The home was dark and quiet. The room's hearth grew dimmer, and the chamber's only steady light was a single, small bulb from the nightstand's lamp. Nearly an hour later, David was again woken by coughing, but this time something was different, and he knew that his body had entered a final phase of digression. He looked on MaryAnne. Her head now rested against his waist, only partially concealing the graceful curves of the face that had first drawn his eye and then his heart. He realized that he had seen that face only a few times in his life, for he had replaced it with an image of something far deeper than physical attraction. He stretched forth his hand to her head and took the tousled, umber strands between his fingers. He spoke to her in whispers as she slept.

"Could we not have spent just a few more minutes?"

Tears began to fall down his cheeks as he struggled to breathe. But they were not tears of pain, but separation. His chest seemed to be constricting more tightly now, and each breath had to be bargained for. A spasm caught him, and he clenched with its pain, his breath turning to pants. When it had passed, he looked back longingly at the woman at his side. It was time.

"I love you, MaryAnne Parkin. I have always loved you."

His chest constricted again, and he grimaced with its contraction.

"Must I go alone?" He struggled to catch another breath, then, unable once more to cough up the fluids that filled his lungs, surrendered his last word. "Mary . . ."

At eleven minutes past four, David Parkin died. There was no one awake to note the hour of David's passing. When dawn came, awakening the city in its golden radiance, a wail echoed through the corridors of the great Parkin house, and Catherine, running to the aid of her mistress, entered the room, where she found MaryAnne on her knees, clutching her husband's waist and sobbing.

CAROUSELS

"From our first babblings to our last word, we make but one statement, and that is our life."

DAVID PARKIN'S DIARY. OCTOBER 11, 1933

nother cavity was opened on the cemetery's knoll, and the stone angel's shadow trespassed the simple granite marker that denoted the resting place of David Parkin. By one o'clock, a crowd of considerable body had gathered for the eulogy. Every living worker at the Parkin Machinery Company, current and retired, attended with spouse and family—a tribute to David's great heart.

At the side of the casket, Catherine and MaryAnne, in ebony attire, held each other in disbelief, as if it all were some ghastly drama.

Inconspicuously, to one side of the gathering, stood a quorum of Negroes who had braved stigma to pay homage to a white man they considered a friend. Gibbs stood to Catherine's side, with Elaine by his. An Episcopalian minister, young and flaxen-haired, newly ordained to the diocese, stood at the head of the casket, reading his eulogy from a worn prayer book that was not his own.

"O God, whose mercies cannot be numbered, accept our prayers on behalf of thy servant David and grant him entrance into the land of light and joy, in the fellowship of thy saints; through Jesus Christ thy Son our Lord, who liveth and reigneth with thee and the Holy Spirit, one God, now and forever. Amen."

MaryAnne stepped forward and placed a flower and a gold pocket watch on the casket's hood before it was lowered into the earth.

Gibbs put his arm around MaryAnne's waist. "I promised David that I would take care of you. I am always here for you, Mary."

She embraced him. "Thank you, Gibbs. He loved you."

At this, Gibbs swallowed and his eyes further moistened. Elaine buried her face into his shoulder.

As the mourners congregated to pay their respects to MaryAnne, a young woman, dressed in an elegant black silk gown, stepped forward to the new widow. A veil fell from the woman's bowler hat, partially concealing a beautiful and youthful countenance, now florid with grief.

"Mrs. Parkin, I wanted to share my condolences."

"Thank you, dear," MaryAnne replied. She looked closely into the stranger's face. "Forgive me, I do not remember you."

"We have never met. My name is Dierdre Williams. I was an acquaintance of David's."

"Thank you for coming."

Dierdre started to turn away, then suddenly paused. She looked back into the widow's face. "You are fortunate to have been loved such."

MaryAnne's sad stare flashed with bewilderment as the young woman turned and walked away to join up with her aunt.

As the last of the crowd dispersed, Catherine took MaryAnne's arm. "Let's go home, Mary."

MaryAnne just stared at the marker for a moment, then bowed her head. "I would like to be alone for a while."

Catherine took her hand. "I shall come back for you."

"I will walk home."

Gibbs embraced MaryAnne once more, then took Elaine's hand and departed the knoll, followed closely by Catherine.

It was only a few moments after the crowd's silent departure when an elderly woman, hunched with age, advanced slowly from behind the trees. MaryAnne recalled having seen the feeble woman standing afar from the crowd and had dismissed her as a visitor to another grave. The woman looked at her as if she would speak, then turned to the marker, knelt down, and placed a small wooden object next to a single red rose. She remained on her knees. She was heavyset and disheveled, her tattered clothes, like their wearer, a remnant of a bygone era. Her silver hair was tousled, pulled back in a careless bun.

MaryAnne felt herself drawn to the woman who knelt at her husband's grave. The woman, aware of MaryAnne's gaze, looked up. Her face was ancient and creased in wrinkles. Yet there was something familiar in her face—something MaryAnne had seen before. And then, in the woman's deep-set eyes, she saw David.

"Rose . . . ?"

The woman gazed at her, her silence neither confirming nor denying.

"You are David's mother."

The woman remained silent. MaryAnne could not help but feel apprehension in the woman's presence.

"Are you . . . real?"

She struggled to her feet, then replied in a solemn, coarse voice. "You are David's wife?"

"Yes."

"What is your name?"

"MaryAnne."

"MaryAnne," she repeated, nodding slowly. "My David married beautiful." She looked down, and the wind caught the hair at the nape of her neck.

"He went back to Chicago to find you."

A strange, sad smile lit her lips. "They think I'm a ghost, in Chicago. I have read that I haunt a theater there." She spoke the words with peculiar indifference. "Tell me about my son."

"He was loving and strong and loyal."

"Everything I am not."

MaryAnne just stared at the wretched woman. "How long have you been here? In the valley?"

"Months," she answered tersely.

"Why didn't you come to see David?"

The woman didn't answer, but suddenly glanced from side to side as if someone had joined them. "You pity me, perhaps. Or maybe hate me."

"Yes, I pity you. For what you traded away. For what you might have known. But I do not hate you."

"You wondered that I was a ghost?"

"I was told you had died," MaryAnne said.

"I am dead to all I have known. To everyone I have known. I roam this world in regret of all that might have been. Dead or not, I am a ghost. I never jumped from that bridge. Looking out over that black water . . ." She paused as if the very memory held terror still. "It should be of no surprise to anyone. My whole life I never fulfilled any promise. Even my dying. It is my curse, to live to lose my son twice." She suddenly stirred from her own mumbling. "I did not come to mourn my son. I lost him a lifetime ago. I came to mourn my choices. And meet one promise." Rose looked down at the offering she had left on his marker—a wooden toy carousel.

MaryAnne sniffed and brushed at her cheek, and the woman abruptly said, "You haven't the right to sorrow. You have had so much."

The words enraged MaryAnne. "So much to have lost. Everything I held dear is now only a memory."

"Memories are what we trade our mortality for. What I would do for just memories."

"Even when they bring such pain?"

Fresh tears fell down MaryAnne's cheek, but the woman only glared at her. Her hard countenance revealed no sympathy. "There are worse things than pain."

To her own surprise, MaryAnne's heart welled, no longer for herself, but for the austere soul of this woman. Unexpectedly, a single tear fell down the hard woman's cheek, and it rolled slowly like a drop of rain on cracked, baked desert clay. "Everyone dies. You have lived. You shan't ask for more."

A gust of wind swept through the grounds in a sudden breath, and the evergreens quivered while the smaller ones bowed in condescension. MaryAnne pulled the scarf up around her chin. "Will you come back with me? To our home?"

There was a sudden change to the woman's demeanor, and her reply came as if she spoke only to herself—answering voices only she heard.

"I do not belong here."

"Where will you go?"

"Away!" And at the word, she looked off in the distance as if her soul had already fled, followed longingly by her gaze. "Away from this miserable cold. To California. It is warm in California . . ."

She began to nod as if she had arrived at consensus with the spirits that shared her soul. She spoke with a voice inadequate to express the lesson her words conveyed. ". . . we were always warm in California."

At this, the old woman turned abruptly and shuffled off without farewell—having forgotten that she had shared in conversation with someone now left behind. MaryAnne's gaze followed her until the hunched form fell from view below the stone fence that divided the cemetery. MaryAnne stepped to the grave, then stooped and lifted the toy carousel with both hands. It was a simple wooden toy, crudely carved and painted, yet capable of producing such wonder in a child as to define an age. Despite the simple workmanship, it was not unlike the toy carousel David had brought back for Andrea more than two decades earlier when she was still an infant. She wondered if David had consciously remembered the toy when he had purchased it for his child and if seeing it had brought him the joy of remembrance or the pain of loss. Or, instead, if something deep inside, forgotten to the waken mind but etched on the tablets of his heart, had drawn him to the carousel, to give his child a symbol of his commitment to her—that he, like the toy, would never leave.

MaryAnne stowed the carousel under her cloak and carried it back to the home. She climbed the stairway to the second floor of the mansion. In her hand she held a skeleton key she thought she would never use again. In the other hand was the wooden toy.

She unlocked the door, then, taking a deep breath, pushed the parlor door open. Like David had been, she, too, was lost in the sudden outflow of memories the sight evoked. She had forgotten how beautiful the room had once been and, though cloaked in a shroud of dust, still was. Her eyes were immediately drawn to the bed and then to the grandfather's clock, remembering the day of its birth as well as its death.

On the fireplace mantel across the room, she found what she had come for—the delicate porcelain carousel David had given to Andrea. She gently brushed the dust from the piece, revealing its intricate pastel and gilt markings. She released the toy's catch and the porcelain carousel turned, its horses rose and fell to the sweet, gentle melody of its music box, then abruptly stopped, its spring unwound. The wooden carousel did not match the beauty of Andrea's exquisite toy, yet the connection was undeniable.

MaryAnne sat down on the parlor's dusty carpet, gazing at the two small toys she cradled in her lap. She wound the smooth silver key of the music box, and the tines again filled the air of the once dead room with the carnival sounds of life. And she wept for the loss of her love.

EPILOGUE

ourteen years after her husband's death, MaryAnne Parkin was buried next to David and Andrea on the knoll of the angel statue. It was at her funeral that I met the remaining survivor of the era—Catherine. Catherine had married four years after David's death and, with MaryAnne's blessings and tears, moved with her new husband to the temperate climate of the small township of St. George, Utah, south of the great red rock monuments of Zion Canyon. Despite the distance, she spoke with MaryAnne each week, and, we discovered, knew much of Keri and me from MaryAnne's letters.

Catherine was petite of stature, as small as Keri, with blond hair turned grey that fell to her shoulders but no further. She had captivating hazel eyes, mimicking her hair's adopted hue, dramatic and tear-shaped like a fawn's. Noticeably, she was attentive to all about her as one who has spent her life in service often becomes. She spoke fondly of MaryAnne and the life they had shared, and she questioned us considerably about our stay. I sensed in her query a longing for the mansion and an earlier time, if but to capture again a single note of the sweet song of a day gone by.

The marble angel statue stands to this day in the Salt Lake City cemetery, midway through the graveyard on Center Street, amidst the willows and sycamores, just above the ground called Babyland, where children are buried. Our family visits the statue each Christmas season, and during one yule visit, our second daughter, Allyson, pointed out a peculiar thing. During the holiday months, the sun at the angel's back so lights the statue that its shadow spreads its wings over the three graves, and the family is united again in the seraph's embrace. If it appears to be a small thing, it is still of beauty. And nothing of beauty is insignificant.

MaryAnne and David Parkin left us many things of beauty, the greatest of which are their lessons of love and life—lessons that time will never forget, nor diminish. David's death was not in vain, for, as he once himself wrote, "life is the greatest of all statements," and in his great sacrifice he spoke volumes, showing us that there are things not only worth dying for, but, more importantly, worth living for. For life's greatest philosophy is not handed down in stoic texts and dusty tomes, but lived, in each breath and act of human compassion. For love has always demanded sacrifice, and no greater love is there than that for which our lives are traded.

And in this great cause of spiritual evolution we are all called to be martyrs, to die each of us in the quest of a higher realm and loftier ideals, that we may know God.

And what if there is nothing else? What if all life ends in the silent void of death? Then is it all in vain? I think not. For love, for the sake of love, will always be enough. And if our lives are but a single flash in the dark hollow of eternity, then, if, but for the briefest of moments, we shine—then how brilliantly our light has burned. And as the starlight knows no boundary of space or time, so, too, our illumination will shine forth throughout all eternity, for darkness has no power to quell such light. And this is a lesson we must all learn and take to heart—that all light is eternal and all love is light. And it must forever be so.

Visit
❖ **Pocket Books** ❖
online at

··

www.SimonSays.com

··

Keep up on the latest new
releases from your favorite
authors, as well as author
appearances, news, chats,
special offers and more.

SIMON & SCHUSTER
A VIACOM COMPANY
www.SimonSays.com

Pocket
Books

2381-01

POCKET BOOKS
PROUDLY PRESENTS
Excerpts from Two Recent Bestselling
Classics by
Richard Paul Evans

The Locket

Available in Paperback
from Pocket Books

and

The Looking Glass
A Novel

A Reflection of Two Hearts

Available now in hardcover from
Simon & Schuster

The Locket

Richard Paul Evans

PROLOGUE

There are those who maintain that it is a shameful thing for a man to speak of sentiment, and the recounting of a love story must certainly qualify as such. But if there is virtue in stoicism, I do not see it, and if I haven't the strength to protest, neither have I the will to conform, so I simply share my story as it is. Perhaps time has thinned my walls of propriety as it has my hair.

If my narrative is, in fact, a love story, I suspect that the world will not likely recognize it—for pulp romances do not often push aluminum walkers or smell of peppermint oil. Still, there are stories that refuse to be interred in silent graves like the lives who gave them breath. The story of Esther Huish is such—commenced and concluded in a town born of gold, a mining camp cradled in the lap of the Oquirrh Mountains in the remote, windswept ranges of western Utah: the town of Bethel.

Bethel is now a dead town, and its history is not one story but two, as towns may live more than once. In 1857 a tramp miner and sometime evangelist named Hunter Bell, expelled for card cheating from the nearby Goldstrike mining camp, was wandering in exile amongst the bulrushes of the Oquirrh foothills when he chanced upon a rich deposit of placer gold. Bell staked his claim and within a month was joined by more than sixteen hundred miners. Learned in the vernacular of the gospel, if not the spirit, Bell bequeathed the town the biblical name of Bethel—the House of God.

Though Goldstrike and Bethel were sister cities, they proved as different as siblings in character as in appearance. Bethel was staid and industrious. Her greatest structure was the local chapel, which, when resting off the sabbath, doubled as the town hall and a one-room schoolhouse. Conversely, Goldstrike's most resplendent structure was a honky-tonk piano saloon and brothel. It was a raucous haven of prostitution, gambling, and murder, aptly nicknamed by the Salt Lake City newspapers as Sodom West. As the larger and more accessible of the two cities, Goldstrike became the center of commerce on which Bethel relied for its train station, milling, and trade.

A year after the turn of the century, as gold production in both cities started to decline, tragedy struck Goldstrike. A fire, started in a saloon's kitchen, ravaged the mining town. It was followed by an ill-timed flash flood that collapsed most of the mines and all but washed away what remained of the once thriving township—a baptism of fire and water the area ministries claimed was apocalyptic, having prophesied that a great scourge was sure to befall the decadent town. Bethel, though spared heaven's wrath, was no longer accessible by railroad and died as well, leaving behind only those too old or too broken—like slag tossed aside after being purged of its wealth.

For nearly thirty years, Bethel (or Betheltown, as Esther and those indigenous to the small town called it) lay dormant, until 1930, when in the wake of the Great Depression, there was a resurgence of interest in the town's boarded-up shafts and Bethel was reborn as a Depression baby.

It was just prior to these days that Esther Huish arrived in Bethel—the young, beautiful daughter and sole companion of an elderly man seeking fortune as a miner. Prosperity eluded the man and time proved that his greatest wealth was his daughter, who, as he grew infirm, provided for him as the caretaker of the Bethel Boarding House and Inn. Esther was an elderly woman when I met her, in the last months of her life. She had become a recluse—preferring to our world an era that existed only in her memory and the diaries in which she chronicled those days. An era evidenced by a petite golden locket. It was an encounter that was to leave me forever changed.

I believe it a great irony that I learned of life from one dying, and of love from one so lonely.

To everything there is a season, said the Preacher, to every purpose under heaven—a time to get and a time to lose, a time to love and a time to hate, a time to dance and a time to mourn, a time to be born and a time to die. Those months with Esther were a season of all these things—and most important, the season I learned of faith, forgiveness, and second chances. One winter in a rest home called the Arcadia.

chapter one

Betheltown

"As I lie in bed listening to the toil of my body beneath the infirmities of age, my heart wanders again to Betheltown and I wonder how it is that, through the same sorcery of time that has brought me to my end, Betheltown has become less heartbreak than joy. And less memory than dream."

EXCERPT FROM ESTHER HUISH'S DIARY

Bethel, Utah. April 2, 1989

As the desert blurred past in the luminous hues of an impressionist's palette, Faye huddled tightly against the car door, her eyes closed and her coffee hair spilling over her face. The last of the music, frayed tones from a hayseed country station, had miles back degenerated into a storm of static, and now the only noises were the car's undulations over the primitive road and the occasional sigh of my sleeping companion. We had already traveled fifty miles past the last evidence of humanity, a rancher's lodgepole-pine fence, into the desert's blanched, stubbled plain, and Faye had not yet asked where it was that I was taking her. Her faith in our journey was not unlike her faith in our courtship, attributable only to some godlike quality of the female mystique—an unwavering virtue of hope and patience—that, if unable to predict our destination, found merit at least in the journey.

I had never been to this corner of the earth—only eight months previously, I hadn't even known of its existence—but the stories I had heard of the dead town had given it meaning, and I confess anxiety at its approach. I was told that the town, steeped in the foothills of the Oquirrh range, was constantly assailed by mountain winds. But there was no wind that day, and the spray of red dust in the car's wake hung in the placid air, liberated from a roadway not trespassed for a year's time.

I was glad for this day, for its blanched, cloudless skies, for though I embraced the land's immense solitude—felt akin to it—it would be foolhardy to venture so far from civilization with the possibility of becoming stranded on washed-out roads. Flash floods were common in these regions, and most of the ghost town's abandoned mines had decades earlier collapsed under their turbulent runoff. The wash of such cataclysm was a souvenir hunter's ecstasy of relics and coins and an occasional grain of gold. It had always been such with the town, as men came to take from the land or to take from those who had come to take from it, and even in death it was so.

Only, today, I had not come to take but to impart.

Before us the coarse road crested, then dipped into a barren creek bed surrounded by the pink clusters of spring beauties and the scattered stalks of bulrush that proved the creek still possessed occasional life. At the creek's shallow bank I left the car idling and walked to the rill and placed a hand to its stony bed. There was no trace of moisture. I examined our intended route, rolled back a single stone of possible hazard, then returned to the car and traversed the bed. A half mile forward, the timber skeleton of a gold mine's stamp mill rose from a mesquite-covered knoll—a wood-tarred contrivance of rusted wheels and cogs and corroded steel tracks over which ore cars had once rolled and men and horses had sweat. I glanced down to a crudely drawn map, astonished that after all these years, and with a dying memory, Esther had remembered such landmarks so distinctly. I wondered if she had just never left.

At the mill's passing I turned west and coaxed my Datsun up the hill, where the road vanished into a buckwheat-dotted plain that spread infinitely to the north and south and climbed the foothills of the mountain into the town itself. As we neared the decrepit structures of the once-flourishing township, Faye's eyes opened and she slid up in her seat.

"Where are we?"

"Esther's hometown."

Faye gazed on in apparent fascination. ". . . what's left of it."

We passed the ornamental iron fence of a cemetery. "Welcome to Bethel—the House of God."

"This is where Esther was born?"

"She came here as a young woman." I looked out at the desolate terrain. "Makes you wonder why anyone would come here."

Faye turned to me. "Why are we here?"

"To fulfill a promise."

Faye leaned back in her seat, momentarily content with my ambiguity.

I parked the car under the gnarled limbs of a black locust tree near the center of the deceased town and shut off the engine.

The morning's drive had taken nearly two hours, but it was the conclusion of a much greater journey, one that had taken nearly half a year. A journey that began the day my mother died.

chapter two

The Arcadia

"The Arcadia is unlike that chill, tile institution
that I was brought here from.
The small difference
between it and a sepulcher was movie night."

EXCERPT FROM ESTHER HUISH'S DIARY

or the third consecutive day, snow fell heavy in driven blasts that cloaked all that hadn't the sense or ability to come in out of it. From my perch at a shallow bay window, I watched the mortician's high-stepped approach through the piled snow. Tucked under the man's arm was a folded vinyl body bag. Midstep, the heavy man lost his footing, flailed, then disappeared in a sprawl of slush and powder, then rose again, cursing as he brushed down his charcoal over-coat. Moments later a gloved fist pounded against the door. The man was ruddy cheeked and broad faced. He was still breathing heavily from his hike, his breath clouding before him as I opened the door.

"I can't find the street numbers. This the Keddington place?"

"You have the right house," I said.

"Body inside, I reckon."

I glared at him. "My mother is inside."

The man kicked his boots against the threshold, then stepped past me into my home. He glanced about. The spartan room was carpeted in a well-worn shag of olive hue, and bare except for three humble pieces of furni-ture—a wooden armchair, a garish red-and-gold uphol-stered sofa, threadbare in its extremities, and a single brass-stemmed floor lamp, its shade burned through where it had once fallen against its bulb. The room was illuminated only from the window.

"Where's your mama?"

I pointed toward the darkened hallway. "The bedroom is there on the right."

The man unbuttoned his coat but did not remove it, and stepped in the direction of my gesture. I followed him to the doorway. Inside the dim room he moved toward my mother's body, shrouded beneath a hand-tied quilt of her own making. He pulled down the blanket, removed one glove, and placed two fingers beneath her chin, then looked down to examine her fingernails.

"When she go?"

I looked again at my mother's face. "Just a few minutes before I called," I replied, glancing up at the shadowed face of the mantel clock. "Maybe three hours . . ."

"Coroner been by?"

"The certificate's on the nightstand."

"Anyone else witness her passing?"

"No. We only had each other."

"I'm sorry," he said, and there was a trace of empathy in his voice. "No other family?"

"I have an uncle. But he's not family."

"Where's your old man?"

"He died a few years back." Then I added without thought, "Not that he was family either."

The mortician's brow furrowed. "How's that?"

I feigned the tipping of a bottle, a habit acquired through years of explaining my father's absence. "We hadn't seen him for more than seven years before he drank away his liver."

The man nodded empathetically as he removed his second glove. He stood and walked to the foot of the bed, drawing the quilt down with him. He lifted his bag from the floor and began working it up over her body.

"Don't mean to be judgmental, but for just losing your only family, you ain't seem much broken up."

I was too numb to feel slighted by his remark. "My mother has been dying since summer. There just aren't any tears left."

He closed the bag up over her head. "Yeah. Eventually it just give out." He stood back as if to examine his work. "There's a few papers you'll need to sign. Legal papers."

We walked out to the kitchen and he spread the forms about the drop-leaf table, pointing me to the lines that required signatures.

"This your place, or you rentin'?"

"It's mostly the bank's. But we put a down on it a few years back."

"Well, if you're thinkin' of sellin', I know a good realtor. They've been tearing down these places and putting up mini marts." He sniffed. "Reckon you'll be headed off anyhow."

"Why is that?"

"Just always happens that way. Demons will chase you off."

". . . Only the ones at the mortgage company. I haven't been able to work since she took to bed last summer. Between the medical bills and house payments, I'm pretty much buried." I signed the last paper.

"You got some employment in mind?"

"Whatever I can find. Work's a little scarce around here."

He reached into his coat pocket and took out a dog-eared business card, penning a phone number and address on its reverse side. He offered me the card.

"Are you hiring?"

"Nah. That's the number to a nursing home. The

manager up there told me just yesterday that she needed help. Tell them that Roger sent ya up. They like me up there."

"I don't have any experience with that sort of thing."

"You been at your mama's side since last summer, you got plenty experience. Tell them I sent ya," he repeated. "I'm kind of a regular."

"What is the place called?"

"The Arcadia Care something."

I stowed the card in my shirt pocket and the mortician stood.

"Hate to impose, but could you lend me a hand here taking your mama out to the car? This blizzard has us shorthanded at the morgue."

We carried my mother's body out under pallid skies to the back of the station wagon. The mortician secured the tailgate, then took a brush from his front seat and scraped his windshield. I watched from inside the house as the station wagon fishtailed from the curb into the icy roadway and took my mother away. I closed my eyes and wept.

Look for
The Locket
**Available in Paperback
from Pocket Books**

The Looking Glass

Richard Paul Evans

CHAPTER ONE

Quaye

There's no love left on earth
and God is dead in heaven
In the dark and deadly days of Black '47.

❈ IRISH FOLK SONG ❈

It's easy to halve the potato where there's love.

❈ IRISH PROVERB ❈

*C*onnall McGandley trudged wearily across the haze-shrouded countryside, his arms crossed at his chest, his pace pressed against the receding twilight. The chill air smelled sweetly of a distant peat fire and he willed himself to not think of its warmth. Dusk brought a bite to the fog and he had pawned his coat in the last town for the paltry measure of maize he carried in the sack flung across his shoulder. He had walked hungry since dawn with hope of securing relief for his family. There was no labor for hire and his coat had fetched only a couple handfuls of Indian corn from a shopkeeper who chased him out of his store after the transaction. He had encountered few on his journey, just the quiet, deserted bogs and abandoned hovels of a dying nation. The music of Ireland, the land of song, was silenced by famine and the only strains now that filled the air were the occasional piercing wails for the dead—the keening of the banshee.

To the side of the road, behind one of the heaped limestone walls that serpentined across the countryside, a woman crawled on hands and knees through a dank bog, gleaning what had been missed in the last picking, chewing anything that was edible: raw turnips, nettles, and charlock. He turned away. The scene was all too familiar—men and women in the final throes of starvation, their mouths stained green from the grass they ate in a vain attempt to survive. It no longer held curiosity. It no longer held even emotion. It was just the way it was. It would not be long before his own family would be evicted from their hovel, to burn with the fever and madness of starvation or die of exposure. His only son already lay hot with typhus.

It had been two autumns since the mist rose from the sea to cloak Ireland. When the fog lifted, the first signs of the distemper appeared, the stalks bent in the fields, a harbinger of a nation's fate. The blight hit in full the following year, destroying nearly the whole of the island's potato crop. The potato was everything to the Irish poor and the Celts could make anything from the tuber, from candy to beer. The potato was as much heritage as subsistence, but even in the best of times, the potato culture was a precarious existence.

It was shortly before the last harvest when McGandley first discovered the blight on his own meager crop of lumpers—the first lesions on the curling leaves, bruiselike markings that had dropped him to his knees in fervent prayer to St. Jude, the patron saint of desperate circumstance. The family immediately harvested, pared off the diseased portions of the crop, and ate or sold what they could, feeding what they couldn't to the pigs. Then they devoured the pigs themselves. But even the swines' bones which they had boiled, reboiled, then gnawed in hunger, were now gone, replaced only with desperation.

Fifty steps ahead, emerging from the screen of fog, a wooden horse-drawn cart was mired in the mud to the side of the road. A squat, dun-haired man stood calf deep in the mud in front of the horse, pulling at its lines and cursing the animal. It was a curious sight, more so as most farm animals had already been slaughtered for meat. The man saw McGandley and raised a hand to him.

"You, there." The expulsion appeared before him in the frigid air.

As McGandley neared, the man grimaced at McGandley's appearance, surmising him a madman. He had encountered many on the day's travel—men and women, often naked, lunatic with hunger.

"Have ye anything to eat?" McGandley called.

The man frowned. "Not outside my belly." He motioned to the cart. "Can ya lend a hand?"

"If yer wanting to get somewhere, man, ye be better off riding yer buggy on the road, not on the side of it." He stopped an arm's length removed and stared somberly at the stranger. "Are ye English?"

"I'm American."

"Bonny for yah. If ye were an Englishman yer throat likely be cut by now. Likely do it meself."

The American studied the man. "The English been sendin' money to the famine aid."

"Oh have they now? I tell ye, caskets be of more use. There's no famine where there's food. The Brits have stolen it all." McGandley's voice dropped to a more ominous tone. "It is well for ye yer not an Englishman."

The American set aside the horse's lines and took a step toward McGandley. "I have money. Help push me from this and I'll pay ya. I must be to Cobh harbor. My clipper sails at dawn."

McGandley's interest was piqued. In the wake of the famine, more than a million Irish had already emigrated, some to the fever camps of Liverpool or Wales, but mostly to the new world, stowing aboard nearly anything that floated. "Coffin ships" the seamen called them. There were times that such vessels arrived with Irish aboard but not life.

"Ye be sailing back to Americay?"

The sailor realized McGandley's intent and regretted the divulgence. McGandley did not wait for an answer. "Take pity on our pathetic lot and take us with ye."

"Ya got money?" he asked.

"Not a bleedin' pence."

The American shook his head. "There's no room."

"But, in the steerage, man."

"Along with your typhus and cholera? There's already a million Irishmen at the dock."

McGandley scratched at the lice on his scalp.

"Ye could stow me girl. She's a wee lass."

"I can't, man."

"Ye could if she were yer wife."

The American spit near his own feet. "I don't need no wife," he said, then he turned back to the horse. "Be a good man and lend a hand. I'll pay ya for your trouble."

McGandley stood resolute and the American glanced about helplessly. He had already been delayed the better part of an hour and was no closer to liberating his cart. With night falling and his pockets full of money from the ship passages he had brokered, it was no time to be stranded in Ireland—the horse a banquet, he a bank. The hungry would find him.

"A woman to watch over ya on such a journey would be a blessing," McGandley pressed. "Me girl works hard. Harder than them slaves ye got chained in Americay."

The American still did not respond and McGandley's stomach knotted. He eyed the sailor. He was an ugly man with a wide, ruddy face spiked with stubble, younger than himself by at least a decade, and shorter by a hand.

"What do they call ye, lad?"

The sailor spoke slowly, reluctant to give anything up to the Irishman. "Jak."

"Well now, Jak, she's a lovely lass. A regular colleen. You can do with her what ye like." He gazed at him darkly. "A real man wouldn't pass the offer 'fore he saw the lass."

The sailor stomached the challenge to his manhood and rubbed his forehead as he considered his prospects. A woman would be a blessing on the voyage, even if he were to just abandon her in the waterfront slums of New York. In the darker venues of the city he might even turn her for a profit.

"She's not got cholera or typhus?"

"Healthy, she is."

"If she's homely I'll leave her dockside."

Ignoring the threat, McGandley lay down his sack and moved forward to the task of liberating the cart, his shoes filling with the black mud as he plied his way forward. He rubbed the lean colt's flank to calm it, dropped to his haunches to inspect its breast collar and tugs, then looked to examine the cart. Its wood, iron-banded wheels were buried no more than a half foot in the muck.

"She's a fine pony," he said, patting the horse. He rose, took up the leather lines and stepped off to the side of the horse, then brought the lines down like a whip against the horse's hip.

"Giddout, yer."

The horse's muscles rippled as it strained forward, tearing its hoofs from the mud. The horse advanced with ease from its confinement, pulling the cart straightway from the mire. When the cart was settled on the road, McGandley retrieved his sack of maize, then returned to the cart, offering the lines to the astonished sailor.

"Why wouldn't the blasted beast pull for me?"

A sardonic smile crossed McGandley's face. "Well now, man, if ye be standin' in front of her, where's the poor animal to go?"

❄

The sun was not yet below the horizon when the cart crossed the stone wall boundary of McGandley's clachan. The hamlet, once alive with the voices of children, was mostly deserted as one by one its families were evicted by hunger or landlord. The American halted the cart in front of a thatched-roof cottage and McGandley lowered himself to the ground. A woman, pale and gaunt, with deep wells of eyes, emerged at the sound of their approach. At her side was a young woman who smiled at the return of her father.

"Da."

McGandley did not respond to his daughter's call, and at the sight of the stranger she moved behind her mother. She stared anxiously at the men, instinctively fearing her father's distance and the coarse, leering man who accompanied him. The mother did not ask who the man was who looked on her daughter, but watched silently, as if she were a spectator at a play-act tragedy.

"Come, lass," McGandley commanded.

The girl timidly obeyed, lowering her head as she stepped forward. She was nearly fifteen years of age, fresh in young womanhood with emerging breasts and full lips, her high cheeks ashen with hunger; her long, copper hair spilled over her gaunt and freckled face.

She was barefoot, clothed in a high-necked muslin dress purchased two springs previously from the cast-clothes hawkers. The crimson dress, now faded and threadbare, fell crumpled to her forearms and left her long legs exposed. She was, as her father had claimed, pretty, more so than the sailor had expected or hoped for. No such woman, young or old, had ever looked on him favorably. She glanced up fearfully at the man, then moved toward her father.

"What do ya call her?" the sailor asked.

The girl looked to her father, fearing his reply.

"Quaye," he said gruffly.

The man wiped his mouth with the back of his hand. "If she was hung for beauty she'd die innocent. What do ya want for her?"

"Passage to Americay for the girl." McGandley looked down at his feet. "Whatever coins yah got jinglin' about for us."

The sailor reached into his trousers pocket and brought out a handful of coin. "What do ya know? Thirty pieces."

McGandley did not look up. He did not share the sailor's amusement.

"I could buy any woman in Ireland for that."

"She's eaten well till recent," McGandley growled. "She'll serve well enough."

The man said nothing, tossed the silver at McGandley's feet, then motioned to Quaye. "C'mon, girl."

Her mother turned away her tear-brimmed eyes, but there was no disagreement. Either way her child was lost to her. Quaye looked to her father in disbelief, but his countenance was hard and resolute. He squatted down next to her. Looking into her eyes, he said softly, "If ye will remember who ye are, ye will find yer way through it." He looked over to the sailor, who watched impatiently. "Now go 'long with the man, Quaye. He be yer husband now."

"Just a moment," her mother said. She pulled from her spindly finger a silver band then stepped forward and placed the ring on her daughter's ring finger, lovingly clasping Quaye's hand in her own. She said softly, "May ye find love to turn it right someday." Then she kissed her gently on the cheek. "Go well, me girl." She breathed in deeply as she stood. As she rose, the sailor stepped forward to claim his chattel, led Quaye by the arm to the cart, and lifted her in, while her parents watched silently. Without another word the man flailed the horse and started off into the darkness with their child, the cart vanishing into the damp fog and blackness.

"*A mbathair ta me norbh,*" McGandley muttered to the night air, then he slowly turned to his wife, his head falling with his words. "Mother, I am killed."

Quaye did not turn back as the cart carried her away from her home.

Look for
The Looking Glass
Wherever Books Are Sold